TWENTY FORTY-FOUR
THE LEAGUE OF PATRIOTS

A NOVEL BY
TONY DARNELL

Inspired by the political theories, works and quotes

of other people who fought for liberty and freedom.

A special thanks to Amanda, Bobby, Lane, Sharon, Tiger and Jessica,

as well as Chris, Ryan and David.

Published By:

12th Media Services, 3651 Peachtree Parkway, Suite E275, Suwanee, GA 30024

Send comments or questions to: editor@2044thebook.com

ISBN: 1680920006

ISBN-13: 978-1-68092-000-0

Library of Congress Control Number: 2014956630

CIP data is available.

V1.02

Dedicated to my wonderful and amazing wife.

Sonya,
Don't let freedom and liberty die!

Terry Newell

Preface

I am not a person who reads any substantial quantity of books. While reading is pleasurable, I rarely possess the time required to finish a book before I have forgotten what was in the first chapter. A successful year of reading is often measured with one or two books, not including the various unread magazines located in the stacks in my office.

During the summer of 2013, information was released which stated the United States government had been illegally spying on their own citizens. Because of this revelation, George Orwell's classic book, *Nineteen Eighty-Four* (*1984*), suddenly experienced a dramatic increase in sales, partly due to *1984* being a story of life in a world where the government controls and monitors almost every aspect of your life.

Unlike most high school students, the reading of *1984* was not a requirement for me. I can't remember what books were required of me to read during that time. But *1984* had been on my list of "I should read that book" for a significant period of time. On June 10th, 2013, upon hearing the book being mentioned in the news, I finally purchased a copy and quickly placed it on a shelf in my office to be ignored.

I don't remember when I decided to finally read the book. I do remember I was traveling by plane, and decided reading would help to pass the time, and the book had been staring at me for a while. And as with all well-written and interesting books, once I began reading, I was captivated by the story and Orwell's incredible style of writing. The book was finished before I returned from my trip, and I read it two more times, a few pages here and there, over the next several months.

The brilliance of *1984* isn't limited to the imaginative story, but in the way the story is told. The story is key, but George Orwell was simply a gifted writer. Of course, his insight into a world which may never happen was almost prophetic, as it was written in an age where the monochrome television was the new pinnacle of technology, and few people owned one.

There is a quote falsely attributed to a man named Charles H. Duell, a former Commissioner of the United States Patent Office. In 1899, Mr. Duell supposedly stated *"Everything that can be invented has been invented"*. The real source of the quote was from an 1899 edition of Punch Magazine (according to Dennis Crouch, a Law Professor at the University of Missouri School of Law). However, this same reasoning goes back to around 931 BC, when Solomon wrote Ecclesiastes. Chapter one, verse nine reads: *"That which has been is what will be, that which is done is what will be done, and there is nothing new under the sun"* (New King James Version).

When one studies the forms of government and political thinking, I believe the same can be stated. All of these government theories and institutions, including socialism, communism, dictatorship, oligarchy, constitutional republic, etc. have foundations which have already been clearly defined. And for each one, there are numerous clever and profound statements of truth and rebuttal which have been declared, negated and debated. People have attempted to create sub-sets of these governments, borrowing and combining characteristics of a few or many to create their own satisfactory version. But if one could state "All potential forms of government which can be defined have been defined", would one be able to state "All political thinking has been thought"?

If one can assume this statement is true, then one of the only remaining original theories available is in the assumptions of the transformations of a society, or of a nation, from one form of government to the other, and the steps required for any combination of such conversion. The only originality available is in how such a change takes place, and the characters involved. For example, in order to displace a monarch to move to a different form of government, the monarch must first be dethroned. In most cases, this is accomplished by force which leads to the execution or exile of the monarch. It doesn't matter what the next form of government will follow, the first step is to simply eradicate the monarch, and it is these steps one can possibly find a unique story or method which has not yet been discussed or proposed.

However, even without a clever story or a new way to regurgitate these same debates and arguments, people must be constantly reminded of the goals of each political system. A socialist doesn't advocate for a touch of socialism, but they strive and struggle for a political and governing system which is complete and total socialism. People seem to forget the failures and horrors of socialism and communism, and naively believe that such societies can thrive, as long as everyone is equal. The duty of those who seek freedom and liberty have the never-ending task of educating and reminding the general populace of what is truly just and correct, and what is wrong.

In *1984*, the reader discovers a world which has already undergone a transformation of some type. The story mentions a revolution and a nuclear war, civil unrest and the like. But the how and the why for each of these events aren't specified to a great detail. Nor were these details necessary for the story to be told. The history of how the characters had arrived was forever lost when George Orwell passed away shortly after the book's publication. We do know some background on the characters and the location was of a dystopian society, possibly in London, but how they arrived wasn't as important as what happened while they were there.

Twenty Forty-Four is not an attempt to be a prequel to *1984*, but rather an attempt to explain one of the many possible scenarios which could bring any nation, or a group of nations, to the place similar to the society described in *1984*. Orwell finished *1984* during 1948, and his story was simply a prediction of life 36 years into the future.

As I wrote this book, many of the political terms and theories and statements expressed have definitely been stated before, as I doubt I am capable of any original and powerful philosophies of my own. I don't consider myself to be a great political thinker, commentator, aspiring pundit, or anything more than simply someone who has a general understanding of the political system they believe is honorable and efficient. Since this is a fiction novel, the majority of my thoughts did not require any research, except to ensure I was not directly plagiarizing someone, and there are no footnotes or credits for any of the ideas set forth. I can only give a blanket acknowledgement that none of the political terms and theories and statements originated in my mind.

While the inspiration for *Twenty Forty-Four* was driven by Orwell's *1984*, it was not the only source of political knowledge. My political thinking has been inspired by quotes and the general political statements from people such as Ayn Rand, Niccolo Machiavelli, Ronald Reagan, and the various current political commentators from the conservative mass media outlets. After over thirty years of following politics, the foundations of political knowledge have simply been ingrained in my mind.

The characters and institutions described in this book, are not in any way directly related to any individual people, living or dead, or any current political or economic establishments. Any allusion on the reader's part is just that, derived from your own personal political views and assumptions.

Tony Darnell

Chapter 1

The waiting area was sparsely decorated, but the furnishings appeared to be fairly new. David wondered if the new appearance could be from lack of use. He had been visiting this office for the past two decades, and even though he was only in here once a month, he couldn't remember seeing anyone else in this room. However, it was difficult to determine the age of this type of furniture. To him, all waiting-room furniture looked the same. The side tables were constructed from plastic and finished to resemble wood, so even as the surface wore down, it still maintained an appearance of wood. There were also two faux-leather chairs, three hastily-drawn landscape prints on the wall, and a dozen old and tattered entertainment and political tabloids. The magazines were too old to accurately determine their frequency of usage.

The time was almost seventeen hundred, and David had been waiting for nearly an hour, which allowed him plenty of time to critique the age of the furniture. Reminding himself it was good to have patience, he wondered if any of his co-workers would have left by now. The clock on the opposite wall embraced his stare for a solid seven minutes, as he was captivated by the movement and gentle clicking sound of the second hand. But as the minute hand slowly climbed towards the top of the hour, he was dreading the drive back to his hotel in rush-hour traffic.

This meeting was really a formality. David was fortunate in that he worked for SoCare, also known as Society Healthcare, which was the national Party's healthcare benefit system. SoCare controlled the vast majority of the hospitals, clinics, doctors, nurses, medical suppliers, pharmaceuticals - anyone and anything related to the healthcare industry. SoCare's main mission was to provide quality healthcare to the masses, or in their case, to attempt to provide quality healthcare services to the masses. Their main agenda was really to regulate and control the healthcare industry, which they did extremely well. David's title was "Benefits Resource Representative" and his primary responsibility was to visit his assigned list of hospitals, clinics and centers to

1

make sure they were aware of the new and available SoCare products and services.

His job was fairly easy, but it was extremely tedious and boring. None of his clients really wanted to meet with him. All meetings were regulated and mandatory for both parties, and were required to be held at least once a month. Most meetings only lasted a minute or two. The majority of his appointments consisted of nothing more than a handshake and the client saying, "Thanks for stopping by. We will see you in a month." David usually spent more time waiting than visiting. And he spent more time in his car than waiting. He often wondered if, and wished, he could perform his responsibilities over the phone, but regulations needed to be followed and without the regulations, he wouldn't have a job. The fact he possessed a good and more importantly, a stable job, always helped to fuel his patience.

None of his clients had ordered anything directly from him in a long time. All of the ordering was now completed online via the network. And even though he received a minuscule commission from each client based on their total purchases, he wasn't making a huge sum of money. The amount was enough to live on and to survive in a semi-comfortable state. But over the past several years he had grown tired of his job. He was tired of his monotonous life and tired of the complex and redundant system to which he was chained. David had held this job and only this job since graduating from college, and at that time he was delighted to be employed. Unemployment has always been high, but it was extremely high back then. Most of his friends simply moved back home to live with their parents, and were working menial but almost-sustainable living-wage jobs. Yes, David was very fortunate. Maybe "blessed" was a more-appropriate term.

Living-wage jobs provided one with enough money, along with your Prosperity Benefits, to barely eek out a nearly-content way of life, and comfortable enough to prevent you from wanting more, especially if more difficult work was involved. The job market still hadn't recovered, and this is why he had grown complacent over the years. He had a well-paying job compared to the amount of work he was required to perform, he never called in sick, and he rarely took vacations. In addition to his little-more-than-meager salary and modest commissions, there was the almost-satisfactory apartment filled with adequate but constantly-aging furniture, a scant number of nice possessions, along with the best benefit of holding a Party job, which was near-immediate tenure. Plus, he was fairly competent in his work, his clients tolerated him with a smile, and his boss generally left him alone.

Only two more months remained until David would be forced to leave his job and take his mandatory retirement benefit. The only fear he possessed was the uncertainty of being able to survive on the various Prosperity Benefits alone, after his salary was taken away. Once he completed his twenty-five year work-benefit allowance, he would be forbidden to obtain another job, unless he worked in the black market, which was also known as the free market. Even then, you didn't want to get caught, as you could lose all of your Prosperity Benefits and even face jail time. For former employees of the Party, it usually wasn't worth the risk.

The clock's hold on his attention was broken by the movement of the office door, which opened with a tiny squeak. Standing in the doorway was a gray-haired but well-built older man.

"David, sorry to have kept you waiting so long. Please, please come in." The man waved him towards the door. David stood up, adjusted his pants and coat, grabbed his briefcase with his left hand and made his way inside, with his right hand ready to be extended. As David walked towards the door, he replied with a smile. "No problem Tim, I appreciate you taking time out of your day to see me." The reply was pleasant, and one he was accustomed to saying. In David's own mind, he always thought the reply was almost robotic, as he simply repeated the same greeting from customer to customer. But with David, no one ever saw it as being fake, and he couldn't really think of anything better to say. David was a genuinely nice person, and his customers recognized this trait, which was one of the reasons his appointment-success rate was much higher compared to his colleagues.

As he walked into the office, a strong miasma of stale cigarettes and dissipated alcohol filled the air, despite the three slightly-open windows. The stench and lingering smoke was overwhelming to David, and his eyes became watery. Tim pointed to one of the leather chairs in front of his desk, "Please, have a seat."

David flashed a quick smiled and sat down. Pausing his spiel until Tim sat down, he went into his sales mode, and another robotic pitch kicked in. "Tim, it is that time of the month again. I need to check to make sure you have everything you need. We do have quite a number of new products coming out, and I can go over them with you very quickly. It might take five minutes." Reaching into his bag, he pulled out his tablet and a binder full of product and services information sheets, while waiting for the reply he knew he would receive.

Tim was an older man, and his face reminded David of a hunter or outdoorsman, with a thick-graying mustache and overly but naturally-tanned skin. He was sitting in a high-backed leather chair, and leaning back with one of his leather shoes perched on the corner of his desk. David was still waiting for the usual negative response, but Tim wasn't providing him with a reply. Opening the desk drawer, he took out a pack of cigarettes, and continuously but lightly tapped the end until one squirmed out of the opening and fell into his hand. Still staring back at David, he balanced the cigarette between his lips and brought a lighter to the tip, without asking David if the smoke would bother him, as he knew he would say it wouldn't. Tim took a lengthy drag, and forcefully exhaled the smoke out of the corner of his mouth, up towards the ceiling to join the residue of his last few cigarettes.

"David, you can put your items back in your bag. I honestly don't see how you keep this up. Every month we meet, and every month you ask to show me the new products. And every month I turn you down. You understand we do all of our purchasing online, and I haven't personally or directly ordered anything from you or anybody else in ten years or more. All of the ordering happens downstairs on level two. You really should be meeting with them."

David shoved the items back in his bag, sat up in his chair and looked down at his lap for a brief moment, as if he was contemplating what he was going to say, before looking back at Tim.

"Tim, you are still the head of this hospital, correct? You know if I go downstairs, I will either be ignored, or I am liable to make someone angry at me. The people down on level two, they aren't the most pleasant people.

Actually, I did go down there once, to the second floor, and they treated me like, well, like they treat all of the vendors. It is as if we have the plague or the mark of the beast. At least up here, I know our meeting will be pleasant, and I can check you off my list, and eventually you will offer me a drink." David grinned.

Tim smiled back and chuckled. "Yes David. Let's cut to the chase. I appreciate the offer, but I am not going to look at your material, and I will offer you a drink. So, would you like a drink? I have a bottle of excellent Duvall whiskey. I already had my assistant fill my ice bucket, as I knew you were coming and wouldn't refuse a drink. And I know how much you like ice. But I still like it neat." Tim removed his foot off the desk, pushed himself out of his chair, and walked over to the side of his office towards a tall round table with thin square legs, which held four bottles of liquor and a stack of glasses. With the cigarette dangling from his lips, he opened the whiskey bottle and poured the dark-reddish liquid into two short crystal glasses, making sure to add several pieces of ice to David's drink.

David was impressed, though he wasn't surprised. "Duvall whiskey? I haven't, well, I haven't had any good whiskey in probably fifteen years. But Duvall, isn't that a rare find? How did you come across that?"

Tim placed the cap back on the bottle, and removed the cigarette from his mouth. "The majority of my non-SoCare vendors, they still bring me gifts. Not every rep is lucky like you and works for SoCare. These other vendors, they think they still have to bribe me every now and then. And yes, I will admit they do. Even though it doesn't really help them. The hospital still has to order the majority of what we need from SoCare."

David sighed out loud, and afterwards, realized it was a bit too loud. "I am not sure if lucky is the correct term. I am coming up on the end of my work-benefit period. I certainly hoped I would have moved forward to a different position, maybe have a chance to do anything else besides this. I have spent the past twenty-five years on the road. Twenty-five years is a long time. Twenty-five years." David stretched out the pronunciation of the last three words, as in disbelief.

Tim ambled over and handed David his drink. Tim raised his glass in the air, towards David. "Well, here's to retirement. Even if it is forced upon us."

They brought their glasses together, until they heard a small clink. Tim took a sip of his drink, and made his way back to his desk. David was a bit shocked. "What a minute. Us? You are retiring as well?"

"Yes David, I am retiring. As you are aware, this is one of the last private hospitals in the country. Let me see, I think we have maybe five or six others scattered around. A few stragglers, hanging on to the ways of the past. But it seems none of us, none of the hospitals, we simply can't keep up with all of the changes and regulations. And especially all of the regulations which involve the endless forms they throw at us. The forms and regulations seem to change from week to week. We have an office of five people who do nothing but make sure we conform to all of the regulations. They aren't even completing any forms, they only check and verify the work of others. You can't imagine all of the daily crap I have to put up with here. Which is why I have the liquor." Tim took another sip.

"And then you have all of this newer and mandatory medical technology and equipment, which aren't very different from the previous models, yet the purchase and implementation costs are exorbitant. Then the reimbursement rates for these procedures from SoCare keep going down. We don't make enough to pay for the equipment, and in the long run, we don't even come close to making a profit, and we haven't made a profit in years. When a hospital can't make their payroll or pay bills, they lose doctors and nurses, and then they can only do one thing, and that is to join SoCare. In a little under two months, we will dissolve our private ownership and officially become another cog in SoCare's proverbial healthcare wheel. They haven't officially told me, but I am fairly certain when that happens, I will be shown the door. Maybe even escorted out by security." Tim amused himself with that last line, and he snorted briefly. "But such is life, I guess." He took another sip of his whiskey and another drag on his cigarette, causing the ashes to fall on his shirt, and he brushed the mess onto the floor.

David finally took a large sip of his drink, as if he needed to catch up with Tim. His mouth was parched, and despite the smoothness and purity of the drink, the whiskey burned a little as it went down, which spawned a small coughing fit, and his eyes watered even more. He wasn't much of a drinking man, as alcoholic beverages were too expensive and he couldn't afford them, at least not on a regular basis. But a free drink should never be refused. A free drink, a free lunch, or a free anything was always acceptable, and pride was not an issue here.

David sighed again, but not as loud as before. "I turn forty-seven this year, and I am not sure what I am going to do. My junky and too-small-for-my-height company car will be taken away, and buying a used car may be out of reach for a while. The rent on my apartment is barely affordable on my current salary. Once my retirement benefits start, I will probably have to move out and rent a room outside the blue zone, and I am not very happy about doing either one. These decisions are tough, but I really need to take time and figure out what I am going to do, and make some plans. My job and my life have consisted of doing the same thing over and over again for such a long time. Part of me is looking forward to a change, but I am not even sure what change would feel like. I try to tell myself it could be an exciting time in my life, but the uncertainty of it all is the great unknown." David realized he probably complained a little too much. But there was a quality, or a trait about Tim which made him feel comfortable, unlike the majority of his clients.

Tim leaned forward and placed his elbows on his desk. He had known David for a long time, and had been studying him for the past year. The conclusion was made that David was a good man, one of the few decent people left in this world. "It sounds like you haven't thought much about retirement, but I certainly have. I plan on moving north and getting a small place in the mountains. A tiny cabin in the woods, hopefully one near a river or stream or even a small pond. My plans were confirmed a long time ago. I want to spend my glory days doing a little fishing. Well, hopefully a lot of fishing. And maybe I can have a small garden, and grow a bunch of vegetables, especially peppers. You can't get a decent banana pepper anywhere. When my wife Peggy was alive, she wanted us to retire to the beach. She loved the beach. She would never go near the water, but she loved the beach, the sand, the sun, the fruity drinks. But to me, the beach is too hot, too sandy and too expensive, even for me. So I guess I am the only lucky one here. I will get a small pension from SoCare, and

I have my Party pension as well, so I should be okay."

David was taken aback. "I didn't know you served in the Party. When was this?"

"Well, David, I am quite a bit older than you. I was in the Party for over twenty-two years, right before I took this job. I certainly wouldn't have this job if I hadn't been in the Party. If you think being on the road is tough, try spending a grueling twenty-two years with the Party. Not to mention all of the years I have wasted in this hospital."

Tim paused, as if he had more to say. Instead, he leaned back in his chair and took another sip of his drink. David managed to finish his drink, probably faster than he should have. They both awkwardly stared at each other, as Tim slowly finished his drink. Tim placed his empty glass on his desk and stood up. "David, have you ever done any fishing?" David shook his head. "Since you haven't decided on what to do when you retire, I am going to make a suggestion. You might want to consider doing some fishing in your retirement. It is very relaxing, but the real benefit is you can eat what you catch. If you have never eaten a fresh trout pulled from a mountain stream, then you are missing out. I have a great fly-fishing book in my car. Let me walk you outside to your car and I will loan it to you. I believe the book is still in my trunk. Let's go check."

David placed his glass on the edge of the desk, grabbed his briefcase, and followed Tim out the door, feeling light-headed accompanied by a slight head rush. He wasn't a drinker, and the whiskey had already started working, warming his body, and after a long day the feeling was good. Tim turned around to lock his office, and they walked down the long hallway to the elevator. As they passed through the lobby, and reached the outside of the building, neither one said anything. Respectfully following Tim, David stayed a step or two behind him, as they walked to Tim's car. Overhead, dark clouds were slowly rolling in from the west, and the sky appeared as if it was going to rain. The balmy afternoon air was already thick with the extra humidity.

Taking a quick look around the parking lot, Tim appeared to be looking for someone, before he opened the trunk and leaned over the bumper. Inside was a cardboard box full of various books and papers, along with a spare tire and tools which were no longer in their designated storage area. Reaching down, he began to shove the stacks of books around until he found what he was looking for, a hardback book titled "*Fly Fishing for Beginners.*" After closing the trunk, Tim turned around and said, "Let's go sit on the bench over there for a minute, so I can show you a trick or two about how to fish." David followed as they sat down on a bench near a small fountain on the side of the parking lot.

The wind started to blow in an attempt to erase the heat radiating from their clothes, but the humidity was already making everything sticky. On this side of the parking lot, the sidewalk turned into a circle, and was flanked by another circle of bushes. The bushes stood guard against a circular fountain pool in the center, with a worn metal bench on either side. David noticed a small dirty-bronze plaque on one side of the fountain which read "In Memory Of Albert Robertson." David didn't recognize the name, but he noticed the fountain was void of all but a minimal number of visible coins, and the bottom was stained green from algae. The fountain was a multi-layered one and was probably very soothing and pleasant when it was turned on, but today the water barely trickled out of the top.

Sitting on the bench, Tim pulled his phone out of his pocket and turned towards David. "I am thinking about getting a new device. What kind do you carry?" David was already sitting on the bench, but he leaned to one side, reached into his pocket, and pulled out a very old phone.

"This is what I have. It is work-issued. I am afraid they don't give us the new equipment. I've had this one for about seven years. But on the good side it's as solid as a brick and does what I need it to do." David handed it to Tim. Tim took the phone, looked at it carefully, as if he was studying it, found a button on the side, which he pressed and held down until the phone turned off. Handing the phone back to David, he repeated the same action with his phone. David was baffled.

Tim handed the fly-fishing book to David. "David, we have known each other for a long time. I have been here for the last sixteen years, and for the first fifteen years or so, we never spent more than a minute or two together. But in the past year, I have been working on a new project, a special project. And that is why our meetings have become a little more open and let's just say, friendlier.

From the first day we met, I could tell you were a good man. I never really saw anything which would make me want to change my opinion of you. So, I decided I wanted to get to know you a little better. And I think I have accomplished this goal over the past year, even if it was ten or fifteen minutes at a time. I believe you are an honest man, which is a scarce quality nowadays. I believe I can trust you. Can I trust you David?"

David didn't understand how trust was related to fly fishing. "Yes, Tim, of course you can trust me."

"Good. Then I will be honest with you. I really didn't bring you out here to read this book on fly fishing. Even though it still might be a good thing to pursue in your retirement. I brought you out here because I needed to talk to you about a different topic." Tim paused and slowly surveyed the parking lot. "Out here, this is probably the only place where we can talk without being monitored."

David was a bit dumbfounded. "You mean your office is being monitored? Is it wired or do they have cameras in there? I knew the Party monitored people, but I thought they were only searching for criminal activity. I never thought they would monitor the inside of an office, especially one in a private business. Every article I have ever read about their monitoring mentioned they were only after criminals and terrorists. Well, it was also public knowledge that monitoring had increased, especially after the terrorists wars started."

"Yes, I know for certain my office is wired. And I wouldn't be surprised if my car was wired as well. Or my home. You would be amazed at how small the cameras are now. But the surveillance is not limited to criminals or terrorists. I know our office phones, home phones and cell phones are all being recorded. Not simply mine or yours, everyone and everything is being monitored. Whenever you go onto the network, every action you take is being monitored and recorded and added to your file. Anything you say, or do on your phone is recorded and your position is tracked. They can even listen to what you are saying when you aren't actually making a phone call. But, this access is limited to when your phone is turned on. They can take pictures with your phone's camera and retrieve them without your knowledge. And of course, you have all of the surveillance cameras, the traffic cameras, the hidden microphones and the mini-sats. This information is common knowledge within the Party. All of these spying programs were a major scandal a long time ago, but the news about it died down for a while, until the beginning of the terrorists wars. But the surveillance never stopped, it only became more intense, more developed, and more accurate. I know most of this from my previous work with the Party. Well, way back before, when there were two political parties. Back before the current single-platform Party was formed. And I still have friends there, in the Party, and they tell me things, they keep me updated on what's happening." Tim reached over and opened the fishing book David placed in his lap. "Now, flip through the book while we are talking, and pause every once in a while, especially if there is a nice picture."

David looked up, and now aware someone could be watching them, he slowly turned his head around, scanning the lot for people, or cameras, before looking down at the book. "I have heard the Party listened to phone calls, but I assumed it was only for national security. You mean they record everything I say?"

"Yes and no. They don't actually listen to the majority of what people say. Computers have this task. They have programs to search for specific patterns and words, and even the tone or accent of your voice. But if what you are saying triggers an event in the system, or if you cause an outburst in your conversation, or if you are arrested, they can go back and basically review your life for the past month or the past year. Or in some cases, the past ten or even twenty years or so. They do the same with video. They can use their network of cameras to track you wherever you go, using facial-recognition software to figure out who you are. There are programs to detect your mass and height, and even the way you walk. In high-security places, infrared cameras can detect if you have something hidden under your clothes. They have tens of thousands of mini-sats floating above us, recording high-resolution video of entire cities. If your life gets assigned to one of those, then forget it. They will know everything about you."

Tim now lowered his voice to slightly above a whisper. "David, I have played along with the Party for a long time. I followed their rules, and I overlooked things I shouldn't have. And when I spoke out against these things, I was punished. So, I licked my wounds, swallowed my pride and decided to keep playing along. But in the process, I lost my moral character. I became a person I am not proud of. And now because of this merger with SoCare, and because of some other things, I have truly seen how horrible the Party has become. It isn't only the Party. It includes everything and everyone who turns away, the same as I did, while allowing the Party to grow and become the evil it is now. In less than two months, I will be as far away from this hospital, from society, from the Party as I can be. And the main reason..." Tim stopped talking.

David mimicked Tim, talking at a whisper. "What? What were you going to say?"

"You see David. I have cancer. And even with all of my connections, even with my status as director of this hospital, I do not believe I will be able to get approved for treatment fast enough. By the time I am even allowed to see a specialist, I will be dead or too far gone for help. I convinced one doctor to take a look at my records, with great risk on his part, and he agreed the prognosis is grim. Even if I am approved by the medical benefits review board for treatment, he doesn't believe I would even live long enough to receive it. And getting approval, with the cancer at this stage and at my age, is almost impossible. I might have six months left, maybe a year if I am lucky. Which is why I am here with you today, and why I am telling you this."

David was confused about this situation, of him sitting here with Tim on this bench, and with Tim telling him these things. Here is a man who, often in the past, while being kind and polite to David, would barely speak to him for more than a minute or two. Only in the past year or so, has he been more inviting, more open during their normally brief meetings. Why is he confiding in me? I don't have anything to offer. I am not a doctor. I don't have access to the drugs. I can't help.

Tim continued, "You see, I don't believe I am alone in my thoughts. From all of the conversations we've had in the past, I believe you might share the same concerns and thoughts I do about the Party. The Party is not what it claims to be. Would this be a fair statement? Would you agree?"

David sat there, still a bit stunned and even more confused. It was unheard of, for a member of the Party or even a former member, to be saying anything against the Party, even while sitting on a bench in a hopefully-unmonitored location. "I don't understand. What thoughts or concerns are you talking about? My interaction with the Party is almost zero. In fact, I have little to do with the Party or even society in general. As far as I know, the Party controls everything, but that's just how it is. I do my job, go home, and I get back out there and do my job again. My life is as far removed from the Party and their controls and pretty much everything else. I just try to focus on my job."

"You live in the blue zone, don't you David?" asked Tim.

"Yes. But what does the blue zone have to do with any of this?"

"Well David, where you live does have a little to do with what I am going tell you. You might remember, a little over twenty-five years ago, we had two political parties. And they loathed each other. It was not a very civil time to be in politics. But one party determined that because of the heavy growth in the cities, or what we now call the blue zones, if one party could win enough of the blue zone votes, they could control the elections. This control included both the national and local legislative bodies. And this theory was eventually proven to be correct, after one party had the power to draw the voting districts in very unique ways. Of course, this type of redistricting had been going on for ages, but the Blue Party took it to the extreme. And after a while, when you control enough votes, and to a degree, when you can control the voting process and even the outcome of elections, in the end you gain control over the country. For the Blue Party, it didn't matter if they had to break the law to do it either."

"The blue zone and red zones were set aside to determine contribution collection and benefit distribution. Remember, back then, the word 'taxes' was used to describe the revenue collected from the citizens. Today the term is called contributions. This is one of the many words which have changed over the years to fit the Party's agenda and mission. The red zone doesn't receive the same allocation of what we now collectively know as Prosperity Benefits, and the red zone residents are taxed at a higher rate than the blue zone residents. The vast majority of the blue zone residents are staunch supporters of the Party.

And even though the blue zone is tightly controlled and monitored by the Party, the residents gladly welcome this subjugation, in order to receive a majority of the benefits."

"At the time, we were in the middle of a great recession, some say it was a depression, and people of all trades were having problems finding work. The Blue Party kept increasing the Prosperity Benefits for the blue zone residents to the point where people made more money sitting at home, than they would at their old jobs. So more and more people flocked to the blue zone from the red zone, until the populations of the red zones were not enough to control or win any of the local or national elections. The party which controlled the blue zones took control of the local areas, and then after two election cycles, they controlled the national legislature."

"Eventually, the other political party decided it was better to join them, instead of fighting them. No one likes to be on the losing team. The leaders of both parties got together, and agreed that instead of spending billions fighting each other, they decided they would simply share the power. Of course, the political donations would still be raised, but it was easier to line the pockets of their friends and family with this money, instead of actually spending it on campaigns. There were still two parties, with two apparently different sets of goals and ideologies, at least for a while. But the agreement which was in place didn't last long. The Blue Party, which was the party in power, already controlled the media and the local and national governments, and so squeezing out the Red Party was easy. The media reported to the masses precisely what the Blue Party wanted them to report. In other words, the media were essentially taking direction from the Blue Party bosses. The media also formed a covert group, an organization, headed by Blue Party members, to ensure the correct message was being broadcast. Everything, all of the news you read about or saw on the television, was being directed by the Blue Party."

"After several years, the Red Party dissolved. Many members simply switched sides so they could stay in power. Many others, like myself, agreed to resign, to not seek re-election and most importantly, to keep quiet. We all left the political scene, and in order to buy our silence, we were all promised and given very well-paying and comfortable jobs."

"But a select group of us outsiders stayed in touch. We formed a small private association and still retained our old platform and beliefs. Our meetings were held in secret, and we did whatever we could do to harm this new single-platform party. And there were a few people in our group who remained with the Party, and these were the ones who switched sides to stay in power. They still preached the Party line, but deep inside they still possessed the old drive and passion that what we were doing, in silently opposing the Party and working against it behind the scenes, was truly for the good of the country."

"We are now at a point where the members of this group have had enough of the Party. We need to escalate our actions beyond what our small group can do alone. And, many of us are too old to actually do what needs to be done. This is where you come into the picture. I can't tell you exactly how many of us there are left, but we are all recruiting people, trustworthy people, like yourself, to help us with this cause. People who aren't happy with the Party and the state of the country. This is why I asked if I could trust you. I already knew the answer, but I needed to ask you for myself. I can trust you, correct?"

David was still perplexed and wasn't sure where this conversation was going. "Yes, of course you can trust me."

To David, it was strange being in this situation, being a confidant, trusted by a former Party member, even one with possibly nefarious goals, and the conversation intrigued but puzzled David. Even after spending the past decade relatively alone, except for the small interactions with his clients, or with the people who served him food, or the desk clerks who checked him into his hotel rooms, his self-imposed solitude didn't isolate him from a true understanding of the Party's nature. He never considered that he or anyone else possessed the power to implement change in any way. Everything and everyone was engulfed by the Party's ideologies, but their beliefs and actions never fully resonated with David, and in a way he always felt like an outcast. Their laws and regulations seemed to be fair, but he could never grasp the logic or lack of logic behind the reasoning for each act. Perhaps now was a chance that someone was going to do something, and he could be a part of it, even if he didn't know what part he would play.

"What do you want me to do?" asked David.

Tim reached into his pocket, and pulled out a folded green envelope.

"Before you give me your decision, I want you to take this envelope, go home and read the letter inside. It isn't very lengthy, but it explains in further detail the task I am asking you to take on. When you are finished reading the letter, I want you to destroy it. The words are printed on a special type of paper called nitrocellulose. The more common name is flash paper. When you touch this paper to a flame, it catches on fire very quickly, almost instantaneously. There are virtually no ashes, and the destruction is immediate."

David reached out and took the letter, and placed it inside the book.

"I want you to read this and to think about what I am asking. I don't want to see you for another month. You should not deviate from your normal schedule. I will see you again on the same day and at the same time we normally meet."

Tim stood up, and extended his hand to David, who accepted his hand and shook it. He began to leave, heading towards the hospital, when David blurted out. "Tim. One last thing." Tim stopped, and turned around.

"I am sorry to hear about your cancer. I really am. I wish you the best."

Tim was touched by this simple display of concern and compassion, albeit a small one, but it was an act that was rare among people nowadays. And the simple words David spoke, confirmed he was the type of man Tim calculated he would be. "Thanks, I appreciate it. But I might have an option or two left. We will have to wait and see. That cabin and those fish might still be within reach."

Tim walked back towards the hospital. David followed him with his eyes as he walked through the doors. Holding the book tightly with his hands like he was protecting it, and with the edges of the envelope peeking out of the sides, his mind started to ponder what Tim was asking him to do. The answer would have to wait until he was back home. Taking one last look around the parking lot, he stood up, walked over to his car, cautiously squeezed his tall frame inside the tiny car and closed the door. Leaning to his right, he slipped the book underneath the passenger's seat, and drove off towards his hotel, as the rain began to fall.

Chapter 2

The traffic David endured on the drive to the hotel was sadistic. The route was filled with cars and trucks incapable of being driven properly, and a heavy torrent of rain washed away any common sense occupying the inside of the vehicles. At almost nineteen-thirty, David finally pulled into his hotel, after spending nearly two hours on a drive of less than twenty miles. The frustration and the unpleasant discourse between the other cars was unnoticed by him, as his mind was still focused on his earlier conversation with Tim.

Tim had asked him, "Can I trust you?"

This single and simple question caused his mind to race in an ungovernable manner. Tim provided him with an enigma without an easy solution. The unknown was in guessing what Tim was asking him to do, especially with the need for secrecy along with the letter which must be destroyed. During the drive, David's mind had been going through the possible scenarios and the ones he attempted to generate weren't plausible. So the decision was proposed, debated and finally confirmed, he would wait until he returned home to read the letter. The necessity of destroying the letter immediately helped him to agree to this delay, as he didn't have a lighter or any matches. The thought of stopping at a convenience store to buy matches occurred more than once, but he decided he needed to read the letter in the privacy of his home. The concern of over-thinking this entire scenario was accepted, as he was probably reading more into the possibilities than what was really going to happen. The front of the hotel suddenly appeared in his view, which snapped his attention back to driving. Decreasing his speed as the car approached the area in front of the lobby doors, he leaned over and reached down to verify the book was still under the passenger's seat, as if there was a possibility it vanished. He would be home tomorrow night, and reading the letter could wait.

David pulled into a parking space at the back of the hotel, next to two overflowing green dumpsters. He consistently seemed to arrive late at his hotels, and the parking lot was always full, and the only available parking was usually in the back. As he exited the car, he detected the stench of the garbage, flowing from the dumpsters, and the smell was nasty. The pavement was still hot, despite the rain, and the soupy-sour smell from the garbage clung to his skin and seemed to penetrate his clothes. He would definitely have to take a shower before going to bed. Pulling his luggage out of the trunk, he extended the handle, and started dragging it across the lot. One of the axels for the two bottom wheels had broken earlier in the week, and was now permanently stuck, so as he pulled it across the lot, one wheel was being slowly eaten by the asphalt. Carrying the bag was contemplated, but wasn't an option as he was too tired. A new piece of luggage would need to be purchased, but he was hoping he could make do since his retirement date was very near. He really didn't see himself wanting to travel or being able to afford to travel when this was all over. And even cheap luggage was expensive.

After waiting in line for what seemed like an obscene amount of time, he checked in with the semi-amicable young woman at the front desk, and headed towards the elevator. Something was out of place, and he noticed the interior of this hotel appeared to have been painted since his last visit. Previously the walls were an almost-putrid green color, which reminded him of rotting vegetables, but now the interior had been painted a uneventful shade of gray. The new walls reminded him of the color of a naval battleship. Gray was such a dismal color, one which appeared to be void of any life or personality. Walking through the lobby, the old vile green paint could be noticed peeking out along the edges of the walls, where the painters must have forgotten how to cut-in paint, or they were simply too lazy to care.

When David reached the elevator, there was a crudely-handwritten sign covering the outside buttons which stated "Out of order - use stairs." The sign wasn't a surprise, as the elevators in the Party hotels were unreliable, and the haggard condition of the sign confirmed the frequency of its use. The desk clerk didn't even bother to mention the elevator was broken. Collapsing the handle on the suitcase, he reluctantly hoisted the heavy bag off the floor, and headed towards the stairs, only to discover the interior of the stairwell had been violated by the same depressing gray. With the noticeable lack of ventilation in the stairwell, the smell was overwhelming, and he could almost taste the flavor of the paint through his nose. There were four flights to clear, and the combination of fatigue and the abundant fumes caused him to stop and rest after climbing halfway. Normally, having to take the stairs wouldn't be a concern. But, he hadn't been sleeping well, and he found himself to be a little light-headed, with almost the same sensation from drinking the whiskey. As he waited for his mind to clear and for his balance to return, he realized he was more than simply exhausted from lack of sleep. He was tired of his job, with the constant and irritating travel, and he was generally despondent with his uneventful life.

After a brief pause he continued up the stairs, and passed through the doorway into the fourth floor hallway. The door to the stairwell had been left open in what was probably a vain attempt to disperse the smell. The power of the gray paint had walked through the door opening, and the air in the hallway provided almost no relief. His room was found at the far end of the hall, and he lamented that his room was always the furthest away from the elevator, or near the ice machine. Being near the ice machines usually wasn't a bad thing, as they were broken more often than not. But when they were functioning, through the emaciated walls you could hear every cube drop into the plastic ice buckets.

David often wondered, were the private hotels the same, covered in the same lifeless paint, with the same indifferent interior? When he traveled, David was restricted to staying at only certain Party-owned hotels. He hadn't traveled on his own expense for a long time, so he accepted the fact he would probably never find an answer to this question which bothered him.

Upon opening the door to his room, a forceful wave of cleaning chemicals hit him in the face, which in turn generated a self-directed curse for having such a strong sense of smell. He naturally flinched at first, but then accepted that along with this particular smell, at least the room might be clean. Too often the maids at the Party hotels would simply make the bed and empty the trash cans. Most of the time they wouldn't even change the sheets or vacuum the floor. Holding his breath, in one motion he tossed his bag onto the bed while continuing to the window. After banging on the lock, he was able to slightly open it, in the hope the crack would invite a small breeze to try and dissipate the chemical cloud. The room was also very warm so he made his way over to the thermostat, and noticed the air conditioning was turned off. He turned the thermostat to the lowest setting, in a vain attempt to cool the room and to counter the blistering heat that would soon be wandering in from outside through the small opening in the window. Sweat was already dripping down his back from the arduous climb up the stairs, and he could tell the room wasn't going to offer him any comfort.

His stomach bellowed a low but long rumble, and he checked his watch. The restaurant should still be open, and a shower would have to wait. The hike back down the stairs was quickly made in order to get a bite to eat. In addition to being restricted to staying at the Party-owned hotels, he was forced to eat breakfast and dinner there as well. The sign near the hostess station read, "Please seat yourself." David found a spot in the corner, and sat in the chair on the opposite side of the table, so his back was against the wall. He preferred a table which offered him a view of the restaurant where he could watch the other guests.

Every once in a while, he would act out in his mind a fantasy where he would casually meet a woman, maybe she would be at the next table, and they would awkwardly start what would turn into a great conversation. And for an unknown reason, their chance encounter would be special for her as well. They would maybe have a drink or three, chat for a while and then go up to her room, and spend the night together. And afterwards, they would discover they lived in the same apartment complex or very close to each other. And after returning home, they would continue seeing each other, exclusively, and he would no longer be alone. The fantasy was played in his head often, with the minor details changed to keep it exciting. Meeting a woman on the road was really his only option, as he rarely left his apartment and never ventured out to do anything in the city.

After carefully scanning the restaurant, and after not seeing any viable prospects, he opened the menu. Reading the familiar selections, he once again reminded himself he would probably never have the courage to go and talk to a stranger. This reason alone usually helped him self-justify his loneliness and inability to act on any desires of the heart. Plus, if he encountered a potential and suitable paramour at this hotel, their presence here would indicate they possessed the same unwanted characteristics he despised in himself. A person with the same type of meaningless job and life he possessed wasn't appealing. David was a little better than average-looking, with a full head of thick brown hair, and a puerile face with hazel eyes. Even though he exercised almost every night he was on the road, his body only managed to maintain a youthful shape, and failed to gain any noticeable mass. But with his self-imposed isolation and insecurity, he lost the majority of the social skills useful with women, the same skills he perfected when he was younger. The only type of social skills he now possessed involved the ones you use when meeting with clients. With his clients, he was a very different man, full of confidence and with a genial personality.

The menus were nearly-identical at all of the hotels. The only reason to even look at the menu was out of habit, combined with a glimmer of optimism that one day, the menu would offer him new and exciting foods he could try. But like always, his hopes were defeated, as the menu contained all the same vapid offerings as the other hotel from the night before.

After waiting for nearly ten minutes, a waitress sauntered over, and even though she appeared to recognize his face, she didn't know his name and didn't even bother to acknowledge the fact she might know him. As she stood by his side, David browsed the choices on the menu, counting the elapsed time in his head, while he pretended to be contemplating his selection, when he already made up his mind. He enjoyed making them wait, as he had been forced to wait. There was a science as to how long a waitress would remain before they would offer you more time to decide and then leave, possibly never to return, and he liked testing their patience. The stalling was halted after twelve seconds, as she rolled her eyes while loudly smacking on the gum in her mouth. David noted his best time with this particular waitress was sixteen seconds, so his record wasn't broken tonight. "I'll take a cheeseburger with fries, and a diet cola with lots of ice. No tomato or ketchup please." She took his order without saying a word, grabbed his menu, and disappeared into the kitchen.

Eating dinner every night at these Party-hotel restaurants was beyond monotonous, with the same nasty and greasy food night after night. He missed the enjoyment of a good home-cooked meal. His longing was due to him not being much of a cook, and he tried to remember the last time he last enjoyed a really good meal. The date was probably a week or so before his wife left him almost twelve years ago. She was fondly remembered as an attractive, decent and kind person; a little gullible, maybe even bordering on being simple-minded, but she was a really good cook. Having met and dated in college, they were married a month after they both graduated. She held a nice job with the Party at their local National Information Office, and her commute was a short distance from their apartment. They had a great time when they were together, but she had grown weary of him being on the road so much. Over time, they eventually grew apart, and parted ways amicably.

Thoughts of her often crossed his mind, if she was still there, honing her marketing and propaganda skills for the Party. The last time they talked was seven or eight years ago, upon crossing paths in a department store. She was still as pleasant and appealing as he remembered, and he wondered if she would be retiring as well. The encounter caused him to ponder if there was a chance they could start seeing each other again. But he quickly dismissed the idea. She had probably married again. During their time together, she would often comment on how she wished he was a Party member. His wife, along with most women her age, as well as the majority of the current population of women, possessed this infatuation for Party members. According to her, and it wasn't too far from the truth, Party members always had a good job with a great salary, and they lead these spectacular and exciting lives. A Party member was what she really wanted, and most Party members wanted a younger wife as well. She probably found an older Party member who would appreciate a younger wife. The only downside for the wives was Party members rarely stayed married for long, at least not to the same person. To a Party member, marriage was like buying a car. You find a nice new one, drive it for a while, and then trade it in after the novelty wore off for a newer model.

The daydream about his ex-wife was interrupted by the clang of a hard plastic plate in front of him, announcing the arrival of his food. He hadn't even noticed the glass of diet cola the waitress placed in front of him earlier, but he quickly noted the lack of a sufficient amount of ice. As the waitress steamed away, he mumbled a soft, "Thanks," and began to eat. The waitress returned after a few seconds, placed the check on the table and left. David noticed she never said a word.

The cheeseburger consisted of a lump of hard bread, a slice of synthetic cheese and a patty of an unknown substance which could be identified as hamburger meat. David lifted the bun, and immediately noticed they failed to include any lettuce on the burger. There was a quick thought of calling the waitress back, but he decided against it, as the lettuce was always a gamble anyway. The lettuce used for burgers was usually taken from the inner part of the head, and always included a large white spine in the middle. David preferred the green-leafy variety which was usually reserved for salads. Replacing the bun, he took a bite of the cheeseburger. As he chewed through the dense bread, the taste of the meat broke through, and consisted mostly of warm grease. The fries were satisfactory, but desperately needed salt and pepper, and could have been warmer as well. As he worked on his meal, his thoughts turned away from his ex-wife and back to what Tim said, "Can I trust you?" Those words, one simple question, had been haunting him.

As always, he quickly consumed his food, which even upon arrival was barely warm. Eating quickly was a requirement if you wanted to attempt to enjoy the food, as the meat product had a foul taste when it was cold. The grease from the burger quickly applied itself to the inside of his mouth much like the dismal gray paint from the walls. The fries brought along their own version of grease, but the meat grease usually won the fight and hung around longer. Even though the food wasn't great, he was really hungry. Lunch was almost nine hours earlier, when he purchased a hot dog at a gas station.

Lunch was the only meal where he could eat outside of a Party-owned hotel restaurant. His per diem for lunch was a small and fixed amount, and when he traveled, he was reimbursed for this set amount whether he ate lunch or not. So on most days, he either skipped lunch or ate something moderately inexpensive. Often, he would bring cans of chicken or tuna or vegetable-filled ravioli from home, and eat it cold from the can while he sat in his car. A container of water was stored in the backseat, along with a plastic bottle to be refilled as needed. David had longed viewed his per-diem as a small bonus. The less he spent on lunch, the more he could save for retirement. Over the past twenty-five years, he estimated he had saved a year's pay from the remains of his per-diem, which brought him a sense of satisfaction. After finishing his meal, he signed the check and made the hike back to his room.

Normally after dinner, he would exercise in the hotel fitness room. Despite the nasty paint smell and bland food, this hotel was one of his favorites because it possessed a half-decent fitness room. All government buildings, including hotels, were required to have a fitness room, as part of the "Party's Keep Our Bodies Healthy" initiative. David rarely encountered anyone else in the fitness rooms, and he enjoyed the solitude. This hotel's fitness room had two treadmills and a nearly-complete set of rusty dumbbells. When he exercised, he would spend a half-hour on the treadmill, and then work out with the weights for another half-hour. But tonight, he was too tired, both physically and mentally, and it was already late. And now he held the combined taste of two types of grease and the gray paint in his mouth. It was going to be a long night.

Chapter 3

David woke early the next morning. As usual, he had trouble sleeping. During his shower, his insides were moaning and gurgling, and still battling the consequences of last night's platter of grease. He dressed quickly, as he wanted to get an early start before traffic. Today was the end of his work week, a Friday, so as usual there were two morning appointments, and the afternoon would be spent driving the four or more hours to get home. His sales territory was defined by a drive-time of no more than six hours from his home office, and his clients were the larger medical clinics, centers and hospitals within this radius. Given the long drive home, he usually tried to finish his Friday appointments early. If he was lucky, he could get home before the local traffic going into the city was a mess, which rarely happened.

With his briefcase in his hand and his suitcase dragging behind him, he made the trek downstairs for breakfast, with a detour to the front desk for a copy of the Party's newspaper. Reading anything was not a normal action during meals, due to his hobby of people-watching, and he seldom read the Party's paper. But the paper would be a good read for later this weekend, to possibly provide insight or evidence on what Tim stated about the Party. And it didn't hurt that the paper was free.

The breakfast buffet was always the same at the Party hotels. The choices usually included a large and deep tray of a substance purported to be scrambled eggs, but with the consistency of overly-concentrated oatmeal. It was a given the hotel didn't use real eggs, as those were too expensive. Therefore the eggs were more than likely a thick protein product which was dyed yellow. The protein base was probably the same product used for the hamburgers, but without whatever food agents used to achieve the different texture and color. The eggs were usually a little watery at the bottom of the pan, and David avoided this by delicately scooping from the top half. When the eggs were overcooked, they morphed into a type of protein cake, and he preferred the cake version. There was always a tray of fake-meat patties, or what the cooks in the kitchen would proudly call sausage. Even when the meat was labeled a ham patty, the taste was not discernible from the sausage patty, which caused him to speculate the only difference was the color of the food dye, and maybe more grease.

The biscuits were his favorite, even though the biscuits were simply hard round pieces of bread, and weren't palatable unless white gravy was poured on top, and left alone for five minutes to soften. The gravy was a favorite as well, and he stopped trying to figure out what it was made from. On occasion he would take a few extra biscuits, and feed the pigeons during lunchtime. By then, the biscuits would be as dry as sand, but apparently the pigeons didn't mind, and the pigeons didn't need gravy to enjoy them.

David filled a plate with a large helping of eggs, meat patties and biscuits and gravy. While he always seemed to be hungry, this morning he ate like he was starving. The eggs were watery despite his meticulous scooping efforts, but the biscuits were perfect. Another trip was made for more meat patties, along with another biscuit and ladle of gravy. Even though the coffee tasted more bitter than usual, while he was in line he grabbed a to-go cup, mainly because the coffee was free. He preferred to drink his coffee black, which is how he made it at home. He was forced to forgo sugar when it was rationed and became too expensive for him to buy or even for restaurants to give away. And the fake-sugar substitutes were chalky and seemed to be made of nothing but fiber, or that was the effect it had on him. The fake-sugar was the type of substance which wasn't good for him to consume when he was on the road all week long.

As he waited for the gravy to soak into the second round of biscuits, the words, "Can I trust you?" kept repeating in his head. Like always, he was positive he was over-thinking what Tim had said. Trusting a person or having a person ask you if they can trust you is such a personal request. You would never ask a stranger for trust, and you wouldn't trust one either. You wouldn't even trust the majority of your friends, at least not all of the time. This simple question, despite not knowing the reasons behind it, triggered feelings of pride and confidence, feelings he hadn't experienced in a while. A long time had passed since anyone asked him to do anything on a personal level, and certainly no one had asked him to trust them. Yet here was the head of a large hospital, a former legislator and former Inner Circle Party member, a man involved in a secret organization, asking him for his trust. This man hadn't really divulged any secret information yet, but if knowledge about this organization was discovered by the Party, it could possibly get them both twenty or thirty years in prison. The fact that David wasn't involved with this group didn't matter, he now possessed knowledge of its existence, and would be just as culpable.

David finished the biscuits, grabbed his luggage and briefcase, and headed out to his car. Once outside the hotel, he observed he was walking very fast, almost running to his car while dragging his luggage behind him, with the locked wheel drawing a black line across the almost-white and sun-bleached concrete walkway. Throwing the luggage into the trunk, he stepped over to his door, and realized he left his free coffee in the restaurant. Checking his watch, he found he was way ahead of schedule, and suddenly he noticed his spirits were high for a change. Such efficiency on his part was definitely worth the reward of a cup of real coffee at one of the coffee shops scattered around the city, and there may even be cause to splurge for a pack of real sugar. On second thought, a packet of sugar was an extra charge, and two packets were almost half the cost of the coffee. There was no sense in getting crazy at this time. Black coffee from a coffee house would suffice.

Even with a quick stop for coffee, David arrived at the first hospital early, and sauntered up to the security desk, only to be notified by the security guard the person he was meeting was not going to be there. The guard instructed him to contact her on Monday, and they would reschedule. This news brought a feeling of relief, but it also left him with two hours to kill until the next meeting, and he was anxious to complete this day and travel home. Once back in his car, he at least had time to finish his coffee, and he tried to pretend he could taste the sugar he never added. But his pretending brought a feeling of remorse that he cheated himself for at least not buying one packet of sugar. The consolation was that the coffee was still much better than what the hotel served. The taste was still slightly bitter, but it was less artificial.

The decision was made to go ahead and drive to the second appointment, where he found a good parking spot under a large pine tree, where the shade would definitely help in this heat. The time was only nine-twenty, but it was already unbearably hot and humid. The next appointment wasn't until eleven, so he pulled out his tablet to check his electronic mail, but noticed he was almost at his weekly data quota. If the quota was surpassed, he would have to pay for the overage out of his own pocket, and such an act was illogical. Browsing the subject lines of the emails, he only read the ones deemed important and decided he could wait until he was back at work on Monday to respond. Besides, even though some of the Party employees could be scheduled to work until seventeen hundred, most would stop trying to do anything meaningful after lunch on a Friday.

The majority of the workforce quit working on Friday at twelve hundred, in order not to go beyond the thirty hours per week work-benefit allowance. The restrictions on work allocations were mandated by the Party so more people, or at least those who had a job and weren't solely surviving off Prosperity Benefits, could have the chance to work. Most people either worked only six hours per day for five days, or nine hours for three days with an additional half-day. The plan was to stagger the work shifts and hours so no one worked the same shift or schedule every week. This restriction also eliminated overtime and overtime pay, which was forbidden. The Party's reasoning was if a business needed an employee to work overtime, then the business should hire another person to work those hours. But, if you worked for the Party or a Party member, your work-benefit hours might be a little longer, as every Party-related work position was considered critical, no matter what your job entailed. All of the rules the Party mandated and enforced upon others were not always applicable to the Party and their employees. David's position within SoCare usually required him to be on the road at least forty-five to fifty hours per week, for the same salary and benefits as if he worked thirty hours in an office.

The switch to the thirty-hour week was a product of the nationalization of businesses which occurred a little over a decade ago. During this period, the country was in the middle of a bloody terrorists war, being fought on their own soil. Also during this time, the country suffered a horrific bacterial outbreak in the food supply, possibly as a result of a terrorist activity but never confirmed. The estimates were between one to three million citizens died or were permanently disabled. No one in the Party really wanted to know the actual numbers, so no one could disprove the lower numbers of casualties the Party was claiming. The Party stepped in and in order to protect the food supply and the citizens, they nationalized all food manufacturing and distribution. The next industry to be targeted was the farms producing the crops, and they quickly succumbed to nationalization as well.

Soon after, the private food businesses and grocers couldn't keep up with the Party's new food, nutrition and health regulations, and so once again, in order to protect the public, the Party nationalized their businesses. The remaining survivors of private enterprise, as far as food or beverages were concerned, were small specialty shops, like coffee houses or tea rooms. In the Party's mind, the revenue generated from these enterprises wasn't large enough for them to deal with the hassle of managing the thousands of locations. Besides, the Party already regulated the coffee and tea imports to the point where the profit margins at these stores were very small. The liquor and tobacco shops had fallen to Party control a half-dozen years before, and these were turned over to the regional Party groups to control. Plus, the owners and workers of these specialty food businesses were heavy contributors to, and faithful supporters of the Party, so control of their businesses and livelihood were spared for now.

Relaxing in his car, he was savoring the last of his coffee. Normally after drinking the Party coffee, his stomach would burn for several hours, much like the whiskey Tim had given him, but without the pleasant side effects. This coffee was almost as smooth as milk and he vowed after he retired, he would treat himself at least once a week to the good stuff, if he could afford it. Coffee this good was nearly impossible to find in the co-op stores. The good coffee was only sold at these specialty shops.

Opening his briefcase, he pulled out the Party's newspaper. The headline read "Party Officials Exonerated in Highway Scandal," and he started reading the story. A group of Party officials with the Society Transportation Department had been accused by a local contractor of demanding bribes for work already been awarded to his company. The judge, the Honorable George Doyle, ruled since the contract had already been awarded, there was no logical reason for the officials to seek bribes. In this case, the contractor must be lying in order to make up for the fact the contractor was unable to finish the project on time. In the judge's ruling, the contractor was stripped of the contract, and the second contractor with the second lowest bid would now take over the project. David guessed the second contractor would not make the same mistake as the first.

The conversation with Tim caused him to analyze this story he was reading. Why would a contractor create such a fabrication? What would he gain with this accusation? His company already won a potentially-lucrative contract. Perhaps this one contractor had grown weary of paying people off? But the story, and the way it was presented to the reader, didn't make sense. The more he contemplated the article, the more he realized this was a typical news story about the Party. The Party is accused of committing a crime or malfeasance, but always in the end, they are found to be not guilty. If what Tim said about the Party controlling the media was correct, then why were these media outlets allowed to even print these negative stories? According to Tim, the media was supposed to be taking their marching orders from the Party. And, above all, this was the Party's own newspaper. Why would they print any information about a potential scandal if it was false? He couldn't quite understand the logic behind it.

The paper was folded and thrown onto the back seat. David looked at his watch, and the time was nine thirty-five, almost another hour and a half to wait for his next appointment. While normally a very patient man, he desperately wanted to drive home and read the letter from Tim. An idea came to him, and he decided to do something he had never done in his career. Grabbing his briefcase, he quickly left the car, and scurried towards the front of the hospital. He slipped through the revolving door, and walked up to the security desk. One of the security officers was on the phone, and the other one was reading a magazine, and didn't bother to acknowledge his presence. David took the registration book, and signed his name and wrote down the time.

Once the security officer was off the phone, David said, "I am here to see Betty Thompson, I have a nine-thirty appointment, and I am running a little late. Traffic was horrible."

The security guard's expression was vacant, as if David was speaking a foreign language. The guard finally translated what David said, and he looked down at his clipboard, using his finger to keep track of where his eyes were focused.

"Your appointment is at eleven hundred."

David sighed loudly and let out a low grumble of self-disgust. "Would you mind calling Betty and asking if she is available now? I think I must have double-booked my appointments. I have another appointment at a different hospital at eleven, and it would be a big help if I could meet with her now."

The guard picked up the phone and after referencing the computer for her information, he dialed Betty's extension. After mumbling into the handset and listening to the response, the guard place the handset back on the phone. "She said she can't meet with you now, and she doesn't need anything. She said to do the normal scheduling process for your next meeting, and there is no need to make up this meeting." The guard turned away, sat back down in his chair, and picked up a magazine.

"I appreciate your help. Have a great weekend." David turned around and almost skipped through the revolving doors, with a big smile on his face.

Chapter 4

David arrived home in near-record time. Normally, he wouldn't get home until eighteen or nineteen hundred at night, if he was lucky and if traffic wasn't bad. The parking lot was almost full, but he was able to find a spot one row over, still fairly close to his building. As his car rolled into place, the clock on the dash flashed thirteen fifty-five. If it hadn't been for having to drive through one of the never-completed construction zones, he could have been here twenty or thirty minutes earlier. The radio had been tuned to one of the Party's classical music stations, and was still softly playing music, so he waited until the song was finished. Listening to classical music was very soothing to him, and the lack of words allowed him to think at the same time, without being too distracted. If he was sad or depressed, he enjoyed listening to Italian opera music. Even though he couldn't speak or understand Italian, the power of the voices made him feel good inside. He didn't experience the same effect when he understood the lyrics. A lost feeling softly arose inside him, one of a sense of great pride and accomplishment from his trick earlier for his last appointment, which helped to shave at least a couple of hours from his day. The last time he was home this early on a Friday afternoon was a distant memory.

Turning off the car, David remained in his seat, staring down towards the floor in front of the passenger's seat. The book was not visible, but he knew it was still there, as he checked it twice during the drive home. A sudden shudder shot through him, like when you notice a spider crawling on your leg. This was followed by a reluctant awareness, the kind which is present when one is was about to lie or commit a crime, and the latter was definitely a possibility. His conscience was having second thoughts about even reading the letter, but he reasoned these feelings should be brushed aside. After all, the only act he was perpetrating was reading something, and reading a letter couldn't be a criminal act. His mind had not decided on an answer to the question of helping Tim, and he still wasn't sure what he was being asked to do anyway. After taking a quick look around the parking lot, he leaned over and reached under the passenger's seat, and withdrew the fly-fishing book. Even though he could see the ends of the envelope, he opened the book for verification, and the envelope was still there, and it was still sealed. The book with the envelope was quickly shoved into his briefcase, and he stepped out into the midday sun.

The heat and humidity quickly engulfed his body and he started sweating almost immediately. Closing the door, he went around to the trunk, removed his luggage, and started for his apartment across the burning asphalt. As he made his way towards the sidewalk across the lot, the stuck wheel on his luggage popped off and unevenly rolled and hopped across the pavement before resting at his feet. Standing above the wheel, and studying the now wheel-less side, he closed his eyes and took a deep breath. The luggage would have to be replaced, something he desperately wanted to avoid. A cheap piece of luggage like this costs at least two days' worth of wages. If he woke early tomorrow, he might be able to make it to the Second Chance store and find a used one before someone else did. Saturday's were when they usually restocked the store.

Collapsing the handle, he picked up the heavy bag, and carried it the remainder of the way. His apartment was on the third floor, and like the hotel, the elevator was out of order. But in this case, the elevator had been broken for over three months. The stairs were in the middle of the building, but were still located outside. Despite being in the open air, the stairwell always radiated a strong urine smell, which was being amplified by the heat and humidity. By the time he reached the third floor, he decided he would have to take a shower before going to bed. Setting the luggage down, he opened the door to his apartment, and dropped his suitcase on the floor. The temperature in the apartment was nearly as hot as outside. David quickly closed and locked the door, and he headed straight to the kitchen, where he pulled a large plastic cup from the cabinet, and filled it with water from the faucet. Walking over to the couch, he placed the cup on the side table on top of a magazine, and placed his briefcase beside him.

He kicked off his shoes with his feet, and removed his tie, careful to not disturb the knot. His wardrobe for work was limited, and he only possessed a handful of ties which were potentially still in style, and he struggled whenever he attempted to tie one. This was his favorite tie, burgundy in color with tiny black dots and made from silk, and the length was perfect, so he tried to save the position of the knot whenever possible. The expensive tie was a gift from his ex-wife, and he wore it to remind him of the happier times in his life. Grabbing the plastic cup, he took a long drink of the tepid water, reached over and opened his briefcase. The warmth of the water managed to resurrect in his mouth the grease taste from this morning's breakfast.

Taking a deep breath, he removed the fly-fishing book from his bag, and pulled the envelope out from between the pages. Holding the letter in his hands as if it were fragile, he remembered what Tim stated about destroying the letter, so he set the book and envelope back on the couch, and headed into the kitchen. Opening the drawer next to the refrigerator, he rifled through the contents; batteries, receipts, band-aids, pens and miscellaneous junk. Towards the back and behind the mess, he found a long lighter, the kind you use to light fireplaces or cooking grills, and he wondered why or where he purchased this, as he had never owned either. With lighter in hand, he quickly retreated back to the couch.

With the lighter at the ready, he picked up the envelope. There wasn't anything written on the outside, and the seal was only a small round white sticker with gray lines, resembling the stickers used for the tops of medicine bottles. Gently peeling off the sticker, he opened the envelope and removed the letter. The paper had a nice clean smell to it, and was very thin and stiff. He carefully unfolded the letter and began reading it.

"We are honored you have agreed to consider our offer. You are one of a small number of people we have considered for this important mission. To be considered is also an honor, as we are only selecting people with the highest of standards, and we hope you understand the seriousness of this invitation. We understand you probably have questions, and the purpose of this letter is to explain what we are asking of you. We hope you will abide by our request to destroy this letter with fire once you have finished reading it."

"We realize and hope you understand, if you do accept our offer, you will be putting your life on the line, for this is a dangerous mission. But first, we want to explain to you why we are asking you to do what we are asking you to do." David paused and re-read the first part again, wondering why they used the word "hope" so much.

"Starting approximately twenty-five years ago, the national political system in our country was much different than how it is today. The country's political system included two main parties, with a handful of minority parties on the side. The control of the government was almost evenly split between the two parties. There were periods when one party was in complete control, and after a few years the control would revert. On some occasions, the control was split and power was shared between the two parties. These two main parties were known as the Red Party and the Blue Party. During this period, the Blue Party was in control of the government, and we were experiencing a great economic recession."

"In an attempt to stimulate the economy, the Blue Party decided to use government contributions to also address another problem, which was a supposed energy shortage. The Blue Party offered government-backed loans to private companies, for the purpose of developing new methods of obtaining energy. However, the energy crisis was also created in part by the Blue Party, in an attempt to obtain more control over the existing energy industries. Regulations were passed which made it extremely difficult for these companies to operate and to produce cheap and reliable energy. These loans were made to allies and supporters of the Blue Party. Within a few years, every single company defaulted on these loans, without producing any new energy sources or theories of the same. The Blue Party also focused on restricting the production of energy through fossil fuels, and pushing more companies to direct their energy usage towards environmentally-friendly energy sources. But these green energy sources couldn't keep up with the demand, and the cost of energy increased tremendously."

"With this rise in energy costs, every product in what was then known as the free-market economy became more expensive. More regulations were passed by the Blue Party in an attempt to control costs and inflation. But the private companies needed to spend more money to conform to these new regulations, which in turn, drove up the price of goods and services even further. Soon, companies started reducing the number of people in their workforce, in order to remain profitable. The Blue Party decided they could solve the unemployment crisis by targeting the construction industry, which by this point was suffering as well. Government-guaranteed loans were offered for new construction of houses and small commercial buildings. A temporary spike in construction and retail jobs resulted from the infusion of capital, and the growth lasted almost three years. But then the housing market collapsed, as the working class couldn't afford these new houses, which were the same houses backed by these guaranteed loans. And the majority of the people who owned these new government-backed small businesses had no real business experience, so these new businesses failed as well. As a result, larger businesses began to suffer and then falter, and the financial markets also collapsed."

"The Blue Party saw this as an opportunity to increase government-sponsored housing. In addition to the millions of homes with defaulted mortgages and which they now owned, they purchased large office buildings which were available due to the recession from the market collapse, and converted them into government-owned micro-apartments. People who couldn't find work and lost their homes moved from the suburbs and from the rural areas to the blue zone, to live in these office/housing developments. The Blue Party expanded and created new social programs, which were encapsulated into the newly-titled, "Prosperity Benefits," and all existing benefits were also extended for several years."

"The Blue Party then turned to the transportation industry and regulated it even further, in a continued attempt to restrict fossil-fuel energy use, and once again these programs produced negative economic results. The next industry to be targeted was healthcare. New and additional healthcare regulations were implemented, with the intent to provide cheaper healthcare for the unemployed and the uninsured. But the effect was many private insurance companies and healthcare providers couldn't keep up with the rising costs of these regulations and mandatory health benefits. After three or four years, the Blue Party quietly assumed control of the healthcare industry, one hospital at a time, and one insurance company at a time. They started buying out or seizing the failing hospitals and clinics, and taking over the bankrupt insurance companies. The Blue Party saw a large window of opportunity, and the regulations kept pouring out of the capital, targeting any industry that was having problems. The more they regulated an industry to solve a problem, the quicker the industry died and was subject to government, or Blue Party takeover."

"It was during this time the Red Party, who was not in power, tried in vain to stop these regulations. They tried to appeal to the citizens, but they were largely ignored because the media outlets were already under the Blue Party's control and influence. The Red Party could not get their true message out to the people, and their efforts were ridiculed and taunted by the media. Decades earlier, the educational system had fallen to the Blue Party, and by this time the majority of the citizens were either too dumb, too naive or too apathetic to realize or care about what was happening. Besides, the majority of the citizens were now surviving on the Blue Party's Prosperity Benefits. During this time, we also witnessed the creation of the blue and red zones. These zones were created as a way to proportionally distribute benefits and funding, when in reality they were created for economic and political control."

"During this period, the Red Party more or less surrendered. A deal was negotiated to keep both parties intact, but the Blue Party would be forever in power. The Red Party was allowed to semi-govern the minor and less-populated areas, which were now called the red zones. The Blue Party would control the majority of the population, and the majority of the Prosperity Benefit recipients, who now lived in the more-populated blue zones. This plan worked for a couple of years, until the Red Party couldn't keep quiet about the continued corruption and lawlessness of the Blue Party. In short, the Red Party made threats, but the Blue Party held firm, and the Blue Party won. The secret deals were made in the back rooms of the capital city, and both parties combined to form what we now know as 'the Party.' "

"It was also during this time when many of the Red Party legislators simply left politics. We were the ones threatening to expose the Blue Party. Looking back, we were lucky to receive the deals that were offered. We would leave the political scene, take regular jobs, and in exchange for being able to continue to maintain the lifestyle we demanded, we would become silent. But today, the nation is at a point to where it can no longer survive without intervention. After almost three decades with a dismal economy, with taxation beyond comprehension, with programs of unjust wealth-distribution, with never-ending regulations, with a national debt approaching sixty-five trillion, our group has decided to try something, anything to get us back to where we were forty or fifty years ago."

"But we have become a group of older men and women. We have the financial resources and the plan, but we don't have the strength or the numbers to fight this battle, and we don't possess the longevity to see it through. This is why we need your help. This is why we will need the help of a thousand others like you. We need you to fight the battle with us. We have the plan, we only need you to execute it."

"We should not have to say this, but this is a dangerous mission, and secrecy is of the utmost importance. Do not mention this mission to anyone. Do not write down anything concerning this letter, nor type anything into a tablet. If you keep a journal, continue to write a normal daily entry, but exclude writing anything about this letter. Remember, the Party is watching and listening. The Party is always watching and listening."

"If you have doubts about what we are saying, please do your own research. We would advise you to not do this research from your home or work, and certainly not on a current device which you own. You should purchase a used device from a stranger, or from a second-hand store or a pawn shop. Connect to the network from a public place, such as the library or a coffee house. But do your research from inside your vehicle if possible. And do not stay at one place for more than an hour. You may need to access foreign databases or news outlets for the more accurate historical information. When you do your research, be wary of any national police patrols approaching your area. If the police are visible, leave your device under your seat and walk into the establishment as if you just arrived there. Be careful at all costs. The Party is watching. We need you. Will you join us?"

David sat back on the couch. This was a lot of information to absorb. Most of this historical information about the political party system was foreign to him. Looking back, almost thirty years ago, when he was still at the university, he remembered hearing the Blue Party held all the answers. All of his professors, highly-educated people who he admired and respected, all stated the Red Party was evil and was only interested in making money for the big corporations. The professors preached the belief that these profiteers were limited to greedy old men, as their recognition or understanding of the definition of a shareholder was nonexistent. The Red Party didn't care about the average person on the street, the middle class, or the common man. The Blue Party talked of things like equality and freedom, but only as long as both of these ideals fit their agenda. If you disagreed with them, you were branded a traitor to society, an outcast, an evil person or an idiot. Many of his fellow classmates were driven away, forced to leave the university by professors who handed out failing grades to those who dared to disagree with their platform and beliefs.

And while during this time he was somewhat apolitical, David listened to what the professors evangelized and at the time it all made sense. Mainly because he never took the time to question what they said or why they said it, or to even figure out the logic behind it. He was too busy trying to work and to pay his way through school, too busy trying to find love and get a career started, too busy trying to survive.

David read through the letter one more time. The letter didn't state what type of help they needed, only they couldn't do it without him. No one had ever really offered him an opportunity to help with anything important, and certainly never an opportunity which might otherwise fail without his help. There was this feeling of being needed, of being wanted, and for the first time in a long time, a feeling of importance and power. After pondering what he read, he remembered what Tim said about destroying the letters.

David took the pages and separated them on the floor. Grabbing the first piece of paper, he held it with his left hand by the top corner. With his right hand, he took the lighter and flicked it, and watched as an inch-long flame appeared. Cautiously, he guided the flame to the bottom of the paper, until the flame finally kissed the paper, which produced a quick but shallow sound, almost like a faint sneeze or rush of air, as the paper caught fire and vanished almost instantly. This entire concept of quickly-burning paper, and at the same time his action in eliminating evidence, was amazing to him. He then proceeded to destroy the rest of the papers.

Chapter 5

The past month had been very busy, as David maintained his regular work schedule, and attempted to go about his normal routine, all while counting down the days until he was to meet with Tim. Time was also spent researching the Party and peeling back the layers of disinformation in order to discover the previously-unreported facts. Revealing such secrets was difficult, and often required him to perform additional analysis to be able to obtain the truth. A pattern of duplicity and hypocrisy was confirmed, and the realization of his ignorance regarding this subject pained him. How could he have been so blind and so apolitical to the events surrounding and restricting his life and his freedoms?

The day to meet back with Tim finally arrived, and the meeting was scheduled for the afternoon. The meeting was on a Thursday like last time, and this was David's last appointment of the day. The decision to join him in this unknown endeavor had been made. The question posed by the letter, "Will you join us?" was even more haunting than Tim's, "Can I trust you" statement, and both were being constantly repeated in his head. Yes, he would join them, and yes, Tim could trust him. Yes, he would support this cause, this mission, whatever it was. His life had been a boring, mind-numbing routine, and he longed for a different purpose, one with a meaning, even if it was dangerous. This assignment and the actions he would be taking against the Party, would definitely be noble and good for the country.

The two earlier morning appointments were a blur in David's mind. The first meeting was brief as usual. Normally he would attempt to prolong each meeting, mainly to kill time and fill the day. But he was anxious to get to the afternoon appointment. The second meeting was a rare fifteen minutes long, and seemed like it lasted for an eternity. The meeting involved a new client, and she asked a litany of ridiculous questions. The next two meetings after lunch were very short, and he was grateful. As he drove to the hospital to meet with Tim, the questions he had been pondering seemed to answer themselves. Or maybe they didn't matter. Maybe he should hold them until after Tim explained everything.

David pulled into the parking lot, and found an empty spot in the back near the bench. From his car, he noticed the plaque had been polished since his last visit, and the fountain was in full flow, and the falling water was indeed pleasurable to watch. There was an urge to get out of the car to check on status of the algae in the fountain, but he decided against it. When he made his follow-up appointment with Tim's administrator, she instructed him to park and wait for Tim to come out of the building. The clock on the dash read fifteen forty-three, which meant he was seventeen minutes early, so he decided to leave the car running with the air conditioner on, as the heat was unbearable. Rain had fallen just a few minutes earlier, and the steam was still gently rising from the pavement.

Since the last meeting with Tim, David had grown this new sense of awareness. Before, he would travel along, oblivious to what was around him, with his mind in almost a programmed state. Now, he seemed to notice everything. Unfortunately he always possessed a strong sense of smell, but now his other senses seemed to have come alive, and he was now more aware of what was happening around him. He watched each person as they walked to and from the hospital. He took notice of the cars in the lot, their make, model and age. A game was quickly invented to try and match the person with their car based upon nothing but their appearance, but his success rate was zero. Turning his attention to the street lights, he tried to see if they had been repaired or replaced, as it would be a perfect place to hide a camera, but he couldn't detect if anything had been installed. Tim stated the Party is always watching and listening, and this was a mantra he now adopted. At first he scoffed at this idea in his head, but the evidence around him gradually verified the statement, and he spent the last month justifying this to himself.

Over the past month, he first noticed the number of cameras out in the open, on the street, along the sidewalks, and perched on the corners of buildings. He was astonished at his lack of attention before, but it wasn't like the cameras were added overnight. Their numbers grew slowly, as if to blend in with what was already there. Most cameras were easy to spot; a long tube, with glass at one end, and an antenna for wirelessly connecting to the network. And the half-dome cameras had the appearance of a black ball cut in two and stuck on a ceiling or the side of a building. The difficult ones to discover looked like a part or a piece of a different object, such as a small round opening near a light, or on the top of a sign. Tim stated the cameras were everywhere, and he was correct. What was unknown was whether all of them recorded sound as well as video, and the only safe assumption was they did.

David looked up and noticed a large man walking through the double doors of the entrance of the hospital. Straining his eyes, he noticed it was Tim walking at a fast pace, looking down as if he expected to trip on the cracks in the sidewalk. When Tim was about twenty feet away, he looked up at David and shook his head slightly side-to-side. David rolled down his window, and as Tim walked by, he said, "Sinclair's Park," and kept walking towards his car. David started his car and left the parking lot before Tim reached his car, turning left and heading towards the park.

Roberta Sinclair Park was a long and thin park, stationed near the river cutting through town, and was mostly comprised of vaguely-drawn parking spaces and a boat ramp. There were worn picnic tables and over-flowing trash cans every ten spaces or so, but almost all of the spaces were empty at this time of the day. If this was a Friday, it might be a different story, but on a Thursday afternoon, there were only a half-dozen cars in the entire park. David guessed not many people used this during the workday. These cars possibly belonged to retirees, out walking their dogs or fishing in the river, which prompted him to wonder why anyone would want to eat anything coming out of this particular river. He found a parking spot near the end of the lot, about twenty parking spaces away from the nearest car. Backing into the space under the shade of some pine trees, he kept the motor running, with the air conditioner turned down to a lower setting. Tim arrived two minutes later and backed his car into a place further down.

Staying in his car, he waited for Tim to look his way or to get out of his car first, as he assumed he should follow his lead. He didn't know if Tim was going to come to him, or what he was supposed to do. Tim sat in his car and studied the area closely, like he was expecting a police team to come out of the bushes or rappel from the trees. He even looked towards the sky, up and down the length of the park, and David guessed he was scouting for any drones or helicopters which may have been hovering above. After he was satisfied, Tim opened the door of his car and started walking down a trail between his car and David's. David waited until he couldn't see Tim, and then stepped out of his car and started down the trail.

When David caught up with Tim, he was standing on the edge of an open field. The field was full of week-old wildflowers, with dried blossoms turned various shades of brown, attempting to remain proudly perched on the ends of tall stalks which were leaning over, like they were half-asleep. The songs of birds could be heard, and David watched as two squirrels chased each other continuously around a tree. The nearest tree line was across the field, a good distance away. David approached Tim slowly, almost cautiously, while at the same time looking around for anyone else. As David moved closer, Tim spoke first, in a hushed tone as if he was disclosing a secret, which was exactly what he was about to do.

"Sorry for the change in venue, but I thought it would be safer here. With our hospital merger less than four weeks away, there have been a number of Party members around. I needed to go on a weeklong trip and I wasn't sure if they started to implement any security features yet, especially out in the parking lot. They install most of those at night, when no one is around."

David stood there, unsure of what he needed to say.

Tim stopped canvassing the woods and field, and turned towards David. "Have you thought about what we asked, and do you have a decision?"

David wondered why Tim didn't ask him if he had any questions, because there were still a couple running through his mind. Maybe questions weren't allowed. Maybe it was all or nothing. David decided to ignore the questions he had stockpiled during the past month. They probably weren't important, and he could get them answered later.

"Yes, I have made a decision. I have given it a lot of thought. Probably too much thought. But I can see exactly what you were talking about."

Tim asked, "So, you did take time to do research?"

David paused again and scanned the area, as if each answer required verification to ensure no one else was present. "Yes. I followed the instructions. I bought a used tablet from a stranger and did all my research from various places over the past month, while I was traveling from city to city. I found dozens of examples, with most of the details coming from foreign news sites. I don't know how or why I never really paid attention to this before, the Party seems to..."

Tim interrupted him. "We can no longer refer to them by name. We can only use pronouns. It is us or them. This vagueness is now warranted, especially since you can never be sure if you are being monitored. But please continue."

"It seems they are either above the rules or they simply choose to ignore them. And the people who are there to keep them in check, which I believe is the media, are simply spinning tales to further their agenda, which I am assuming is also the media's agenda. But what I found so amazing is the majority of the people have blindly bought into it as well, including me, until this very moment. Their lies have been bolstered, supported even, and repeated so much, by themselves and by the media and by the people, their lies have become the truth. And the real truth is never revealed or even sought. Also, it seems in the minds of the public, the intentions of the Party..." David caught himself when he mentioned the Party by name.

David spoke softer, as if he could erase his mistake, and he continued. "I mean, the intentions of these people, what they promise to do, these promises always weigh more than the actual results. They are never held accountable for promises which were never kept or were broken. Or even when they flat out lie to the public. Even in the local news sources, I was able to find quite a lot of harmful information against these people. But what I don't understand is why they would allow these negative events to even come to light? Why do they allow the media to report on these scandals? In the end they are always found to be innocent, but why expose this information to the public?"

Tim kept searching the area while David was talking. "You see, David, as hard as they try, they have yet to be able to control this information from reaching all of the media sources, especially the independent outlets who aren't big fans of their agenda. The main media groups still have to provide the public with information about them, and the public still likes to hear about bad news.

The public relishes in the dirty laundry they see on television or the garbage they read in the tabloids. The media outlets have higher ratings and they sell more tabloids and advertising when they present negative information. Have you noticed the news programs always report on whatever morbid deaths have occurred? Do we really need to know about a woman and her five children who died in a house fire? No, but what also sells is when they tell us the husband may be charged with murder, along with the crime of not having adequate fire prevention in the home? Or do we need to know when a person, or a member, was found in a hotel with another person or member, who was now dead? There is no longer any privacy in death."

Tim paused as if he heard something, and did a quick survey of the sky. "But these scandals and problems also serve them well. The media keeps reporting these stories, and the public hears, time and time again, that they are accused of misbehavior or unlawful acts. It especially works in their favor when the news is broken by one of these aptly-named rogue media outlets. In the end, this reporting makes them look good. Because even after they are accused of a treacherous act, even if the evidence is clearly there, they know the members involved will either be found to be innocent of all charges, or the story will simply fade away and go unreported by the main media outlets. These end results makes the accusers look bad, and it makes them look good. One day, and one day soon, you will only hear good news about them. The accusers and these rogue outlets will have either gone away on their own, or the public will no longer believe them or take an interest in what they say, or they will be taken out by these people. These goals, they are a constant work-in-progress by these people, a strategy they have planned and executed slowly for decades. They are extremely good at what they do, and so far, they have implemented this plan very well."

David noticed even after Tim finished talking, he was still looking around the woods and the field. The uncertainly of being watched was tense, disturbing in a sense, and David felt vulnerable for the first time. Tim finally stopped scanning, and turned to face him, pausing in a way as if he was judging whether or not David could continue to be trusted, even after telling him all of this.

Leaning in towards David, he whispered, "If you decide to take the next step. You can't go back. Your life, as you know it, will never be as before. You will either fail miserably, or potentially help to alter the course of history." Drawing away, Tim checked the area once more.

David thought he would be nervous when he gave him his answer. But he was feeling pride and enthusiasm in wanting to be a part of whatever it was he was going to join. "I have made my decision, and the answer is yes. I want to join, I want to help. And I am willing to do whatever is necessary. And I understand the risks, and they are acceptable. But I do believe this mission is necessary, and admirable at the same time. Someone or some group has to do something, and I definitely want to be part of this."

Nodding his head, Tim said, "We will walk back to our cars. I will have two boxes for you to take. One box will be fairly heavy. Do not open this box yet. Keep it in your trunk until after you have opened the smaller box, which will be much lighter. When you get home, go to a closet or your bathroom and open the small box. Do a scan of whatever room or space you are in before you open anything. If you see or if you notice anything out of place, then go to a different room. Investigate whatever is unusual. If it turns out to be nothing, then continue with the small box. Read everything with your back to a wall. I do not believe they have found out we are talking, and I do not believe you are being monitored yet. Inside the box, you will find further instructions on your next steps. There are two envelopes. One envelope contains instructions for you to follow while you are still employed and the other one is for when you retire from SoCare. It doesn't matter in which order you read them. You will walk back to your car first. When I get to my car, and after I have opened my trunk, you can then open your trunk. You can do that from inside the car, correct?"

"Yes. I can."

"We will not see each other again. Next month, you will visit with a person from the purchasing department downstairs. See the first floor receptionist for the name, but it should be a man named Alex Bidden. Now, walk back to your car, and get in. Remember, only open your trunk after I have opened mine. I will make the transfer, close your trunk, and drive off first. Wait five minutes after I leave, and then you may leave. I will stay here for a minute or two. Good luck."

David took a last look at Tim, as if he was memorizing his face. Maybe he was looking for a sign to tell him, or to warn him once he reached his car, he should drive off. But it wasn't there. Despite the apparent danger he was now willingly associated with, he still trusted Tim, and he felt this was the right thing to do. David started walking, slowly away from the field, into the trees and towards the path. Looking at his watch, it was sixteen thirty-three, and he kept cautiously looking around, but saw no one else. Out in the parking lot, he noticed a small number of new cars in the lot, but most were parked at the other end. Once he made it to his car, he unlocked the door, sat down and closed the door. He felt under the steering wheel for the trunk release lever, as if it wouldn't be there. A small feeling of panic crept up on him, and he didn't know why, but it was overtaken by the excitement of this pending adventure. Searching the parking lot, he was sure no one saw him, but he decided to check the sky for drones or helicopters.

Tim approached a couple minutes later. He stopped about fifty feet away and was watching the parking lot, and David noticed him in his rear-view mirror. David wasn't sure if his paranoia was kicking in, but in this case, being paranoid was a good thing. He was positive from now on, paranoia would always be his ally.

Tim opened his trunk with his remote, and at the same time, David reached down and flipped the lever, opening his trunk. Tim first moved the heavy box into David's car, and the weight of it caused the car to sink. The second box transferred quickly, and Tim closed both trunks. Tim walked to the door of his car, opened it, sat down, turned on the ignition and began to move. As he passed by David, he glanced over, made brief eye contact with him, and continued driving away.

David watched as Tim's car sped down the parking lot, and finally disappeared from view. He rolled down his window and took out a cigar from his briefcase. The cigar was a gift from a fellow worker, who recently had a baby, and he had been holding on to it for a few months. The aluminum cigar tube was unusual, as most baby cigars were plastered with, "It's a boy!" or "It's a girl!" on the side. This tube displayed a painting of a woman in a red frilly dress, along with words in a foreign language he didn't understand, but assumed it was Spanish. The woman and the dress suggested a dancer, and for a moment he was almost mesmerized by her face and figure, as he never really looked at her closely before. The woman was captivating, and he laughed as he pondered, "I wonder where she lives?"

Years had passed since he had been attracted enough to a woman to even contemplate trying to get the courage to ask her out for a date. The insecurity he unwillingly obtained from the divorce always waylaid whatever dating plans he thought he could have. Unscrewing the top of the tube, he looked inside as if he almost didn't expect a real cigar to be there. The aroma of the tobacco was slight, so he brought the canister to his nose and inhaled. While he was not really a fan of cigarettes or their nasty smell, he enjoyed a good cigar. This one was sweet, almost like being in a flower garden on a hot day. He capped the tube and put it back into his briefcase. "Not now," he thought. "Not now." The cigar would be saved for a more important date and time.

The four-hour drive back home was uneventful as usual, and traffic was unusually light. David wanted to stop and open the small box, but he didn't. Temptation came again when he stopped at a truck stop in the red zone to treat himself to breakfast food for dinner. At first, he thought he could probably take a peak at what was inside the boxes while he paused to eat, but after a study of the parking lot, he counted at least five cameras out in the open. The presence of the cameras made him wonder why were five cameras needed at a greasy diner right off the interstate? His new-found paranoia caused his patience to kick in, and he decided to wait. For dinner, the restaurant served what David believed to be real sausages. The little links contained what appeared to be pork meat, and they were fried nice and brown, and even the grease tasted good.

The time was almost twenty-one hundred in the evening, when David was finally rolling through the gates of his apartment complex. A spot was found relatively close to his apartment, and as the car came to a stop, David waited while he examined the parking lot. Mrs. Ortiz was outside in the grassy area, walking her dog, which was unusual for her this late at night. He decided to wait for her to go inside, and once she finally did, he grabbed his briefcase and popped the trunk lever. Opening the car door, he walked around to the back. The appearance of the two boxes was a little unnerving, but he quickly grabbed the smaller one, and closed the trunk. There was no need to test the elevator, so he eagerly raced up the stairs to his apartment door. As he fumbled with his keys, he placed the box down on the concrete floor. He finally succeeded in opening the door, and he shoved the box inside with his foot, before darting into his apartment. After the door was closed and locked, he looked through the peephole as if he almost expected to see a person standing there. There was no turning back.

Chapter 6

Once inside his apartment, David gently tossed his briefcase onto the couch, and took his place beside it, weary from the long drive. Tomorrow was going to be one of those rare Fridays where he wasn't traveling, but instead the day would be filled with a training session on how to complete some new reports which were being issued. These sessions were deemed a waste of time, as the reports would always be two or three months late in being deployed to the field. Soon after, newer versions would be introduced, and additional training would be involved. These reports and forms were part of a never-ending cycle of change and frustration for him. And by the time these latest reports were distributed to the field, he would probably be retired.

David normally went to bed early, and he liked to watch a half-hour or so of television, usually sports or nature shows, before going to sleep. Even though he was physically tired, he knew he wouldn't be able to sleep until he opened the box. Picking up the box, he carried it to his bedroom, where he turned on the lights with his elbow and gently placed the box on his bed. Remembering what Tim stated, he slowly scanned the inadequately-furnished room for signs of disturbance. Everything appeared to be normal. But then again, he really didn't know what he was looking for. If the Party was going to hide a camera in his bedroom, he probably wouldn't be able to find it without an exhaustive search. The box had a slim piece of tape across it, barely holding down the flaps and it was easily removed. Inside the box were two large green envelopes. One had the word "Now" written on it, and the other was marked with "Later." David assumed the first one was for pre-retirement, and the other post-retirement, as Tim had mentioned. Grabbing both envelopes, he decided to head to the bathroom to read them.

He closed the bathroom door, and then softly closed the toilet lid, sat down and again scanned the walls and the fixtures. The shower was to his left, covered with large white tiles on three sides and embellished with a dark yellow grout, stained from the years of black mold which David seemed to fight every other month. The "Now" envelope was a thick, large green envelope with a string for a clasp. He carefully untied the string, and looked inside, which held two additional smaller green envelopes. One of these other envelopes contained what felt like paper, and the other appeared to contain flat plastic items. He opened the thin one first, and inside was a letter, which he unfolded and began to read.

"David, these instructions will prepare you for your initial action. Since you have only a short time left in your work benefit, there is pre-retirement work you may perform. Assuming you opened this envelope first, you will find the other envelope contains teller debit cards. During your work travels, you will need to go to various teller machines and withdraw money using these cards. The maximum you may remove per day will vary per machine, but you should withdraw the maximum each time, once per day per card. You should vary your withdrawals from bank to bank, and never use the same teller location within a single trip in the same city. Do not use these cards for any other task but withdrawing money."

"You should also purchase several hats, at least seven, and several pairs of large sunglasses. Every time you withdraw money, wear a different hat and glasses. Take care to not look directly at the camera within the teller machine. Check to see if there are any additional cameras posted outside, and avoid looking directly at them as well. Again, make sure you only use each card once per day. Do not deposit the money into any bank. Find a secure place inside or outside of your home to hide the money. If necessary, obtain several glass jars with lids and bury the money in the woods outside of your apartment or in a local park, but be diligent so no one notices you. You will use a large portion of the money for your recruiting purposes, and these other stashes may come in handy one day. The debit cards all use the same security code, which is 5497537.

"I have also included a pre-paid cellular phone, which will be active for one year. The GPS chip on this phone has been disabled. You can still be tracked using cell-tower triangulation, but this location method isn't as accurate and so they usually do not rely on it for tracking. They do have access to this information, but for unknown reasons, they seem to ignore it and rely solely on the GPS information. However, like all forms of communication and all types of electronic devices, they are recording what you say and are tracking this equipment at all times. Do not make any calls or send any personal messages on this phone. This phone is only for me to contact you, or for you to contact your associates. There is a list of codes and their meanings, and the most important code is the number nine. If you receive a text message with the single number nine as the message, then our mission has been revealed to them. You will need to be prepared to go into hiding, to disappear. If you receive this warning, destroy the phone immediately and leave, no matter what you are doing. You should always have a survival bag packed and near you at all times. You may want to consider hiding extra survival bags throughout the city as well. Good luck, T."

David opened the envelope with the debit cards, and counted ten cards. David thought for a moment. The normal maximum withdrawal limit was at least one thousand a day per account, while some other banks allowed for larger withdrawals. He had almost two months left before he retired. If he maximized their usage, he could potentially withdraw over five hundred thousand with these cards, if he wasn't caught, and even more after retirement. With the realization of the amount of money he was to withdraw, he discovered his mouth was dry, and a sudden but noticeable headache had arisen, and his hands started shaking slightly. Placing everything on the floor, he went to the kitchen for a diet cola and three headache tablets. With this situation, a stronger drink option would have been preferred, one like the whiskey Tim gave him. He contemplated going to the national liquor store, but such an act was not his normal behavior, and now was not the time for deviation.

Returning to the bathroom, he picked up the other thinner, green envelope with the designation of "Later" scribbled in pen, opened the clasp and pulled out several pages of what appeared to be a letter.

"This letter will provide you with instructions on your next steps. The next step of your journey will be the preparatory phase, during which time you will read and learn the instructions from the *Guide*, which is the small black book you received. The guide's purpose is to prepare you for the recruiting phase, as well to provide preparation and survival information, should you have to go into hiding. This letter also contains your orders for phase one. As a level-one associate, your job will be to recruit others to execute our targets."

"The goal of this association is to reverse the current socialist agenda and move back to a capitalistic and free state, where individual responsibility is mandated and freedoms are restored. We also want to bring our government back to the state where the people control them, versus the other way around. The news you hear and see everyday is being manufactured and controlled by them. The news is not a true reflection of what is really happening. Our mission is divided into two phases, simply referred to as phase one and phase two."

David paused for a moment, before reading the last paragraph again. There had to be an assumption that, "them" meant "the Party," and he remembered what Tim stated about using pronouns or indirect references instead of the word, "Party." He continued to read.

"This country is at a breaking point. One fourth of the country is working to support the other three-fourths, and neither will be able to survive much longer unless drastic actions are taken. Our freedoms and rights are being abolished for the good of their agenda. They are almost at a place of no return, at a point where nothing can stop them. The majority of what you see, read or hear is a lie. We have a system where laws only apply to those who are not in power. Where a slip of the tongue can put you in prison for the rest of your life, if they don't decide to simply kill you. Where a protest can cause you to disappear in the middle of the night. We must fight back. We must do whatever action is necessary."

"However, we will not be fighting them directly. They are too large, too numerous, and too strong at this point. What we must do is weaken their support structure. We must attack their feet, until their feet can't support the weight of the body, and then the body will come crashing down. They are like a hive of honeybees. You can try attacking the queen, but another bee will take the queen's place. You can attack the workers, but there are too many, and the fallen workers are easily and quickly replaced. You can't attack the hive structure, for it is too large and has no weak points. The way you kill the hive is to kill their source of power, their source of nutrition, and their source of life.

The way you kill the hive is to kill the flowers. If you kill the flowers, the hive will perish."

David stopped reading. The word "kill" was disturbing, and it was at this point he realized he never really thought about exactly what they were going to ask him to do, and he never bothered to ask. There were a few ideas, but he assumed it would be something non-violent, like protests or speeches or making phone calls. Maybe he had been too trusting, too wide-eyed about being part of the mission, but he really never settled on what types of actions might be taking place. Yes, the word "dangerous" was mentioned, but up to this point, the word "kill" was absent. There was too much excitement about joining something with meaning and a purpose and after all, Tim trusted him and put his faith in him. He thought about this word "kill," and what the ramifications were to take another life, even if he wouldn't be the one performing the action. There was an uncertainty if he could still say no at this time, but the main reason for accepting the offer was the mission was honorable, even justifiable. The purpose was easily definable and noble, restoring the original freedom and rights which had made this country great.

"To find the flowers, you must understand how the flowers help them to maintain the power. Information is power to them. Control of information is power. Control of the due process of law is power. Control of who is prosecuted and who is released is power. They make the laws, the regulations, the processes, but other people are the ones who carry out their demands. Other people are the ones supporting what they are doing, often blindly and without question."

"The mission is to find these flowers, these blind followers and eliminate them. But you can't do it alone. Your job will be to recruit others to do this work. You must find others who have been unjustly hurt by the laws, the regulations, and the processes. These are the people who will follow you and will eagerly strike back. And these victims aren't difficult to find, but you must be diligent in your research and select the proper candidates. If one of your choices presents any hesitation to join our cause, leave the person immediately and find another recruit. The proper ones are out there."

"You should not find anyone you know personally, and never disclose your real name. You will know their name, and possibly where they live and work, but the need for this knowledge only flows downhill. The goal is to build an army of these resources, which we call "Associates." And we will all implement our first strike on the same day, with one person assigned for each individual target. There will be a time where other targets may be identified and taken out as well. Planning and preparation is the key to success."

"In the other box, we have provided copies of a small book titled, "*The Guide for Restoring Freedom,*" hereby referred to as the "*Guide.*" The *Guide* contains the simple rules and advice for action, which will help you be successful in your mission. You will take the additional copies of the *Guide* and provide them to your associates. The associates should read the *Guide* at least once and pass along a copy to their recruited associates. Do not take any notes about what you read in the *Guide*. Do not make copies of any pages. Read the *Guide* several times if you must."

"You are a level-one associate, and you will choose five people, known as level-two associates, and provide each one with six copies of the *Guide*. In turn they will choose five additional recruits, known as level-three associates, and they will pass along their extra copies of the *Guide*. If the recruiting for phase one is executed successfully, we should have thousands of associates in place, and thousands of initial actions will occur. After phase one, you may be asked to continue to recruit, but it will be much more difficult, as our cause may be known. The first strike is the most important."

"Our first strike, again known as phase one, will be aimed at those who support them from the outside. Judges, lower-level government employees, media personalities, celebrities, supporters - anyone who has a high profile and either controls the dispersement of information about them or their activities, or controls the outcome of their unlawfulness, or supports their cause on a regional or national level. Remember, we are going after the flowers. The flowers will grow back, but we will keep cutting them down. Soon, no one will want to be a flower, except those who aren't already in their favor, for they will understand and recognize that if you support them, you are taking a big risk in doing so. You can ignore the little flowers. Individual flowers which have no direct influence over a larger group of the population are insignificant. They will wilt and die on their own, or they will run away and hide."

"You should never mention the name of our group to anyone. As a level-one associate, we will disclose this name to you. But all of these initial actions must be performed so it appears they are being done by anonymous individuals, without ties to any single organization. There will be a time when this group and the name will be made public, and all of your associates in the field will understand at that time. They will either realize it, or they are too ignorant and then they do not need to know. You must remember, and your associates must remember, we must successfully execute both phase one and two on specific dates. The target date for phase one is Saturday, October the first. All initial actions need to take place on this day. Phase two has a start date, but it doesn't have an end date. Phase two should be started on Saturday, November twenty-sixth. Phase two will involve eliminating the lower-level members, and more information on who to target is explained in the *Guide*. Again, phase two is different from phase one. Phase two will never end, at least not until we have restored this country to its former glory. Phase two will not end until we as a nation, once again, desire freedom and liberty over security. Phase two will not end until the people once again have the power, and multiple political parties are in place. Remember these dates. After you destroy these letters, do not write these dates down." David paused for a moment, and then read the last line in the letter.

"Welcome to the League of Patriots."

David looked up at the wall in front of him. A wave of silence was suddenly noticeable in the room, and his ears were ringing. This was a lot of information to absorb. How in the world was he going to find these people to help in this cause? How would he know what to do? He read the letter again, this time a bit slower. Yes, the *Guide,* the answers must be in the *Guide*.

Chapter 7

David was busy during the past five weeks. With only two weeks left until his work benefit elapsed, he had been working his territory, visiting his clients and living life as normally as possible. The teller cards were being used, once per day, and the maximum amount was being withdrawn each time. A certain skill was needed when using the teller machines. A skill he believed he created and now mastered, which dealt with approaching the teller machines located outside the banks, and determining where to stand so the camera couldn't get a good view of his face. The machines located inside stores were much harder to negotiate. Per the *Guide*, multiple hats of different kinds and colors, and a variety of cheap sunglasses were purchased for these covert actions. And a coded log of which hat and which sunglasses he used was created, so he could vary the pair after each visit. He was withdrawing at least ten thousand a day, and he believed he hid his actions very well. Per the *Guide's* suggestion, the money was being buried in old canning jars in the woods behind his apartment. The only other deviation he made from his normal schedule was performing research to locate possible associates.

Using the teller money, he purchased three more tablets, so their use could be varied and rotated. David found an application which would route his network activity through foreign public network servers, so any searches would appear as if the incoming connection was made from another country. David was getting very good at this part of the mission, or at least he thought he was, and the clandestine activity was exciting to him. But there was always this nagging feeling he would slip up, make a mistake, and the Party would catch him. Every day or so, a touch of paranoia would creep up, causing him to pay more attention to what he was doing or where he was going. The paranoia was welcomed, as it kept him alert and cautious, especially when he became too relaxed. And there was a new daily ritual, involving the purchase and enjoyment of real coffee from a coffee house, along with the occasional splurge for a pastry every now and then.

The time was Friday afternoon, and David was on his way home from another week in the field, traveling on a national highway in the middle of nowhere, fighting traffic which should not have been there, given the rural area he was in. The congestion was not even close to breaking, and David was giving serious thought about what he would do if he was caught by the Party. If he was apprehended, then Tim more than likely had been caught as well. The Party's handlers would certainly interrogate him, and try to figure out who he had recruited, and what the mission encompassed. Knowing they would probably resort to torture, he would resist telling them anything for as long as he could, as long as he could bear the pain. Yes, torture would definitely be invoked. Eventually, he would break down, and after they extracted whatever information they wanted, he would either face life in prison or be put to death, and he already chose death over prison. A vow was made. Unless they caught him by surprise, he would not go down quietly. He would be prepared to run, to hide, to do whatever was necessary to stay alive, or die trying to escape.

His reverie was interrupted by the ringing of his work phone, and glancing down at the screen, he could see a picture of his manager. A call from him wasn't unusual, and the frequency of his calls were never predictable. David answered the phone and as usual, his boss was curt with his message, as if he had a fear of talking over the phone. He wanted to see David first thing on Monday morning, but he didn't provide a reason for the meeting before ending the conversation. With David's pending retirement, the most likely scenario was more paperwork to complete, or maybe he needed to discuss his retirement benefits. Either way, David wasn't worried about the meeting. Interaction with his boss was infrequent, which was a benefit in itself. David was a model employee. He completed all of his reports on time, if not earlier than required, and this meeting should be nothing to be concerned about. If his activity had been discovered, it wouldn't be his manager who would be contacting him. The Party would be paying him a visit, probably in the middle of the night, or he simply wouldn't see them coming up from behind him and throwing him into a van, or shooting him on the spot. The last option was preferred, as it was quick and relatively painless, and the end would be unannounced.

The clock on the dash had been mocking him for the past hour, constantly reminding him of the traffic still flowing at a slow pace, and was now flashing the time of seventeen thirty-three. His stomach had also been talking to him, as earlier he opted to skip lunch to finish his teller withdrawals instead. Two of the last three appointments for the day were notorious for making him wait, and he wanted to withdraw the money away from his home area. On the weekends he started driving north to the mountains, inside the red zone, for his withdrawals. Many different routes had been prepared, so a teller machine would only be visited every three weeks. His stomach rumbled again, this time a bit louder, and so he decided to take the next exit and stop for dinner. Home was only a short distance away, but with this traffic, the conservative estimate for the remaining travel time was at least two hours.

David was still in the red zone, and he pulled off the highway, allowing his car to coast to a stop at the end of the off-ramp, where he spotted a truck stop on the opposite corner. This particular truck stop was immense, with separate gas stations for both large trucks and cars, and a separate building with a restaurant. The parking lot was overrun with cars and trucks, all tangled together, as they jockeyed into position for a gas pump. There didn't seem to be any order to this mess, as people seemed to have lost their ability to form a straight line. After weaving his way through the confusion, he found a parking spot on the far right side of the building, near the back. His hunger pangs subsided, so he decided to do some research, before heading inside for dinner. There was still the necessary scanning of the parking lot for cameras, and it was all-clear, so he pulled out one of the tablets, and connected to the network, making sure to start the application directing his connection to go outside the country and then back in.

A few days ago, he thought he finally found his first associate, but there was some information he needed to confirm first. After about twenty minutes without success, he slid the tablet back under the passenger's seat, ambled inside and ordered his favorite meal of fried chicken and steamed vegetables. The food tasted homemade, and the vegetables weren't soggy, but firm and crisp. This restaurant would definitely be a place to remember.

As he ventured back out onto the highway, the traffic appeared to be even thicker than before. He tried to take his time eating dinner, but the food was very good, and the slow enjoyment of a good meal was unfamiliar to him. There was a pleasant surprise of free coffee refills, so he attempted to nurse a second cup of coffee as long as possible, while watching the patrons from a corner booth. The passing of time appeared to have stalled, and he peeked down at his watch, as he was intentionally ignoring the rudeness of the dash clock, as if the time on his watch would be later, but it was only seven minutes before nineteen hundred. With the traffic continuing at this slow of a pace, he still might have another couple of hours to go. Thinking once again about the mission letter and how it mentioned the word "kill," he was still struggling with the thought of taking another person's life, even if he wasn't doing the killing. Justification of this action would need to be produced, at least in his own mind. The letter stated that the country was heading to a point of no return, to a place where the Party controlled everything and everyone, even more so than they do today.

For this mission, was killing justifiable? Was there ever a reason when killing was justifiable? Perhaps when there was formal declaration of war, then killing was a necessary and a legitimate act. Thinking back to his college days, he tried to remember what he learned in his history classes, of the past wars and the fighting which occurred not only in this country, but all over the world. College was over twenty-five years ago, and it was at least that long since he studied history, or studied war, but he remembered being taught war was never good. Wars had been fought since then, but he never really paid much attention to why or even where. Wars were usually started by countries seeking land, or power, or resources or all of these things. Wars were started over religious beliefs, with a convert-or-die theology on one side, and where the purpose on the other side was to eliminate this threat of evil, such as the terrorists wars fought a decade or so ago. But in the end, an honorable country usually defended themselves in a war to protect the country, to protect the citizens, and to ensure whatever original freedom and rights the country established were preserved.

And isn't this what the mission was about? The mission was to protect the country from itself, or at least from the government which infringed upon and slowly dissolved these same freedoms and rights. The government which was originally created to represent the people now only represented itself. Every war has a goal, and war is certainly justifiable when it is necessary. Even though this mission wasn't a war, or at least it wasn't being called a war, it definitely had goals worth fighting for.

But was the achievement of this goal really necessary? All of the freedoms and rights which people possessed, did they really want or deserve either? Rights were endowed upon people by God, and any action by the government against those rights only reduced the liberties and freedoms associated with these rights. The majority of the population didn't believe in God, and only believed in the Party. To them, rights and freedoms were granted by the Party, and both were only good if they were for the good of society, and not the individual. The Party was their friend, their benefactor, and in fact many couldn't survive without the Party. Would they be able to understand what was happening and why they were fighting? If the mission was a success, would they cheer the champions, these liberators of freedom, or curse them like they do now? Do the majority of the citizens, who seem to relish being controlled by the Party, do they really want things to change? Do they even understand they are slowly being enslaved, or are they content with their position in life, no matter how inadequate it is? A mission to free an oppressed populace is often as difficult and dangerous as enslaving them. The problem with any freedom movement is you can't force people to accept freedom, especially when a promise of security is their other option.

From what David could recall, many decades ago, when soldiers returned home from war, a parade would be held to celebrate their victory and their return to their families. David's grandfather was in one of the wars, but David wasn't sure which one. He did remember when he was younger, perhaps less than ten years old, his grandfather told him stories about coming home to a parade, and about how life was much different back then. People looked up to his grandfather, respected him, and treated him differently, in a positive way, for being a soldier. His grandfather never spoke of the horrors of war, but only of the sweetness of victory. But over the past half-century, returning soldiers were treated with disdain and hatred. Even the soldiers who won the terrorists wars were treated like second-class citizens upon their return, and called names like baby-killers, mercenaries and war-profiteers. If David participated in this mission along with the other associates, and if they were successful, and if their participation was made public, would he be cast as a hero or villain?

David contemplated for a long time about the possible end results of his participation. The mission had to be successful, and they would have to win, but if they were successful at stopping the Party, what would happen next? Too many people were dependent upon the Party, and the benefits which easily and freely flowed their way. If the Party was gone tomorrow, would the people survive? Would they know what to do after being spoon-fed for so many years? What was more important, freedom and liberty for those craving it, or a society where people favored security and nothing else? People were barely surviving now, and if the Party was destroyed, they still would be barely surviving. Maybe those people tethered to the Party needed to be cut free, and if they didn't survive, then perhaps their deaths were good for those who did survive? Instead of survival of the fittest, would it be survival of the independent and responsible?

If the Party was gone, and if people suffered, wouldn't the other citizens, the ones who didn't have to survive off the Party, wouldn't they certainly come to their aid? After all, the Party as it is today wasn't around hundreds of years ago, and people certainly survived back then. Life was definitely a lot more difficult, but people survived and society, the nation as a whole, survived and even thrived. Yes, David assured himself, people would survive, or at least those who wanted to survive would make it. As it is now, the general population was barely surviving, and when times were tough, people helped one another. Deep down, people were good to each other, especially in times of need. The mission was necessary, success was necessary, and therefore killing was necessary. And in his own mind, David concluded he didn't care if he was branded a hero or a traitor, as this was the proper thing to do, the correct action to take. After all, people in charge of this operation were a lot smarter than him. People like Tim, they were the ones who devised this plan. They were the ones who really knew what was going on. They knew what needed to be done, and David certainly trusted Tim. And he certainly and strongly believed the mission and the goals were worth the consequences. He was willing to bet his life on it.

Chapter 8

David arrived home right before twenty-one hundred. He unpacked and gathered his dirty clothes together in a laundry bag. Venturing back outside into the heat of the night, he went downstairs to the laundry room to wash a load of clothes. David hated doing laundry. The laundry room was dark and damp, and there was always this musty smell lingering in the air. His clothes had a habit of absorbing this odor, so they never smelled clean, regardless of how much detergent or fabric softener was used. Luck was on his side tonight, as there were two machines available. Fumbling around in his pocket for change, he fed both machines. At the moment, there were three dryers available, but the unknown was whether or not in an hour, if these dryers would still be available. In order to save money, residents would often wash their clothes in their tubs or sinks, and then use the dryers to finish the task. Access to the dryers was never a sure thing.

David started the machines, and went back up to his apartment. The laundry room was always a lot hotter than the outside, and he immediately started to sweat. He headed to the refrigerator, grabbed a diet cola, and proceeded to the bathroom. Kneeling down, he pried away the bottom trim on the sink cabinet to retrieve his copy of the *Guide*. With the book and drink in one hand, he closed the toilet lid and sat down. He took a quick survey around the room, to look for any evidence the Party implanted a monitoring device, and everything looked normal and in place. Then there was the realization he should have probably done this survey before retrieving the book, which caused him to closely recheck the perimeter of the tile floor for dust, in case a camera hole had been drilled from the sides or above, but the floor appeared clean. This would be this third time he read the *Guide*, but even after two previous readings, he wanted to read it again, to be sure he understood everything. The black leather binding and one side of the book was covered in dust and hair, despite being isolated under the cabinet, and he grabbed a towel to wipe it clean, before carefully opening it to the first chapter.

Chapter One - An Introduction to Our Mission

The mission of this organization is to attempt to revert the minds of the citizens, the actions of the government and the country back to a state where the citizens still wielded near-absolute personal authority over their lives, still enjoyed an acceptable level of freedom, and to a state where the government would serve them in the limited capacity which was intended by the founding creators of the original government. Our nation is at a point where the government does whatever actions are necessary to further their socialist agenda, while the rights of the citizens are being overturned, and often by their own choosing. While we believe our goal is noble, it will not be without human cost to both the citizens and to our associates. What we are attempting requires great risk, but the risk can be averted if we have even greater preparation. Any individual task can be successful if the associate takes extreme and absolute care in the planning and execution of the action. However, the success of any great mission has always relied on the participants being willing to sacrifice part or all of their own personal freedoms and lives, in order to secure the freedoms of others.

This country has always, with the exception of the past twenty-five years, had a two-party political system. The country had multiple and separate branches of government, with separation of powers, and with checks and balances in place. Each branch had a responsibility to watch over the other branches, with each branch being equal in the eyes of the government. But after the turn of the twenty-first century, the Blue Party started covertly and unlawfully enacting their agenda across all branches. These subversive acts were not completed overnight, but slowly over a period of decades, methodically and secretly implemented under the noses of an uneducated and apathetic populace. We will attempt to provide more details and evidence on how each branch of government was overtaken in separate chapters in this book, and therefore the information detailed which follows is not absolute. In this chapter, we will provide a short summary for each branch, with more complete details to be revealed later.

The executive branch was the first branch to blatantly supersede their authority. One of the tenets of the executive branch was to faithfully execute the laws of the legislative branch. But there were times when the control of the legislative branch was split between the two parties, so new laws couldn't be passed. During one of these periods, with the Blue Party in control of the executive branch, the executive branch decided to either ignore the laws which had been passed, or to modify the law as needed, or to simply create laws on their own. The Blue Party also used blackmail as a way to threaten and control those Red Party members who had not faithfully executed their oath of office or had demons in their current or past lives. It was also during this period when the executive branch, along with their various departments, was able to modify and to control the outcome of elections via fraud and other methods so the results were in their favor.

The legislative branch, the control of which was divided between the two parties, began to fail in their responsibility of overseeing the laws as they were being executed by the executive branch. Instead, the Blue Party legislative members became a group of spokesmen with a goal of only protecting the executive branch. These members were content with doing nothing more than defending the illegal actions of the executive branch by spouting off a list of talking points, which were provided to them by the executive branch. The actions of the majority of the Blue Party legislators, when it was time for the creation or approval of new laws and regulations, were also being controlled and directed by the executive branch. The executive branch also extended its reach by allowing their own departments to issue regulations and penalties without legislative approval. In short, with the failure of the legislative branch to properly oversee the executive branch, the executive branch had gradually taken over the entire system of the national government, excluding the judicial branch.

The judicial branch was the last noticeable branch to stray from their original purpose. There had always been tension between the legislative and executive branch, and the judicial branch was considered long ago to be the only branch largely isolated from a political agenda. The interpretation of laws was not supposed to be evaluated against a political agenda. But the judicial branch gradually started to ignore their charter of justice being blind, as judges began to *decide cases not based upon the law, but upon these political agendas. Of course, the agenda was provided to them by the Blue Party and also created and directed by the executive branch.*

Socialism had taken root in the executive branch, but the effect was beyond political or economical. The Socialist mindset also infiltrated our national security interests. Our enemies became our friends, and our friends became our enemies, at least in the minds of the Blue Party. The citizens of former enemy nations and members of terrorist groups, who in the past slaughtered our citizens on our own soil, were now being funded, supported and applauded. These same enemy nations then attacked our former allies, and our executive branch stood by and did nothing.

The Blue Party and the media viciously attacked any individual or group who supported the Red Party, or those who spoke out against the Blue Party. Organized religion, specifically the Jewish, Catholic and Christian groups, were the first to have their beliefs restricted and then eventually annihilated by the Blue Party. Freedom of religion became freedom from religion. The Blue Party had long supported any fringe group, no matter how obscure, as long as the group did not support the Red Party. Therefore the Blue Party willingly associated themselves with groups considered outcasts or even illegal thirty or forty years prior.

The Blue Party recognized they were losing elections in certain areas of the country by only a slight margin of percentage points. Their stifling economic restrictions and wealth-redistribution policies weren't having the desired effect, and they needed a way to close the gap, especially in areas where they could not control the counting of the ballot box. By accepting any fringe anti-Red Party, anti-capitalism, or anti-religious group, they were able to slightly reduce the gap. But it still wasn't enough.

They needed a way to import Blue Party supporters into these areas. They tried pressuring the businesses along with their unions to help. The businesses didn't see the return on spending millions to relocate entire factories, simply to provide the Blue Party with additional voters. And the union members were historically territorial, and didn't want to move to simply satisfy the needs of the Blue Party. The Blue Party finally had a brilliant idea. Due to the Blue Party's previous lack of immigration enforcement, the country already had tens of millions of well-established illegal workers and immigrants. They pushed for instant citizenship of these foreigners, and then to ensure their vote in favor of the Blue Party, they also provided them with inflated and targeted Prosperity Benefits.

But the immigration-to-citizen conversion numbers still fell short of what was needed. So the Blue Party once again threw open the borders like a curtain, and hundreds of thousands of poor, uneducated and destitute people poured into the country. The smiling Blue Party officials were waiting near the ignored checkpoints and border crossings, with citizenship and benefit cards in hand. These new citizens were then distributed to the areas in need of Blue Party votes and support, and the executive branch illegally directed outrageous amounts of money to relocate them. But along with a new abundance of loyal voters came a flood of aliens with exotic diseases and medical problems. As these immigrants were distributed across the country, they helped to spread these diseases amongst the general population. Hundreds of thousands of people died, and it helped turn the tide against the Blue Party, but only for a short period of time.

There was another fatal drawback to the open-border policy. Along with the influx of the Blue Party-loving immigrants were thousands of terrorists. The Blue Party knew this was happening, and they knew exactly who and what groups were coming into the country. Every one of these new arrivals was secretly tracked. The Blue Party actually wanted these terrorists to engage in terror activities. Their plan was simple. These acts of terrorism would cause the populace to further embrace the greater security and surveillance policies being pushed by the Blue Party. What the Blue Party failed to take into account was the citizens in the red zones were armed, and most of them were heavily armed. As the first wave of terrorist attacks happened in the red zones, the residents fought back, capturing anyone who looked like a terrorist and executing them on the spot. The Blue Party was already prone to ignore whatever happened in the red zone, and for the most part, they continued to do so. These acts of self-preservation by the red zone citizens only fueled the rumors that living in the red zone was dangerous, which in turn helped the blue zone and the Blue Party's image.

But then the terrorists moved into the gun-prohibited blue zone, where they found a much easier prey, and they continued with their attacks. This situation didn't bode well for the blue zone citizens and the Blue Party, and the Blue Party was forced to hunt down and eliminate these terrorists. The terrorists wars lasted for several years, and cost billions of dollars and hundreds of thousands of lives. Of course, there were those terrorists who had already fallen victim to the easy availability of citizenship and abundance of Prosperity Benefits. This group simply forgot about their holy war, and settled in for nice, comfortable lives. The level of benefits they were receiving were much better than a life on the run, and certainly better than life back in their home country.

And of course, free speech was also attacked by the Blue Party. The right to free speech was intended for a citizen to be able to say anything, even at the risk of offending another citizen, without a fear of retribution. If you espoused a belief or an idea which went against the Blue Party, you were branded as evil, close-minded, bigoted or racist. Certain words were targeted for elimination, and the simple use of these words would have you branded as an idiot or a zealot. The words "hate" and "greed" were powerful weapons used by the Blue Party. Other harsh labels were used to identify those who disagreed with their philosophy or platform, a platform of beliefs which also included many previously-shunned groups. If you disagreed with the philosophy or platform of the Blue Party, you were non-inclusive, a capitalistic pig, a moron, anti-social, or homophobic. Banned were any words or ideas which disparaged or offended an individual or group who supported the Blue Party. These offensive and insensitive words were forbidden, and could not be used by any individual or group of people without fear of retaliation. The real goal was not only to restrict speech, but to create a mindset where thinking negative thoughts was just as harmful. Speaking your opinions or beliefs requires one to think beforehand, and if harmful words were caused by thought, then the Blue Party would find a way to restrict free thinking as well.

Another purpose of political correctness in speech wasn't to protect people from being hurt or offended. This was evident as the Blue Party looked the other way when their members or groups violated their own code of conduct. The purpose of political correctness was to be able to, at any given time, declare that a word or phrase was socially or morally unacceptable. And political correctness helped to train the public into accepting and justifying (without thinking or opposing) a ban on a word or words deemed offensive. Implementing a ban on future words or phrases would then become easier and easier to achieve without needing to provide a reason. And the list of approved or banned words changed and grew constantly. This gave the Blue Party the power to control and limit what would otherwise be known as free speech, especially if what was being said was not in the Blue Party's interests. Political correctness was a powerful weapon which the Blue Party, along with the public and the media's help, skillfully wielded. However, the control and restrictions on free thought would take longer to achieve and enforce.

Religious organizations were forced to provide goods and services in strict violation of their religious beliefs. Religious principles and morals were deemed as archaic, old-fashioned, magical nonsense and simply ridiculous. The war on a peaceful and caring religion has always been a clear prophecy of the fall of any free nation. To the Blue Party, science held all of the answers, even if the science was incorrect or fabricated. In addition to religion, the Blue Party used science as a way to stifle entire industries, while promoting only those industries which promoted their agenda or lined their pockets with money. They accomplished these goals by providing huge grants and research facilities to the scientists who in turn, provided them with whatever scientific information they needed to promote their agenda.

In lieu of a tangible deity, people were instructed to worship the Earth, Mother Nature, the trees and the animals, which allowed the Party to determine what was moral or unjust. The killing of animals was taboo, and the use of fur would solicit physical attacks against the wearer. The sacred Earth was also deemed to be dying at the hands of the greedy industrialists and capitalists. Saving the Earth and its inhabitants was only going to be achieved by saving the climate, which was being attacked, altered and harmed by the evil capitalists and their businesses and pollution-spewing industries. Climate reports, climate modeling and weather forecasts were skewed in favor of their agenda. And if you believed anything to the contrary, or questioned these scientific results and studies, you were branded a heretic and an extremist.

Despite all of these events, there was a period in which the two political parties, the Blue and the Red, decided they could work together. The truth was the Blue Party was headed towards a position where they would continue to grow their control over the legislative branch. And the Red Party didn't want to continue to face defeat, election cycle after election cycle. Therefore, the Red Party made a deal with the Blue Party. They would quit the stonewalling and the filibustering of the Blue Party's legislative bills. In return, the Blue Party would allow the Red Party to pass a small number of acceptable but restrictive bills of their own, in order to keep their constituents in favor, and more importantly, to keep the Red Party members in power.

But this peace accord barely lasted two election cycles. The Blue Party went back on their word, and the Red Party was forced to either surrender or join them in their cause. The Red Party members quickly and conveniently lost faith in their ideals and beliefs, and simply surrendered. A minority of the members quit the political process altogether, and the remainder simply changed uniforms. Instead of the Blue and the Red parties, the public was informed the parties were merging, laying down their differences so they could work together, in unity, to do what was best for the country. Instead of labels for each party, they were simply now referred to as the Party. One political party, united for the good of the people and the survival of the country.

None of this would have been possible without the media's help. A half-century earlier, the media was unbiased to a degree, when news was limited to print and radio. Back then, the majority of the media was a true watchdog of the government, providing information to the people which could steer political policy or turn the outcome of an election. And when a political scandal broke, the media fed on it like a wild animal, regardless of who was at fault. Scandals sold magazines and newspapers, and drew people to the evening radio news.

The invention of television changed the definition of what it meant to be in the media. Being seen was much more convincing than being heard. The creation of the television personality and the news reporter changed everything. A new star was born, one not based upon their acting skills or intelligence, but upon their appearance and how well they could read their view of the news to the public. And of course there were the regular actors and actresses who became famous in the dramas and comedies being played out on the screen every night. Many people, along with a good portion of college students, believed the quick road to fortune and fame was to be on the television or in the movies. Majoring in liberal arts or journalism was often much easier and always more noble than getting a degree in business or law. Journalism also gave these people an outlet for their own socialist agendas, and a way to think with their hearts. No longer would stories of the unfair and unjust be swept under the rug. Journalists were going to save the nation from the horrors of war and crime and poverty and racism. Also, being famous and rich was one of the goals, and the easy way was through television or movies. With the growth of local media outlets, one stood a better chance at being a part of the local news show than starring on television or in the movies. Students were drawn to and flocked to journalism as a career. But the journalists, both professional and otherwise, focused more on their liberalism and socialism beliefs, than actual journalism.

If journalism wasn't your love, other newly-created areas of study were introduced, providing easily-obtainable degrees which unfortunately, didn't offer the recipients a viable path to a promising and stable job after college. When these graduates couldn't get a fabulous job in the entertainment or news industry, they also found they didn't possess the knowledge or skills to even obtain a decent job in any other area of business. The majority of them reluctantly moved back home with their parents or cohabited en masse in cheap apartments. With an already bleak job market, their thoughts quickly turned to the easiest safety net available, becoming dependent upon the hard work of others, and having the government provide them with Prosperity Benefits. Once this path was chosen, those not already in lock step with the Blue Party's platform, their ideals and beliefs easily gravitated towards supporting their providers and their only means of survival. Other graduates returned back to the schools to teach, and brought with them their liberal ideas and their love of big government. The population went from a decade of fighting against the establishment to the next decade of not questioning what it did or how it acted.

Along with the explosion of television and movies, both the ignorant and educated quickly turned into a quasi-celebrity-worshipping cult. People who were famous, these people who many of their worshippers had sought to become, those who acted in movies or television, or those who were in an entertainment group - these celebrities suddenly became political scholars and agents for the Blue Party. It didn't matter that the majority of these celebrities barely finished primary school or only possessed a year or two of higher-education. The masses flocked to them, and hung on their every word, and were mesmerized by their fantastic lives. The lower and middle-classes lived their lives vicariously through these celebrities. The marriage of the rich and beautiful and the politically famous had occurred, and the Blue Party was firmly in control of this union. The media and celebrities soon took their talking points directly from the Blue Party. If you were in either industry and spoke out against the Blue Party, you suddenly were blacklisted or found it difficult to find work. If you kept quiet and played along, you could continue to reap the rewards of fame and fortune and political glory.

It also didn't hurt that the Blue Party held a tight grip on the entire education process. The foundation of education is no longer in educating students with a goal of improving their knowledge and thinking skills. But rather, the goal of government education is to shape one's intelligence to a level where a person has difficulty understanding the logic in a political or social position or in a law. The ability to understand and apply logic is replaced instead with thinking by emotion. The student is also taught to easily and readily agree to whatever is popular or sounds fair, as long as the action and consequences being proposed is equitable to all people. The opinions on any subject changed from "I think" or "I believe" to "I feel."

From pre-school through college, the teachers and their unions walked along, hand-in-hand with the Blue Party, who promised them raises and lower grading standards. More money and less work is always attractive to those who have grown dependent upon the toils of others. Not all teachers were on board with this program, and like the celebrities, they found they needed to get with the program, or find work in the private schools, or simply leave the profession.

So, in the span of three or four decades, the Socialists won a secret battle, one the majority of the population didn't know was being fought. It didn't matter if their policies didn't work, or if unemployment was high, or if the national debt was out of control, or if prices were rising and the standard of living was falling. All that mattered to the Blue Party was they were in power. They created an environment with a majority of uneducated voters who loved them simply because they were the Blue Party - the party of the common man. The Blue Party was the party which promised that everyone, independent of stature or education or wealth or ability - everyone would be equal. From each according to his ability, to each according to his need. And the masses believed and defended every word. To be an avid supporter of the Blue Party meant you were the only true supporters of freedom and liberty, when in reality, you did not possess either. The advocates of the Blue Party sought equality for everyone, while agreeing to exclude the equality requirements for those in power inside the Party. And the Blue Party leaders were seen as demigods holding and possessing all of the knowledge that was true and flawless.

Once the Red Party was eliminated, and the new singularly-named Party was in power, once they had control of the media and the entertainment elites, once they had control of the education process, they started their plan of equalization. And if you, as a citizen, didn't agree with their views or agenda, you were continued to be labeled a hater, an evil person, or a traitor. Free speech was only free if the Party agreed with what you were saying. Tolerance was preached heavily by the Party, but the application of tolerance was a one-way street.

But there arose a problem. The country was too large to continue to apply and to enforce these socialistic principals upon everyone. Prosperity Benefit Zones were then developed where the Party could more easily control the masses and what was being provided to them, and what rights were also being restricted or taken away. If for no other reason but spite, the Party named the more-populated city areas the blue zone, and anywhere else was labeled as the red zone. Because of the high unemployment in both zones, the ever-increasing Prosperity Benefits were tilted in favor of the blue zone occupants. Many citizens fled the red zone for the blue zone, unaware the Party was drawing them in and under their control. Once they had enough people in the blue zones, the Party could slowly begin to ignore the red zones. The occupants of the red zones were not important, and their actions were not meaningful, as long as those in the red zone suffered a little more than those in the blue zone. Eventually, the plan was the red zones would become barren, as people would leave and concentrate in the blue zones. And *once you were in the blue zone, your actions and the actions of your fellow citizens would be easier for the Party to monitor and control.*

David put down the *Guide*. The realization never occurred to him before, but his work territory was almost exclusively in the blue zone. The requirement one had to drive through the red zone to get to another blue zone was apparent, but he rarely traveled to or spent any time in the red zone. The only exception being when he would drive up in the mountains to use the teller machines, and he never ventured from his route. An epiphany surfaced, and he chuckled to himself as to why he didn't realize this before, as he already read the book the previous times. The *Guide* mentioned he should concentrate his candidate search to the red zone, and it now made sense. The red-zone residents were probably already biased against the blue zone and the Party. By joining this mission, these people would have nothing to lose, if the red zone was indeed falling apart or neglected as the *Guide* mentioned. Life in the red zone was purportedly horrible, and over the past two decades, there had been a slow but steady migration to the blue zones, partly in order to take advantage of the higher Prosperity Benefits offered to blue-zone residents.

David placed a half-piece of toilet paper in the guide as a bookmark before he closed the book, slid it back under the cabinet, and put the trim back in place. There would be more time to read tomorrow night. The plan was to travel to the red zone tomorrow to use the teller machines, but now he was going to head out a bit earlier, as one of the potential associates he identified lived in the red zone. He needed to locate him and he was running out of time.

Chapter 9

David just finished a meeting with Tim at his hospital, and the outcome was incredibly successful. Tim placed orders for multiples of all of his products and services, and David was beaming. The order was the largest ever taken, and possibly the largest order in the history of his department. As David strolled through the hospital lobby, he bounced through the large doors and out of the hospital. Stepping out into the blaring sunlight, he held his hand up to his eyes to block the sun. Through the glare he noticed the parking lot was filled with police cars, officers, national troops and armored vehicles. Tim was behind the line of police cars, standing by the fountain with a loudspeaker, instructing David to surrender, and there was no use in running. The police were positioned outside of their cars, with their guns drawn, aimed directly at him, and he was surrounded. David studied the scene in the parking lot, much like he was sizing up the situation, before smirking and deciding to make a run for it, and then taking off and running towards his car. As the torrent of bullets flew past him, he was able to make it to the safety of his car, a large black sports vehicle, similar to what the Party gave to its members. He jumped in the car and slammed the door shut. The bullets were ricocheting off the windows, and he accelerated very quickly and left the parking lot, causing a few policemen to jump out of the way.

David was now driving through the streets of a downtown area, which were void of any other cars or people. In his rearview mirror, there was a wave of police cars trailing behind him, with their blue lights flashing and their sirens screaming. The black car quickly moved out of the city, and was driving on one of the national highways. The road was full of cars and trucks, and he was weaving in and out of the traffic, with the police right behind him. Up in the air, and directly above him and on all sides, were dozens of Party drones and helicopters. Their rockets were exploding on the road all around him, tossing cars and trucks and throwing up huge chunks of concrete and asphalt. For an unknown reason, he was impervious to their weapons, as if a higher-power was shielding and protecting him, sympathetic to his plight, and there was a revelation he was going to make his escape, and he was going to live.

David continued driving at full speed, and easily increased the distance between him and the police cars. As he topped a hill, he looked further down the road, where it continued towards the bottom of a small valley, and he saw a bridge crossing the river. Increasing his speed even more as he approached the crossing, he could now see the police established a roadblock, with heavy armored cars and trucks blocking his path. He slowed down, trying to figure out which way he should go, when he heard a voice to his right. Tim suddenly appeared in his passenger's seat, and was talking to him. "Today is going to be a hot one, so if you are taking the kids to the community pool for fun in the sun, be sure you wear plenty of sunblock. We might see some clouds roll in..."

David opened his eyes to the sound of the weatherman continuing his spiel, and he could feel his heart throbbing, and he was covered in sweat. The voice continued, and startled him once again, and he realized the voice was coming from his alarm clock, which was set on one of the national radio stations. Movement was impossible, as if his entire body was paralyzed, and he was almost afraid to move. His heart was racing from the dream, so he remained still, allowing his heartbeat to drop back down to a normal rhythm. The voice on the radio switched from the weather to the news, and a woman was now talking about the recent rash of hate crimes in the red zone. Her voice was nice and mellow and smooth, describing these gruesome crimes with incredible detail, but it was as if she was reading a lullaby to a baby. After his heart returned to an almost-normal tempo, he finally moved and reached over and turned off the radio.

Normally on a Saturday he would sleep in until nine hundred. But since his last meeting with Tim, he began to treat Saturday like a normal workday. The clock read seven minutes past six hundred. Reaching up, he turned on the lamp on his bedside table, in an attempt to help prevent him from falling back asleep. When he finally moved, he noticed the air inside his apartment was thicker than normal, and the sweat had attempted to glue the sheets to the back of his body. The air conditioner was normally set on eighty to save money, and since he was on the top floor of his complex, he suffered in the summer but benefited slightly during the winter. Rising from the bed, he stumbled over and glanced at the thermostat, and the readout still displayed eighty. The fact the thermostat wasn't broken was a relief, but he was still noticeably hot, and maybe the sweat was only a product of his dream. Also, the apartment manager wasn't at work on Saturday, and they would never send a repairman out on the weekend. The meeting with his manager was on Monday, and he certainly didn't want the maintenance man snooping around in his apartment without him being there. He set the thermostat to seventy-eight, enough to slightly cool the room while he took a shower.

By six-forty, he was dressed and ready to go. He decided to splurge, and get breakfast at a local coffee shop. Even though he had all of this money from the teller machines, he was still very strict in sticking to his normal budget, and using the teller money for non-mission purchases was forbidden. The *Guide* stressed you should never, if at all possible, deviate from your schedule or expenditures. When he started drinking coffee outside of the Party hotels, he made sure he paid cash for every other purchase, so no one could see a sudden rise in expenses. This detail was probably too small for anyone to notice, but he didn't want to take any chances. Paranoia was now his friend.

Walking outside and along the way to his car, he discretely scanned the parking lot to see if there were any strange cars around. The sun was above the horizon, but was blocked by the tall buildings surrounding his apartment complex. David could already tell it was going to be a hot day, confirming what the weatherman stated earlier. The mountain area was usually cooler than the city, and he began to look forward to these weekend trips.

David made his withdrawals along a predetermined route, changing hats and sunglasses between stops, and he even changed his shirt several times. His preference for shirts were bland ones which included solid colors - blue, dark green, maroon or white. And the *Guide* offered a handy tip, which involved applying rubber cement to the one finger he used to punch the buttons on the teller machines, to avoid leaving any fingerprints, as wearing gloves in the warmer weather would be suspicious. After an hour and a half, he was finished with his route, so he made his way over to a public library to use the network.

A perfect spot in the corner of the parking lot was available, under a large oak tree, providing him with a nice shady place to use his tablet, but not too far away to be able to receive a signal from the library's network connection. This would be his first attempt at recruiting, which prompted a desire to refresh his memory one final time. Notes about each candidate were compiled on one of his tablets, written with a rudimentary code he created. The code consisted of simply substituting the most commonly-used vowels and consonants with each other or numbers, combined with his own version of shorthand. The experts from the Party could easily crack this code, but if a regular person found or stole his tablet, they probably wouldn't be able to decipher what he was writing. Or at least he thought this was true. By now, he could write and read his code with ease.

David identified his first potential associate, a man named Gary, and he easily found his address through the public property tax records. The difficult part was in figuring out a way to meet and talk with him, and if possible, away from his home. David left the library and drove north for about an hour, and then continued through a small town towards his target. Gary lived in a small subdivision of about thirty houses, with most of them being small log cabins in a valley, engulfed by small but steep hills. As David slowly entered the subdivision, he looked to his left and noticed a small dirt and grassy area at the front of the subdivision.

The area appeared like it was originally designated for a house. David guessed this lot never sold and from what he could tell, the lot appeared to have been commandeered by the neighborhood and turned it into a makeshift but shoddy playground for the kids. There were three rusty swing sets and four rope swings hanging from the same number of trees. David quickly checked the playground, but couldn't see anyone in the overgrown vacant lot, so he pulled into the dirt parking area out front. This location would provide him with a good vantage point, and with his binoculars, he started scanning the houses down the street. The use of the binoculars was risky, as he didn't want any neighbors wondering who this stranger was, sitting in a car looking at their houses. Gary's house was nice, but like the rest of the neighborhood, the yard was desperate for maintenance. An old blue pickup truck stood guard in the driveway, and it was assumed this was Gary's truck. The license plate was too small to read, but there was a large dent in the back right panel of the truck's bed, which could be used later to identify the truck.

With the location of his recruit verified, David quickly left the lot and turned right out of the subdivision, back in the direction of the town. There was a small country store located a short distance down the highway, so he drove there to wait for Gary. The store was near the crest of a hill, and from the parking lot, David was provided with a good view of the subdivision entrance. Now all he needed to do was wait, and hope no one noticed him sitting there. As usual, it was a good idea to inspect the exterior of any building for cameras, so David stepped out of the car, and walked towards the entrance. The building did not seem to have any visible cameras, and the location was deep in the red zone, so the need for security out here was not warranted. After he finished his surveillance of the store, he turned back towards the subdivision, to make sure Gary had not left. He noticed a stack of real estate books in a rack near the front of the store, so he walked over and hastily grabbed three different issues, and went back to his car. The *Guide* explained that you always needed an excuse for being in a place you normally wouldn't be, and now he had one. If he was stopped by the police, his ruse would be that he was thinking of buying a small cabin and retiring in the mountains. The magazines provided him with a reason to sit in his car, watch the entrance to the subdivision, while he pretended to browse through the listings.

David was slowly flipping through the magazines, keeping an eye out for Gary, and he gradually slipped into a fantasy about actually attempting to buy one of these cabins. A small cabin might be affordable, and the smaller the place the better. With a cabin and some land, he could plant a garden and grow vegetables, and he could even try hunting and fishing. There was sure to be a learning curve for both, as he had never attempted either one. But in each listing, after it listed the details of the property, the selling points focused on how nice the soil was for a garden, or how close you were to being able to hunt or fish. The daydream was interrupted by the sight of a blue truck passing him to his right, and David was able to see that the truck had a dent in the back right panel, confirming it was Gary, or at least it was the blue truck. David quickly drove onto the highway and followed him, but not too closely.

The truck stopped at a small hardware store not too far down the road. Gary parked in front of the store, hopped out of his truck, waved to an old man across the parking lot and went inside. David pulled his car over to the side of the store. This scenario and his speech were rehearsed dozens of times over the past week, with the only unknown being the responses from Gary. Rehearsing what he was going to say boosted his confidence, but all of a sudden he was very nervous, and his mouth became dry and he was debating if he could pull it off. A picnic table and a gazebo were in the tall uncut grass on the side of the store, and David determined this would be a good place for the meeting. Both had signs showing they were for sale, but he could tell from the discolored and cracked wood they had been sitting there a while. Taking a deep breath as if to summon whatever courage he could muster, he grabbed a large paper sack from under his seat, left his car and sat down on the bench closest to the door, but still a fair distance from Gary's truck. As David waited, Gary's story replayed in his mind.

Gary grew up in this area, went to the local high school, played on the football team, and married his high-school sweetheart a year after they graduated. He worked off and on in construction for a year before deciding to join the national military. The plan was to give the military a try, and maybe even make it his career. The other career options in his home area were not great, with or without higher education, which Gary did not possess. He and his wife were stationed at a military base southeast of where he now lived. They rented an older house in an mature but run-down neighborhood which at one time would have been considered lovely. The area wasn't the best part of the blue zone to live in, but it was affordable, and the majority of the neighbors were decent people. His wife, Patty, was working at a local department store. They were saving to buy a small house a little closer to home, back towards the red zone, where they could start raising a family.

Gary had been deployed overseas for his third six-month tour, and Patty was pregnant with their first child. Gary had been gone for three months, and they tried to schedule the pregnancy so he would be home in time to see their baby being born. Even with the floundering economy, they lived a good life, and better than most of the people who graduated with them.

One overcast afternoon, Patty was leaving to go to work. Since they couldn't afford a car, she normally took the government bus to work, and then a co-worker or her manager would give her a ride home at night. The closest bus stop was less than a five-minute walk from their house, and it was a walk she made every day for almost the past four years. As she left her house and made her way to the sidewalk, she barely noticed a large older-model car drive very slowly past her. She didn't think too much about it, as most of the cars in this area were older, and she continued walking towards the bus stop. Her attention was focused down the street towards the stop, and she was checking her watch to make sure she wouldn't miss the bus. She didn't see the slow-moving car pull into a driveway and then turn around. With her mind preoccupied about being late for work, she didn't notice the car slowly pull next to her and stop. And she didn't see the man get out of the car and quickly walk up behind her. She finally reacted, although not from fear, but only when she heard some footsteps and started to turn around. The man pulled a long tool out from behind his back and hit her once on the top of her head. The force of the weapon stunned her, and she lost her balance and started to fall, but he caught her from the side, and hugged her body before she hit the ground. Wrapping his arms around her, he started dragging her towards a vacant house. In this empty house was where the man assaulted and strangled her. Patty was twenty-four years old.

Her body probably would have gone unnoticed for a while, except she dropped her house keys into the dirt as she was struck, before losing consciousness and being pulled to the house. Later that afternoon, a teenage boy found the keys while walking home from school, and his mother recognized the key ring, with the round metal tag embedded with the national military emblem, and Gary's name in the middle. After placing some phone calls, and after the neighbors couldn't locate Patty or find anyone who knew where she was, she reluctantly called the police. The police arrived, and the young man took them to where the keys were found. One of the officers discovered what appeared to be a line of dried blood on the sidewalk. More officers were dispatched, along with search dogs and rescue drones, and they quickly found the body in the basement of the vacant house.

An investigation was started and the police began the long process of questioning the neighbors. Most of them had been at work, and as usual, no one witnessed anything. The gang of police were still there when a resident who lived near the crime scene, a man named James Hill, informed them he captured the attack on video. His house had been burglarized several times over the past year, and he recently installed several security cameras, in a vain attempt to catch the thieves. One of the cameras was located in an upstairs window, pointed out and down at the street, and it was this camera which recorded the attack. The police followed the man to his house, where he copied the video onto a memory stick. Back at the police headquarters, the video was placed into evidence and reviewed, and one of the detectives was able to use photo-enhancement software to identify the license plate of the murderer.

An all-points bulletin was issued for the car and the owner, and every officer within a hundred miles was in on the search. The sky was buzzing with the ominous sounds of search drones and news helicopters. A patrol unit spotted the car outside a local bar, and within minutes, a police assault team stormed the location, where they quickly took the suspect, Johnson Bryce, into custody. In the trunk of his car they found a small pipe wrench, with specks of Patty's blood on the handle. At the police station, Johnson quickly confessed to the crime. The media praised the police for their swift and successful capture of this career criminal, but not much was mentioned about the sadness from the loss of such a young life. Johnson possessed a long history of mostly minor offenses, but now if convicted of murder, he could be put to death.

The news of his wife's murder devastated Gary. The military granted him an emergency leave, and he came home to bury his wife and unborn child. Because their combined income was barely over the national burial benefit level, the bodies were cremated and placed in a shared community grave. Not surprisingly, the local community and their home town was startled and saddened by this tragedy. And also not surprisingly, the local and national media covered the story for almost a week. While the area where they lived was known for petty crimes, burglaries, small-time drug deals, it had been a while since something like this happened, at least not to a pregnant young woman. These news articles were how David learned about what happened, but it wasn't the murder which made Gary a viable candidate. There were plenty of murders in the blue zone.

Johnson Bryce was to be put on trial for murder and would face execution if found guilty, and as usual, the media was there to cover every minute and every related storyline. The trial had been delayed several times, for various reasons set forth by the defense, and the delay bought Johnson almost two years of time. Gary wanted to be home for the trial, so instead of continuing his career in the military, he resigned after his last tour, and was given an honorable discharge. His plan was to attempt to re-enlist after the trial, and then try and start his life over again. If he was successful in re-enlisting, he was hoping for a permanent overseas deployment, as he didn't think he could have a new beginning if he lived nearby. Gary even decided he would try to be deployed to a war zone, where he could possibly die a hero, and his agony over her death would finally go away.

A trial date was finally set. Even though the crime was over two years old, the media resurrected that day and the events off and on for a solid week before the start of the trial. Events like this were a ratings booster for all media outlets, and of course, the citizens in the area were mesmerized once again with the details. The past event and the trial were all anyone could talk about, at least for this particular week. There was always a tragedy or a scandal in the works for next week. Security for the trial was tight, as the entire town was whipped into a frenzy by the media. People were gathering and staging protests outside of the courthouse, where many of the participants volunteered to be the executioner.

The trial judge was a man by the name of William Raymond, a Party-appointed judge and a former Blue Party regional legislative member. The honorable Judge Raymond possessed a great abhorrence towards the military and anyone who supported the military, including the families of soldiers. He was also a staunch opponent of the death penalty, a widely-known fact which provided great satisfaction to the defense team. They knew his position on the death penalty, and like any good defense team, when faced with overwhelming and conclusive evidence, they devised their defense strategy around this particular judge.

The trial began, and the courtroom was filled to capacity with protestors and curious onlookers. The jury was sworn in, and the judge read aloud the indictment, listing all of the charges being brought against Mr. Bryce. The judge then asked the prosecution for their opening statement.

The lead prosecutor rose from his desk, sauntered over to the jury box, and began with a summary of that day's events for the jury. The defendant, Mr. Johnson Bryce, brutally assaulted and strangled this poor young pregnant woman, for no reason whatsoever, and they possessed the video and the physical evidence to prove it. As soon as the video evidence was mentioned, the defense put forth an objection. One of the defense team's lawyers stood up, and stated the objection was pursuant to the legal code 118-02-14. The police did not have a search warrant for Mr. Hill's house, where the video of the alleged initial altercation was taken, and Mr. Hill did not have the authority to record people driving on a public road or walking on a public access way, which in this case was the sidewalk. The defense stated Mr. Hill was well within his rights to record anyone who stepped onto his property, but once he started recording people in a public area, permission was required from each person involved, prior to those persons being recorded on video. And Mr. Bryce had certainly not granted Mr. Hill permission to record him. Since the video was taken illegally, and since there wasn't a search warrant to search Mr. Bryce's car, then none of the subsequent evidence could be admissible and used against the defendant.

The defense was putting forth an argument that if the video was not admissible as evidence, then the vehicle tag number the police retrieved from the video could not legally be used to locate Mr. Bryce's car. And because the car was found illegally and the search of the car was performed without a warrant, the wrench they found in Mr. Bryce's car was inadmissible as well. And nor was the subsequent confession made by Mr. Bryce. The prosecutor would need other evidence to prove their case. The defense thereby made a motion to dismiss the case.

The prosecution table was shocked and somewhat incredulous. They asked the judge for a five-minute conference amongst themselves. Besides knowing how ridiculous the defense objection was, they also knew the history of the judge they were dealing with. They were hurriedly reviewing and

85

discussing the other evidence available and related to this case. Since the suspect was captured so quickly and confessed immediately, the police didn't bother to perform any forensic work on the body. They had their suspect, a bloody murder weapon, a video, and a signed confession. The police budget was already tight, so the detectives opted out of performing any lab work as well. They didn't even bother to match the blood on the weapon to Patty. And since the body was cremated, there wasn't any additional physical evidence they could locate by exhuming the body. They finally agreed this objection wouldn't stand. It couldn't stand. This was ludicrous. After the break was over, the judge ordered the court back into session.

Gary was in the courtroom as this objection was being raised. He was sitting on the back row, eight rows behind the defense table, as the police wouldn't let him sit any closer to the defendant. He could clearly see the back of Mr. Bryce's head, and he had a direct view of the judge, perched high upon his bench. As the defense was laying out their objection, Gary seemed to think he saw the judge smile, ever so slightly. The judge's normal scowl turned into a straight line, with one side turned slightly upwards, and his eyes briefly widened. This reaction lasted less than one second, before his face turned sour again. Gary was positive he saw it.

After the prosecutor's meeting was over, the objection was read again by the defense. The judge lingered for a moment, and then spoke. "Counselor, I am going to overrule the remark about the police needing a search warrant for the video. The homeowner..." The judge paused, lifted his glasses from the end of his nose, and tried to focus his eyes on the video monitor in front of him. "The homeowner, Mr. Hill, produced the video evidence willingly and offered it to the police. Also, the police entered the house upon the invitation of Mr. Hill." A sigh of relief could be heard from the prosecution table, and members of the team were holding back their enthusiasm.

"However, I will need to take a recess to review the other parts of your objection. I am not completely familiar with the law about recording people without their consent in a public area. The court will take a one-hour recess while I do some research, but I want the defense and the prosecution to remain in the courthouse. This should not take long." The judge stood up to go to his chambers, and the bailiff announced in a loud booming voice, "All rise." As the judge stood up to leave, the crowd erupted in a murmur of whispering voices, and several of the women in the audience gasped.

The prosecution was stunned, and the defense table quickly huddled together. Both teams were now whispering and talking in their respected groups. All of the prosecutors took out their tablets and were typing furiously, and silently dictating orders to their assistants. Mr. Bryce leaned over to listen to his lawyer, and he glanced at the back of the courtroom. His eyes met Gary's, and Bryce smugly cocked a smile. Gary was in a state of disbelief, combined with a slowly-rising rage. He was thinking this certainly can't be correct. This can't be a real law.

The judge returned after only twenty minutes. The bailiff once again bellowed, "All rise," as the judge entered the room. After the judge instructed everyone to sit, he pulled his chair up closer to the bench, and placed his elbows on the top. Pulling the microphone over to his mouth, he said, "I have reviewed the laws regarding recording video in a public area, and yes, the defense is correct. The defendant's car was on a public road, and Mr. Hill did not have permission to record Mr. Bryce. Even though the video shows the initial attack on the victim, the attack took place on a public-owned right of way, a sidewalk. Because of the angle of the camera, we do not see any actions done by the defendant after both the defendant and the victim move off the sidewalk and off camera. If the video was from a national surveillance camera, it would be a different story, as this law does not apply there. But the video wasn't from a national camera. Therefore, I have to rule the video may not be used as evidence, and any subsequent evidence obtained from the video, the automobile and license information, will not be admissible. Also, since the information from the video lead to the capture of the defendant, as well as the discovery of the murder weapon and the subsequent confession, I will have to rule these may not be used as evidence as well."

The courtroom was astonished and silent in disbelief. The judge turned towards the prosecutor's team. "Does the prosecution have any more evidence to present?" The lead prosecutor was looking down at the table, dumbfounded by what he heard. The prosecution didn't have any more evidence. There weren't any witnesses, there wasn't any physical evidence from the body, and there weren't any forensics. There was nothing else. He slowly rose from his chair. "No, your honor."

The judge nodded his head in the affirmative. "If there is no further evidence to be presented, how would the prosecution like to proceed?"

The lead prosecutor reluctantly said, "Your honor, we have no other choice but to drop the charges and dismiss the case."

The defense team was quietly but politely celebrating their victory. Mr. Bryce was silent as well, almost stunned, and he couldn't believe it worked. Leaning over, he whispered thanks to his lawyers, and then slowly looked behind him. Gary was no longer in the courtroom.

With this decision, the media outlets had another field day. Upon further review of the law, the media discovered the prohibition of recording a person without their permission mainly focused on the commercial aspect. One could not record someone else and use it in a commercial venue without the subject's permission and just compensation. The law did not state anything about using the video as evidence for a crime. In fact, the actual legal meaning of the law was fairly ambiguous, and the judge used this ambiguity to his advantage. The judge stuck by his decision, and stated there was nothing anyone could do about it anyway. He claimed a guilty verdict against the defendant would be thrown out upon appeal. Over the past two decades, the decisions handed down by juries were treated as recommendations, instead of binding legal verdicts. Judges were no longer elected, but appointed by the Party, and were given complete and absolute power in their courtrooms. The majority of judges also shared the view that when a law is broken, more often than not, society was guilty rather than the lawbreaker.

And now after the fact, even if the prosecution was able to obtain additional evidence, the defendant now couldn't be charged twice for the same crime. And the media, the majority of whom were also against the death penalty, defended and praised the judge for his actions. The judge received his day or two of fame along with some unwanted added tension. But Gary's life was nearly destroyed.

Gary left immediately after the judge's ruling. Upon hearing the case was dismissed, he knew if he didn't leave, he might try to kill Johnson Bryce right there in the courtroom. But with Johnson now a free man, Gary would need to be patient, to simply seek revenge at a later date and time. Of course, Gary's plan was locked away in his mind, and he never mentioned his thoughts or feelings to anyone. His grief-driven silence during the entire ordeal was understandable, and he refused to give interviews or talk to the media. But David speculated that revenge must have been running through Gary's mind, and revenge was probably still consuming a lot of his current thoughts, even though a lot of time had passed. Unfortunately for Gary's plan of revenge, Johnson Bryce left the area shortly after the trial and virtually disappeared, as he knew what his fate would be if he stuck around.

Chapter 10

The glass door of the hardware store opened, and David watched as Gary appeared, with a small plastic bag in his hand. Gary paused for a moment to put on his sunglasses, and David shouted, "Hey Gary!" while waving for him to come over. Gary looked over at David but didn't recognize him, as his face was hidden by a camouflaged hat and sunglasses, and both were standard apparel for this area. Gary walked over towards the picnic table, and as he approached, he returned a polite, "Hey," while still trying to figure out who this person was. But as he got closer, Gary realized he didn't know this person. This still wasn't an unusual situation. In a small town, everyone knew everybody in one way or another, and you generally forgot people you met from time to time.

David motioned for him to sit down. "Good to see you, you got a minute to talk?"

Gary removed his sunglasses, and David removed his as well. Gary stared at him for a minute. "Sorry, I can't seem to remember your name." This wasn't unusual for Gary, as Patty's death changed him in ways he was still trying to figure out. Most days were a haze, and remembering people's names or faces, or remembering things he needed to do was a daily hardship.

David stood up half-way and extended his hand. "I'm Steve Jackson. You got a minute to talk about a job?" Gary reluctantly shook David's hand, as he didn't know anyone named Steve Jackson. David motioned for Gary to have a seat, and they both sat down.

Since Patty's death, Gary was working mainly in the construction industry, but work wasn't steady and he was bouncing from job to job. Unemployment in the region was at twenty-four percent, but the truth was the majority of people simply quit looking for a permanent job. And, you never really knew the actual rate of unemployment, as the Party-supplied figures were never accurate. Many people were working as day laborers where they were paid in cash and where they could avoid paying the high work-benefit taxes. They coveted this non-reportable income, as it would still allow them to collect their Prosperity Benefits, after their Displaced-Worker Benefits expired.

For the past two decades, there had been a string of food shortages, which in turn drove the creation of private mini-farms. The private red-zone grocery stores were having problems obtaining enough food from their commercial suppliers, as the majority of them had been nationalized. And it was becoming more and more difficult for private stores to obtain anything from any other Party-owned companies. So, the majority of the red zone citizens turned to these mini-farms and to themselves for providing their families with food. The food generated from these small private farms were only sold in the red zone areas, at the private grocery stores, but mostly at the more-profitable little wooden stands on the sides of the roads. And these farms needed a constant supply of workers, and therefore the need for labor was usually satisfied by local residents. Tired of working on a sporadic basis, Gary was willing to talk to anyone about a job, even a complete stranger.

David put his sunglasses back on, and wasn't sure exactly where to start. He had been rehearsing this moment for the past several weeks, once he identified Gary as a candidate. David began to talk and he hoped his rehearsals would pay off. "Gary, first off, I am very sorry for your loss, for what happened to Patty. I can't imagine what you have been going through. I understand times are tough, and I'm guessing your life has been hard these past five years." Gary was non-responsive, and he put his sunglasses back on.

"I really don't know what you are feeling. But I understand, and I can sympathize with you." David waited for a reply, and they were both silent for a moment.

Then Gary finally spoke. "Yeah, it has been rough. There are days where I don't want to get out of bed. Well, there are weeks where I don't want to get out of bed. I have tried to move on, get past it. But it has been difficult."

Gary continued to talk for another ten minutes, telling David about how he was angry back then, consumed with rage, and wanted revenge. But when Johnson Bryce vanished, it left him with a feeling he would never recover from this situation. He talked about how he turned to alcohol, and then drugs to try and help ease the pain. But none of it worked. As he poured out his soul, David wondered if Gary really ever had the chance to talk to anyone about what happened, or about his mental state, or his thoughts or feelings. Or maybe he has told this story over and over again to anyone who would listen, and the people he knew were tired of hearing about it. And now, Gary had a new person to talk to. David couldn't figure this part out.

Gary finished with, "Well, that's about it. I take it day to day, job to job. That's all I can do."

David could tell from the cracking in Gary's voice this event was still heavy on his mind, and he still hadn't been able to shake his demons. Now it was time for David to offer a chance to make things right again.

"I can understand something has been bothering you since the event and the trial. A feeling you can't quite figure out. You mentioned it briefly, and I could have guessed you still have revenge on your mind. You don't really care what would happen to you, if you were able to finally extract this revenge. Or, you may be holding back, thinking revenge isn't the way to go. Maybe you are too good of a person. But, I believe your thoughts of revenge are your main concern, and this is what is bothering you, and what is gnawing at you on a daily basis. But I also believe your revenge is directed at the wrong person. While revenge on Mr. Bryce seems like the logical way to go, I believe you have a different goal which is more easily attainable. Especially given the fact Mr. Bryce has vanished." Gary was listening very closely, and he leaned over the bench, turning his head so one ear was closer to David.

"Gary, what happened to Patty was an atrocity, but what happened in the courtroom was even worse. Justice died that day, when the judge let that murderer go free. You know the judicial system has changed. Justice is no longer blind. Political agendas now drive the courts. These self-righteous judges are no longer following the law. They are creating their own laws, legislating from the bench. If they don't like the law, they find a way around it, or a way to decipher it to their advantage. These judges do everything they can to push the Party agenda. In your case, at that time, the Party and your judge were against the death penalty. Well, the Party won't abolish the death penalty as they still use it when it is convenient for them. But when it isn't in their interest, as with your situation, the Party and their followers abhor putting anyone to death. I wouldn't be surprised if the Party provided the defense with their argument, and maybe even talked to the judge about it before the trial. And the prosecutor was either too stupid or too scared to protest what happened. With all that being said, let me get to the part about this job I was talking about."

"I am going to be blunt here. You see Gary, I am a volunteer in an covert organization which is on a mission to change all of this. We aren't a militia group. We don't have an army or a cache of weapons. All we have are individuals like yourself who want to bring our country back to where individual freedom and following the laws mattered. Where justice meant the laws were upheld despite your political feelings. Where politicians created laws that served the people, and not the other way around."

"Gary, I know you served in the military. I know you fought in the terrorists wars. But we aren't terrorists. We don't harm the innocent. We aren't trying to start a civil war. We are only removing from society those who have decided to not follow the law. Our enemies are individuals who have a political agenda which goes against everything this country was founded upon and has stood and fought for. We are fighting for the same freedoms that when you served, you swore an oath to protect. We need you, and others like you. Everyone has their own mission, their own battle and their own goal. But together, these individual events, if properly planned and executed, they will help us win the overall war. In your mission, your personal mission, your enemy is not Johnson Bryce. In your mission, your target is Judge William Raymond. He is your enemy, and he is this country's enemy. He is your target. He is your revenge."

Gary was still silent, absorbing everything David said. David was able to keep his composure, and was very calm and confident. His years of talking to disinterested clients, trying to convince them to look at brochures or purchase something from him, his experience was now paying off. He was as comfortable talking with Gary as with any of his customers. He continued his focus on Gary, who was looking down at the table.

"It is very simple Gary. We are a secret organization. We don't even know how many people are in our group. There isn't a membership list. We don't have any meetings. No single member can identify more than five other members. And once I leave here, I probably won't ever contact you again.

Anonymity is part of the plan. And my name isn't Steve. I have my own personal mission, and I am also tasked with finding four other people such as yourself. This way, if any one of us are captured or discovered, our enemies won't be able to find us all. We don't have a single large plan of attack, as each act is driven by each individual member. Really, the only thing we all share, the only thing we have in common is a goal. Our goal is restoring individual freedom and justice, true justice for everyone. We need you Gary, the time has come for you to serve your country again."

Raising his head, Gary removed his sunglasses and rubbed his eyes. David could see his eyes appeared bloodshot, and he could tell this was an emotional time for him, and he no idea how he was going to react. "Do you have any questions for me?"

Gary didn't say anything right away, and David let him think. After a brief period, he said, "You are talking about killing people. They may not be innocent people, but how is this not terrorism? How is this not better than the terrorists who have been doing stuff like this for the past fifty, sixty years?"

David took off his sunglasses and adjusted his gaze so he stared right into his eyes and replied, "Gary, terrorism is the act of killing innocent people, and at times even killing soldiers or police officers, to drive fear into the hearts of a population. A terrorist may claim a religious or political cause, but they do what they do because they hate our country and what we stand for, which is freedom, liberty and justice. The end result of terrorism is only terror. We believe terrorism is used to propagate a cause, and in this day and time, more often than not, we think it is a religious cause. And in most cases, it is. But the people who are running this country, they have their own form of terrorism, but they have fine-tuned and hidden it so you don't even know you are being terrorized. Freedom is dying a slow death from a thousand cuts."

"So, how are we different? What we are doing is removing from our society those people who are not following the law, and the reason they aren't following the law is for political purposes. They are as harmful to our country as the criminal who steals or kills. These people, are in effect, fighting their own discreet war against freedom and liberty. They have the same cause as these terrorists, in they hate our country. Or at least they hate our country as we used to know it. This hatred of freedom, of capitalism and of prosperity, this is their religion. This judge could be considered a traitor, in as far as he is aiding and abetting an enemy of the country, a country we once knew and loved. Our enemies are those who are driven to stifle and then eventually displace individual freedom and liberty. They desire a place where a select group has the power, and the people have none. Where everyone is equal, no one prospers over another, except for those in power. And if we don't do this, if we don't act, then what have we been fighting for? Look back in history, at all of those people in the military who gave their lives for our freedom, all of these years and all of those lives lost will have been a waste. And that's why we need you Gary. That's why we need you."

David paused. He could tell Gary was contemplating what he was saying, and his mind was trying to figure out if what David was saying was true, or if he could make himself believe it. "Gary, the only reason Johnson Bryce went free, the only reason he wasn't executed for his crime, was the judge had a political agenda against the death penalty. That was it. And the law he used to cover up this agenda didn't even apply to the case at hand. The judge, a man who is supposed to follow the law, lied about the reasoning for dismissing the evidence. And the media, who have the same political agenda, covered up this neglect and branded this judge a hero. The judge became a hero in the media's eyes for setting a murderer free. Justice was not served. A horrific crime was committed, the criminal was not punished and your life was turned upside down. And if you do a little research, you will find this wasn't an isolated case. This judge is known for reducing sentences for violent crimes. Instead of placing the blame for a criminal's action on the criminal, he places the blame on society for failing the criminal. This judge, and many others like him, blames society for not providing the criminals with enough social benefits and resources, as if that would have prevented the very crimes they commit. The criminal was sick, but these people believe it was society's failure which gave him this disease. As long as this judge lives, justice will continue to be suppressed. And because of people like this criminal, and like this judge, our country will continue to decline to where laws won't matter. The government will decide what is right and what is wrong. And a socialist government has no morals. But there is hope, Gary. We are that hope. It is our job to save our country."

As David was talking, Gary was rocking his body in place and nodding his head ever so slightly up and down, like he had a nervous tic.

Gary asked, "So, what are you asking me to do, exactly?"

"We need you to join us in our mission. We need you to take care of this judge, before more murderers go free and more innocent people have their lives destroyed. We need you to find others like yourself who have been wronged not by society, but by the people who believe they are above the law and who favor the group over the individual. Find those individuals who have been wronged by people who possess a political agenda of steering this country away from our founding principals. People who admonish the truth, the truth that this country is, or was a great country. We can bring the country back to how it was in the past. But we can't do it without fighters like yourself. We need you Gary, we need you. The country needs you. Your country needs you."

Gary was shaking, his emotions of remembering what happened to Patty, and the fact he couldn't or didn't do anything, these feelings were overwhelming him. "I am not sure. I don't know if I can do this or not."

"I understand Gary. I understand. But ask yourself this. Is Patty at peace? Is your unborn child at peace? Have you done everything in your power to make sure justice will finally be served? Have you done everything you can, in order for you to finally be at peace? Your mission will simply be to remove this judge from society. Eventually, Johnson Bryce will get his justice from his cronies or his enemies on the street. Your mission will also be to identify and recruit others like you, people who can correct the wrongs which have occurred. And you need to get them to join our group. That's all you have to do."

Gary said, "I don't know exactly how to do this. Even if I said yes, I don't know what to do without getting caught. I don't know. I really don't know."

David smiled inside, but maintained a serious look on his face, taking off his sunglasses and reaching into the paper bag he placed on the bench. He pulled out one of the copies of the *Guide*, and handed it to Gary. David leaned over, and said, "That is why we have the *Guide*. The *Guide* will explain everything and it will show you the way. This book has the answers to your questions. It has the plan. It will tell you what to do. You will not fail."

Gary took the book and held it with both hands, and his eyes were fixated on it. His hands were almost shaking, and he rested his arms on the table. If this book could show him the way, then he had to try, for himself, for Patty and for his unborn child. His mouth was parched, his eyes were holding back the creation of tears, and the current of emotions he was feeling deep inside seemed to provide him with the answer he couldn't bring himself to give. Without moving his gaze off the book, he said, "Count me in."

David pulled a large green envelope out of the bag and handed it to Gary. Inside were additional copies of the *Guide*, along with a pre-paid cell phone with the GPS chip disabled. David explained if he was caught or if there were problems, if possible, he would send a text message with only one number, the number nine. If Gary received this message of only the number nine, he would simply need to disappear. The *Guide* will explain everything else, including other codes which could be sent in various ways. The envelope also included ten thousand in large bills. This money was to be used only for his mission, and he should also give the five associates he recruited their portion of the money.

As David stood up, Gary didn't move, but remained seated, with the *Guide* in his hands, fascinated by the apparent knowledge it might hold, answers to help him find peace. David walked over to the other side of the bench, leaned over and whispered his final words to Gary. "Gary, this is it. You are now with us. Now you have committed yourself, there is no turning back. The group doesn't like people who quit or betray us. But, you will be successful in your mission, you will not fail, and that is an order. Good luck."

And with those words, David walked back to his car, got inside, turned on the engine, and drove away. When he was a few miles down the road, he discovered his breathing was now heavy and long, his heart was thumping, and as he looked down at the steering wheel, he noticed his hands were shaking.

Chapter 11

Monday morning arrived, and again David was up at six hundred. A combination of exhilaration from his successful meeting with Gary on Saturday, along with a slight concern over the meeting with his boss made for a restless night. After a quick shower and shave, he put on his best old suit and tie, and ate a bowl of dry cereal for breakfast. David loved milk in the morning, especially whole milk, but the price of a gallon of real milk had reached a point where he could not afford it, and he no longer even considered buying it. There were various milk substitutes, but they either tasted like gritty and pasty water, or the liquid was too thick from the added starch. Besides, the generic brand of cereal was expensive enough. The taste was like shredded cardboard with artificial sweetener glued to one side of the cereal pieces, and it left a sour taste in his mouth. But, according to the box, the cereal was nutritious and full of fiber, and the cereal certainly tasted like fiber.

After his meeting with Gary, David returned to his apartment on Saturday full of jubilation and excitement. On the way home, he stopped at a red zone flea market and bought a movie on a data stick. It was a science-fiction thriller he remembered seeing as a child, and he needed to take his mind off what happened earlier, and what might happen on Monday. A trip down memory lane would definitely help. Even though in his mind he accomplished the impossible, his thoughts had been racing and he knew he would never fall asleep. He also discovered and purchased a bottle of local wine, and was amazed at how inexpensive it was, compared to the wine at the national liquor stores. There was some hope and worry it wasn't brewed in a bathtub or a radiator and it wouldn't kill him. The Party warned about buying food or drink items from the red zone. Even with the success of recruiting Gary, he still needed to recruit at least four more associates, and he figured he could use a good drink, or at least a strong one.

David also purchased a new coffee maker, as well as a can of fairly-decent but pricey coffee at the local national cooperative food store. The trips to the coffee houses were pleasant, but the costs were adding up. The money from the teller machines was still being withdrawn, and he was keeping the money separate from his own. But the purchase of sugar was still out of reach.

David arrived at the local SoCare office with fifteen minutes to spare before his meeting. As he pulled into the parking garage, he noticed it was already packed, which was unusual for a Monday. The search for an open space took him down three levels before he found one in the corner. Since he spent so much time on the road, he rarely went into the office. Usually he would have to visit when they had a team meeting to discuss the new products or new paperwork, or if he needed to attend a training class. Overall his spirits were still elevated, and whatever nervousness he had about the meeting dissipated. There had been enough worrying done over the past week, and if this meeting brought bad news, there was nothing he could do, and whatever was going to happen would happen. Plus, he only had two weeks left on the job, what could possibly go wrong?

David made the trek to the garage elevator, and pressed the button for the lobby. Once in the lobby, he walked past security, and used his identification card to continue through a turnstile, before heading towards the main elevator. The SoCare office was in a fairly large skyscraper in the middle of downtown, and his boss had a sizable office on the 35th floor. The elevator opened, and he along with eight other people crammed themselves inside. The ride was a bit tight, and the air in the elevator took on a smell of a damp and moldy basement. When the elevator arrived at his floor, he pushed himself past the others to exit. Turning to the left, he lifted his identification card up to the access reader, and entered through the main glass doors. The receptionist wasn't there yet, and missing her was a small disappointment. David didn't know her name, but she was in her middle twenties, and was quite attractive. Seeing her was usually the only pleasant thing that happened when he visited the office.

Making his way down the hallway, he took a spot in one of the cubicles reserved for remote workers. His meeting was at eight hundred, and he had five minutes to spare. He dropped off his briefcase and hurried to the small kitchen, where thankfully a pot of coffee had already been brewed. The office coffee had a habit of being lukewarm and slightly bitter, and usually required three packets of artificial sweetener. Today's version was accompanied by a strange plastic aftertaste, which David blamed on the sweetener. The foul coffee was discarded and replaced with another cup of the same, but this time without the vile sweetener. As he tasted the second cup, his deduction was correct, as the sweetener was the culprit.

At one minute before eight hundred, and with the coffee already angrily burning his stomach, he grabbed his briefcase and walked down the rows of cubicles to his bosses' office. The door to the office was open, and he stuck his head around the corner to see if his boss was inside. His boss looked up from his desk and noticed him.

"David, come on in and have a seat. I will be with you in a minute. I need to finish this form."

"Good morning Steve." replied David.

David sat down in one of the leather chairs opposite the desk, placing his briefcase on the other chair, before deciding to move it to the floor. Something had changed, and he noticed the desk was a bit different than what he remembered from his last visit, and the clean appearance gave the impression it was new. The wood was darker, as if the stain had been recently applied. Up on the wall behind the desk were a pair of different paintings with frames which still shined and weren't covered in dust. While Steve hunted the letters on his keyboard with his two index fingers, David studied the grain in the wood, and determined the placement of the lines was too random to be fabricated. As the clicking sound of the erratic typing became obvious, David wondered why his boss never learned to type. Typing was a requirement in school when David attended, and Steve was certainly as old as him. Reaching over for his mouse, Steve clicked it once, and spun his chair around towards David.

Steve always spoke very slowly, as if he was in no hurry to finish the conversation. David was always amused by this, and he wondered if Steve's brain was actually asleep as he spoke, forcing another part of his nervous system which had no control over speaking to take up the slack. There appeared to be an internal struggle to think about each word before he said it, as if he was translating each word from some foreign language but lacking the proficiency to do so. Or maybe he was being controlled by another person in a different room, and he had to wait for them to type out what he was going to say.

"Okay David, good to see you. Thanks for coming in this morning. I understand you have, what, two weeks left with your work benefit?" David nodded. "Well, I have to discuss an offer with you, and you don't have to give me an answer right away. But I do need you to decide within the next day or two. Last Friday, right before I called you, I received a call from the head of the Party's Information Services Group. This person recommended you for a position as a Regional Services Director. Now, even though you only have two weeks until your work benefit elapses, Party business always overrules regulations. With this position, and with his recommendation, we are able to offer you a five-year extension on your work benefit allocation. And of course, with this new position will come an increase in your salary benefits, and a fairly sizable one in fact. We will also be able to adjust your work and retirement benefits up to a level nineteen. I think you are currently at, what, a level nine?"

Sheepishly, David replied, "Um, no, a level eight."

"Well then, this is certainly good news for you. With level nineteen, in five years, your Prosperity Retirement Benefits will be much, much higher. And you might even move up a notch or two before then. And you will also get Outer Circle membership." Steve reached over to a stack of papers, pulled out a green folder, removed a single sheet of paper, and started scanning the information on it. It always took him a little extra time to read anything.

"This new position will give you a..." He stopped, his eyes opened wide, and his eyebrows raised slightly. It was almost as if his eyes needed to refocus.

"Wow. This promotion will give you a very nice pay raise. I think I will let HR go over the details with you. I don't want to discuss the specifics, but it appears level nineteen pay for this position is quite good. And instead of a general pool vehicle, you will be issued a new director-level vehicle every two years, along with increased per diems and an expense account. You will also gain an office and a personal assistant."

He paused again, scanning the rest of the paper several times, before looking up at David. "If you decide to take this position, you will need to go meet with HR to review your benefits package." Steve put the paper back in the green folder, and stuck the folder back on top of the stack of papers.

Leaning back in his chair, he continued, "David, essentially your job will be similar to mine, but with a different group of men, uh, I mean people."

Steve said, "Men," but he caught himself. Any word which specified a gender was banned by the Party. The words men and women were to be stated as either people, persons, humans or beings, or any other non-gender-specific term. This was in order to place everyone on an equal level, as individualism was not one of the Party's main tenets. A person could belong to a particular group, but all members of all groups were equal and their rights and privileges were consistent. Of course, this did not apply to members of the Party, as David now recognized.

"You will be overseeing a group of managers, their software engineers and a dozen or two contractors as well. These people you will be managing have been focusing on installing our latest medical records and accounting software for all of the SoCare medical centers in your current territory." Steve grabbed the green folder again, and removed the paper, reading the details again to confirm what he said, before continuing.

"Yes, it is basically the same territory you have been covering. The software replaces whatever system the centers have been using and interfaces with the main SocBenefits application database. As you may know, we haven't finalized the installation of this new software in all of our centers. In fact, I believe our finished progress is a little under sixty percent. Your engineers and the contractors are responsible for installing the software, and converting the data over from the old system. This of course, is good news for you because the installation of the software is mandated by the Party for every center. Instead of a normal sales goal, you are commissioned on the number of installations achieved each quarter. And another department handles any hardware integration you might need. You may run into them, but you won't be working directly with them, the managers on your team will handle that relationship."

"Anyhow, the overall project implementation was supposed to be finished two years ago, but we ran into the inevitable minor snags we usually encounter with some of our contractors. We now have a five-year extension to complete the project. Your job will be to make sure these installation engineers stay on schedule. Make sure they fill out their reports, and then you will send a weekly report to your new boss and Ahmedzhi Khan, who is with the project management group, to make sure they are kept aware of the new installations. All of your responsibilities will be explained in a resource function package you will get from human resources. Any questions?"

David was surprised and didn't know what to think. The last twenty-five years were spent on the road, in the field, doing the same mindless job, traveling the same boring route, visiting the same uncaring customers and enduring the same lousy hotels and obnoxious food. And now, with two weeks left, they were offering him what was known as an "Outside-Party" job. The job name was not because you worked outside, but because you were granted membership in the Outer Circle as it relates to the Party, and more importantly, as it relates to your level of authority within SoCare. And as a member in the Outer Circle of the Party, the membership also brought along a different set of benefits.

The Party is divided into two groups, or classes, with three levels in each class. The Inner Circle, or IC, is comprised of those in power. The top level is reserved for the nationally-elected or the Party-nominated people, composed of the national politicians and judges from the different branches of government. The top level also includes the cabinet members, and a select group of their direct subordinates. The middle level includes more national employees who report to the members of the top level, as well as the regionally-elected politicians, including the governors and judges. The bottom level included all of the remaining national employees who worked for elected or nominated officials, with a pay level of at least twenty-two, and then only if they were lucky enough to be included in the Inner Circle. If not, they were a member of the Outer Circle. Most of these employees were included in the Inner Circle. Being a lower-level member of the Inner Circle was more prestigious and powerful than being an upper-level member of the Outer Circle.

The Outer Circle, or OC, is comprised of all national government workers who do not directly work for elected or appointed officials, but still worked at a pay level of fifteen or higher. The OC also includes non-national workers, local politicians and judges, as well as people in the media or celebrities. The level structure is the same as the Inner Circle, but what determines your tier or level is how much you have done for the Party, your pay level, or how famous you are. Most of the media personalities or celebrities are low-level members of the OC. Being included in the Outer Circle is a big honor, if one cares about being a member of the Party. If you aren't a national employee, membership is by invitation-only from a member of the Inner Circle. And membership for anyone at any level within the Outer Circle could be revoked.

David was more than astounded, and he could feel his temples pulsating slightly, and hear his heartbeat inside his head. He just agreed to be in the League of Patriots, to take part in a plot to destroy the Party, and now he was facing an incredible promotion, along with Outer Circle Party membership. In effect, he would be fighting to destroy an organization of which he was now a member. As David's mind wandered, his boss was staring at him, waiting for him to speak.

David finally snapped out of his stupor. "Yes, this is a great honor, and I certainly appreciate this opportunity. Of course, I will accept the position. I am honored. Thank you very, very much."

"Oh, don't thank me, I had nothing to do with it. There must be a member fairly high up in the Party who must like the work you have done, and of course, I have always considered you my best employee. By the way, since you have accepted this position, you start immediately, as in right now. So, you will need to go down and see Lu Zheyong in human resources on level three. He will get your paperwork completed and provide you with your office number. If you have any questions about benefits or anything else, he will explain that as well."

Standing up, David shook his former manager's hand, grabbed his briefcase and left his office.

David spent almost two hours in human resources. The paperwork didn't take long, but he had to wait to receive his new Party credentials, consisting of an identification card and a security badge. In the bottom right corner of both was a single blue circle, with a line drawn through the bottom third of the circle, indicating his status within the Party. This was his Party-level designation, and also a get-out-of-trouble card. With membership in the Party, if he was pulled over for a traffic violation, he wouldn't have to show his driver's license. His Party identification card would be all he needed from now on. Unless he committed a serious felony, like murder or armed robbery, he pretty much had immunity from prosecution on most misdemeanor charges.

David was given several large green envelopes, a binder and a copy of the Party's rules and regulations. Lu instructed him to read and to be familiar with as much of the information as possible. New employees of the Party were granted extra time in learning their new positions, but ignorance of the Party's rules was not excusable. He also was given a statement showing his new salary and bonus. David compared his new compensation plan against his old one, and he would be receiving a six-hundred and twenty percent increase in his base salary, and a five-hundred and fifty percent increase in his bonus versus his previous commissions. And the way Lu explained it to him, his bonus was almost guaranteed. The feelings of astonishment and shock over his increase in salary had yet to wear off, and there was a difficulty believing he would be earning this large of an amount of money.

After receiving his Party credentials, he made his way out of the HR office, and took the elevator to the 22nd floor. Walking down the long hallway, he was having a difficult time in locating his new office, room 22135. His time was spent looking at the interior offices, but he finally located his along the outer wall, almost near the corner of the building. And as he stood in front of the door, he noticed someone already installed a crude temporary name plate. His name was printed on a piece of glossy beige-colored paper and was carefully taped to the door. He pushed the door open in a guarded manner as if he expected someone else to be inside, as perhaps the name plate and this entire ordeal was a cruel joke being played on him. The layout was similar to his former manager's office, and he was instantly mesmerized by the furnishings. Walking over to the desk, he noticed it appeared to be nicer than what his former manager had, and the chair behind it was definitely larger. His eyes finally moved off the desk, and he noticed the large window, so he moved over and stood as close as he could to it. As he leaned against the glass, he discovered the nice view of the park in the next block over. Standing there, he was still processing what happened to him. While he was watching the people down below on the street, and letting it all sink in, he heard a soft voice behind him.

"Mr. Gagnon?"

The voice startled him. Turning around, he saw a young woman standing in the doorway. She was tall and thin, wearing a nice skirt suit, and her face had the symmetrical shape of an oval, while being framed and protected by her long and fair hair. Even from across the room, David was fixated by her blue eyes. She made the receptionist David missed earlier appear plain.

David cleared his throat. "Yes?"

The woman casually moved forward towards David, almost in slow-motion and he immediately noticed her high-heel shoes. She stopped near his desk, and extended her hand, but David wasn't looking at her hand, as he moved his gaze back up to her face.

"My name is Stephanie, and I am your new admin."

David cautiously walked towards her, took her hand, and gave it a gentle squeeze. As he stood close to her, he caught the trace of a scent, possibly her perfume. Slowly and discretely, he deeply inhaled once more through his nose, and dctcctcd a gentle and fruity aroma, possibly the essence of an apple or a berry, but he couldn't figure out which one. He finally realized he needed to respond, and he probably should let go of her hand.

"Hello, Stephanie, very nice to meet you. But please, call me David."

She giggled slightly and looked away for a second, as if she was embarrassed. Her initial demure manner was quickly tossed.

"Okay. David." She said those words in a bashful way. "I am your new admin, and my office is across the hall."

She turned and moved to the other side of his desk, picked up two pieces of paper and handed one to David. "I have prepared for you a list of the phone numbers you will most likely be calling. I should have your new cell phone, laptop and tablet to you in three or four days. You will need to use your current phone until we can upgrade it. And here is my business card, with all of my phone numbers. I would suggest you put this in your wallet in case your phone dies or is lost or stolen."

David took the business card, which displayed her office and cell phone number on it, along with a title simply labeled "Administrator." He took out his wallet and slipped it behind the lone credit card.

Stephanie handed David the other piece of paper. "Here is a copy of the executive cafeteria's menu for today. Lunch is served from eleven-hundred to fourteen-hundred hours. You will need to show them your identification when you enter. The cafeteria is on the 30th floor. Do you know how to work the phones?"

David nodded as he continued to unknowingly stare at her.

"Now, I think that's all I have right now, but if you need anything, please let me know. I know this is probably a lot for you to take in, with it being your first day and all."

David was still holding the menu and the list of phone numbers. She added, "If you need anything, please let me know." David watched her begin to walk away. He had only known her less than two minutes, but he was dumbfounded by her beauty. And he was intrigued by how fast and smooth she talked, almost as if she rehearsed what she was going to say. As she was nearing the door, she spun around on one foot and asked, "Open or closed?"

David was still in an enchanted state. "Excuse me?" David didn't quite catch what she was saying.

"Your door. Do you want me to leave it open or close it for you?"

David stuttered a bit, "Open, open is fine, thanks."

She smiled and started to turn away, when David blurted out, "Stephanie. Would you do me a favor and have lunch with me? I might have some questions I need answered." He wasn't sure why he asked her to lunch so quickly, and he was surprised by his forwardness and his ability to even speak coherently in a time such as this. Maybe it was because he was a bit nervous about going down there on his own. Or maybe it was because she was extremely attractive. He had no idea why.

Her eyes lit up for a split second before returning to a normal position, as if she was trying to hide her expression. "Why of course David. Please come and get me when you are ready." She smiled, spun around again and walked away.

David stood there, almost unable to move, in a condition of self-induced paralysis. His mind had been in a daze all morning, and now this happened. This entire situation must be a dream, and she wasn't helping the situation. Finally he managed to move, and he stepped over towards his desk, placing his briefcase on the floor before sitting down in the high-backed leather chair, and pulling it towards the desk. It was almost as if he was seeing the furniture again for the first time. The dark wood grain on the top of the desk caught his attention first, then the paintings on the wall, and then the two leather chairs on the other side of his desk with the brass tacks along the arms and around the seat. A plant on a stand in the corner behind the chairs suddenly appeared, and he tried to guess the type, as it looked like a fern, but he wasn't certain of it. He was never good with plants, and he surmised if the plant was left to his care and attention, it would be dead within a month.

The top of the desk was empty, except for the two pieces of paper Stephanie had given him. He reached down and opened one of the drawers on the right side of the desk, and it was already stocked with various office supplies. His briefcase was moved up and over to the left side of the desk, and he opened it and removed the large green envelopes from human resources. He kept the one marked "Responsibilities of Position OrMy-123534", and set the other two aside. It was probably a good idea to start learning what they wanted him to do.

David opened the envelope, removed the inch-high stack of papers, bound with a huge metal clip at the top, and placed the stack on his desk. A deep sigh was unconsciously generated as he removed the metal clip, studying the thick stack of paper, and he was amazed at the national government's enormous use of it. For the past four or five decades, the use of paper was declining with the growth of technology. Paper was extremely expensive, and the production of it was heavily regulated, as in order to make paper, you have to cut down trees. The passing of the *Forestry and Atmosphere Preservation Act* made it a crime to cut down a tree of any size without a permit. After the act was passed, the paper industry was devastated, paper prices soared, and thousands of forestry and industrial jobs were lost. People were arrested and fined for simply cutting down a tree on their own property. Most paper was now made from plant and crop waste. The new product wasn't as smooth as the old paper, and tended to fall apart in areas of high humidity.

The act also made it illegal to burn wood or any wood by-product in a fireplace or stove, as the output of carbon dioxide was deemed harmful to the planet. The ban included burning pretty much anything, including coal and charcoal, and even campfires were illegal. The act really had no effect on the coal industry, as it had already been regulated to death, and the majority of the coal mines closed years prior. The only source of coal was via the black market. Most people in the red zone ignored all of these laws, and the Party usually turned a blind eye to what happened in the red zone. But while the red zone residents were conveniently ignoring as many laws as they could, at the same time they were constantly looking over their shoulder.

David looked down at the papers, and he turned over the first page and started to read. The document began with a bunch of legal-sounding words which David had a hard time pronouncing and understanding. The convoluted horde of long words mentioned and referenced non-disclosure, proprietary software, and penalties for misuse of information, mixed in with unfamiliar legalese that made whatever they were trying to convey difficult to comprehend. David hadn't even finished reading the first page when he stopped. Something was missing. Coffee, yes, he could use another cup of coffee. Coffee and more specifically, caffeine was needed to help clear the fog from his head. Gently placing the sheets back in order on the stack, he walked out of his office and across the hall.

David stopped in the doorway of Stephanie's office. "Stephanie, I am going to get a cup of coffee. Do you want anything? I am assuming the kitchen is in the middle of this floor?"

Stephanie quickly rose from of her seat. "Mr. Gagnon, uh, I mean David, I can get coffee for you." She winced at herself, as if she should have offered to get him a cup earlier. She rushed over to him, took her right arm and placed it on his back, and gave him a little push. With her left arm extended, she directed him back towards his office, and escorted him inside. He went over and sat back down at his desk.

Stephanie smiled. "I will be right back." She took a couple of steps and then performed a small twirl back towards him. "How do you like your coffee?

Sugar? Cream?"

David was surprised and delighted when he heard the word sugar. "Yeah, if it is real sugar, then yes, sugar please, but no cream. In fact, I will take three packs of sugar." As she left, David instantly felt a little better. Sugar was such a small perk, but having it with his coffee everyday was going to be a welcome treat. He might even need to borrow a few packs to take home.

Chapter 12

David was able to finish reading twelve pages from his manual. There was so much information, so much legal jargon, it was difficult to understand it all. After finishing the first cup of coffee, he sent Stephanie out for one more, but this time with only two packets of sugar. A long time had passed since he experienced real sugar, and the taste was very sweet, and this was the best coffee he had tasted in a very long time. He couldn't remember the last time he drank coffee which wasn't at least a little bitter. On the rare occasions in the past fifteen years or so when he tasted sugar, the flavor was as if someone cut it with flour or starch. A covert trip to the kitchen would be necessary so he could take at least a pocketful of packs home with him.

As he checked his watch for the time, he noticed the watch band was frayed on the sides. The watch was at least twelve years old, and besides having to change the battery every six months, it was a decent watch. And every year or two it would require a new band. Maybe he could wait a while, until after his first paycheck, and get a more professional-looking and non-digital watch, perhaps one with a second hand. The time was eleven-thirty-three, and the effects from his first cup of the bad coffee had subsided, possibly flushed away by the better coffee. The new feeling was definitely one of hunger, and he pondered if it was too early for lunch. He decided since the cafeteria opened at eleven hundred, any time after was appropriate. He rose from his desk, ambled over to Stephanie's office and stopped in the doorway. "I know it is a bit early, but can you do lunch now?"

Stephanie's gaze quickly moved from her monitor towards David, and her expression held an almost-excited and surprised look. "Yes, I can do lunch. And no, it isn't too early." Stephanie rose and followed David to the elevator. When the doors opened, he made a gesture with his hand for her to enter first. She kept her head down and grinned at his uncommon display of manners. The doors closed, and David pressed the button for the 30th floor.

As the elevator moved, Stephanie said, "I have only been here for a little over two years, but this is the first time my manager has asked me to have lunch with him. I hope I don't get too excited and embarrass you."

This amused David slightly. "Is there a policy against it?"

"I don't think so. I know other admins who eat lunch with their manager, usually once every couple of weeks or so, maybe more. They tell me their lunch hour is usually spent doing busy work, filling out reports and things like that. I believe it is more a convenience for them if they work through lunch together. I don't know why, but my last manager never invited me to lunch."

The news that other managers took their admins to lunch was comforting to David, and it eased his nervousness of being alone with her. "Well, how about this, we won't discuss business at all. Besides, I don't really know what I am doing yet, and I haven't thought of any questions to ask you." David then remembered his possible need for her to answer questions was the reason for asking her to lunch in the first place, but maybe she wouldn't remember that detail.

Stephanie smiled again, and was looking down at her shoes. As the doors slid open, a brief rush of air filled the elevator, and David could smell her scent again. Maybe it isn't a fruit, was it coconut?

As they walked down the hall, David spotted two large wooden doors, marking the entrance to the cafeteria, and a small security desk to the right of the doors. David was wearing his Party identification around his neck, and held it up towards the security guard. As soon as the guard saw the circle on David's badge, he leaned in for a closer look. "Good day Mr. Gagnon. Enjoy your lunch." The guard gave him a directional wave towards the door.

David opened one of the doors, and again he allowed Stephanie to enter first. As he walked into the room, he was immediately impressed with its size. The executive cafeteria was expansive, much larger than he anticipated. As he quickly scanned the room, he could see the food was served buffet style, with separate isolated food stations, all stationed along the side wall. David was searching for the station which held the plates when Stephanie noticed him and mentioned, "I believe the plates are in each food station. You tell them what you want, and they will put it on a plate for you."

David had browsed the menu earlier, and decided on fried chicken and vegetables, a standard meal for him but also one of his favorite combinations. Stephanie opted for the pulled pork barbecue with french fries and a side salad. David chose a table over on the far end of the cafeteria, where he could sit with his back to the wall and look out and watch everyone. Stephanie duteously followed him to the table. As soon as they took their seats, a waitress came by and took their drink orders. David asked for a diet cola with extra ice, and Stephanie ordered bottled spring water.

Neither one said much as they sat down and began to eat. David possessed a habit of eating in a hurry, but as he chewed his first bite, he noticed all of the other employees appeared to be relaxed and chatting and they appeared to be taking their time. So, he decided to do the same. After all, he wasn't on the road, and wasn't really in a rush to go anywhere or do anything. As David took a few bites of the chicken and vegetables, he thought for cafeteria food, this was better than any food he had eaten in a long time. As for eating slowly, Stephanie took the opposite approach. She was eating quickly, like it was her first meal in weeks, and she finished before David made a dent in his food. Once she finished and noticed the abundance of food still on David's plate, she realized she probably ate too fast, and was embarrassed. David noticed the situation and that she appeared to be uncomfortable. He told her since she was finished eating, maybe she could tell him a little about herself.

Stephanie was born and raised in the blue zone, and both of her parents worked for the Party. Her mother died when she was about eleven, though she didn't mention to David how she passed. Less than two years later, her father married a much younger woman. Her stepmother didn't have a job, and simply played tennis or bridge and drank wine or cocktails all day. But even with her love for adult beverages, she was a pleasant drunk and wasn't abusive to Stephanie. They had a decent relationship, but Stephanie wisely kept her distance. Her father divorced her stepmom four years later and never remarried.

Attending the Party's local university, she earned a degree in Business Administration. After not finding work on her own for three years, her father helped her to get this current job as an administrative assistant. Her former boss was much older than David, and was a mid-level member of the Outer

Circle. David couldn't help but notice she mentioned the Party often, and would always identify a person along with their status in either circle. She stated her aspiration was to be a member of the Party, and she didn't care if it was in the Outer or Inner Circle. But she also admitted she would probably never reach this goal. Even though she seemed to accept her fate and wasn't bitter about it, David could tell it really was her dream all the same.

David listened to her stories and continued eating at a slow pace, and was enjoying the taste of the food. Unlike the Party-hotel food, this tasted different, and he wondered if it was because this cafeteria served Party members. At the same time, he was also watching all of the other employees, mainly to keep from staring at her, which was a difficult thing to control. She was quite attractive with a pleasant personality, and possessed a very nice figure. David calculated she was in her late twenties or early thirties, given the timeline she described. She stated she wasn't married, and rarely dated, but instead spent a lot of her free time at Party social activities, meetings and protests. From the way she described herself, David thought she was a little insecure and didn't believe she was very smart. But David had a feeling she was fairly intelligent, and "book smart" were the words which came to his mind. While David finished his lunch, she continued to talk about herself and her goals in life. It was apparent she was nervous, with him being her new manager and with this being her first time in the Party cafeteria. His nervousness had long subsided.

After they finished their meals, a waitress promptly came over and took away their plates. Leaning back in his chair, he was very content, with a belly full of chicken, vegetables and diet cola. They passed a massive dessert section earlier, and he didn't think he could eat another bite, but he would definitely have to do dessert tomorrow. There was an assumption the cooks probably used real sugar in the desserts, since sugar was readily available in the office kitchen. Stephanie finally stopped talking, and was taking her straw and fidgeting with the ice in her glass.

David asked, "Is anything wrong?"

"Well, I just realized I have been talking non-stop for the past half-hour, and you haven't said a word. You must think I am silly."

"No, not at all. I was busy eating, that's all. It was good to hear about you and where you grew up and your history and goals."

In a normal conversation with a non-Party member, Stephanie would feel obliged to ask David about his background. But Party members never talked about their lives or their past with a non-Party member, and it would have been improper for Stephanie to ask him any questions.

David turned to her. "Did you want any dessert?"

Stephanie's face lit up with a slight grin. "Would you mind?"

"Of course not. In fact, I think I will have a cup of coffee. I never finished my second cup this morning."

Stephanie sprung out of her seat. "Thanks. I will get your coffee for you. Two sugars again, right?" David nodded in agreement, and watched her walk away. He liked it when she walked away from him, but he needed to remind himself he was her boss.

After lunch, David was trying another attempt at reading his responsibility papers, and was at a point to where he could finally understand what they wanted him to do. His job was fairly simple. He would be overseeing a team of nine managers, and each manager had a team of twelve or more software engineers, not including any contractors. David would receive reports from each manager every week, and he would take their information and enter it into another application which fed into a database. His position didn't seem to involve anything to do with budgets or performance reviews or any other typical managerial work. From what he could tell, all he needed to do was to monitor the progress of the installations and fill out these weekly reports, which didn't appear to be complicated. He calculated he would only have about thirty or forty hours worth of work to do each month, based upon the number of reports and data involved. The figure might be less once he figured out how to use the reporting application.

He placed the responsibility packet back into his briefcase, and the time was now almost fifteen hundred, giving him two hours to waste before he could go home. Since he didn't have his computer, he was trying to figure out what he could do to kill the time. With his feet, he turned his chair around and scooted over to the window. He turned his gaze to the outside, and off in the distance, he could see airplanes from the national airport, gently rising above the skyscrapers. This airport was one of the busiest in the country, and a plane would take off or land about every thirty seconds. There was a peaceful enjoyment in watching the planes. At random times, a Party drone would float by, skimming along the tops of the office buildings. Like most people, David wasn't a big fan of the drones, and he felt uneasy whenever he saw one, no matter how far away it was.

Airplanes were almost as mysterious, as he had only flown twice earlier in his career, on the rare occasions when he would have to travel outside of his area for training classes. His memory of the experience of flying was distant, and he tried but couldn't recall what it was like to fly. He did remember how small the seats were. David was above-average in height at almost two meters, and his knees pressed up against the seat in front of him. Then there was the stingy little bag of chips or pretzels, and when they served him a diet cola, since the drink from the can was warm, the ice removed all of the carbonation out of the beverage, so it was flat when he drank it.

The fog from this morning had lifted from his brain, and was replaced by boredom and more daydreaming, as he watched the planes take off and come in for a landing in the distance. His thoughts were interrupted by a knock at the door. David rotated around in his chair to see a young man standing at the front of his office.

"Mr. Gagnon, I am Curtis from the transportation department. Your car is ready."

David didn't understand. "I'm sorry, my car?"

"Yes, I have your new car ready for you. I will show you where it is parked, and I can give you a tour of the features. Also, I will need the keys to your old car. Is there anything you need to get out of it?"

In his car, he had been storing his tablets and the daily teller withdrawals not yet hidden, but since he was coming into the office, everything was removed. Whenever you drove your car to the office, it was subject to being searched by security. His car had often been searched in the past, and he wasn't taking any chances. David stood up, and followed Curtis down the hall. They rode down the elevator in silence, and exited on the top floor of the parking deck. David followed the man over to the left side of the parking area. Curtis stopped at a large black sport utility vehicle, unlocked it and opened the driver's door. David just stood there and stared at the car.

For the past twenty-five years, David had been driving a tiny white enviro-car. The car was underpowered and with a front seating area which was probably too small for this young man standing beside him, much less a person of his height. Thinking about his old car reminded him of the small seats in the airplane. Now, he was looking at a very large car, with a vastly larger interior space and legroom. With the energy crisis, he wondered why the Party utilized such large and inefficient vehicles.

Curtis stood there, still holding the door open, and wondering what David was doing standing there. "If you would like to have a seat, I will go over the features of the car with you."

Walking over, David sat down in the driver's seat. Immediately he could feel the softness of the leather seats through his cheap suit. The seat wasn't rough like the thick coarse fabric in his old car. He looked around at the dash, and noticed what appeared to be real wood embellishments all around the console. There was also a large display panel in the middle of the dash, and an array of little buttons. The use of the wood and the leather was surprising to him as well, but it was another example of rules and regulations being ignored by the Party.

"Do you need me to show you how to operate anything?"

David replied with a smile, "Yeah, sure, if you have time." Curtis walked around to the other side of the car and sat down in the passenger's seat. He spent about twenty minutes explaining all of the features, the majority of which David didn't even know existed in a car. When he was finished, they both stepped out and met at the back of the vehicle.

Curtis said, "We don't have your parking name plate ready yet, but this is your reserved space, number twenty-two."

David was amazed and delighted. He would no longer have to drive around looking for a spot, and then walk forever to get to the elevators.

He then reminded David, "I still need the keys to your old car."

David reached into his pocket, took off his apartment and mailbox key, and handed him the car key and fob. "I parked it on level three."

"No problem sir, I will find it." David thanked him and they walked back towards the elevators. David went up to the lobby, and Curtis took the stairs down to level three.

David walked back into his office, and when Stephanie saw him, she followed him inside. "I didn't realize you were still here. Is there anything I can get you before you leave?"

"Leave? What do you mean? I have another hour of work."

Stephanie looked at her watch. "But it is after sixteen hundred. I didn't think you would need to stay late on your first day."

David was unsure what she meant again. "I am not sure I am following you. My hours are eight to five."

Stephanie gave him a devilish look, as if he was playing a joke on her. "Didn't HR explain your hours? David, your hours are from eight-thirty to four, every day except Friday, which is a half-day for you, and you have an hour and a half for lunch. And of course you have the weekend off as well. I am the only one of us who works from eight to five everyday, except for Friday, when I only work a half-day there as well." David wondered why Stephanie was working beyond the Party-regulated work benefit hours, but he decided to forget it. He remembered a select group of the Party employees weren't subject to this regulation, but he wasn't sure how those restrictions were applied.

David said, "Well, if that is the case, I guess I will go home. I will see you tomorrow." David reached over and picked up his briefcase, put the envelopes inside one of the pockets, and walked out of his office. Stephanie closed his door and held her identification badge up to a sensor to the right of the door, and pressed a button to lock the door. After she heard the soft click of the lock being engaged, she returned to her office.

David was feeling incredible as he took the elevator down and as he walked out to his new car. The key fob was much different than the old one. It was a little larger with options his old one didn't have. The fob could be used to start the car, open the rear door, open the windows or moonroof, and there was a red emergency button. As he climbed in, he instinctively went in backwards with his legs sticking out, and then slowly brought his legs inside. With his old car, he would have to sit down and force his legs inside, where his right knee would press up against the dash. If the car hit a bump in the road, his knee would knock the corner of the hard dash and the resulting pain would linger for hours. He concluded his old car was the source of his knee problems. With the new car, he had four inches of extra space between his knees and the dashboard. He studied the interior one more time, pushed the start button, backed out, and started towards home. Traffic was fairly light this time of the day.

Chapter 13

David was at home, laying on his sofa, sipping a diet cola, and gawking at the bags and bags of clothes he placed on the floor in front of him. After arriving home from work, David went back out to a clothing store in the mall which was next to his house. During lunch earlier, he noticed all of the other Party members wore really nice clothes and suits. Not all of them wore suits, but the ones who did had suits that appeared to be made of silk or wool or a type of micro-fiber. David's suit was about ten years old, and even though he probably only wore it once a month, it was looking worn.

David purchased five suits, three sports coats, ten button-down white cotton shirts, four pairs of shoes, four belts, ten pairs of pants and eight ties. He even picked up a replacement piece of luggage. The sacred vow that the money for the mission would only be spent for the mission was temporarily suspended, and he paid for his clothes with this borrowed cash. His current financial situation did not have the ability to complete such a large purchase. He decided he would pay the mission money back after his new pay increase had taken effect. He strolled into the shop still wearing his cheap suit but with his new Party identification clearly visible. No one asked any questions as to why he was buying so many clothes, or why he paid with cash. The clerks were polite and courteous, and called him sir, which he relished. Now, alone on the couch, his mind was trying to process what happened to him earlier in the day.

In all of his years of working for SoCare, he couldn't remember anyone at his level being granted a work-benefit extension. He remembered one manager from his department who received one, but he died a short time later. Of course, after many of his co-workers retired or left for another job, he really never talked with them again. So, maybe it does happen, and he just wasn't aware of it.

His thoughts turned to the situation with his mission. Despite having this new and wonderful job, there was no need to disassociate himself. A commitment was made, and he confirmed in his mind several times, if not hundreds of times, that his involvement was the proper course of action. A new problem arose, in that he wasn't positive if he was going to be traveling as much, and he still needed to keep hitting the teller machines for money. And he really needed to be careful, since he now possessed a vehicle which was easily identifiable as a car belonging to a Party member, and he certainly couldn't be seen stopping at teller machines all over town. The solution was simple. He would need to figure out how to buy a used vehicle, one he could at least use at night and on the weekends to go and withdraw money.

He also needed a new place to live. His lease was due to expire in two weeks, to coincide with his retirement. Several previous weekends had already been spent on the possibility of renting a basement apartment from various strangers out in the red zone, and he met with several nice people. The deal was to be finalized this week, but now that wasn't an option anymore. He needed to find a place closer to work.

David reached over to the side table, and picked up one of the real estate magazines from his visit to the mountains, when he met with Gary. He started slowly flipping through the pages, but this time he was paying more attention to the listings and their features, and he noticed a number of really nice mountain cabins. Because of the depressed real estate market which had been going on for the past three decades, these cabins were fairly inexpensive. Of course he could not afford one on his retirement benefit allowance alone, but with his new increase in salary, he could probably buy one and have it paid off before his five-year work-benefit extension expired. That is, if he didn't have to go into hiding.

A revelation occurred in which he could get a different place here in the city that was a little larger than his current apartment, but he could also have a weekend place up in the mountains. Plus, this mountain house could be a place to go if he needed a place to hide. On second thought, he probably couldn't hide there, as it would be in the public records that he owned the property, and the Party would be able to easily find him. But he still liked the idea of a place for the weekends, and it would also provide him with a home base for recruiting his associates.

With his new status as a Party member, he now qualified for a Party-guaranteed mortgage. These special mortgages were only available to Party members, and were guaranteed by the Party National Bank. The only qualification you needed was to be a member of the Party. The banks didn't check your income, job status, credit rating or anything else. Approval was guaranteed, and only took two or three weeks. A regular mortgage would take several months, and you were required to fill out numerous forms and applications. He would definitely need to take a weekend trip north and find a cabin. Maybe a cabin with a one or two acres of land, enough land to grow his own vegetables, and maybe he would get some chickens. Fresh eggs were another one of his favorite foods, but they were also in the same self-prohibited category as milk, beef and sugar. He didn't know what was involved in purchasing or raising chickens, but he could figure the details out later. Fishing was another possibility, like Tim suggested, and so was hunting, even though he wasn't sure what animals were hunted up there. The majority of the mountain area was in the red zone as well, which would make it easier for him to finish his recruiting, if he could find the right people.

The longer he looked at these cabins, the more he decided he would go there this weekend. Plus, he needed to try and do his regular teller withdrawals outside of the blue zone, and he already decided he needed a used car to do that. It was a given he would definitely have to go out to the red zone to purchase a used car.

The plan was settled. A trip to the mountains this coming Saturday was in order, and he would take a look at one or two of these properties. His favorite so far was a nice three-bedroom log cabin, with a detached three-car garage, on top of a small mountain. From the time he received his first company car, he had never parked in a regular garage, if you didn't count the one at the office, and he hoped this place was big enough for the large SUV he now drove. The description stated the property was on twenty-five acres of land with mostly hardwood trees. There was a small stream which flowed along the bottom of the property and fed a two-acre lake. David hadn't lived in a house since high school, when he lived with his parents. Besides the cramped dorm room in college, he had only lived in only two different apartments since then. He was looking forward to the change.

Chapter 14

David arrived at work early on Tuesday, five minutes before seven hundred. Even though his normal working time wasn't for another hour and a half, there was his habit of going to bed early and getting up early. His mood was elevated, and he was wearing one of his new suits, with a new shirt and tie, new belt and new shoes. As he was getting dressed, he realized he should have bought new socks as well. His current ones were too thin, and his feet were already hurting from the new shoes. But he was feeling good, and he actually wanted to go to work this morning. At the same time, he thought his newfound appreciation for his job was odd, given the situation with his mission. Maybe it was the increase in his salary and benefits, or maybe it was his new car, and he didn't mind being stuck in traffic as much. It was probably all of these things, and having Stephanie as his assistant was a nice benefit as well.

Sitting in his chair, he took the paperwork out of his briefcase. The need to learn all of his responsibilities was still outstanding, but so far, his obligations didn't seem to amount to much. And the more he read, the more the document became extremely wordy. An entire page was required to explain how to fill out a form on the computer, not including what information needed to go into what fields. The document would need to be read and parsed several more times and notes would need to be taken, translating what he thought they wanted him to do in words he could understand and reference later. But so far, most of what he figured out was that his job involved completing a group of, what he already considered to be useless, status reports. As far as he could tell, all he needed to do was to simply copy a stream of near-endless figures and updates from his employee's field reports into another form. He thought it would be easier if his employees simply used the same form he was going to have to use. But then if that happened, he wouldn't have a job to do.

The next forty minutes was spent continuing to decipher his job responsibility information. The field reports wouldn't start arriving until next week, and Stephanie mentioned his laptop and cell phone wouldn't be here until the end of the week. He was startled by the sound of Stephanie at his door.

"Good morning David," she cheerfully announced.

David looked up at her. When they first met, David thought she just was another attractive girl. And even though he had only known her for a day, every time she talked, he could feel himself liking her even more.

She spoke again, before he could reply to her greeting. "Wow, you look nice today," and she realized her gaff. "Well, you looked nice yesterday, I meant to say I like your suit and tie. Are they new?" Before David could respond, she continued talking. "Would you like a cup of coffee? They should also have a platter of pastries in the kitchen. I can bring you one."

David continued to stare at her, noting an appearance of innocence, and almost a sense of purity. Like most of the other girls he met at work, she was probably attracted to the power in the Party, and drawn in by the feeling she was helping to change the world. Even after only being around her for a day, he determined despite her apparent intelligence, she was probably quite naive as well.

David smiled, "Yes, coffee and a pastry, that would be nice. Thank you." She returned his smile and hurried off.

David's thoughts turned to his mission, contemplating that if he spent all day in this office, everyday, it was going to be difficult to complete his tasks. The immediate need was to recruit associates, and this was really the most important part of his mission, besides not getting caught. Before being offered and accepting this job, he already completed his research on seven possible recruits, and a number of suitable candidates were finalized. The difficult part was in finding a way to meet them.

Stephanie returned with his coffee and a bear claw. "I put the bear claw in the microwave oven for you. They taste so much better when they are a little warm. And here is your coffee, with two sugars." She placed both on his desk.

"Thank you very much."

She disappeared for a moment, and came back in with a green folder. "I have a list of the new centers which have begun the conversion process this quarter. There are only two in your area and work began on both last week. I don't have the project plans yet, but I do know we have engineers and contractors already on site at both places."

David took the folder and opened it. Inside was a single sheet of paper, with the names and addresses of the centers. As David scanned the information, he noticed Tim's hospital was on the list. David wondered if he could take a chance and ask Tim these questions which were bothering him, questions the *Guide* didn't answer. He wasn't sure how Tim would react, but he thought he could give it a shot. Maybe he could at least let Tim know he was in his area, and then he could determine by his reaction if it was a good idea or not to meet. Plus, this would give him a chance to get out of town to use the teller cards.

He called for Stephanie, and she hurriedly came in and stood by his desk. "I believe I need to pay these centers a visit, to make sure they are getting things started on the right foot. I don't have my computer yet, do you have any idea how I could book my travel?" In the past, David needed to fill out numerous online forms and get approval from his manager whenever he traveled, which was every week. This task was another part of his old job he hated.

"Booking your travel is part of my responsibilities, so I can do that for you. I will need to know how many nights you will be staying and what centers you will visit. I will take care of the details."

David handed her the paper. "Let's start with these two. I only need one night near the second office. The drive to the first office should only take three or four hours and the other office is a short drive after that. If I need to change anything, I will let you know. Also, I couldn't find anything in my job packet about my travel allowance or per diem, any idea how much it is?"

"If it is anything like my old manager, I don't think you have a travel allowance exactly, or a per diem. Use your company card and I will take care of filing your expense reports. When are you leaving?"

"Right now. Well, I will need to go home and pack. I will leave from my apartment. Will you send me the hotel details?"

"Of course. Have a great trip and I will see you in a couple of days."

David shoved his paperwork back into his briefcase and headed out the door. As he was walking down the hall, he still wasn't sure if this was the right thing to do.

David arrived at Tim's hospital a little after thirteen hundred. He walked up to the security desk with his Party identification in his hand. The guard looked up at him, as he placed his identification on the desk. "I am here to see Tim..."

The guard interrupted David before he could finish, as he recognized David from his previous visits. "Tim doesn't work here any more. He retired two weeks ago." The guard was surprised when David presented his Party identification, as after seeing David all of these years, it wasn't obvious he was a Party member. David never dressed nor acted like one.

David was a bit disappointed. "Well, I guess I need to see Kevan Richards. I think he is on the fourth floor." The guard never even looked closely at his Party identification, the appearance of it was all he needed to see. David signed into the register and put his identification around his neck and headed to the elevator. He wasn't sure what he was going to do now. The entire drive was spent thinking of how he could ask Tim these questions which were bothering him. He hadn't even thought about what he was going to say regarding his actual reason for being there.

The fourth floor receptionist was like all of the other ones working in any Party building as she was young and pretty. David wondered if she was as innocent and naive as the rest, just like Stephanie. David hadn't even made it to her desk when he heard a person behind him call out his name.

"David!" He turned around to see a man walking towards him, and as the man approached, he stuck out his hand. "Kevan Richards, nice to meet you. Your admin called to let me know you would be paying us a visit." David shook his hand, and Kevan started walking down the hall. David wondered how Kevan knew what he looked like, as they had never met before.

"I have reserved the main conference room for us." David followed him down the hallway to a large room with a huge conference table which could seat about thirty people. David took a seat, and placed his briefcase in the chair next to him. Kevan sat on the opposite side of the table, directly across from David. Another young and attractive woman entered and Kevan noticed her. She was Kevan's assistant, and he shared her with two other managers. Kevan turned to David. "Would you like a cup of coffee?"

David replied, "Yes, with two sugars." The woman and her appearance made David wonder, "Does anyone ever hire any ugly administrators?"

Kevan gave his order to the admin, and she left the room. Kevan turned back to David. "It is a pleasant surprise to have you here. They only completed the merger last week, and we started working as quickly as we could."

David wanted to say, "Merger? The Party regulated their way into taking over this center." But he held his tongue.

Kevan continued, "And, congratulations on your promotion. The project plan normally doesn't call for a director's visit, at least not until we have finished the data export. We won't have that ready for a few weeks."

David tried not to appear surprised at this information. He had no idea what he was to be doing with these hospitals, and he didn't know how long any of the projects would take. Stephanie mentioned the lack of any available project plans, and even if he could get copies, he wouldn't know what to do with them. Some improvisation would be needed.

David ad-libbed his pitch. "Well, we are trying an escalated method for these conversions. As you know, we were granted an extension for completion, but I was brought in to make sure we don't miss any of our goals. I will need to see your project reports, and I would like to talk with the engineers from our department who have been assigned here. I want to make sure they have everything they need from us. And I guess this is also a good way to meet the members of your team. You and I probably would have an initial online meeting, but it was going to be a while before I received my computer. So I figured a face-to-face meeting would be a good start."

David stared at Kevan. This was a gamble, because he really didn't know if this is what he was supposed to do. The job information packet never mentioned the need for David to travel. But Kevan now reported to David, and Kevan wasn't a member of the Party yet. He was four years and two levels away from being in the lower level of the Outer Circle. David thought if he was wrong in what he said, he could plead ignorance. But with Kevan's status of almost being a Party member, and with David being his manager, he figured Kevan wouldn't doubt his intentions or deny anything he requested. And he was correct.

Kevan nodded. "Yes, of course David. We will do whatever we can to help you, and give you whatever resources are available."

At that moment, the woman entered with the coffee. As she handed David his coffee, she gave him a big smile. David assumed the smile was received due to the Party identification hanging around his neck.

Down on the second floor, the office space was nothing but rows of cubicles. David followed Kevan to a smaller meeting room on the side of the building, and David walked over to the window. The room had a nice view of a small lake and what looked like a park with walking trails, but the trees next to the building blocked most of the view. Kevan returned with three engineers, and everyone took a seat.

Kevan started with, "This is David Gagnon, the new regional director of our group, and he is here to review our project plan. He wants to make sure we have everything we need, and we stay on schedule." David was studying all the engineers, and noticed none of them appeared to be very happy. Each wore an expression on their face like they were scared and about to be fired. Or maybe it was simply complacence, he really couldn't determine which one.

David said, "Well my job here isn't to impede your work, I want to make sure we are on the right track. I know we have a project plan, but we need to make sure we stay focused. In the past, we haven't done as good of a job as we should have. So I am here to offer assistance in obtaining any additional resources or whatever you think you might need."

No one said a word, as if Kevan warned them to be silent. Kevan finally spoke, "That's good to hear. David, what would you like to do first?"

David leaned back in his chair, without an idea of what should be done, but he needed to say something, anything. "Well Kevan, what do you think I should do first?" The question was spoken in a tone as if he was testing Kevan.

Kevan pondered the question for a few seconds. "Why don't we go down to the war room and take a look at our data-mapping process, and we can explain to you what we are doing."

David replied, "That is exactly what I was thinking."

Chapter 15

The unsuitably-named war room was a former conference room filled with ten faded plastic desks with multiple computer monitors on top. The three engineers quickly sat down at their desks, and immediately started typing on their keyboards. Kevan walked up to one of the engineers, spoke quietly to him, and then motioned David over.

"David, this is Rajesh. He can give you a quick explanation on what we are doing here." David walked forward, and Rajesh stuck out his hand.

"Nice to meet you David, please, have a seat." He pointed to an empty chair at the next desk. David sat down in the chair and rolled it over with his feet.

Rajesh moved the application windows around on one of the monitors, until he found the one he wanted to show David. Originally from India, Rajesh was a husky man with a thick mustache and a head of thinning hair. As David moved closer, he detected a hint of curry and garlic. Rajesh pointed to his screen, and then began to talk. David noticed he didn't have much of an accent.

"David, the procedure is fairly simple. What we are doing is mapping the database fields from the old system to our new system. Each hospital and clinic has a different data schema, with hundreds of tables and thousands of data fields. Then, once we have everything mapped, we will export the data as standard SQL or a comma-delimited text, depending on our source database. Then we use another program to parse the data so the old fields match the fields in our new system. Next, we import the data into the new system. Once all of the data is imported, we can start quality analysis and stress-testing the new system. Once QA gives us the green light, we put a hold on the current system, export the data again, re-import it, and then go live. At least that is how it should work."

David thought the last sentence was stated with a touch of sarcasm, and he was surprised by the tone of his voice, or maybe it was only his imagination. With all of the technical jargon, he was having a hard time following what

Rajesh was saying, and the last part was the only thing he understood.

"What do you mean, that's how it works? Is the project plan not working properly?" David had no idea what the project plan involved or what was supposed to be happening. He had never seen, much less worked on, a project plan before. And he was trying to remember what Rajesh said earlier, as he spoke very quickly. What the heck was SQL or comma-whatever? He would need to remember to research those terms later.

Rajesh responded, "Well, the specifications are the main problem because in the new system, the specs keeps changing. The data fields keep moving around to different tables, or they will invent a new table which has a format which doesn't quite match any data we have. So we have to change our current data format to match the new data format, and then parse the data once again to fit. It is like trying to hit a moving target."

David still wasn't sure what he meant. "You mean they keep changing the new software and the old software doesn't convert the data properly?"

Rajesh smiled as if David understood their problem, and as if he was going to be able to solve it.

"Yes. That is our problem. Can you get them to stop changing the code and specifications so we have a stable version we can work with?"

David was unsure if he had this authority, and he was uncertain who he would contact to present this request. But he said, "I will certainly pass along this suggestion. But I need more information about what exactly you are converting."

Rajesh reached over on the side of his desk, and grabbed a heavy green three-inch binder full of paper, using both hands as he handed it to David. David wondered why the plans weren't in a computer program or in an electronic format, instead of being printed.

"Here is the database schema for all of the applications of this hospital which we are converting. We are dealing with medical records, pharmacy records, health regulations, accounting, pension accounts, vendor information. Everything has to be converted over to the new system."

David's ears perked when he heard the word accounting. Was it possible his teller transactions were included in this system? After all, Tim gave him these cards, and David assumed the card accounts were tied to this hospital. This was one of the questions he wanted to ask Tim. Where was this money coming from? Wouldn't someone from accounting or the security team notice the withdrawal of thousands and thousands each day?

David looked at Rajesh. "I would like to learn a little more about the systems you are converting. Could we take a look at the forms?" David paused as if he needed to think. "Well, I don't want to waste your time looking at everything, how about we look at say, the accounting system?"

Rajesh seemed pleased that upper management was taking an interest in their work, and David noticed Kevan already left the room.

"Yes, David, I can show you how to access the information. You can then see what we are up against. There are so many fields and data in the accounting piece alone, it really is overwhelming. The names of most of the fields are also hard to figure out. The conversion guide isn't any help at all. Let's use this computer over here. I can login and let you look around."

Rajesh pointed over to the computer on the empty desk to the left. David rolled his chair over, and Rajesh followed in his chair. Rajesh found the application window and started typing. He then pointed to a form on the screen. "There you go. This is the main dashboard. Here you can search all of the different fields. And as you can see, most of the fields don't even have a name which means anything. We have to try and figure out what the names mean, what the values are, and what they are used for. Let me know if you need any help."

Rajesh scooted back to his own desk. David stared at the screen, not knowing what he needed to do. He began reading all of the buttons and links, until he found what he thought was a search button before selecting it. After a short delay, a form appeared. There were numerous field choices, and he decided to start at the top, under "Name," as that field was the most obvious. He glanced over at Rajesh to see if he was watching, but he was typing furiously on his keyboard. David wondered if he should try searching for the names on his teller cards, but he was unsure if the Party kept a record of what searches were made. He certainly didn't want to blow his cover, especially if security was monitoring what was being searched.

David swung his chair around towards Rajesh. "Rajesh, if I start poking around here, that isn't going to alarm anyone in security, will it?"

Rajesh laughed. "Are you kidding me? None of this stuff is monitored by security. We don't have a real security department here. That is why we are moving the data over to the new system, where it can be properly monitored. Don't worry, no one is going to know what you are doing. If they ask, I will say it was me. But, try not to delete anything. If you have any questions, stop what you are doing and I will help you." Rajesh turned back to his keyboard and continued typing.

While his reply eased David's mind, he was now worried that once the data was transferred, someone might take an interest in why these people were withdrawing tens of thousands a week in cash from teller machines. Looking over at Rajesh again, there was no other choice than to think he was telling the truth. He moved the cursor up to the search box. All of the names on the cards were embedded in his memory, as he had used them every day for months.

He typed in the first name, and then hit the search button, and a list of records appeared. The screen only displayed the first twenty-five records, and then there were links for several more pages of records. He clicked on the first line and a new screen appeared with more information. David started scanning the screen. The results displayed the person's name, along with a debit in the amount of a thousand, and the numbers were in red. For an unknown reason, almost all of the other fields were blank. The bank name and the account number were both blank as well. The date of the transaction was there, but that was all. Then he noticed a field with the label of "Designation," and it contained the word "InPtyLvl2." As David looked at the text closely, the meaning came to him almost immediately, and he said to himself, "Inner Party Level Two."

David sat back in his chair and stared at the screen. The words, "Inner Party Level Two," kept repeating in his head. "Inner Party Level Two, Inner Party Level Two." These teller cards belonged to the Inner Party, and Tim was only in the Outer Party. David ran his hands through his hair and scratched his head, before covering the lower part of his face with one hand, and then he wiped the edges of his lips.

This knowledge that the cards belonged to the Inner Party was shocking.

What was Tim doing giving him ten Inner Party bank cards? Was Tim trying to get him killed? His mind started racing, and he was thinking about what they would do if he was caught with these cards. There probably wouldn't be a trial. The Party would send a person to sneak up and shoot him in the back of the head as he walked to his apartment from his car. Or he would simply disappear in the middle of the night. Or even worse, he would be caught, tried, convicted and sent to the labor camps in the mountains, forced to break rocks with a dull pickaxe or whatever it is they make the prisoners do out there.

David thought about every possible scenario, and he ran each one through his mind, before finally deciding Tim was certainly smarter than this. Tim wouldn't jeopardize the entire mission with what could be described in any way as a sloppy act. Tim knew what he was doing, and he needed to trust him, and there was really no other choice. The other names were searched, and one by one, each result contained the same sparse information: the cardholder's name, the amount of the transaction and the date, along with the same designation of "InPtyLvl2," - Inner Party Level Two. He took a deep breath, and exhaled slowly before confirming Tim knew what he was doing, otherwise the Party would have definitely caught him by now. Tim covered his tracks and there was no way he was getting caught, as long as he kept wearing a hat and glasses and being random in his pattern of withdrawals. Those were the instructions Tim provided to him.

David clicked the clear screen button, and then clicked the button marked, "Home." Staring at the screen, he noticed a link labeled, "National Patient Search," and he became curious. The hospitals records were mandated to be localized for each hospital, or to maybe each regional service area. In all of his years of working for SoCare, there was never a mention of a national patient registry. The Party-controlled hospitals might have all of their data together, but this was a private hospital. Why would their patient information be combined with the national Party hospitals? Or was it? After all, there were privacy laws against a national registry of this kind. Or at least there were such laws at a previous point in time.

He clicked the link and a new screen appeared. Since he had never been to this hospital as a patient, he decided to search for his name. In the name field he typed, "David A. Gagnon," selected his home region, and hit the search button. A progress bar appeared, along with the words "Searching National Patient Registry, Please Wait." When the search was complete, a list of the results appeared, with fourteen other similar names in this region, along with their benefits identification number. His eyes ran down the list, and he found his record. He clicked on the link, and almost immediately, he was now looking at all of his personal information: his name, address, city, phone number and national identification number. There were links below his information which connected to all of the Party Prosperity Benefit departments. All of his information was there. There was even a picture of him, and he recognized the picture as being the one from his driver's license. He noticed the field named, "Designation," and it contained the value "OtPtyLvl1," - Outer Party Level One. There was a link below labeled, "Health History and Information." He clicked on the link, and a window popped up with an alert at the top which read, "Proprietary Information - User Verification Required," and below the window were two fields, for a user name and password. David certainly didn't have a user name and password, so he clicked the cancel button.

David sat there in amazement of how much of his information was available to anyone with a terminal in this hospital. At least his health information required a password, but he surmised employees or Party members here probably had access to this information as well, and it didn't matter if that person was in the Party or not. David had a realization. This was certainly a wealth of information he could possibly use in his mission. The health information wasn't valuable, but if he could gain access to this software or to the Party's version of this software, he could use it to research his associates and where they lived or worked. Or, even better, he could also use it to research the targets, to make it easier for his associates to locate them. Then again, maybe the health information was valuable. If one of his targets had a medical condition, it might be easier to exploit their weakness versus having an associate put a bullet in their head. But the knowledge and ability to accomplish such a feat was unknown to David, so he would have to find someone in the medical field to help with these types of situations.

His mind started up again, trying to figure out all of the ways he could utilize this information. He needed to find a way to gain access to this data once he was back in his office. This would certainly be a lot easier than traveling around to coffee shops, and doing his research from his car. The background research would still need to be performed, but the hardest part of his searches was finding out where a candidate lived, unless they owned property. But he needed to figure out a method so his searches wouldn't be tracked. If Party Security decided to do an audit of his searches, then he would be in trouble. He would have to determine a way to get around the security aspect, but it was a problem to worry about later. He wanted to perform one final search. Moving back to the search page, in the name field he typed, "Johnson Bryce," and hit return. David smiled when he saw the results on the screen.

David discretely turned his head towards Rajesh, and noticed he was over at another engineer's desk. He reached into his briefcase and pulled out one of his tablets. He then spent the next twenty minutes performing more searches and transferring the information into his device. Having access to this system was going to be extremely valuable.

Chapter 16

David left the hospital a few minutes before sixteen hundred, having spent the remainder of the afternoon watching Rajesh work, and listening to him and the other engineers complain about changing data fields and values and a bunch of other terms David didn't quite understand. But Rajesh and the rest of the team thanked David for stopping by, and they seemed to be genuine about it. David was amused that they were optimistic he was actually going to be able to help them. He would need to figure out if he could actually do anything, but he didn't know what needed to be done or what person he could talk to. Maybe he would figure it out when he visited the other center tomorrow.

Earlier, David received his hotel information from Stephanie. This particular hotel was one he had never visited, and it was located an hour's drive away in a different city closer to tomorrow's appointment. David entered the address into his device, and followed the directions. The location of the medical center was known, but this hotel was in a part of town he never frequented. He normally stayed at the Party's hotel a block away from the center, but this hotel was seven miles away, closer to downtown. The downtown area was saturated with tall buildings, with gray or blue glass exteriors, and all of them possessed the same uneventful style. The hotel was the same as the neighboring buildings, tall and sleek, but there were several glass elevators which ran along the outside of the building. He pulled into the hotel's parking lot and drove up to the lobby entrance. A valet in khaki pants and a short-sleeved shirt with the hotel logo on the chest ran around to open his door before he even had a chance to put the car in park.

As the valet opened the car door, he greeted David in a cheerful manner. "Welcome to the Pantheon, Mr. Gagnon." David was surprised the valet knew his name.

David reached down and flipped the switch which opened the rear door. The valet went around to the back of the car, and once the door opened, grabbed his new luggage and placed it to the side. A bellman was standing by and he walked over, took the bag and then quickly disappeared inside the lobby. The valet grabbed David's briefcase, closed the back door and walked back to David, handing him the briefcase and a valet ticket.

"Have a nice night." The valet quickly jumped into the car, slammed the door and sped away. David watched as the car slipped into the parking garage, and he turned and faced the lobby, wondering where his luggage had gone. He finally spotted the bellman inside, walking away with his bag. David strolled through the automatic revolving door, which was made of shiny and polished brass and the glass was etched with the hotel's logo.

As David approached the front desk, the desk clerk noticed him. "Good evening Mr. Gagnon, how are you doing today?"

This recognition was a little unnerving for David. "I am fine, thank you. I believe I have a reservation." David reached back for his wallet, and took out his company credit card, unaware his Party identification was still hanging around his neck. Before he could hand the clerk his credit card, the clerk handed him a room key.

"You are in room 1207. The elevators are over to your right. Take the elevator to the twelfth floor and exit to your right. Your room is the third one on your right. Your bag should already be in your room. Dinner is served until midnight, and the bar is open until two hundred. If you need anything please dial zero. Is there anything else I can get for you?"

David took the key with his left hand, as he was still holding his wallet and credit card in his right hand. "Do you need my credit card?"

The clerk smiled. "No sir. We already have your card on file. We will send a copy of the bill to Stephanie. There is no need to stop by in the morning and check out."

David put the credit card in the wallet, and the wallet in his back pocket, and realized Stephanie must be efficient at her job. When she made the reservation, she must have sent them his picture. Or perhaps they have a database of Party members, given this is not a typical Party hotel, but one reserved for Outer or Inner Circle members. Either way, it was the fastest he ever checked into a hotel. And the clerk was pleasant and actually called him by his name. The other Party hotels were always short-staffed with bland-tempered clerks. And it seemed no matter what time he arrived, there was always a line of four or five people waiting. Ambling towards the elevators, he noticed he was wearing his Party identification around his neck, solving the riddle of him being recognized.

As the doors opened, David was impressed. The elevator was huge in comparison to any normal elevator. All of the sides were glass, and as it quickly rose upwards, David faced the back of the elevator and watched as the ground was moving farther and farther away. Looking out onto the city, the view was beautiful, with all of the big glass buildings so close to each other. He wondered what it would look like at night, with all of the lights from the cars down below and the buildings lit up all around him. The ride was quick, and as he felt the elevator coast to a stop, he heard a soft ding, and the elevator doors opened behind him. David turned down the hall, found room 1207, slid the card into the slot, and opened the door.

The lights were already on in the room, and he could hear the air conditioning straining to keep the room cool. He walked in past the bathroom, and as he turned the corner, he spotted his bag sitting on a little cushioned table at the foot of the bed. The expanse of the room caused him to stop in amazement, and as he slowly panned around, the space appeared to be bigger than his entire apartment. There was a section on the left which contained a large couch, and two side chairs pointing towards a large television mounted on the wall. There was also a coffee table and a vase which appeared to be filled with fresh flowers.

To his right was a small bar, with a sink and a large steel container and four glasses on a silver-plated platter. Underneath the counter was a refrigerator with a glass door, and a mini-bar cabinet with a similar glass door to the right. David bent down to see inside the refrigerator, and it was stocked with his favorite diet colas, possibly another kudos for Stephanie. He opened the door to the mini-bar, and inside was a variety of snacks and small bottles of various alcoholic drinks, but without prices. David looked on top of the mini-bar for a menu or list of prices, but he didn't see one. Closing the door, he noticed the king-sized bed, covered with six large pillows. On the bed was another small silver tray with four wrapped pieces of candy or chocolate. David was hoping it was chocolate. Along with sugar, chocolate was incredibly expensive, and also on the self-prohibited list. There was a large painting over the bed, and on each bedside table was a small vase with fresh flowers and a large lamp. Turning to his left, he noticed the entire outer wall was one large window, stretching from the floor to the ceiling. In the corner, on the other side of the bed, was a small table desk and an office chair. And another large television was mounted on the inside wall, across from the windows.

David couldn't move, as he was almost paralyzed with admiration. This room was nicer than any hotel he had been in, and was definitely nicer than his own apartment. His cell phone rang, and he was startled by the sound. Reaching into his pocket, he grabbed his phone and pressed the answer button, and brought it to his ear.

"Hello?" A familiar voice was on the other end.

"David, this is Stephanie. I hope your drive was pleasant. I wanted to be sure everything was okay with your room. Is the room to your satisfaction?"

"I just arrived, and yes, everything looks great." He wondered how she knew he was in his room.

"Did you have a good day? How were your meetings? Is there anything I need to do for you before I leave?"

David peeked down at his watch, and the time was almost eighteen hundred, which caused him to wonder why was she still at work. "My day and my meeting went well, thanks for asking. And, no Stephanie, I don't need anything else. But I do appreciate the call."

"Okay, great. I wanted to be sure you were okay before I left for the day. Please don't hesitate to call me if you need anything."

"Thanks Stephanie, I am pretty sure I will be okay, but thanks for offering. Have a good night."

Stephanie said goodbye and he slipped the phone back into his pocket. A feeling of great satisfaction arose inside him, and he was thinking he could get used to this, and he wondered if the mission was really worth it.

The next morning, David woke early and enjoyed a great breakfast in the hotel restaurant. Instead of watery scrambled eggs baked in a banquet pan or with the texture of a sponge, the restaurant served real eggs. Breakfast consisted of three eggs, scrambled to order, along with several pieces of real bacon, which he hadn't eaten in years, as well as biscuits which were soft and fluffy, with real maple syrup. The coffee was incredible, served with sugar cubes on the side. David had never seen sugar cubes before, and he asked the waitress what they were, and as she explained, she called him by name. The quality of the Party-member hotels was definitely higher, and while this was surprising, it only helped to strengthen what he already knew. The rules for the Party members were vastly different than the rules for the people who simply worked for the Party.

That morning's meeting with the second center was about the same as the meeting from yesterday. One of David's other direct-reports, a man named Edgar, was in charge of this conversion. David went through the same routine as yesterday, but with more confidence. This time, he was able to ask one of the engineers how he could access this center's system from his office. The engineer wrote down the instructions, and provided David with the engineer's own user name and password until he could get his own credentials. David was confident he solved his problem of being able to access the system, at least for a while. Any searches David performed would now be attributed to the engineer, and the security department probably wouldn't even bother auditing the engineers who were working on the project, if they even audited anyone.

David arrived back at work on Thursday, right before lunchtime. The comfort of the hotel room as well as the excellent food in the restaurant prompted him to extend his trip by one more night, even though he was only a two-hour drive from home. To him, staying at such a nice hotel was almost like a vacation. Now that he was back in the office, he spent the remainder of the morning reviewing the project binder from Rajesh, looking up words and terms he didn't understand. An invitation for lunch was offered to Stephanie again, and she was just as delighted as the first time. His laptop and new cell phone were delivered after lunch. Stephanie was excited to show him how to access the management application, where he would be filling out his reports. He spent the remainder of the day reading the project plans, but he was still lost in all of the technical jargon.

Friday was a mindless repeat of Thursday. David read the project plans in the morning, took Stephanie to lunch, and continued reading the project plans the rest of the afternoon. He decided he might need to download a computer book or manual or something which could help him learn what he was reading or presumed to be doing, as none of it was making any sense. After lunch, he logged into the healthcare system and found the addresses of three more possible recruits. Having this type of access to data was going to make his mission so much easier.

Chapter 17

David's first week in his new job was over, and Saturday morning arrived. Today was the day David was going to look at a cabin in the mountains, and he was anxiously awake by six hundred. After a quick shower, he ate a breakfast of the cardboard-fiber cereal and was ready to leave for the mountains at seven. Wearing jeans and a golf shirt, he put on a pair of old hiking boots, in case there was any dirt or mud. The weather forecast called for a typical hot and humid day, but he surmised that if he was walking around in the woods, jeans might be better than shorts.

Grabbing his phone and keys, David went outside to the parking lot, and as he approached his car, he was still amazed at his new situation. With a new car, a much higher-paying job, a beautiful assistant, and incredible hotels and great food when he traveled, life was definitely great. Despite all of the goodness and optimism, at random times, second thoughts about the mission would develop in his mind. But he already decided it was too late to back out now, and he tried to ignore his doubts. Upon opening the car door, the familiar aroma of a combination of plastic and real leather was detected, and he inhaled deeply with enjoyment, while wondering how long the inside would still have the new-car smell. His old car wore a lingering and defiant odor like a wet dog on a hot afternoon.

The ride to the mountains was pleasant, with surprisingly little traffic. David pulled into a gas station, coasting over to the side of the lot, before stopping and taking out the real estate magazines. With the realization that it might be too early in the morning to call a real estate agent, he decided to go inside for a cup of coffee and maybe a doughnut.

The coffee wasn't bad, but they only offered packaged doughnuts, and the first one was a little stale. He considered warming it in the microwave which was near the wrapped sandwiches, as Stephanie did with his bear claw, but the inside of the oven was covered in filth. The powdered sugar on the doughnut was very sweet. Near the cash register, he found another real estate magazine which was different from the ones he had, so he decide to browse through it before making the phone call to the agent. He slowly flipped through the magazine, looking at each house or cabin, and reading the concise descriptions, trying to kill as much time as possible. After he finished, the clock only displayed eight fifty-two. Even with his high level of patience, he was too excited to wait any longer. If he called and the agent was asleep, but more importantly if they became mad or upset, then he could always wait a while and call a different real estate agent.

David opened the other real estate book and flipped to the page with his favorite cabin, and dialed the number of the agent. To his surprise, the woman who answered the phone stated she was already awake and dressed, and would be happy to meet with him. He speculated she might be lying, as her voice sounded raspy, as if she was asleep. But her grogginess turned cheerful when he mentioned the purpose of his call. David assumed she probably hadn't made a sale in quite a while, and was probably surprised anyone called. He told her where he was located, and she directed him to drive a little further and they would meet in the downtown square. She said he was only about five minutes from there, but it would take her about thirty minutes to meet him.

David arrived at the town square, which contained an old courthouse nestled in the middle, and was surrounded by empty parking lots. He circled around once and decided to park in the center near a bench. The air was already a little warm outside, so he decided to wait in the car with the air conditioner turned on. His favorite feature of the car was the air conditioner, it was incredible. His old car only produced slightly colder air than the outside air. You could hang meat in this new car if necessary.

Almost a half-hour passed before a long dirty-white sedan pulled up next to his car. The passenger's window rolled down and a woman leaned over to try and make eye contact, before shouting, "David?" Nodding his head, he turned off his car and stepped out, locking his car with the key fob as he opened the passenger's side door. As he sat down and closed the door, a strong sour smell hit him in the face. David kept the door open as long as possible without being awkward, in an attempt to allow some fresh air to follow him inside.

When he finally closed the door, the woman tilted her head towards

David, and extended her hand. "David, Susan Adams, nice to meet you." As David accepted her hand, he noticed her hair was in a pony tail, which confirmed his assumption she was asleep, since she didn't do anything with her hair. But then again, it was Saturday, or maybe that is how women dressed here. After returning her greeting, he opened the magazine and pointed to the listing for his favorite cabin.

Susan looked at the listing. "Oh, yes, this is a great place. I know this one very well, and I think you are going to love it. It's not too far from here either."

David thought she probably says that about all of her listings, or any listing she has an opportunity to show. Susan drove around to the road on the opposite side of the square, and headed away from town. David gave her a quick glance, without being too obvious. She was fairly attractive for her age, but he guessed when she was younger, she was probably a knockout. Her bottle-blonde hair failed to hide dark roots which were long overdue for a visit to the beauty salon. She wore a dusty and dark green jacket, white button-down shirt, and blue jeans. And she was thin but with a chest which was probably store-bought.

After a brief and almost uncomfortable delay, she started talking and asking a lot of questions. "Have you been in the market long? Are you from around here? How many houses have you seen? What is your budget and time frame? Are you married? Do you have any kids?"

David answered the questions politely but with very short responses, trying to give her a hint he wasn't the talkative type, but she kept at it. As they were driving along the highway, she began to point out anything and everything she saw, as if she were a tour guide and a real estate agent at the same time. Perhaps she was trying to sell him on the community and local attractions, as well as the cabin.

"Now, up on your right, there is a road side vegetable store. We have them all over the place. This one is usually only open on Friday and Saturday, like most of them around here. But this particular one, they have the best tomatoes. But don't buy them if they are even slightly green. You might think they will ripen, but they won't, even though tomatoes usually will ripen after they are picked. But these do not. Make sure they are nice and red and without bruises. They bruise easily, and once they bruise, they go bad very quickly. But don't wait until Saturday afternoon to visit. They usually sell out of everything by noon. The only thing they will have left is the bad pickings which no one wanted."

David was staring out the window, enjoying the scenery, trying to tune out her voice. But as she continued talking, David observed she had an unfamiliar but nice country accent and her voice was very soft and pleasing, and she reminded him of his mother.

"During the fall they have a bunch of good corn as well, but make sure you open the husk and check out every ear. We have a real problem with corn bugs. I don't know if they are weevils or beetles or what, I guess it depends on what month it is. But they sure can mess up a good ear of corn. So, you shouldn't buy a whole bunch of corn without looking at every ear. And once in a while in the summer they will get a load of peaches as well. Best darn peaches you will ever eat. Bigger than your fist. But make sure they don't have mold on them. If it has been raining a lot, they'll have mold. You have to check each one before you buy it, and check on the bottom as well. The bottom is where the mold hangs out."

Instead of being annoying, David was beginning to like this woman with her soft twangy voice. Given her appearance and the way she talked, David assumed she probably lived her whole life within a five-mile radius of this town. The vapid air which was straining to come out of the vents dissipated the sour smell a little, and David was hoping the odor hadn't stuck to his clothes.

As Susan drove, she kept talking and talking. But David finally accepted this apparent wealth of unsolicited information and found it might actually be useful, if he did buy a place here. Fresh corn was rarely available at the national grocery stores, and he definitely liked peaches. Tomatoes weren't his favorite, but his experience with tomatoes was limited to the canned generic brand which had a tendency to be stringy. Fresh ones might be better.

Susan continued, "Over here on the left is an antique store. I am using the word antique loosely, because they sell mostly junk, but once in a while you can get a nice piece of furniture really cheap, especially after an older person dies. When they do, their kids will bring all of their stuff here for Buddy to sell.

145

Buddy runs the place. It really is more like a permanent garage sale. Or, if you are looking for knick-knacks or things to put on a shelf in your new cabin, they have those as well. You can probably also get a deer or a boar or even a bear head to put on the wall over the fireplace. On Saturdays, they have this car show. Well, it isn't really a car show. People do bring their old cars to show off, but most people bring their cars to sell or trade. And they also have..."

The last part caught David's attention, even though he was half-listening, and he interrupted her. "I'm sorry, did you say people sold their cars here?"

"Yes, every Saturday, from about nine in the morning until around lunchtime, or until everyone gets tired from being out in the sun, or if they get too drunk and decide to go home or go out in the woods and shoot at animals or the trees. They usually have about twenty or thirty cars here for sale. At times they only have five or ten. If it is raining, then they usually don't show up at all. The regulars show up real early to get a spot in the front row, and they are the ones who bring their old antique cars, but they usually want too much money. And no one has money to buy antique cars any more. They always have a price on them, but I think they bring them here to show off and socialize. You need to get with the people behind the first row or two, as these people are the ones who are really wanting to sell or trade."

"They use the empty lot next door. And in the store Buddy has hot dogs and cold drinks and on sunny days there is a guy outside who sells boiled peanuts. We call him Jones, and he is probably about ninety years old. I don't know if Jones is his first or last name, as he doesn't really talk much. His vocabulary is hard to understand, and he normally repeats the word 'yeah' a lot. I'll tell you what, those are the best boiled peanuts I have ever tasted. And if you know the right person, you can even get a jar or a jug of sweet corn liquor."

She paused for a moment as a car pulled out in front of her, and she needed to slow down. David wondered why she didn't warn him about buying the peanuts. Every other item came with a warning attached to it.

"But, if you do buy those boiled peanuts, make sure they aren't too salty. Later in the morning, Jones, after he has drank too much, he puts too much salt in the boil. He gets the shaky hands the more he drinks, and that is how you can tell if the peanuts are going to be too salty." And there it was, watch out for the extra-salty boiled peanuts.

As she kept driving, David had a feeling this was perfect. He could come out here to the red zone and buy a used car with cash. He could skip registering it in his name, use it until the tag expired, and then either sell it or abandon it. There wouldn't be any records and his name wouldn't be attached to it. Plus, there was the chance he would only need it for a few months anyway, until after phase two, especially if he needed to go into hiding.

Susan kept on talking, this time about trees and all of the critters in the woods. David went back to his daydream about what he would do if he bought a cabin. As the roads started getting curvy and the woods became thicker, Susan needed to slow down her speed. David noticed an occasional dirt road that would appear on the sides of the highway, leading off into the woods. The roads didn't have any street name signs or houses on the corners, which stuck David as being odd.

David asked, "Where do these dirt roads lead that are on the side over here?"

Susan didn't even need to look. "Oh, those are forestry roads. That area over there and on the other side here is a national forest. The roads are for the forestry people to use, to drive up there and count trees or wildlife or whatever. Or they go up there to look for moonshiners. Those roads go on for miles and miles. When we were teenagers, we would go back there and have parties and get drunk and make out. There are a dozen or so nice waterfalls back there, and a bunch of small lakes. We used to go skinny dipping in the lakes. The roads were open for the locals and tourists to visit, but the government said people were littering and eating the fish they caught and shooting at trees, so they are off-limits now. You have to protect Mother Nature and all that stuff."

The roads intrigued David. If his situation with the mission was really bad, he could possibly disappear down one of these roads and hide out if he needed to. He was still in the process of finishing his bug-out bags, and he could possibly hide a couple out there as well. The *Guide* explained you needed several emergency survival bug-out bags, in case the Party was on your trail and you needed to run. You were also supposed to have several hide-outs you could use. David had been working on the bags, but he hadn't found time to scope for hide-outs yet. A hide-out could be a room at a friend's house, or a cheap non-Party hotel, or any place where you could stay for a night or a week or more. He was thinking if he bought a cabin, he could use the weekends to explore and to find suitable places to hide. Having land around the cabin would allow him to hide a cache of food and water. Depending upon the layout of the land, it might be possible to build a small survival shed or a place to hide a tent and supplies, in order to have a place where he could sleep and cook food.

Susan kept driving for another ten minutes, and she continued talking. David couldn't determine if for her, breathing was even necessary to produce speech, as she didn't appear to stop talking long enough to refill her lungs. She finally turned off the main highway onto a small paved road which went down a small hill, and then crossed a wide and heavy-flowing stream. David noticed the weight limit on the old bridge over the stream was eleven tons, and he made a mental note to check to make sure his new car wasn't that heavy. He was unaware as to how much these larger cars weigh, but he was almost positive it didn't weigh eleven tons. This fact would be something to verify if he ever drove here.

After the stream, the road split, and Susan stayed to the right. The road became much narrower, as if it was built for one or one and a half cars and not two. Every hundred meters or so, the road widened, so if two cars were using the road, one could pull over and let the other one pass. They went up a fairly steep hill before leveling out onto a plateau, where the road became even more narrow. The plateau contained a wide and grassy field, full of grass and weeds which looked like they hadn't been cut in quite a while, if ever. Susan stopped the car and gave David a warning. She leaned over the steering wheel, and pointed her finger up in the air.

"Okay, this property is at the top of this mountain. It is a pretty steep drive, and I am going to have to drop down a gear or two, and then go a little bit fast to make it up the hill. But don't get scared, I have been driving these mountain roads all my life." David was correct. She has lived here her whole life.

Susan put the car into first gear and floored it as fast as the whale of a car could go. They traveled up a pretty steep hill before leveling off, and continuing up another steep hill which curved off to the left. The road kept going uphill, and Susan kept gunning the engine. The road finally leveled off into a huge round area, covered with asphalt and a thick layer of leaves and scattered branches. Susan stopped and parked the car on the right side of the circle.

"Now, that wasn't so bad, was it?" she asked.

"No, that was fine." David was a tad scared at first, but decided she probably knew what she was doing. But on the way up the last hill, he turned his head to look out his window and closed his eyes.

As they opened their doors and stepped out, Susan started towards the cabin, but stopped in front of the car to wait for David, as he was standing by his car door and looking around the property. The cabin was off to the left of the circle, and there was a separate three-car garage on the right side, with a small covered walkway connecting the two. The entire area was blanketed by a canopy of huge hardwood trees, with an occasional white pine that towered over the other trees. The cabin was nestled in between several huge trees. The ground was also covered in a thick layer of brown leaves, and there wasn't a patch of grass to be seen.

"Shall we?" asked Susan, as she motioned for David to follow. He was admiring the beauty of the outside of the cabin, with the wrap-around porch, and everything was made from logs, even the posts circling the porch.

A lockbox was dangling from the front door knob, which Susan opened by placing a fob near it. A door popped opened on the bottom of the box, and the keys fell out onto the porch. Susan took the keys, unlocked and opened the door, then held it open for David to go first. As he entered the cabin, Susan began the tour.

"This is a three-bedroom, two and one-half bath log cabin, and it has a partially-unfinished but full basement. The basement is an open floor plan and is already stubbed for a full bath."

Susan continued talking as they walked through the hallway towards the living room, and she pointed to the left. "This room is your downstairs half-bath, and over here to the right, is the living room, with a real stone fireplace. This house was built almost thirty years ago, and the fireplace and wood stove was installed before all those crazy environmental save-the-planet regulations. I doubt anyone would come here to see what you were burning anyway. If the chimney gets stopped up with creosote or if the flue lever breaks or gets stuck, I know a guy who cleans the insides and he can fix pretty much anything if something goes wrong. And Ricky lives a few miles from here, and he can get you a big stack of firewood. Remember, don't burn any pine logs in it, or you are liable to catch the place on fire."

The living room was nice and open, and the dining area and kitchen were off to the side. Susan continued her tour. "The kitchen was updated about five years ago, so the appliances should still be good. You can probably put a four-chair dining table set right here, because you want to be able to look out to see the view when you eat."

To his left, he noticed two sliding glass doors. Walking over, he attempted to open them, but he was unfamiliar with this type of lock, so Susan came to assist. After opening the door, David stepped out onto the covered deck. The view of the mountains and the valley was breathtaking, and the horizon appeared to be a hundred miles away. David could barely make out the other cabins way down below, but even with the many trees blocking his view, he was positive there were more out there. This area was too beautiful to be left alone.

David was envisioning the cabin being a great asset. Depending upon the attitude and reception of his neighbors, he should be able to find one or two friendly people he could trust if he needed to run and go into hiding. The woods would definitely provide plenty of places for stashing a portion of his money, if not all of it. Choosing to go outside his apartment and into the woods to bury the money wasn't the best solution, as there were too many potential witnesses around. And with twenty-five acres, a number of hideouts could be built in the woods as well. Susan followed him out onto the deck.

"Your property line on the south side is behind us, about thirty feet on the other side of the garage, and it goes along a ridge to the east and west. The twenty-five acres includes all you see down below, all the way down to the grassy field. I think you have almost three acres of the grassy field, but I would have to check the plat. The stream follows a slope on the west side, and ends up at your pond."

David was astonished. "Did you say your pond as in my pond?" David remembered there was a pond in the pictures, but the short description never stated anything about the pond being part of the deal, and he simply assumed it wasn't included.

"Yes, there is a pond. It is almost two acres or so, right next to the field. You couldn't see it because there is a dam there, and they planted a bunch of those fir trees on one side. The sale includes the pond, and the stream is on your property, but it is a national forest stream, so it is protected. But the pond was put in a long time ago, before that big environmental law was passed, so you are grandfathered there as well, at least for now. You can fish in it, but I wouldn't drain it or take water from it, in case the forestry police show up and catch you. And you have the national forest on three sides of your plot. So, you don't have to worry about anyone building anything next to you."

She chuckled softly. "Not that they would in this market anyway."

David was now sold. This cabin would be the ideal place to spend his weekends, and he could buy a used car and keep it here. The location would allow him to scout for more associates in this area and over in the northern part of the state. He could grow vegetables, and maybe even get those chickens for fresh eggs. He could fish in the pond and in the other larger stream they crossed earlier. And, if he could figure out how to buy a rifle or shotgun, he could do some hunting as well.

The ownership of any type of gun was forbidden in the blue zone, except for Party members and the national police. In the red zone, you could pretty much own any type of weapon you wanted. Gun purchasing and ownership was tightly controlled, and guns were only available after a lengthy background check and an extended waiting period. While the Party didn't care what the red zone citizens did with guns, they still wanted to make buying one as painful as possible. But the red zone citizens were very patient.

Party members were allowed to purchase and carry a handgun in any zone, but very few of them did. And almost all Party members wouldn't even think of owning a rifle. The Party permitted the red zone citizens to own guns and they could even kill each other all day long, and it wouldn't bother them. They needed to control the majority of the citizens, and the majority lived in the blue zone. Normally, when a government disarms their citizens, it is not an act of protection, but an act of distrust which is met with loathing and scorn, but only by those people that are armed. The citizens of the blue zone welcomed these gun restrictions, and willingly and voluntarily relinquished any hope of, or any ability for self-protection over to the Party. Even with the ban on personal gun ownership and the severe penalties if you violated this law, the blue zone was rampant with gun-related crimes.

Susan could tell David liked the property. She took him to see the master bedroom on the main level, and the two bedrooms upstairs. All of the bedrooms faced the back of the house, and each one provided a great view of the valley below. The bathrooms were large, and the closets were almost as big as the kitchen in David's apartment. Susan was correct in her assumption, as David was really impressed.

As they headed down the stairs, Susan said, "Just wait until you see the full basement. It is really large and open. And it has a really nice survival room." David wasn't sure of what she said. It sounded like she said the basement contained a survival room, but he wasn't positive what it meant.

Susan led David down the basement stairs, which were carpeted but a little worn. As she reached the bottom, she turned on the lights. As David left the stairs and walked into the main area, he was amazed at the size of the basement, it was very large and open. There were three very long and thick wooden beams supporting two-dozen smaller beams which ran the entire width of the basement, so the layout was almost one large room. Susan continued in her tour-guide mode.

"This is a full basement, as the floor plan matches what you have upstairs. It is stubbed for a bath over in the corner, and they already ran outlets around the perimeter. Your water heater is over in the other corner, but you might want to build a little room around the area, if you decide to finish the basement."

David was strolling around, letting it all sink in. The basement was definitely twice as large as his current apartment.

Susan walked towards the back of the basement. "And here David, is your survival room." David was correct, she said survival room, but he still wasn't sure what a survival room was.

"Survival room?" asked David.

"Yes, the majority of houses built in this area in the last twenty, twenty-five years, they all have a survival room. The real estate people tend to call them storm shelters, you know, to make it not sound so bad, but it really is a survival room. If you don't have a survival room inside your house, then a lot of people build them outside, buried in their backyard. So, usually the listing won't state it has a survival room, but there is a pretty good chance it probably does. And this one has an interesting story. You see, this place was previously owned by a man who made moonshine on the side. He used to make it out in the woods, but then he decided it would be easier to make it indoors. Most of the regular drones can't see through concrete."

"And, you simply can't have a big old still in your basement. So, when he built this house, he decided to add a survival room under ground. But he elected to use his survival room for his moonshine operations."

Standing at the back wall, Susan flipped open the cover of a thermostat, and underneath was a small keypad. She punched in a code, and part of the concrete wall started moving, gradually hiding itself behind another concrete wall. After the wall moved six feet, it stopped. David slowly and cautiously walked towards the opening.

"The room is built under the asphalt driveway up top. All of the sides are reinforced concrete, and you even have a reinforced concrete ceiling. I don't know how thick the ceiling is, probably at least a foot or so, but you can park three or four cars or trucks up top and you wouldn't even know it. Now, if you don't need a survival room, I don't know what you could actually use this for, maybe as a storage room. Or, once in a blue moon, we do get some nasty weather, so you really could use it as a storm shelter. But this over here is the best feature of this room."

Susan went to the left side of the room, and stood by a large door. David noticed it looked like a regular household door, but it was made of metal. She opened the door, and David looked inside. Behind the door was a long hallway, with rows of metal shelves on either side. The lights to the hallway automatically came on when the door was opened.

"Every survival room has a separate and hidden entrance and exit, aside from the main door. Well, at least the good ones do. This hallway has room for more storage, and at the end is an exit on the back of the house, on the steeper side of the mountain. This is how he would get his raw materials and liquor in and out of the house, in case the police were watching him from the front. And the thick tree cover provided him with protection from the wandering eyes of a drone or helicopter. At the end of this hallway is another door, but a little smaller. Then outside, on the other side of the door, it is disguised to look like a big rock face, like on the side of a cliff. If you buy the house, I can tell you or show you how to open it from the other side. And, of course, I can give you the code for the main door."

Susan closed the door and went to the main door. "And up top here near the main opening, are two big buttons. If you need to open or close the door from the inside, press the green button. In an emergency, press the red one and the door will close extremely fast. Make sure all of your body parts are inside before you do that." Susan pointed to eight small televisions on the wall. "These monitors are hooked up to hidden cameras outside. Everything is controlled from this device over here by the bookshelf. When you turn this on, you can see all around the house and find out if anyone is outside. This is standard on most of the better survival rooms. You don't want to risk going outside if the police or a bunch of terrorists are waiting for you."

David observed the rest of the room. There was what appeared to be a kitchen in the corner on the far wall, with four cabinets and a countertop, and a small sink at one end. And to the right was a shelf, and a small bookcase at the end, with a couple dozen books on it. There was another door to the left side of the kitchen area, and he opened it. Inside was a cramped but full bathroom, with a shower, metal toilet and metal sink. Despite the bathroom being inside a survival room, it appeared to be professionally installed. Closing the bathroom door, he went out into the main basement area, where Susan was standing.

Susan pressed the keys on the keypad, and the concrete door started sliding back into place. This was all unfamiliar to David. He had never heard of a survival room, but now he saw the benefits of having one, and it would definitely be a great resource.

"Why is he selling this place?" asked David.

"Well, even with all of this fancy hideout stuff, the police still got him. And now he is up at Blue Ridge doing fifteen to twenty in the work camp. And since this house was involved with the illegal liquor trade, the government took the house and is selling it."

The story made the cabin even more interesting, but David had one more question. "If this survival room was such a big secret, how did you find out about it? I would think it would be a pretty hard thing to discover, unless they caught him in there. Did they catch him in there?"

Susan smiled. "Well, while most houses have a survival room, the owners do try and keep them a secret. But no, David, they caught him out on the highway transporting about fifty gallons of shine. Besides running liquor, his day job was in construction as a general contractor. He was able to build this room without any of the building inspectors knowing about it. Or if they did know about it, he probably paid them off. The police still don't have any idea about this room, even if they now own the place. And I need you to keep it to yourself as well. I wouldn't have shown it to you, but I have a feeling you really like this cabin."

David wondered why she would mention this room to him, when he hadn't even said he would buy the place. Or maybe she says that to everyone, and the room isn't really a big secret. Maybe the secret was part of the allure or part of her sales pitch, or maybe she made up the moonshine story. Normally he would have ignored the uncertainty of her story, but it made him ask, "Well, then how did you find out about it?"

Susan softly cackled and walked over closer to David. "Well David, I knew this man for a long time. He was also a friend of my brother, and I was one of his best customers. But enough of the chit-chat David. I am here to sell a house. I can tell you like this place. What do you think? Do you think this can be your house?"

David was amused by her closing lines. The cabin was very nice, and given his potential future circumstances, this room could come in handy if he needed to go into hiding. He studied the layout of the basement, and was replaying the upstairs tour in his head.

155

After pausing for a moment to think, he replied, "I do like the place. And I am guessing the price is fair. I will need to see about getting a loan. I first want to make sure I can do that, and then I think we have a deal."

Susan's face became more spirited. "Well David, I know several if not most of the managers at the national banks around here, and I can probably help you with your loan, or at least point you in the right direction."

"Well, that sounds good. I don't think it would matter which bank I used, since I will be using the Party mortgage loan program."

Susan's expression appeared to freeze, and her face turned white. She stammered and almost struggled to talk. "Oh, uh, I didn't know you were in the Party, I am sorry. Um, yes, you will want to talk with someone about your loan. Now, you can still use one of the national banks here. They can still help you. And I do know several managers who you will want to talk to."

Susan was surprised she was talking to a Party member. The Party made her very nervous. But David seemed to be a little different than the other Party members she encountered, as he didn't seem to have the attitude or cockiness most Party members displayed proudly. She thought he seemed almost normal.

They stood there in silence, and Susan was staring at David, and it made him uncomfortable. She slowly moved towards him. "David, if I can give you a bit of advice. Don't mention you are in the Party to anyone who lives around here. You will make more friends and less enemies that way. You can say you work for a national department or bureau, but you see, the people in this area don't really like the Party. Or their members."

She was surprised she even offered this warning to him, especially since he was a Party member, but David seemed to be different. Something inside made her feel at ease telling him this. She hoped he didn't take it the wrong way. But to survive out in the red zone required knowing what was acceptable, and what wasn't.

Susan's advice caught David off guard, but it shouldn't have. This area was an entirely different world, outside of the blue-zone bubble where the Party was king. The suggestion was sincere, and he welcomed her honesty. "I appreciate your advice. I am not like most Party members. For me, Party membership just came with my new job. But I will take your advice. Thanks."

Susan's face regained a bit of color. "Well alright then. Let's write this contract. Congratulations!"

David returned from his trip to the mountains, and was sitting on the couch in his apartment. The purchase contract for the cabin was signed, and he would call one of the local national banks on Monday. Susan gave him names and numbers to call, but he decided it might be better to use a bank located in the blue zone instead. He assumed most Party members did business inside the blue zone as much as possible, if not always. David's next task was in locating a new apartment, which might entail taking a day or two off work to find one closer to the office. In his prior job, since he was traveling so much, it was easier to live near the outside perimeter highway which surrounded the blue zone, and it was cheaper. Since his salary was much greater than his previous job, he decided he could afford a place downtown.

The problem of needing a different vehicle to make his withdrawals was still present. When he and Susan drove back past the antique store, he noticed the crowd surrounding the cars for sale, but he didn't bring any money with him. Plus, his company car was still in town. Next Saturday, he would definitely return with enough cash to attempt to buy a car. In the past week, he only managed to visit the teller machines three times. A different car was also needed to allow him to finish recruiting his associates, as he was fairly certain his company car was being tracked. And his new company-provided cell phone was being tracked, and everything he said or did in the office was probably being recorded. He tried to remember to turn off the cell phone whenever he left the office. Paranoia settled into his daily routines, and it was now a reflex.

Chapter 18

The next week at work for David was rather mundane. Even though David wasn't scheduled to arrive until eight-thirty, he couldn't shake his habit of getting up early, so he would arrive around seven-forty-five each morning. Once Stephanie discovered her manager was coming in earlier than she was, she started trying to arrive before he would. She would have a cup of coffee with a lid and two sugar packs on his desk waiting for him as he arrived. And, without thinking too much about it, he invited her to lunch everyday, not even considering she might be taking these invitations the wrong way. Plus, he certainly enjoyed her company, and after a while, he began to miss her when he left work. These thoughts of her were difficult to get out of his head, and it was tough to fight these feelings.

David made it through another uneventful week at work. Saturday morning arrived, and he tried to sleep in a little, but he awoke at eight twenty-two. He went to bed early the night before, and decided he would sleep without setting his alarm, and this was the latest he slept in a while. Today was the day he would visit the car show at the antique store and see about buying a used vehicle. His pockets were filled with ten thousand from his teller money, all in hundreds. Now he needed to find a way to get up to the mountain area where the store was located.

Making sure his work cell phone was turned off and on his desk, he used one of the pre-paid cell phones he purchased to call a taxi company. The *Guide* suggested it was a good idea to buy additional phones, so you could use them if you needed to do anything unusual. The *Guide* explained how to open the phone, recognize and then disable the GPS chip, so the phone couldn't be tracked.

Earlier in the week, David went to a coffee shop in the afternoon and using one of his tablets, created a list of ten taxi companies which serviced his home area. He needed to call six companies before he found one willing to take him deep into the red zone. And even then, he was required to pay double the fare both ways, in cash.

The taxi driver was instructed to meet him at a convenience store located a mile from his place. Like his earlier trip last weekend, he was dressed in hiking boots, jeans and old t-shirt, in an effort to try and blend in with what people in the red zone would wear, even though he really wasn't certain exactly how they dressed. Using small backpacks, he finally completed his bug-out bags, so he grabbed one and made the walk to the store, with the taxi arriving a short time later. The exact address to the antique store was an unknown, so he gave the driver directions as he drove. When they were a hundred yards from the store, he asked the driver to pull over in the parking lot of a vacant building. David paid for the ride and stepped out of the taxi, watching it as it drove away, before disappearing from view. The heat outside was already unbearable, otherwise he would have stopped further away. But he was already sweating from the taxi driver's inability to understand how to operate the air conditioning.

The time was a little after eleven hundred. Since Susan stated the car show ended around lunchtime, he didn't want to get there too early. The goal was to find a person who was desperate to sell their car, and one who might be willing to give David the paperwork without a sales contract or whatever was required to close the deal. David made his way down the road towards the store, and as he walked up to the first row of cars, he started searching the lot and the building for cameras. The chance of this place having any cameras was low, but this act was now performed regardless of where he was. He didn't see any visible cameras, and so he assumed it was a safe area.

The first two rows of cars were very nice and were mainly older-restored cars, or ones with new paint and a fresh wax job, but these weren't the type of cars he was looking for. His preference was for an older car with a good engine, but he didn't want anything flashy, as the car needed to blend in. Since he didn't know anything about cars, he would have to try and find a seller he could trust, if that was even possible out here. He casually talked to a few of sellers and feigned interest in a couple more cars. Even though their cars were good, they were too fancy and expensive for the purpose he had in mind.

As David made it to the last row, in the back of the lot near an old wood building which was falling apart, he saw what he thought was the perfect vehicle. The car needed to be a popular model, so there would be an abundance of them on the road, and therefore not easily noticed. It had to be old, but not too old, and it had to be reliable. The black truck he was looking at was perfect. During the taxi ride, he noticed almost every other car in the red zone mountain area was a truck. Most of them were dark colors, like blue or black. And, if he was going to buy a mountain cabin, a truck would also be useful for hauling whatever needed to be moved, especially his survival supplies. Now he would have to find out how much it cost.

There was a young man standing by the side of the truck, dressed in camouflage, and smoking a cigarette. His hair was long and stringy, and he was wearing a green baseball cap with a team's logo on the front. His skin was very dark and tan, and by his appearance, David assumed he hadn't taken a bath in a long time, or he was playing in dirt earlier.

David approached him, and not really knowing what to say, started with, "Nice looking truck. What can you tell me about it?"

The man threw his cigarette on the ground, stepped on it and ground it into the dirt with the toe of his boot, before transforming into a used-car-salesman.

"Oh, you got a good eye, this is a really nice truck." The man was stroking the hood of the car like a cat. "She is only fourteen years old, and I just rebuilt the engine, so it ain't got many miles on it. And I already upgraded the suspension and shocks, so if you go mudding and hit a rock, you won't go flying up in the air. The engine is three hundred eight-five horsepower, so it will haul really good down the road. You ain't gonna find another truck like this, especially in this condition. And I don't smoke in it, so it don't smell like an ashtray."

David could tell this man held a real fondness, even perhaps a love for this truck, and he was definitely proud of it. His accent was very similar to Susan's, but not as smooth and silky, and there was a pronounced and distinct nasal resonance. David went over and opened the door. The inside looked clean, but the seller could have cleaned it recently. The outside appearance was nice, given he mentioned doing something with mud. David closed the door and walked around the truck, inspecting the body for any damage. Standing near the back, he looked down and noticed a trailer hitch, and two bumper stickers.

One sticker read, "I live to 'shine" which David thought was pretty inspirational for a guy to have on his truck. But he didn't recognize the drawing on the right side of the sticker, which looked like a house with a curly smoke plume. The picture was really of a still, which is a device for making moonshine, or illegal whiskey. The other sticker showed a picture of a gun, with the words, "Cold Dead Fingers," a statement which confused David, and he was unsure what it meant. The stickers could be removed later, or left alone to add a bit of character. As David walked around to the passenger's side, he asked if he could take a look at the engine. The man was in the process of lighting another cigarette, and he continued doing so as he walked over and opened the driver's door, holding the cigarette with his left hand as far away from the truck as possible, to avoid soiling the interior. Reaching into the cab, he pulled a lever, and the hood popped open. David walked around to the front of the truck, and the man raised the hood. As David was looking at the engine, he noticed it did look new, or at least it was very clean. But then again, what did he know about engines? David gave the man a look of satisfaction and nodded his head. The man kept the cigarette in his mouth and used both hands to close the hood.

The man started his sales pitch again. "The engine is a six-point-two liter V8, and like I said it has three hundred eighty-five horsepower. This thing will outrun most anything else out there. It is super fast. You ain't gonna find another truck out here as fast as this thing. I also got a winch down here, in case you get stuck in a ditch. I've never been stuck in a ditch, so you could say the winch was almost in new condition." With his foot, the man pointed to the winch at the bottom front of the truck. "And the winch controls are inside the cab, on the passenger's side. The tires are new, I got them retreaded about five months ago. These here are off-road tires, but they do okay on the street."

David was impressed, even though there was no point of reference for being impressed. Now here was the challenging part. He only brought a little under ten thousand in cash, as he had to pay for the taxi, and he didn't know how much these trucks cost, or what they were worth. If the price was under the amount of money he brought, then he would definitely complete the transaction. David turned towards the man, who was now on this third cigarette in as many minutes.

"How much do you want for it?"

The man inhaled deeply, and then slowly exhaled the smoke through his nose. David noticed his clothes seemed to absorb the smoke. "Well, this is your lucky day. I got debts I gotta pay off on Monday, or I'm going be in big trouble. And I don't want to go back to, well, let's say I don't want to suffer the consequences. So, this beauty can be yours for only..." He paused as if he was trying to figure out how much he could get out of this stranger. "How about, six thousand?"

David was thrilled. This amount was much less than what he thought he would have to pay. But the next question could be a deal-breaker.

"Do you have the paperwork on you?" David never owned his own car before, as he always drove a work vehicle, and didn't know what paperwork was needed.

The man smiled, reached into his back pocket, and pulled out a folded piece of paper. "Yep. I got it right here. If you got six thousand, I can sign it over right here and now."

David paused and took a look around the yard. Not many cars had left or been sold, but it was still difficult to see him from the street or the store. And not too many people were paying attention to him or the young man. Most of the locals were looking at a restored baby-blue convertible. David noticed most of the men were gathered around a young woman who decided that wearing only a bikini top and a pair of short-shorts would help to sell her car.

David took a step closer to the young man. "Do we need to write a sales contract?" The man displayed a bewildered look on his face.

"Sales contract? What? No, we don't need no sales contract."

This answer pleased David. He reached into his pocket, and carefully pulled out seven stacks of the bills, with each stack of one thousand held together with a paper clip. The man was reluctantly pointing the title towards David, and as he brought out the money he said, "Okay. Here is seven thousand. I am giving you an extra thousand for your memory. As far as you know, you sold your car to a little old lady who wanted to buy it for her grandson. Is it a deal?"

The young man grinned a yellow smile, showing David he had lost numerous front teeth, and replied, "I hear you. I never seen you before in all my life." The man reached into his pocket, took out the keys, and handed them to David. The money was shoved into one of the pockets on the leg of his pants. The man shook David's hand. "Nice doing business with you. You take care of her. She's a good truck." The man took one last look at his truck before heading towards the back of the antique store and disappearing into the woods.

David climbed into the truck, and started the engine, which produced an extremely loud sound at first, but then lowered to a nice steady hum. He was very satisfied with his purchase, and this truck was going to be valuable. He could now drive wherever he needed and he could start hitting the teller machines again. It wasn't even noon yet, so he figured he might as well drive into town and visit as many banks as he could.

The ride of the truck was relatively smooth once he was out on the highway, and after the engine had time to get warm. It didn't appear to drive or handle as nice as his company car, but it would certainly work for what he needed. The guy was correct, it was a good truck and the sound of the engine gave the impression it could go very fast. David was tempted to see how fast, but he didn't want to risk getting pulled over. The plan was to make his teller runs, and then head back home.

David had completed this same teller route before, back before he was in his new job, and when he had his old car. There were five teller machines in the downtown area, and another seven on the other side of town, spread around a large shopping area centered around a big warehouse store. David could park his car at the local cooperative food store, and easily walk to all five of them. He pulled into the parking lot of the co-op, which was located in a large shopping center, and found a spot near the back of the lot. David's routine for this location involved walking to the end of the lot, and then up on the sidewalk next to the building. This path would help to bypass the cameras outside the co-op, and were pointed out at the parking lot. The first teller machine was located in the front of the store, and there were only two cameras in the lobby. David would enter through the right-side door, with the teller machine on his left against the far wall. One of the cameras was perched above the door, pointed at the teller machine, and the other camera was pointed out into the store. If he was careful, he could walk up to the teller machine and the camera would only record his back.

David walked inside and casually made his withdrawal. As usual, he was wearing a hat and sunglasses. Keeping his head down, he walked out the door and back into the parking lot, reversing his earlier route, down the sidewalk to the end of the center, and then out into the parking lot. The path to his car would then be shielded by the other cars, and hopefully from the cameras as well. As he neared the row where he parked, he went to his right and headed towards his truck, about ten meters away. As he turned, he noticed a police car parked in the far corner of the lot, facing his truck. The officer appeared to be staring right at him. David felt a little uneasy, but he figured it was only his paranoia. After all, he had done nothing wrong.

Continuing to walk past his truck, he doubled-back between the parked cars in the row. This route would allow him to approach the truck from the front, where he could get a better view of the officer. David could see the officer was positioned so he was looking directly at the back of the truck. There was really no way around it, he would have to go ahead and get in the truck, and hope the officer wasn't really interested in what he was doing. As he went around the front of the truck, he reached for the door and he saw the officer sit upright in his seat. David stood there as the officer switched on the blue lights, causing him to quickly jump into the truck.

David started the engine, and threw it into gear. The police car already started moving, and so he stepped hard on the gas pedal, causing the tires to squeal and produce smoke as he fled the parking area. As he approached the exit, David looked to his left to see if there was any oncoming traffic. The road was clear, so he didn't even slow down as he made a right-hand turn onto the highway. Checking his rearview mirror, he saw the police car drift out onto the highway and was now in pursuit.

David's heart and mind were racing. How in the world did he get caught? Was the Party monitoring this particular teller machine, or had he been followed since he left his apartment? Did they have an officer waiting all day and night for him, waiting to see when and where he would use the cards? Or was he followed? This particular machine hadn't been visited in almost a month. Maybe someone from the national police noticed him buying the truck?

All of the possible scenarios for how and why he was caught was running through his mind, and he increased his speed, heading north and away from town. The police officer was close behind him, and the siren was now blaring its distinctive sound. David glanced at the speedometer, and he was already traveling almost 80 miles per hour. Out loud, David said, "Let's see if this thing is as fast as the man said it would be," and he pressed down harder on the gas pedal, watching the speed increase until he was doing a shade over 100 miles an hour. In the rearview mirror, David could see the police car was having a hard time keeping up with this speed. Luckily for David, the budget for the local police in the red zone hadn't kept pace with the blue zone. Most of the red zone police cars were worn-out older models, and thankfully, they were slower.

David had to reduce his speed as the roads were starting to curve around the mountains, and he was trying to think of an escape route. The area north of town was very unfamiliar to him. He had only been up here once, when he went to look at the cabin. If there wasn't a opportunity to lose the officer, he could make a dash for the woods, and probably beat him in a foot race. For the past fifteen years when he traveled, his nightly workout involved running for thirty minutes a day or longer. David hoped this guy didn't fit the typical stereotype of a police officer, and was a little heavy and maybe even past his prime.

As David looked in the mirror, he noticed he separated himself from the officer by a good distance, and was wondering how long it would take before they sent out the drones or the helicopters. Police chases like this were a big hit on television, as they almost always ended with a drone or a helicopter taking out the car in pursuit. The first option was to release a small mini-drone nicknamed a "shocker", which would fly to the car and attach itself and then provide a directional electrical shock to disable the engine. If the car was an older model, with the body still mostly made out of metal, every so often, the shock would be too great and it would electrocute the driver. If that happened, the car would go out of control and crash. If the shock didn't work, and if the driver was known to the police and had a criminal past, then the drones would use small missiles to take out the car and the driver. Those scenarios certainly made for good television. And once a drone or a helicopter was involved, there was always video for the news, crash or no crash. Quite often, they would interrupt the regular programming to show these chases in progress.

David was still trying to determine what to do, scanning the skies every chance he could, when he saw a dirt road up ahead. Susan mentioned the dirt roads were used by the forestry service, and they could run for miles into the woods. These roads may be the only way to lose this police car. David slammed on the brakes, and skidded as he left the main highway and started down one of the dirt roads. As he accelerated, red dust from the road filled the air behind him. The blue lights were attempting to penetrate the clouds, but he couldn't make out the form of the police car, and there was no way to determine how much of a lead he held at this point.

The road started to become curvy, and David couldn't go more than thirty or forty miles per hour, before he would have to slam on the brakes to slow down and take a turn. He was hoping this truck was a much better vehicle for traveling down this type of road than the officer's sedan. And the canopy of the trees was getting thicker, which would make it harder for any Party aircraft to spot him. The road started getting bumpy, and was filled with various-sized rocks which had fallen from the hill next to the road. It was apparent that this road probably hadn't been used in a while, but the rocks could be to his advantage. The truck was lifted high enough to miss the rocks, but the police car might not be so lucky.

The road straightened, and David could now see a large stream to the right of the road. As he increased his speed, the road ahead appeared to come to a dead end. He quickly slowed down and the truck skidded to a stop, with the dust catching up and passing him. Checking the rear view mirror, he was unable to see any blue lights behind him, but he was positive the police car was still in pursuit. As the dust cleared, he could see that the road made a sharp turn to the right and down a small hill, and continued through the stream onto the other side. Turning the truck to the right, he inched the truck forward, until the front tires were now in the water. The stream was flowing very fast, and he couldn't see any white caps from where the water flowed over any rocks. David assumed the water was deep, but there was no way to know how deep. The faint noise of a siren was growing louder, and as he looked down the stream to his right, the blue lights were visible off in the distance, breaking through the dissipating dirt clouds.

David's two choices at this point were to either make a run for it on foot, or to try and drive through the stream. Putting the truck into a lower gear, he gradually moved into the water. The truck made it about halfway when it suddenly dropped down, and water began to seep into the cab. The front of the truck started moving to the left, before lurching downstream for a foot or two. He gave the truck more gas, and thought for a second he might have floated, but the tires found the bottom of the stream and the truck jerked forward. David eased up on the gas, and drove the truck up the small bank to the other the side of the stream.

David could see the road continued straight for about a hundred meters before turning, and he continued down the road as far as he could until he could barely see the area where the stream was located. Looking back, he could see the police car enter the water. The officer started into the water slowly, and as he entered the middle of the stream, the rushing current suddenly lifted the front of the car and moved it to the left. The car began to float and turn, until the entire car was pointing downstream, where it traveled for a meter or two before coming to a stop. David guessed the car must have hit a rock or a log. The officer climbed out of the driver's window and onto the top of the police car. He was soaking wet, but still managed to draw his pistol and aim down the road towards David. As soon as David saw the weapon, he stomped on the gas, and the cop fired his gun until it was empty. Luckily for David, the cop's aim was way off, or maybe he barely missed him.

David advanced down the road as fast as possible, while scanning the skies for aircraft. The treetops were still thick, but David estimated he didn't have long until they sent a drone or a helicopter, or even a search team for him. After about ten minutes, he saw what appeared to be an old road veering off to the right. The path appeared as if it hadn't been used in a long time, as it was covered in leaves with small bushes growing over the edges and in the center of the lane. He directed the truck down the road, and kept going until the road ended in a thicket of bushes. David shut off the engine, and sat there. His heart was thumping in his chest, and he noticed after he removed his hands from the steering wheel, they were shaking. The only course of action was to continue on foot.

David grabbed his bug-out bag, and opened it to make sure it was one of his completed kits. The bag contained a liter bottle of water, a water-purifying straw, an emergency thermal blanket, a small mess kit, parachute cord, a towel, a camping knife and a fire starter kit, along with the remainder of the money from the truck purchase. The *Guide* recommended always traveling with a bug-out bag, and to always have a sizable amount of cash with you, in case you have to go on the run.

David thought it was a silly idea to take the bag with him today. He had procrastinated on making his bags, but now he was certainly grateful to have one. He would have to hurry and make his way on foot. If you were being chased by the Party, they usually caught you. They had the drones and the helicopters and he was certain they had a good map of the area and his capture was only a matter of time.

David removed the towel from the bag, added water from his water bottle, and wiped down the steering wheel, the dash, and all of the controls. He wasn't sure if the towel would remove all of his fingerprints, or if there would be any DNA for them to find. The towel and water were shoved back in his bag, and he hopped out of the truck. Locking the doors with the key fob, he was in motion to throw the keys into the bushes when he decided to hide them, in the odd case they wouldn't find the vehicle and he come back for it later. David searched the ground until he found a rock the size of a dinner plate. Flipping the rock over, he dug a little impression in the dirt with his heel, and placed the keys in the hole. Returning the rock to its original position, he covered it with leaves, and marked the location by a dead pine tree a few feet away. The tree would be used to help remember which rock concealed the keys, even though there weren't many other similar rocks around.

He took out his prepaid phone, and it was still turned off. Even with the GPS chip disabled, he kept the phone off when he was away from his house, and was relieved they would not be able to track him by this phone. To be certain, he opened the back and removed the battery. The highway should be to his west, but he wasn't sure which way was west, as the sun was directly overhead. A quick scan of the woods revealed he was in a flat area between two small mountains. He decided to head to the top of one of the mountains, to provide a better vantage point in order to see a road or a landmark. Being closer to the top of a mountain would possibly make him more visible to any aircraft, but this was his best option. Either way, he already spent four or five minutes here, and that was too long, it was time to move.

After three hours of walking, David almost made it to the top of the mountain. When he first started, the mountain didn't seem to be far away, but he had to make his way through thick bushes and briars which blocked his path. Since the sun had moved along in the sky, he could determine his direction was definitely heading west. Numerous planes passed overhead, but he hadn't heard the unmistakable sounds of a drone or helicopter. Making his way over to the west side of the mountain, he imagined he could hear the sound of cars in the distance. Even with the shade of the trees, the air was brutally hot and humid, and walking through the woods was much different than running on a treadmill, so a break was in order. Taking his water bottle out of his bag, he quickly drank half of it. He resolved to not stop for more than ten or fifteen minutes, as he needed to find a way out of the woods before nightfall. After the brief rest, he headed down the mountain in the direction of where he thought the highway would be located. Once he was near the highway, he could then stay hidden in the woods and continue to head south. He didn't have a plan for how he was going to get back home, or even if he should go home. The Party was certainly going to be waiting for him. At least there was plenty of time to think about what to do.

Chapter 19

David hiked for nearly two and a half hours when he finally heard the distinct sound of vehicles. The highway was just beyond a small valley which rose to a ridge line, and he could see the tops of the cars as they drove past. Climbing back up the mountain but away from the highway, he stopped when he was even with the road and sat down behind a large oak tree, and leaned against the wide trunk. He was tired and his feet were sore and tender. Drinking his water, he watched the cars drive by, fully expecting to see a patrol car pass. The assumption was they were still looking for him, but the traffic was mostly trucks and the occasional motorcycle. Despite his open view of the highway, he couldn't make out enough of the road to even try to determine his location. After waiting for a half-hour, he continued his southward direction, keeping a safe distance between his path and the road. The daylight would be gone in an hour or two, and he wasn't going to stop until it was too dark to see.

The sun finally set behind the top of a mountain, and he estimated there was about twenty or thirty minutes left of daylight. The path was now flat, and as he made his way through a large field of overgrown bushes and thorns, he could see a building in the distance. The building wasn't on the main highway, but on a side road which intersected the highway. David was tired and extremely thirsty and hungry. The water was depleted an hour ago, but his bag, which was light at the start of his journey, now felt like it weighed twenty kilograms. There was some consideration to dropping it, but its discovery might provide the search team with evidence.

The temperature had fallen, but the wind had increased, and the idea of sleeping in the woods didn't seem feasible. An alternative plan would be to wait until the store closed, and sleep behind it. An assortment of wooden crates and pallets was lazily stacked near a dumpster, and he wondered if it might be possible to create a small shelter, with the hope it wasn't trash-collection night. The pain in his stomach was getting sharper, and it had been gurgling for the past hour. There was no other option but to take a chance and see what kind of store it was, as food and water seemed to be more important than not getting apprehended.

David nervously made his way around the building to the front, and only saw two cars in the small unpaved parking lot. He determined it was a convenience store, with a small stand on the side for selling fruits and vegetables. David attempted to scan the outside of the building for cameras, but he really didn't care if any were present. Given the size of the store and the location, he was pretty confident this type of place didn't have any cameras. Cameras might be used inside for security purposes, but there weren't any other options. Opening the door, he walked inside, and observed an old man sitting behind the register, reading a tabloid magazine. A customer dressed in blue overalls was over to the side, playing a gambling machine. These machines were legal in the red zone, and were usually how most of these smaller stores made any money, since the payout was very low and the odds were heavily stacked in their favor.

David made his way to the back of the store, and found the bottled water in a large cooler. He immediately grabbed a liter bottle, and was thankful it was cold. Opening it, he quickly drank a third of the bottle, before stopping to catch his breath. He was almost too tired to drink, and the cold water caused an immediate and painful headache. Before replacing the cap, he scanned the other refrigerated coolers, where he spotted a row of bagged sandwiches. Most of the sandwiches wore expiration dates from last month or prior, but he located one which only expired last week, and he decided to take a chance. With a simple sandwich, he readily accepted the fact that if the food was spoiled, the worse outcome was he might vomit later. His shirt was covered in sweat, which leaked down the back of his jeans, and he still had on his hat, but removed the sunglasses. If the police had visited the store, there was a chance the old man would be on the lookout for someone in his condition, and they might have even left a flyer behind. At this point, he didn't care.

Approaching the checkout area, he placed the items on the counter, near the register. The old man put down his magazine and scanned the prices for the sandwich and bottle of water. As David reached for his wallet, he noticed a phone behind the man with a handwritten sign which read "Local calls - pay per minute," and David had an idea.

"I need to use your phone," he said as he handed the guy a hundred. "And what is your address here?" The old man reached under the counter, and retrieved a book of matches. He flipped the matchbook over, put it on the counter and slid it towards David. On the back was the name of the store and the address. The old man grabbed the phone and placed it on the counter. David quickly found and removed Stephanie's business card from his wallet. Calling her was going to be a big risk. If the Party was after him, they might have contacted her or she might know about it, and she probably wouldn't be in a position to warn him. With her loyalty to the Party, if she knew what happened and if they had contacted her, she might not even consider helping him. David might be a traitor in her eyes, worthy of whatever punishment was to be given. Or, they might simply be listening to her phone calls, waiting to see if he would call her for help. He could only hope that if they were listening, and if they told her what happened, he could possibly tell by the sound of her voice. He stumbled over to the side of the store and dialed her cell phone number.

Stephanie was single, and like the other single girls involved with the Party, she spent most of her free time on the weekends volunteering. These Party-volunteer functions included events such as a protest, a parade, writing nasty letters to the few remaining private companies, or handing out literature. Stephanie usually spent her weekends at the local Party headquarters in whatever capacity was required. She rarely dated, and like David's ex-wife, had her sights set on an older Party member. And since the ratio of young and willing women to older and available Party members was fairly high, Party members certainly held the advantage, and they utilized it as often as possible.

Stephanie participated all morning and afternoon at a protest against one of the last remaining private grocery stores in the blue zone. The cause for picketing was for no other reason than the store carried non-national produce, meaning they sold produce grown on the few remaining non-Party farms. After inundating farmers and food stores with an endless stream of regulations, the majority of both industries folded or were about to go out of business. The only way to stay alive was to join the Party's National Grower's Union and become a member of the national grocery cooperatives. The cooperatives were subjected to a different set of regulations, which were more relaxed, and their businesses were even subsidized by the Party. Though most of the farms were located in the red zone, anything related to private ownership was considered evil, in the eyes of the Party and their followers.

She stayed outside at the protest all day, even in the blistering heat. Now, with the evening being a little cooler, she was out for a jog. Her apartment complex was expansive, and she could get in a good workout simply by running around the parking lot. Even though the property was Party-owned, she didn't feel safe jogging at night, and would time her run so she was finished as the sun was setting, and the area wouldn't be too dark. She was finishing her run and was in front of her apartment when the music from her device was interrupted by her phone ringing. She stopped running, reached down to grab the phone off her waist and tapped the answer button. In between deep breaths, she was able to gasp out a weak, "Hello?"

David heard someone say hello, but it sounded unsteady and forced, so he didn't say anything in return. After a few seconds of silence, Stephanie repeated herself, but this time she wasn't as out of breath.

"Hello?"

David finally replied. "Stephanie? This is David."

Stephanie's eyes widened. "David, hi! Sorry about that, I was finishing my run, and I was out of breath. I could barely talk."

Her statement made David a bit nervous. "Run?"

"Yes, I was jogging, and I was right near my building, about to head upstairs when the phone rang."

David speculated her reply could be a plausible explanation, but he really couldn't tell anything from her voice. "Stephanie, I need a big favor. I need a ride. Can you go inside and let me give you the address of where I am?"

Stephanie was already moving up the stairs towards her apartment. Waving a fob in front of the door, it unlocked and she darted inside. "Sure David, give me a minute." As David waited, he was attempting to hear if there were any other voices in the background.

Stephanie came back on the line. "Okay David, go ahead with the address." David gave her the address, and she said she could use her phone for directions, and she would be there right away.

Before she could hang up, David asked, "Stephanie, what kind of car do you have?"

"It is a little white enviro car, two-door."

The description sounded exactly like the same type of car he used to drive with his old job. "Okay Stephanie, I will see you soon. I really appreciate this. Thanks." David ended the call and handed the phone back to the old man, who looked at the clock on the wall, and handed him his change. David asked him if he could wait outside, and the old man said there was a picnic table on the other side of the fruit stand. As he left the store, David wondered why every convenience store in this area came with a picnic table.

Chapter 20

After almost an hour and a half of painful waiting, David watched a small white two-door car pull into the parking lot. The store was closed, and the area was dark, due to the absence of street lights anywhere on the road. The store's sole outside light flickered above the entrance, radiating a tired and a dirty-yellow glow. David had been studying the road, and he didn't see any evidence of anyone following Stephanie. Her car was too small for another person to be hiding inside. Perhaps the Party hadn't approached her yet and was waiting for him at his apartment. The next course of action was being deliberated, but he needed to return to the blue zone and be closer to his apartment, as well as the money hidden in the woods behind his place.

If he didn't appear right away, there was a chance she might drive off, so he walked away from the picnic table, staying in the shadows and close to the fruit stand. Stephanie was watching the building, when a figure came out of the darkness, and she rolled down her window enough to be able to hear the outside. His face was tough to see at first, but when she recognized him, she yelled with enthusiasm, "David!" He gave her a little wave as he crossed in front of her car, and he continued to look around, as he walked over to the passenger's side. Before opening the door, he peeked in, and confirmed there wasn't anyone else in the car.

"Hello there. It is really good to see you." Turning around, he backed his body into the tiny car, and bumped his left knee on the dashboard. Stephanie quickly turned the car around, and started heading down the road, back towards the blue zone.

"Stephanie, I really appreciate you coming all the way out here to get me. I really, really owe you one." He was working on a reason, an alibi, for why he was out here. She probably wouldn't even ask, and he really didn't owe her an explanation, but he felt he should say something.

"I was on one of those tours of one of the parks when I got lost from the tour group, deep in the woods. I had been walking for a while, but my phone didn't have a signal, so I turned it off to save the battery. I finally stumbled upon this old store, and the man was nice enough to let me use the phone. I would have called a cab, but..."

Stephanie cut him off mid-sentence. "David, it isn't a problem. You don't have to tell me what you were doing. I just finished my run, and I was about to come in for the night anyway. No problem, I am glad to help. Sorry if I might smell a bit, but I didn't even take time to get a shower."

David took a quiet but deep breath through his nose, and he couldn't smell anything. Or at least he couldn't smell anything unacceptable. He imagined she probably smelled like fresh-cut flowers when she sweated.

"Don't worry about it, you smell fine to me." He reprimanded himself and thought, "You idiot. Don't say that."

Despite the rule against asking for personal details from a Party member, Stephanie's curiosity was hard to contain. "So you were lost, huh? That must have been horrible. If you want, I will call the tour company on Monday and get you a refund. They should have a policy in place to make sure people don't get lost, especially out here in the red zone. The crazy people out here could have shot you, or robbed you and left you for dead."

David chuckled inside. Her premonition was what all blue zone residents thought about red zone residents. They think the red zone people are a bunch of hicks who shoot people on sight, or knife them in the back if the chance is presented. David wondered if he could help change her mind. Doubtful, but maybe he could.

"It isn't bad here. Don't believe everything you hear on the news. Everyone I have met so far has been very nice."

Stephanie retorted with a sarcastic, "So far," as if the next person who passed them was going to run their car off the road and kill them for no reason. David decided to change the subject, and get back to what was really important, to try and see if she had been contacted yet.

"Anyway, thanks again for the ride. You really saved me here. I have been gone most of the day, has anything exciting happened?"

Stephanie started telling David about her day, about the protest, how many people were there, and the signs they made the previous weekend. And how they threw rotten fruit and small rocks at a truck delivering produce from a private farm in the red zone. While most of the Party protests were non-violent, they didn't see anything wrong with a little fruit or rock-throwing from time to time. And as she drove, Stephanie poured over every little detail of what happened, and the stories her group shared of their past protests. Stephanie was really proud of her involvement with these demonstrations, and she could remember in great detail what happened at each one. As she rambled on, David was trying to determine if this was nervous talk, as if she was hiding the fact that there was a man or a group of men back at his place, ready to hit him over the head and make him vanish. Or perhaps they already contacted her, and she agreed to help, and the men were waiting back at her place.

As they drove south, the more he considered what the Party would possibly do in a situation like this, the more he decided she hadn't been contacted yet. The Party would much rather take down a target out in the red zone, in the middle of nowhere, in a place where they could shoot David in the head, and then blame it on a red zone hillbilly. And besides, back at the office, when given the chance, she talked non-stop as well. If she was nervous, if she knew what happened, she would probably be quiet and subdued. Plus, in his mind, he thought she might have a small crush on him. He had been taking her to lunch almost every day, and she acted like it was her birthday every time. Several times, he interpreted her comments as light flirting, but he wasn't positive, only because he simply wanted it to be flirting. If she had been contacted, she might have tried to warn him or said an unusual statement as a sign. If the car was bugged, she could pass him a note, or mouth some words. But she continued talking.

As they passed the border of the blue zone, Stephanie finally asked, "Where is your apartment? Where do we need to go?" David hesitated when he heard the question, wondering why she would need to know this information, until he remembered she was giving him a ride home. Before he could answer, she said, "I live in the Tivoli apartments, which is right off this next exit." She said that as she pointed to a green road sign which read, "Tivoli Road - Next Exit."

Was this a suggestion? Were the police back at his house, and Stephanie was trying to tell him he shouldn't go home? Or was she saying this for no reason? Either way, David decided maybe it was better if he could avoid going to his place.

"Oh really? I would love to see your place."

Stephanie didn't move her head, but her eyes darted towards him and back onto the road, and she cracked a mischievous smile. "Okay, I can give you a quick tour, but the place is a little messy. I usually try to clean it on Sunday night, when I have free time. And I haven't cleaned it in a while."

David acknowledged he might be taking a big chance with this move. The men could be waiting for him at her place, but something inside kept telling him she had not been contacted yet. Maybe he could stay there until he figured out what to do. He really didn't have any other options at this point.

Stephanie became quiet, and stopped telling the protest stories, as if she became shy all of a sudden. David didn't know what to think. Instead of acting bashful, was she really nervous about what was waiting at her apartment? Or was it because her place was really messy? It was too late to change his mind, so he decided to keep an eye out for any large black cars, and then he remembered the drones. Leaning over towards his window, he peered up in the sky, straining to see if he could detect the flashing lights of any aircraft. Perhaps there was a drone, one of the smaller and silent kinds, following him back to her place. His paranoia kicked in again. Maybe this wasn't the best idea after all.

Stephanie pulled into her complex, and they silently waited while the large iron gates opened. Most of the residences inside the blue zone were owned by the Party, and if you worked for the national government, you more than likely lived in a Party-owned apartment, townhouse or condominium. If you were in the Outer or Inner circle, then you definitely stayed at a Party-owned place. But, the higher your ranking within the Party, the nicer your residence would be. Party members were still allowed to own second homes, such as a beach house or mountain cabin, but your main home was usually owned by the Party, due to the Party-backed mortgages. The Party enjoyed having control over the place where you lived, even if their only hold on you was through a debt. A little control was better than no control.

David was still scanning the parking lot, and glancing up in the air when

Stephanie pulled into a parking space. She turned off the car, and turned towards David. "Ready?"

David's voice cracked. "Yes."

They each opened their doors, and David expected a group of men to appear from nowhere and tackle him to the ground. Or maybe they would just shoot both of them. But as he stepped out of the car, nothing happened. He stood there for a moment, with the car door open and one leg still in the car, as if he could jump back in for protection. Stephanie was already several meters away from the back of the car, when she stopped and turned around.

"David, are you okay?"

David snapped out of his trance. "Oh sorry, yes. I was looking at the building. It's very nice. It looks a little like my place." He reluctantly closed the door and followed her to the building and up the stairs.

Stephanie opened her apartment door, and as they entered the small foyer, David noticed the air inside was nice and cold, compared to the muggy weather he had been enduring all day. The air conditioner in her car was like his old car, as it only provided air just slightly colder than what was inside the car. But there wasn't anything wrong with the air conditioner in her apartment, which caused him to wonder how much her electric bills were each month, and if she was somehow getting around the usage quota. During the summer, he kept his thermostat on eighty, which kept him well within the monthly electricity ration. During lean times it was set on eighty-two, and ration or not, he could barely afford either setting. David walked into the main area, and took a look around the room. Her apartment was almost exactly like his. There was a small living room, a kitchen over to the right of the door, and then a small hallway which probably led to the bathroom and a bedroom. As he walked in, Stephanie closed and locked the door.

As he was continuing his survey of the room, Stephanie said, "Make yourself at home. The remote is probably hidden in the cushions on the couch. If you want, you can watch a little TV. I desperately need to take a shower. If you need anything to drink, I think I have some mineral water in the fridge." She glanced at the small clock on the side table next to the couch. "It is almost twenty-two, you can watch the news if you want. They might have coverage of our protest." She said the last line proudly.

David's eyes widened. Why didn't he think about this before? The news might mention or have video of his car chase, and he could possibly find out the status of his situation. Maybe they hadn't identified him yet, after all, he just bought the truck. The only way they could know it was him is if they were aware of the teller cards. Every police car was equipped with a camera, but David was so far away, maybe they didn't get a good view at him, and the facial-recognition software failed. It was possible they could have used the mini-sat video images to backtrack the scene and then identify him, but that takes a lot of work. The mini-sats were usually reserved for investigating terrorist activities. Or that is what the public was told.

The mini-sats were miniature surveillance satellites the Party placed in orbit. The exact size or number of these satellites was not made public, but the rumor was they deployed thousands of them, maybe even tens of thousands, orbiting the earth and recording everything happening in every major city. The video was constantly streamed to collection stations, where members of the Party's Internal Safety Division could retrieve almost-live video of most anywhere in the country. The resolution was so high it had been stated they could even read the Party's newspaper from space. After a terrorist attack, the national police would review the video, and rewind the action to find out where the terrorists originated from, and even find out what apartment they lived in. Then it was up to the national police to go to the site and look for evidence, or more terrorists.

David wondered if his chase was shown already on the previous news shows, since it happened so early in the day. But the media and the public loved a good car chase, even if it didn't result in a crash or anyone being killed, so there was a chance the story and video would be repeated on the later news programs. The odds were greater if they didn't have another, more violent and exciting video to report. Stephanie walked into the back, and David sat down on the couch. Like she said, the remote was hiding between two cushions, so he found it and turned on the TV, and changed the channel to the local news station. Glancing down at his watch, the news would be on in less than three minutes. His heartbeat was echoing in his ears.

If he was on the news, and if identification was made, he would only have a little time, so he started planning his next move. If they knew it was him, then he couldn't stay here. Stephanie would need to be convinced to loan him her car in order to get back home, and he would promise to return it tomorrow. The car could be left outside his complex, possibly at the nearby convenience store. He would then attempt to sneak into the complex, and go outside behind his place, to the woods where he buried his jars of money. Once the money was secured, he would drive back up to the red zone, and when it was daylight, there might be a chance to convince an older person to rent him a room, until he could figure out what to do next. This was the only option he imagined would work.

As he was contemplating all of the details, the local news theme began to play, and the screen displayed the list of anchors with their smiling faces, and his heart was about to explode. This was it, this was the moment of truth. The camera panned the news desk and another one finally settled on one of the anchors, a very attractive woman with a head of large blonde hair.

"Good evening. I am Danielle Pearson, filling in for Andrea Robinson tonight. Our top story of the evening is an update on the Prosperity Benefits scandal involving four members of the top level of the Inner Circle. Earlier today, the National Investigative Truth Bureau was seeking answers as to why..."

David turned down the volume, as he really didn't want to hear anything about another Party scandal. A simple car chase wouldn't make it as the top news story, unless the person being chased was killed or something exploded, and then only if they had clear video of it happening. Since he didn't watch much local news, he wasn't sure how long it would be until they possibly showed his chase, or if they would even show it. Painfully, he watched as the anchors mouthed the news stories, and was desperately trying to think of an alternate plan for escape, if his primary plan failed. After the first commercial break, the camera opened back on the blonde anchor. David turned up the volume to hear her say "...a dramatic car chase through the red zone mountains." And then, as she was speaking, grainy video from the police car, showing David's truck driving down the highway and along the mountain road, appeared on the screen.

"Earlier today, a Konah Sheriff's deputy was involved in a high speed chase near the Mount Konah National Forest. The deputy reported the chase involved speeds of over one hundred miles per hour. The suspect took the deputy on a run down a winding mountain road, until the deputy finally lost the suspect when the deputy's car became stuck in a mountain stream. The officer was able to shoot at the fleeing vehicle, and you can hear the gunshots, but the suspect and the suspect's vehicle were gone." David closed his eyes for a second. This was it. He was finished. David immediately felt nauseous, and the sandwich from the convenience store was working its way back up his throat.

The anchor continued. "Three hours later, members of the National Protection Team caught up with the suspect and surrounded his house. The suspect, identified as twenty-four year old Matthew Ward Davis, was inside this house." The video switched to a view from either a drone or a helicopter. The camera zoomed in so you could see the huge armored vehicles, the police cars, the officers with their body armor and assault rifles drawn, and of course, the small house which offered very little protection to the people inside.

"As the Protection Team approached the house, you can hear several gunshots. It seems the suspect opened fire on the team, who then immediately returned fire."

You could now hear dozens of muffled gunshots coming from the television speakers. The armed men were all walking slowly towards the house. It appeared as if most of the officers emptied their guns, as many were reloading as they walked.

The anchor was back on the television. "After less than fifteen seconds, the gunfire stopped, and the officers deployed several stun grenades into the house through a window, and then the Protection Team stormed the house. Mr. Davis, who was wanted on several failure-to-appear warrants, was a known moonshiner and petty thief. He had an extensive criminal record, and he was pronounced dead at the scene. Thankfully, no Protection Officers or onlookers were hurt from the gunfire. Here is a look inside the house, at this grisly scene." The video was now showing the dark insides of the house, riddled with bullet holes, the air full of dust and smoke, and the sunshine peeking in through the holes in the walls. And of course, the video made sure to stop and focus on the young man who sold David the car. His body was near a window, with broken glass and splinters of wood all around. His clothes, along with the carpet around his body, were stained red with blood.

Danielle now turned to the other anchor. "Wow. Wasn't that exciting, Jim? It goes to show you, living in the red zone can be hazardous to your health." Both anchors laughed. The screen switched to the male anchor, Jim, who was announcing another Party scandal, where a married Party member was caught with several underage girls in a non-Party hotel room.

David hit the mute button and sat there, in a daze, trying to figure out what happened here. Did the police confuse him for this man named Matt? David then remembered the car title. He reached into his pocket for his wallet, opened it, and pulled out the folded piece of paper. He was now kicking himself for not destroying it or leaving it with the vehicle, even though he never signed it. He unfolded it and looked at the name on the title, and although the signature was illegible, yes, the owner's name was "Matthew W. Davis." Did he just dodge a major bullet? He chuckled softly, and then said to himself, "No pun intended." Did the police chase him only because he was in this guy's truck? Maybe the chase had nothing to do with the teller machines and nothing to do with the Party. Perhaps this guy simply sold his car and was preparing to get out of town, or go into hiding, or pay overdue court fines. David's entire body felt lighter, as if a huge weight was being lifted off him. There was a good chance he had nothing to worry about after all. His relief was so great, his mind didn't even contemplate the need to have any compassion for this dead man.

David's body sunk back into the couch, and his mind went blank. All of the escape scenarios he had been thinking about were gone. A flood of satisfaction ran through his body, and even though his mind instantly calmed down, his heart was still pounding away in his chest. He continued to stare at the television screen, watching as another woman presented the weather, and he really didn't know what to do next.

With David's eyes glued to the television set, Stephanie walked slowly into the room, wearing a thin pink bathrobe tied tightly around her waist, and with a towel in one hand, drying her hair. She sat next to David on the couch.

"Why is it muted? Did they show anything about the protest yet?" Her voice woke David up from his stupor.

"Uh, not yet, they were going over the weather. I think it will be a nice day tomorrow."

Stephanie frowned. "Bummer. If they are already at the weather, the next thing is sports and then the stupid economy. They probably won't cover it. I didn't think they would. I didn't see any news trucks down there anyway. I was hoping they would have picked up the video we shot and sent to the media person at the Party headquarters." She leaned her body over, so her face was in front of his, in an attempt to redirect his gaze away from the television and towards her. "Would you like a glass of wine?"

Wine? Yes. David desperately needed a drink. Even though he was in the clear, and his mind somewhat adjusted to the fact he would not die tonight, his heart and nerves had yet to respond to what happened. He took a quick look at her, before leaning to the right, and turning his eyes back onto the television. "Yes, sure, wine sounds good. Thanks." His mind was void of any awareness, and he didn't notice she was in a bathrobe, or that her long blondish-brown hair was still a bit damp. Stephanie hopped up and went into the kitchen.

From behind the counter she asked, "Are you hungry? Would you like some cheese and crackers? I received my dairy ration yesterday, and I stopped on the way home after the protest and spent it all on cheese. This is the real deal, not the fake-processed junk. I bought Camembert and goat cheese. I really love goat cheese. I could almost eat this as a meal by itself. I was barely able to get a half-pound of each, but it is worth it. The fake stuff is so horrible, I don't know why they even make it, or who would even want to eat it."

Dairy products were in short supply, along with beef and pork. Most of the corn normally destined for animal feed was being diverted to the Party's Green Energy Initiative, where they would produce ethanol from the corn and paper and cardboard from the stalks. The scarcity of animal feed caused the price of items like milk, butter, cheese, bacon, ham and steaks to be extremely high. The prices and demand were so inflated that these products were rationed in the blue zone, via the cooperative shopper member cards. Each co-op tracked everything you purchased, and the stores wouldn't allow you to go over your allotted quota. A person could always travel to the red zone, and take a chance on whatever dairy products were produced there, but very few staunch Party members or supporters ever did.

David's churning stomach didn't really need the wine, much less the cheese or crackers. But he was hoping maybe the wine would help to calm his nerves, even though the sandwich he ate earlier still wasn't agreeing with him. And he didn't like to turn down free alcohol, but he decided cheese might not be a good idea. "I believe I will have to take a pass on the cheese, but I will take a glass of wine."

Stephanie smiled and poured the wine into two old jelly jars, almost filling each one. She went back into the living room. "Sorry I don't have real wine glasses. I bought a set last year, but they were cheap and the dishwasher cracked them after four or five washes. I like these old jelly jars anyway, they are nice and thick and they hold more wine." She let out a bit of a chuckle, handed David his wine, and took her place back on the couch next to him. She held out her glass for a toast. "To the Party."

David was taken aback by her toast, especially since it was combined with her smiling face. But having her next to him brought a little comfort from this day of madness. Raising his glass up to hers, he reluctantly repeated, "To the Party."

Stephanie took the remote from his hand, and turned up the volume, still hoping they would mention her protest. She really wanted the news program to show the video of her hurling fruit and rocks at the delivery truck. She had this fantasy that if she could only make it on the news, a member high up in the Party would see her, and then either invite her to join the Party, or take a romantic interest in her. But the newscast didn't mention any protests, and she was disappointed.

David almost gulped down his wine, and he really needed it to go to work, in order to calm his nerves. The aftertaste was a little sour, but he didn't care. Since he wasn't much of a drinker, he could feel the effects almost immediately. The wine reminded him of his last meeting with Tim, when they shared the whiskey. He glanced over at Stephanie's glass, and she barely made a dent in her wine. As the wine went to work, he was still trying to think of what to do next. Despite what he saw on the television, he wanted to go home, to make sure no one was waiting for him. Even though he assumed he was in the clear, he wanted to be positive. He wanted to be able to sleep knowing he wasn't going to be shot in the head from behind.

Neither one of them talked during the remaining part of the news. David was still leaning back on the sofa, and Stephanie as well, but she also drifted a bit in his direction. She moved closer to him and was sitting sideways, with her feet on the couch, and the short bathrobe barely covered her thighs, but he didn't notice. His eyes were still fixated on the television, as these thoughts ran through his head. After the news, a rerun of a comedy show came on the television. They watched it through the first commercial break before Stephanie took a series of rapid small sips to finish her wine.

She stood up, and reached out her hand to David. "Are you ready for the tour?" David turned towards her, and finally noticed she was in a bathrobe, but given his mental state, he still didn't think anything about it. She took his hand, and he moved off the couch.

"Follow me." She led him down the narrow hallway, stopping in front of the bathroom door, before twirling around and pressing her back against the wall, and pointing to her left.

"Here is the bathroom." David gave it a quick glance, before she spun around and went into the bedroom, still holding his hand. "And here is the bedroom." She shuffled in and to the right, and let go of David's hand, before moving over to stand in front of the closet doors. David continued his slow walk, and stood at the foot of the bed. The room reminded him of a girls' dorm room in college. On the wall were pictures of Party-supporting celebrities and posters of Inner Circle Party members and other political groups he didn't recognize. The bed was almost too large for the room, and was covered with a thick-pinkish comforter, numerous frilly pillows and a white pillow in the shape of a cat. As he stood there, his head was floating, and he could definitely feel the effects of the wine.

David's eyes kept darting around, trying to fixate on one thing at a time, as if there would be a test later of what he had seen. He heard her say, "Well, what do you think?" He politely nodded his head. "It looks very nice. I like the posters, and I like what you've, uh, done with the place."

Stephanie giggled. "No silly, I wasn't talking about the room."

David didn't understand what she meant by her last remark. Turning his head towards her, he could see she dropped her bathrobe.

"I was talking about me."

David was silent as he stared at her, with his mouth slightly open and a dumbfounded look on his face. Her body was amazing, thin and athletic, and in incredible shape. The wine was really playing with his head. His mind ran through a series of a dozen thoughts in less than a second, but given his current state, his brain couldn't process what was happening, the situation was too much of a shock. Her smiling face turned serious, and her eyes were staring directly into his. She softly repeated "Well? What do you think?"

The only response David could muster was a soft, "Wow." He stepped over, and closed the door.

The next morning, David woke up and was disoriented, as if last night was a dream, and he couldn't remember where he was. He held his left wrist up, searching for his watch, but it wasn't there. Leaning up, he peeked over a large mass of hair towards the alarm clock, and the time was only six-fourteen. His head softly fell back on the pillow, and his face landed on her hair. He moved the hair aside with his left hand and rubbed his head into the pillow. His right arm was positioned under her pillow and her head, and he was more or less trapped, but it wasn't like he wanted to leave. The temperature in the apartment felt colder than last night, and the presence of her body was nice and warm under the sheets.

He attempted to recall what happened, why he was there, why she gave herself to him. The last time he was in this situation, in bed with a woman, in a cold room with a warm body beside him, was almost a distant memory. The feeling of laying in bed with her, of spending the night here was almost as pleasurable as the main act. Waking up with a woman in bed next to you and having their body touch yours was an incredible pleasure in itself. He wondered how long he could stay here, enjoying her warmth, before she moved away or left the bed. There was no need to get out of bed, no where to go, and he was certainly going to try and prolong this bliss. He closed his eyes, but he didn't want to go back to sleep, he wanted to continue to enjoy the intensity of her body.

She moved a little, almost like a twitch, and he opened his eyes again. He was still on his side, facing her back, and she scooted towards him until every part of their bodies seemed to melt together, as if they were one body under the sheets. His eyes drifted shut again, and he tried not to move, when she rolled her body over and faced him. Her movement caused the covers to raise enough to let in a nice draft of cool air. She snuggled close to him, with her head below his, and she wrapped one of her arms around his waist.

She mumbled, "Good morning."

David didn't say anything. He didn't know if he should pretend to be asleep, so this moment wouldn't end, but ignoring her probably wasn't the best move. He finally decided to respond. "Good morning."

Stephanie started lightly stroking his back with her right hand, and he was enjoying her touch as her fingernails gently scratched his skin. She then moved her hand around his waist to touch him. With her eyes still closed, she smiled. "And it appears as if someone else is having a good morning as well."

David grinned, and he thought "Yeah, why not?"

Chapter 21

David and Stephanie spent all Sunday at her place, and only left the bedroom for more of the expensive cheese and crackers. She finally gave him a ride home late in the evening. As she pulled up to his apartment, she asked if she could have a tour of his place. David replied that unlike her apartment, his place was truly a mess, and he would have to take a rain check. She said she understood. He opened the car door, and turned to her to say goodbye, when she leaned forward and gave him a long kiss.

She whispered, "See you tomorrow."

David smiled back and got out of the car, giving her a goodbye wave as he walked towards his building. Only then did he start to second guess what happened last night, this morning, and the majority of the day. Entering his apartment, he flopped down on the couch, still trying to recall the last time he was with a woman. There were four or five women after his divorce, but the relationship never lasted more than a month. After the last horrible experience, he decided to wait six months, maybe a year before trying to date again. Six months turned into a year, and then two and then three. The distant memory of dating, of having a pleasant conversation with a woman, of experiencing a feeling you were wanted and loved, those memories were but a faint recollection. Eventually, deciding on when to date again turned into a promise to himself that when he retired, he would definitely start dating again, if he could find a way to afford it.

A new problem might surface tomorrow at work, as he was unsure how uncomfortable it would be when they were both back in the office. As great as she was, and even though he liked her, he really didn't need a complicated relationship to go along with the mission. The difficulty would be in trying to figure out what she was thinking, or why it happened. The answers would have to wait until tomorrow to see how she acted, or what she would say if she even said anything, and he would need to carefully choose his words and his reactions.

Basking in the silence filling the room, he detected a new sense which he now possessed, one born over the course of this weekend's events. The sense was an awakening of his mind, an awareness of everything around him, as if his body opened and was absorbing every minor detail surrounding him. His apartment, which up until this moment, was satisfactory, now was viewed as mediocre and horrible. And with the realization that money didn't have to be a concern anymore, there was no use wasting what few months or years were left by living with such low standards. He was no longer the same man he was just a few months or even a few days ago, but he was reborn, full of confidence and courage. The question yet to be answered was how long would this new David survive, before his old demons returned.

Now more than ever, he was determined to succeed in his mission. Despite what happened with the truck and the chase, he still had his recruiting to complete, and a second vehicle would be required. And he also remembered he needed to find a new place to live this week. With a new job and a new woman in his life, a nice and more upscale apartment was due. But on such short notice, it was unknown how he was going to accomplish this task.

On Monday, David arrived at work earlier than normal, right before seven hundred, as he needed to use the network to search for apartments. It was going to be difficult finding a place located in a decent part of the blue zone, nicer than his old place but not too expensive, and close to work. His first paycheck had been deposited the previous Friday, and he was amazed at how much more money he would be receiving. The original plan was to get a place only a little better than what he currently had, but he changed his mind, and decided to get a significantly nicer place. There was a chance he was probably only going to be there for a year anyway, maybe even less. He kept reminding himself at a not-so-distant future point in time, the Party would find out about the League of Patriots, and he would have to go into hiding. There was no reason to not spend the last few months in comfort.

Stephanie arrived at seven-forty, and went straight into her office and locked her purse inside her desk. David saw her pass by his office, and wondered why she didn't say hello. She went into the kitchen and returned with coffee for herself and David. Walking into his office, her face appeared to be different. She was smiling as usual, but it projected a different message from the smile she possessed last week.

"Good morning David. Here is your coffee, with two sugars."

David sat upright, leaned back in his chair, returned the smile, and took the coffee from her. Stephanie sat down in one of the leather chairs by his desk. They sat in silence, awkwardly avoiding talking by testing the temperature of their coffee by blowing on it and taking small sips. Stephanie spoke first. "So, are you busy today? Do you need me to do anything?"

David wasn't sure if he should mention this weekend or not, and the wonderful time he had with her. But he decided to wait for her to mention it, as it was the safest route to take. He took a look at a small stack of papers on his desk. "I don't have a lot of real work to do today, at least not until my field reports come in. I came in early to try and search for a new apartment, but there doesn't seem to be anything I like. And I can't find one that's available and is also close to work. Well, I want it to be close to work, but not too close. I can't afford the ones that are real close."

Stephanie's attention was fixated on him and his voice, but she wasn't really focusing her stare on any one part of his face, it was more like she was admiring him. David noticed and even with her saying only a few words, her appearance and the way she sat in the chair were different in some mysterious way. Of course he attributed it to what happened between them, and he was wondering what was going through her mind. Discussion of the subject would be postponed as long as possible, as he really didn't want to talk about it, because even though it was great for him, his insecurity was having a hard time interpreting her motive, if she had one.

She switched off her thoughts of admiration, and reverted back into her administrator mode. "There are some people I can call who might be able to help you. If you can tell me what you are looking for and your budget, then I can do the research for you. When do you need to move?"

David let out a snicker. "Well, I need to move this week if possible."

Stephanie leaned back in her chair, took a deep breath, exhaled, and then a look of concern appeared on her face, like she was scolding him for not doing his homework. "Well, then David, I guess I have my work cut out for me. Let me start working on this."

David explained his requirements, his preferred areas and his budget. Stephanie left and went into her office, leaving David alone to continue wrestling with his mind over what happened the past weekend. The preferred outcome was their situation wouldn't make either one of them uncomfortable at work, and so far, everything appeared to be normal. This type of relationship situation was foreign to him, and he never dated anyone from work. David turned back to his computer, and noticed some of the field reports were already posted.

David started working on moving the information from the reports into the main system. He still didn't understand why the field engineers couldn't use the main system for their reports as well. It would save him a lot of time, but then again, he wouldn't have anything to do. He finished entering the last report when Stephanie walked in.

"Excuse me, David. I have found the perfect place for you, but we need to go see it today. The building is about ten minutes away from here, and it has everything you wanted, and it is available this week."

David was impressed. She couldn't have been gone for thirty minutes. And the time was barely after eight hundred.

"Well, if you don't have anything pressing at the moment, do you think we can go take a look at it?"

Stephanie tried not to show it, but she felt a rush of acceptance inside, and she half-grinned. David noticed her half-smile, and resolved that while she had a quirky smile, he was definitely captivated by it.

"Yes. I mean, no. I don't have anything urgent right now, so let me call the agent back to see when we can take a look at it." She darted out of the room and into her office. David fumbled through his briefcase for the car keys, and then put his briefcase into a filing cabinet and locked the drawer. As he walked into Stephanie's office, she was hanging up the phone.

"Okay, I called the agent and she will meet us there. Let's go."

David and Stephanie pulled into the parking garage of the apartment building. Like Stephanie mentioned, it was located less than a ten minute drive from work, and close but not too close to a national highway which ran through the middle of the blue zone. The apartment was in a tall building, one David estimated to be at least fifty stories high. They stepped out of the car and entered the building.

Stephanie said, "The agent's office is in this building. I told her we were coming over immediately, and she is going to meet us at the apartment on the 38th floor." Stepping into the elevator, David pushed the button for the lobby, where they would have to take another elevator from the lobby to the 38th floor. David was a little uneasy about living up so high. This appeared to be a relatively new building, and since it was owned and built by the Party's Construction Union Group, he didn't trust it was built correctly. He wasn't worried it would fall down, but there had been news reports of shoddy electrical work and resulting fires, and not being able to escape from a fire was his main concern.

The elevator doors opened on the 38th floor, and they were met by a woman in a dark blue skirt suit. The woman seemed to recognize Stephanie, and as they approached, she stuck out her hand.

"Stephanie, David, how are you doing today? I'm Julie White." David and Stephanie shook her hand, and David was surprised by her firm handshake. "Please, follow me."

David and Stephanie followed and stopped two doors down from the elevator. The door lock was operated by using a fob, which Julie waved in front of a pad on the wall. The moving lock let out a nice solid click, and the door popped open. Julie pushed the door open and motioned for them to go in first. As David and Stephanie entered, he was immediately struck by the large living room, and the fact it was furnished. The layout reminded him of the last Party hotel he visited, but nicer. The living room alone appeared to be larger than his entire apartment.

Julie started her pitch, and she talked faster than his last agent, Susan. "This is the living area, and it comes fully furnished, so everything you see today will be included with the lease." Julie walked over to the windows, and pressed a button on the floor with her foot, activating the curtains, which slowly

193

separated to reveal floor-to-ceiling windows and a sliding glass door. David confirmed the layout was like the last hotel he visited, but much larger as there were more rooms in the back, and he concluded yes, they probably used very similar floor plans.

"You have a wonderful view of the city from here, and your windows face south, so you won't get a lot of the heat from the afternoon sun. But if you go out on the balcony in the evening, you will be able to see the sun setting over to your right." Julie pressed another button, which automatically opened the heavy glass sliding doors, and Stephanie eagerly stepped outside. David was a little hesitant at first, but Stephanie gave him a nod, directing him to join her. He cautiously walked out onto the balcony, which was fairly spacious and included a small table with four chairs, and covered by the balcony above it. David didn't really like heights, but he had to admit the view was incredible, and he could even see his office building from here.

They went back inside, and Julie continued with the sales talk. As she was pointing out all of the features, David was silent. Like with Susan, these types of meetings made him uncomfortable and he wasn't in a talkative mood. Behind the living area and down a hallway, was a large master bedroom with a deep walk-in closet. The bathroom contained a shower with a separate jetted tub, his and her sinks, and another small closet off to the side. David was wondering if Stephanie had chosen this place for the two sinks, one for him and one for her. Overall, the apartment was unbelievable. As they made their way back into the living room, David finally broke his silence with a question.

"Julie, I haven't rented a new place in a long time. Why is it furnished?"

"This is an apartment we normally rent by the month for visiting Party members. They will usually stay for a month or two, usually when they are on temporary assignment, or they stay here while they find a permanent place. Normally we don't accept long leases, but Stephanie told me you were in a bind, and we decided we could help you out."

David looked over at Stephanie, and she gave him a wink.

"And, we were able to work it out so it fits your budget." Julie walked over to the kitchen, and started opening the cabinets.

"You should have most of the kitchen items you need for cooking. The majority of the previous tenants didn't cook much, and I'm fairly certain they ate out every meal. If you don't have everything you need, let the concierge downstairs know, and he will get it for you." Julie moved back into the living room.

"We also have new sheets and towels in place, and the housekeeper comes in on Mondays and Thursdays. She is usually here about nine hundred and stays for two or three hours. Place your dirty clothes in the hamper in the bathroom closet, and she will take care of it for you. It usually takes a day for the laundry to be returned. If you have any dry cleaning, and if your maid is not scheduled to visit, you will need to drop it off downstairs with the concierge, but your maid will bring it up for you when she visits. Any more questions, or are we good to go?"

David didn't know what to think. The place was better than what he was searching for and better than anything he could have found on his own, and the price matched his budget. Something didn't feel right about the situation, but he really didn't have the time nor the will to find a different place. Plus, after phase one started, there was a good chance he would have to go into hiding anyway.

Turning towards Julie, he said, "The place is perfect. I will take it."

Julie went over to the kitchen counter, and opened her thin briefcase. She pulled out a tablet, pressed a few buttons, and pulled out a stylus. She stroked the screen until the agreement was on the last page, and she then put the tablet and stylus down on the counter.

"David, all you need to do is sign, and you can move in immediately."

David glanced over at Stephanie, and she was beaming with a face of satisfaction and pride. He walked over, picked up the stylus, and scribbled his name and signature.

Julie stuck out her hand. "Congratulations."

On the way back to the office, David thanked Stephanie for her incredible job at finding him such a great place so quickly. But he still didn't know how he would have time to move his belongings this week, and he might have to take a day off of work. Stephanie suggested since the new apartment was furnished, he should donate all of his old furniture to the Party's Second

Chance store. She could arrange for someone from the store to meet him at his apartment, and they would remove all of the items he didn't need or want. He would only have to move his clothes and personal things. She was sure if she asked, they would bring him some extra boxes. She could also have a cleaning service come in afterwards and tidy up the place so he would get his deposit back. And lastly, she even volunteered to help him move. David wasn't used to things moving this fast, but he agreed to all of her suggestions. He really didn't have a choice.

Chapter 22

The crew from Second Chance arrived at David's apartment at sixteen-hundred on Wednesday. The day before, Stephanie stopped by their local branch and found boxes for David, and he spent last night packing his personal items. He was a little depressed, after packing everything he owned, his belongings only filled five boxes. For the past twenty-five years, he hadn't really spent any money on himself. Whenever possible, his money was saved and not spent, in a desperate effort to be able to enjoy his retirement years.

One of the workers brought a hand truck and helped David move the boxes to his car. The worker was only able to fit four boxes on the hand truck, and David carried the last one, so loading the boxes only required one trip. After placing the boxes in the car, the worker went back inside, and David was standing by his car alone, with his entire life in only five boxes, all of which fit in the back of a car. The situation was dispiriting, as he realized he deprived himself of a life full of belongings he wanted to buy, and experiences he yearned to take, but opted not to. But even now, there wasn't any regret of the choices he made, in being frugal and doing without what others spent so freely on. He always knew, or he thought he knew, in the end he would be alone. There wasn't anyone else he could rely on, and he never really wanted to solely depend on Prosperity Benefits. As he pondered his life, his decisions, his choice to join the mission, the possibility he could die or be killed or go into hiding at any moment, he realized while he was polite and kind to everyone he met, he really ignored the person who meant the most, and that was himself.

David sighed and closed the back door and locked the vehicle. By the time he trudged back upstairs, the workers already removed the majority of his furniture. Three more trips were needed to carry his clothes down to the car. Along with the furniture, he also decided to donate most of his old clothes, and after seeing what remained, there was an understanding he might need to go shopping again. After forty minutes, the workers were finished, and David thought it was the fastest he had seen any Party employees work. But then again, he really didn't have much to donate. He felt sorry for whatever person would want his things, as they must be in a horrible situation if they found his old furniture and clothes to be appealing.

David drove to his new apartment, found his assigned parking space, and removed one of the boxes out of the back. Even with five trips for the boxes and three for the clothes, he estimated it would take less than an hour to finish. Stephanie was scheduled to arrive at eighteen-thirty, as he invited her to go out to eat as a thank-you for all of her help. Up until now, they had only eaten together in the office cafeteria. And after this past weekend, given their new status, whatever it was, he concluded he should probably take her out to an upscale restaurant. A thank-you card wouldn't suffice in this situation.

David finished unloading and was now drenched in sweat. With only a half-hour to get ready, he took a quick shower, but decided to skip shaving his face. He thought a little stubble would enhance his baby-face appearance, even though he was never impressed with his looks. His clothes were all in a pile on his bed, so he quickly put them away in his closet. As he was deciding on what to wear, he realized he didn't have any nicer casual clothes. Everything was either for work, or for simply sitting around his place and doing nothing constructive. Since he planned on taking her to what he thought was a semi-fancy place, he opted to wear a pair of nice slacks and a sport coat. Yes, he would definitely have to go shopping for more clothes soon.

David was ready to go at eighteen-twenty. One of his personal rules was he despised being late for anything, and his nervousness pushed him to get dressed quickly, as he certainly didn't want to keep her waiting. But now, sitting on his couch, he unexpectedly gave himself ten minutes to worry about his date. He really couldn't decide if it was a date, or simply two co-workers going out to dinner. After all, he positioned the invitation so it was really a thank-you dinner, and not a date. But would she think it was a date? Yes, of course it was a date, it had to be a date, after what already happened between them.

His mind was swimming with pessimism for not properly thinking this through. Should he have bought her flowers? Maybe he should have picked her up at her place. No, she offered to meet him here, as she knew he would be unpacking. And he couldn't really greet her at his own door with flowers, where would she put them? Plus, he didn't have a vase. Of course, he could have bought a vase with the flowers, and they could have left them here while they went to dinner. The conclusion was he was over-thinking this entire situation. He needed to go out and have a nice meal and stop worrying about everything, but he knew that wasn't going to happen.

David was startled by a knock at the door, and checking his watch, she was right on time. Taking a deep breath, he walked over and opened the door, and was surprised to see her in an evening dress. At work, she always wore a skirt suit, often without a jacket, but it was always a professional and subdued look. The dress was cherry red and sleeveless, and appeared to be made of a soft velvet material, and simply put, she was beautiful. As they stared at each other in a moment of awkward silence, he whispered, "Wow," pausing for a few seconds before adding, "You look incredible." His insecurity told him he shouldn't have said that. After all, he was her boss. He tried to backtrack.

"I mean, you look very nice. I hope you didn't mind what I said. Sorry about that." Stephanie could immediately tell he was feeling a bit awkward, and he appeared to be blushing.

Stephanie shook her head, but in a playful way. "David, seriously? After what happened last weekend, you think I would mind if you said I looked incredible? By the way, you look very handsome tonight. I like the stubble." She reached up and gave his face a little stroke with the back of her hand.

David was out of his league, and he didn't know how to respond. "Well, I made reservations for us at nineteen hundred. I hope you like beef. We are going to Christopher's, and I heard they have great steak. Um, so, I guess we better head on over."

Stephanie took two steps back into the hallway. David closed the door, and waited for the lock to engage. As soon as he heard the clicking noise, he turned towards Stephanie, and they started walking slowly down the hallway. David's nervousness was apparent, and she decided to ensure he had something to drink to calm his nerves, maybe some wine with dinner would help. After all, it worked the last time.

As they waited in front of the elevator doors, neither one of them spoke, and the silence was awkward for him. Stephanie stared at him with a treasured look, but he couldn't bring himself to turn her way, even though he could feel her eyes on him. Finally, after what David thought was forever, the elevator doors opened. David motioned for her to enter first, and he followed behind her. Turning around, he pushed the button for the lobby, and then stepped to the back of the elevator.

As the elevator began its descent, Stephanie moved closer, and stood in front of him. "David. There is nothing to be nervous about." She then leaned forward, stood on her toes, wrapped her arms around his neck and gave him a long kiss. She drew back and stared into his eyes.

"This is me, remember? Quit worrying about whatever you are worrying about, and let's have a good time tonight."

With her arms around him, David was close enough to smell her perfume, or body lotion, or whatever it was, and it was a wonderful scent. She was wonderful. Amazing was more like it.

"I'm sorry. It has been a long time since I have been on a date." Again, he was uncomfortable with what he said, and tried to backtrack again, and he nervously stuttered a bit.

"Uh, I, didn't mean to say date. Unless you thought this was a date. I wasn't really sure what this was, and I didn't want you to think the wrong thing. I hope it is okay with you if it is a date. If it isn't, then that's okay too."

Stephanie sighed, and her smile disappeared, and she straightened his face so it was even with her, and in a serious tone she said, "David. Yes, this is a date. And I am excited it is a date. But if you don't calm down, and quit worrying about all of this, then it isn't going to be a very good evening."

David had to force himself to keep his eyes focused on hers. He couldn't remember the last time he was this nervous with a woman. Her face was still very close to his, and she was indeed stunning. He leaned his head forward, until it touched hers, and in a soft voice said, "Okay. This is a date. I am glad we have that settled. Let's have a good time."

Moving his hands up from his side, he cupped her head, slowing pulling her face towards his, and returned her kiss with a deeper and slower and more powerful kiss. When their lips parted, he didn't have any trouble keeping his focus on her, and he noticed her eyes were still closed. Her eyes gently opened, and she said, "Wow."

The doors opened, and they walked to the garage elevator and then down to the garage to his car. David walked around the car to her door, and opened it for her. She was impressed by this simple gesture. Even thought Stephanie didn't date much, she couldn't remember the last time, or really any time, when a date opened her door for her. Closing her door, he walked around and climbed into the driver's seat. He backed out of the spot, made his way out of the garage and drove to the restaurant, even though it was only five blocks away. They could have walked, but it was too hot to walk. Plus, walking around in the city late at night wouldn't have been a good idea.

David pulled up to the valet, handed him the keys, and they went inside. David was not accustomed to using the valet service. Sometimes he was forced to use it at the hotels, when the regular parking area was full, but he never liked the idea of having to pay someone to retrieve his car. He always tried to avoid tipping anyone unnecessarily if he was paying for it. But now, with his increase in salary, using the valet was a welcome perk. After all, this was a date.

As they approached the hostess's station, a young woman was punching away on a tablet. She noticed them walking towards her, and turned her attention their way. "Mr. Gagnon, welcome to Christopher's. We have your table ready." It always surprised David, since he joined the Party, wherever he went, the employees knew who he was, and they called him by his name. He wondered how they were they able to recognize him. Were they able to find his picture in a Party database? Or did the hostess simply guess his name? Maybe he was the only person with a reservation for two at nineteen hundred. He realized he worried too much about these things when it really didn't matter. After years of being ignored by waitresses and desk clerks and the rest of the world, it felt good to be recognized. Even if they did find his picture in a database.

Christopher's was well-known for their meat. Beef was in such short supply that it was usually available at only the best Party-owned or Party-affiliated restaurants. Other restaurants offered what they called steak, but it wasn't really beef. The menu usually listed an item as a steak, but it never mentioned the cut. You would never see filet, rib-eye or New York strip on the menu. Their version of steak was a type of protein product which was pressed, formed, colored and flavored to resemble and taste like cooked meat, and it was better if you didn't know what it was made from. And you could never order it medium-rare or medium or well-done, it was cooked one way and served to you.

When David made the reservation, he asked for a table with a little privacy, if such a table was available. The hostess led them through the maze of patrons and tables, to the back corner of a smaller dining room behind the main room. David accepted that this table was about as private as they were going to get, and he really wasn't expecting their own room. The restaurant was only half-full, and the nearest people were three empty tables away. As they approached the table, David quickly walked over and pulled out Stephanie's chair for her. She flashed him a smile, and sat down. David took the seat right next to Stephanie, with his back to the wall. The hostess gave them two menus, and handed David what appeared to be a small book. David was confused at first, but then he was able to decipher the gold scrollwork embossed on the front. The book was simply labeled "Wine."

David opened the book, and listed were many different selections, on at least a dozen pages. He rarely purchased alcohol with his meals, and he only knew of three or four types of wine, and was completely ignorant about any of the brand names. Setting the book aside, he would have to figure out the wine choice later. Stephanie was already busy looking at her menu. David opened his menu, and was reading the list of offerings. The first detail which caught his eye wasn't the availability of numerous choices, but the high prices. Quietly, he calculated this meal would probably cost him a week's pay at his old job. Despite his increase in pay, he wasn't sure if he could ever get used to paying this much money for food, no matter how good it tasted. Once again, he needed to remind himself to quit worrying, and to try and have a good time.

Stephanie was engrossed with her menu, trying to decide what to order. "Do you see anything you like?"

David wanted to say, "the exit", but that probably wouldn't work in this situation. "I haven't really decided yet." He started browsing the steak options, and he forced himself to not look at the prices. The last time he ate a real steak was probably fifteen or so years ago, and he didn't remember the prices being this high.

"I think the cowboy ribeye looks like a good choice. Yeah, I think I will get the ribeye. And I think I will get it medium-rare." He didn't understand what the cowboy part of the description meant, but he thought good meat was only supposed to be cooked "medium-rare." At that moment, a waiter seemed to appear out of nowhere.

"Good evening. Welcome to Christopher's. My name is Stephen, and I, along with Julio will be serving you tonight. Before I ask for your drink preferences, assuming you are here for steak, please allow me to recommend an exquisite twenty twenty-two Chateau Lafleur, Pomerol Bordeaux which arrived yesterday. It is a medium-bodied wine, very fresh and soft, and with an opulent finish. It is an excellent choice with any cut of meat. If you are going to enjoy one of our seafood selections, then we have a nice twenty-six Domaine Leflaive Puligny-Montrachet Les Folatières, which is very light and crisp, with a honeyed density and seductive spice notes."

David bobbled his head and didn't reply, as if he was pondering the suggestion. The waiter was talking too fast, and he didn't understand a word he said. But he could solve his wine-selection problem, and simply take the waiter's advice on the wine.

"I do believe we will be having beef, so, yes, the first suggestion sounds good. In addition to the wine, I would also like a diet cola, with plenty of ice." The waiter appeared to be confused about David's request for a carbonated beverage, to go along with this particular choice of wine. But, he certainly wasn't going to second-guess a patron. David turned to Stephanie, and realized he should have let her order first. He apologized, and she asked for a glass of mineral water. The waiter offered her a few suggestions, and she picked another foreign-sounding name David didn't recognize. The waiter turned and vanished into the kitchen.

Stephanie placed her menu on her lap. There was more awkward silence. Stephanie correctly deduced she would need to drive the conversation, or it was going to be a long and silent dinner.

"So, did you get everything moved out of your old place? Have you unpacked anything yet?" David was relieved she spoke first. He was much better at answering questions than making small talk in a situation like this.

"Yes, the workers came by, and they took everything that wasn't nailed down. I finished moving right before you arrived. But I haven't really unpacked, not that I have a lot to unpack. I did put away most of my clothes, and I can unpack the other items later this week, or maybe this weekend."

Stephanie kept the conversation going. "Well, if you need any help, I am free this weekend. I might have an activity to do Friday night, but after that, I am all yours."

David noticed she was smiling again, and he wondered if she must have a permanent grin. His insecurity kicked in. She couldn't be this happy all of the time. At least he couldn't be the reason why she is smiling so much. Perhaps she is on some type of medication, or she drank a little wine before she came over.

The waiter arrived with a glass and a bottle of mineral water for Stephanie, as well as a diet cola for David. The bottle of wine and glasses were carried by another waiter, and David assumed it was Julio. Stephen placed the glasses on the table, and opened the wine. Pouring a small amount of the Lafleur into David's glass, he placed the cork on the table, and stood at attention.

David inspected the cork, to make sure it was stamped with the same name as the wine. Raising the glass, he swirled the wine around, and held it to his nose. Even though he drank very little wine, he remembered you were first supposed to smell the wine, to make sure it wasn't sour, before taking a small sip. This particular social skill was learned at this week-long coming-of-age camp his mom forced him to attend when he was thirteen. David was positive he was going to hate it, until he learned the camp was also filled with thirteen year-old girls. At first he feigned interest, but eventually he paid attention and learned a few things, and now he imagined he was correct about what he remembered. Even though he was socially awkward at this later stage in his life, tonight he was proud he possibly recalled these facts about how to handle choosing wine at a restaurant. Hopefully Stephanie would notice and be impressed.

David turned to the waiter. "Yes, of course, this wine is wonderful." The waiter poured a half-glass for Stephanie before returning to fill David's glass.

Stephanie raised her glass, leaned forward, and extended it towards David. "Shall we propose a toast?" David held his glass up to hers, and his mind went blank. He tried to think as he started to speak, but all he could mumble was, "To, uh..." and he paused.

Stephanie finished his sentence. "How about, to us?"

David was surprised by this display of affection, but at the same time, he was relieved she didn't toast the Party again.

"Yes, of course. To us." They gently clinked their glasses together, and while she stared at him, they brought their glasses to their lips at the same time, almost in sync with one another. David took a much bigger taste than Stephanie. He needed it.

David didn't realize it, but dinner was a seven-course meal. From the camp, he vaguely remembered what a multi-course meal was, but he didn't really remember in which order everything was served. The dinner took almost three hours to finish, and by the time it was over, it was almost twenty-two hundred. As Julio was removing their dessert plates and coffee cups, Stephan brought David the check. When David opened the check presenter, he ran his eyes down the bill, and was shocked to see the price of the wine. The food was expensive enough, but the wine cost five times as much as the food. He would remember in the future to not let the waiter choose the wine.

As they left the restaurant and went outside, the valet already brought their car from the garage, and was waiting for them. David was confused, as he usually had to give the valet a ticket, and then wait five or ten minutes for his car, but they must have a different system here, and it was a good feeling to not have to wait. The valet opened the door for Stephanie, and David walked around to his side and got in the car. David gave the valet a large tip, as the wine already started it's magic. Pulling out of the parking lot, they headed back to his apartment.

Even though the dinner was a success, David was worried about a new problem, the fact he drank two-thirds of the bottle of wine. As the wine flowed during dinner, he was definitely more relaxed, and Stephanie was deliberately not keeping up with him. Now he was worried about getting pulled over. Even with his Party status, he didn't want to chance getting questioned, and was thinking it was lucky he chose a restaurant so close to home. They pulled into the garage, and David parked the car. The awkward feeling returned, almost as if the wine's spell wore off in the past ten minutes. He turned to Stephanie, and was about to speak, even though he really didn't know what he was going to say. Once again, Stephanie took control.

She looked into David's eyes, and with a slight grin said, "Yes, of course I would love to go upstairs. I would like to see what you have done with the place."

David understood the reference. Whatever insecurity he was dragging around all night had immediately vanished, and he smiled back at her.

Chapter 23

David awoke at six hundred, to the sound of a woman almost shouting the news at him. The alarm seemed to have grown larger speakers overnight. Blindly reaching over towards the nightstand, he fumbled for the snooze button. He turned his body in the bed, and reached for Stephanie, but she wasn't there. As he opened his eyes to confirm her absence, he heard the faint sound of running water in the bathroom. Swinging his legs over the side, he sat up and turned off the alarm clock before slowly standing and shuffling to the bathroom. As he opened the bathroom door, a gentle rush of steam enveloped his face, and over to his left, Stephanie was taking a shower, with the glass shower doors covered in mist. She anticipated the end of the evening last night, and brought a small overnight bag with her makeup and clothes for work. He sluggishly stumbled over to the toilet, and was thankful it was in a small separate room with a door. After finishing, he went over to the sink to wash his hands, and in the mirror he noticed Stephanie was watching him. She cracked opened the shower door, and as the steam rushed out, she said, "Would you like to join me?" David didn't take time to reply, as he quickly peeled off his underwear and joined her in the shower.

David didn't have any food in the apartment, so they decided to eat breakfast in the office cafeteria. Today was the first time he had eaten breakfast here, and he wondered why he waited so long. The quality of the meals served for lunch should have been a good indicator that breakfast was as good. The food was amazing compared to what he had been eating for breakfast at home, or even on the road. Stephanie attempted to make small talk, and David apologized for being so quiet. While the meal last night was incredible, and the wine was excellent, the hangover was neither and he was suffering from a pounding headache. She smiled and said she understood.

After breakfast, they sauntered back to their offices. David really had nothing to do. With his report finished, all he could do was wait for the next round to start trickling back in on Monday. Stephanie always seemed to be busy with work, but David never bothered to ask her what she was doing. He rolled his chair over to his favorite time-killing spot, which was by the window. As the clouds and the planes floated by in the distance, his mind drifted to the mission. Recruiting took more time than he thought, and only one person had accepted, and the date for phase one was closing quickly. Another vehicle was still needed, and would need to be bought this weekend. But instead of buying from an individual, the next car would be from a car dealer. There wasn't any use in trying to hide the fact he bought a second vehicle. A truck was still preferred, as one would be useful in hauling things, such as furniture and even a stack of firewood, or whatever else he might need to move. The mountain cabin would be the reason for purchasing a truck, if anyone from the Party asked.

His thoughts were interrupted by the ringing of his desk phone, and he allowed it to ring two times before he answered the call. On the other end was the closing attorney for his cabin. His loan was approved early, and the paperwork was ready for him to sign. One of the closing attorneys would stop by his office in an hour to complete the paperwork. As David hung up the phone, he confirmed in his mind he needed to buy a truck this weekend. Also, he hadn't been able to consistently withdraw any money lately. There were numerous teller machines around his office, and when he had the chance he would take a walk in the afternoon and make his withdrawals. But he would only wear sunglasses, as a baseball cap wouldn't look proper on a guy wearing a suit, and would only draw attention to himself. He still avoided looking directly at any cameras, but there were dozens of other cameras on the street corners, at the top of light posts and on the sides of the buildings.

David was thinking about his plans for the weekend, but now there was a problem. With this new relationship getting started, he was guessing Stephanie would be wanting and expecting to spend the weekend with him. There was a chance he could probably sneak off tomorrow and purchase the truck, but he couldn't drive around and make his withdrawals if she was with him. He needed to devise a plan where he could complete the withdrawals, and it wouldn't matter if she was with him. After considering the situation and his options, he devised a possible solution.

Pushing his chair back to his desk, he parked it and walked into Stephanie's office. She was busy typing on her keyboard and focused on whatever she was doing, and he cleared his throat to get her attention. She didn't move her head, but gave him a quick glance with her eyes.

"Stephanie, I need your help, but it is with a personal matter. I am closing on a mountain cabin today, and I am going to need a pickup truck. Do you have time to help me?"

The look on her face turned from emotionless to one of confusion. "A mountain cabin? You bought a mountain cabin?" Her response was surprising, and he realized during all of their time together, he probably should have mentioned this to her.

"Yes, I bought a cabin. I didn't tell you about it before, as I wasn't sure if I would be approved for the loan or not, since I have only been in this job for such a short time. But I received a call from the lawyer, and I close on it this morning. And I need your help, because I want to buy a truck to use on the weekends."

She seemed to accept that reasoning, but her expression changed to a concerned look. "Is this mountain cabin, is it really up in the mountains? Like north of here, in the red-zone mountains?"

David sat down in the side chair near her desk. "Yes, it is in the red zone, a little over an hour and half from here. But it is a beautiful cabin. It sits up on top of this mountain, and the view down into the valley is incredible. There are lots of trees and plants, and a stream, and a lake, and nature everywhere. I think you will like it. In fact, I am going there this weekend." He paused for a moment, to let the fact he had plans for this weekend sink in, and to see how she would react. She didn't respond, as if she was waiting for him to finish, to say what she thought he should have said. He decided to submit, and he asked her, "Would you like to go with me?"

Her expression changed, and she slowly flashed her smile again. "Of course I want to go with you, that does sound like fun. I can't remember the last time I have been to the mountains, or the last time I was in the woods. I think it was when I was in the Girl's Junior Union, and we went there on a hike." After not being able to remember any details of her last outdoor adventure, she turned on her chatty mode. "So, you close today? Is it furnished? If not, then we should probably go out tomorrow and buy furniture. I know a place which has quality furniture, and I am pretty sure they would deliver to the red zone. How many bedrooms does it have? Does it have a fireplace?" She was asking so many questions, and she wasn't waiting for David to answer before asking another one.

David finally interrupted her. "Okay, okay. Hold on. No, it doesn't have any furniture. And yes, I could use your help in picking out what I need. It does have a fireplace, and yes, it burns real wood. And yes, that is against the law, but they must be able to get around it up there. There are three bedrooms and two and a half baths. But for now, of the three bedrooms, we really only need to furnish the master." David assumed she would like hearing that. Even though they had only been together less than a week, he figured there was already a level of commitment here, even if he didn't know what it was.

Stephanie opened a new document on her computer, and started typing a to-do and a to-buy list. Her excitement was obvious, and again she started with the questions as she was typing them onto the list. "Okay, so what kind of truck do you want? Is the master bedroom big enough for a king-sized bed? What is the color scheme?"

David had to stop her again. "Wait, one question at a time, please." She giggled softly to herself. David loved it when she laughed. Her laughter made her seem so innocent and trusting. But David hoped she was different from all of the other girls who worshipped the Party. He wasn't sure if she was that way, but he really wanted her to be different. Granted, his personal knowledge and interaction with anyone of the opposite sex was limited to people from work or his clients. He was wanting there to be more to her than just her love for the Party.

They sat together in her office, huddled around the monitor, and for the next hour, David told her everything he could remember about the cabin, and she typed several pages of notes. He explained since he really didn't have any decorating sense, she could choose what she thought they needed. She liked it when he said the word, "they," even though he wasn't really aware he said it. David's desk phone rang, and he jumped up and ran into his office. The phone conversation only took a few seconds, and then he went back into Stephanie's office. "The lawyer is here with the paperwork for the cabin. I will be right back." Stephanie vaguely heard what he said, as she was already out on the network, searching for furniture.

Chapter 24

Friday morning arrived, and David and Stephanie planned to sneak out of work early to go and buy the furniture. Even though they normally only worked a half day, David decided they could head out an hour or two early to get a jump start on the weekend. David's manager, Brad, was located in a different city, and he had yet to meet him. They chatted once a week over the phone, but David got the feeling this man didn't really care what he did, as long as the reports were finished on time. The more he talked to him, the more he found his boss to be indifferent about anything they discussed. Even if the reports were a week or two late, David thought he probably wouldn't say anything. David assumed leaving work early wouldn't be a problem either. There wasn't really anyone around to report him.

Stephanie gave David a list of items she thought they needed, along with a cost estimate. Stephanie located a discount furniture store about an hour north of the city, in the red zone. Stephanie was reluctant to do any business in the red zone, but this was the only store willing to deliver to his cabin on the weekend. She also found a car dealership located somewhat on the way to the furniture store. Stephanie spoke with the manager, and he stated they had the truck David was looking for, and would hold it for him. The manager made it sound like he was doing her a favor, when he promised to not sell the car to anyone else until David arrived. But with the ever-sluggish economy, there was a very good chance they probably wouldn't have sold it anyway.

David and Stephanie arrived at the dealership, and parked in a spot near the front entrance. Before they opened their doors, a salesman already walked outside to meet them. He introduced himself with a smile as Carl, and Stephanie told him their appointment was with Robert, who was the sales manager. Carl's cheerfulness vanished, and he replied he would let Robert know they were here. Carl turned and went back into the dealership through one of the large glass doors.

Earlier at the office, David told Stephanie he didn't want to spend all day at the dealership. Stephanie negotiated the deal over the phone, and instructed the manager to prepare all of the paperwork in advance. All they wanted to do was to sign the papers and leave with the truck. The manager arrived, made his introduction, and led them both into his office.

David and Stephanie sat down in the two chairs in front of the manager's desk. The manager found David's folder, and brought out a small stack of papers. Stephanie announced that while they were doing the paperwork, she was going to go look at a new sports car. The manager took time to explain what David was signing, and David signed and initialed where he was instructed. The entire process took less than ten minutes.

Besides the ill-fated truck, David had never bought a car on his own before. With his job, he was always provided and had driven a company car. His co-workers often told stories of how painful it was to sit in the dealership for half a day or more, haggling over the price, and then spend several hours arranging the financing. David was impressed Stephanie managed to have this process take as little time as possible. David guessed she was more interested in furniture shopping, and getting up to the cabin. As David finalized the deal, the manager took David's copies and placed them in a large green envelope.

The manager handed David an envelope with his copies of the paperwork, along with the keys, before standing up and extending his hand. "We appreciate your business. I hope this transaction went smoothly for you." David looked at the man, and then without standing up, shook his hand.

David said, "I have a question or two, do you mind?" as he pointed with his open palm towards the manager's chair. The manager seemed perplexed, but he sat down. David stood up, walked over to the door, closed it and sat back down in the chair.

"Is this a safe place to talk?" The manager was puzzled, and he slowly nodded yes. "I need to know if this truck has the mandatory satellite tracking service included, where the government can track my vehicle." The manager leaned back in his chair, and looked at David, as if he was studying him. "Yes, of course. By law, all of our vehicles have the SoHelp Friendship Service installed. This unit is required by law when driving in the blue zone. As you know, it is installed for your benefit and protection. What are you going to do if

213

your car breaks down, or if you are in an accident, and it is late at night? This service allows you to receive emergency assistance faster. The device and the service are really for your safety and protection."

David could tell he was only regurgitating the standard talking points provided by the manufacturer, which really came from the Party. This tracking device and service was mandated by the Party more than a decade ago. A decade earlier, private parties or insurance companies installed their own systems for crash detection and the tracking of vehicles. But several members of the Party decided it wasn't fair these devices and services were only available in expensive cars or only the rich could afford them. So, the Party mandated every new vehicle be equipped with this device, and the Party would provide the emergency services needed. In reality, the Party used it as another means to track people. If you were caught driving in the blue zone without such a device, you faced a heavy fine and possible jail time. The law didn't apply to residents in the red zone, as the Party didn't care where they went or what they did, at least not at this moment. And as for the emergency assistance benefit, the Party didn't care if the red zone residents had access to this or not.

David leaned forward, placed his elbows on his knees, and brought his hands together, and began to talk in a low voice, a notch above a whisper. "I don't plan on driving in the blue zone with this truck. How much is it to disable this feature?"

The manager sat in his chair with his hands in his lap, staring at David. David could tell he was trying to figure out if this was a trap or a sting operation. Dealers could lose their sales licenses or face jail time if they were caught disabling the tracking device. David leaned back in his chair, as if to give the manager a better view of his body. He was positive Stephanie told the manager he was a member of the Outer Circle. Otherwise, he probably wouldn't have going through the trouble of completing the majority of the paperwork prior to their meeting. This was probably the first time a Party member ever asked this particular manager to do anything against the Party rules. Or at least this was the impression David was getting from this man.

Finally, after considering David's question, and deciding David probably wasn't an undercover agent, the manager replied. "Well, we can't physically remove or permanently disable the device. But, we do have an alternative. We can provide you with a switch to allow you to temporarily turn it off and then back on. Of course, this switch is purely for diagnostic purposes. There may be cases where you need to have your car's computer upgraded, and we wouldn't want any errant electricity to damage the tracking unit. But by law, when you drive this vehicle in the blue zone, the device must be turned on."

David was pleased with this answer. He almost expected the manager to curse at him or report him to the national police. But the answer led David to believe the man provided this special service before, as his answer appeared to be as rehearsed as his pitch on needing the device. The manager continued. "However, this switch is an add-on, it doesn't come with the vehicle. And your, uh, friend didn't mention this requirement to us."

"Yes, she didn't know I wanted this feature, and it would best if she didn't find out. And how much does this service cost?"

The manager cleared his throat. "A normal switch mounted on the dashboard is fifteen-hundred. A well-hidden and more discrete switch is two thousand. And unfortunately, we can't add this to your loan. This service must be paid for in cash."

David was beginning to like this man. Even with the constant fear the Party bestowed, people were always willing to look the other way or break a minor law, especially if they could make a little money doing it. David said, "Well, obviously, I am going to need the second option. I like being discreet. I have a little shopping to do nearby, could I come back and pick up the truck in an hour or two?"

"Yes, we can have it ready for you in about two hours, it shouldn't be a problem. You can discretely pay me when you pick up the truck, and I will explain how the switch works."

David felt a tinge of satisfaction. He stood up, walked to the door, opened it and went out into the showroom. Stephanie was sitting in the seat of a red sports convertible, admiring the dash and fiddling with the buttons. When David saw her, he thought she looked good in the car. As he watched her, he imagined they were driving around together, in this car, maybe driving to the beach. Every time he thought about her in another way other than being

215

her manager, he would have to remind himself their relationship might never last, with his involvement in the mission.

"Are you ready?"

She grinned and looked up at him, and enthusiastically replied, "Yes. Let's go buy lots and lots of furniture!" On their way out, David mentioned the truck was being cleaned, and they would pick it up after shopping. Stephanie didn't even question this statement. In fact, she never questioned anything he said. David thought this was odd, as his ex-wife was curious about anything he did. If they went out to eat dinner and he ordered chicken, she would ask him why he chose chicken. When he was married, every decision he made had to be justified, or at least clarified, several times. He liked the fact Stephanie didn't seem to care, or she didn't want to know. Maybe it had to do with him being in the Party, and she knew not to ask.

The furniture store was about thirty minutes away, past the boundary of the blue zone. They found a parking spot in front of the store, which was a huge warehouse with a large glass entranceway. David wondered if the store was even open, as there were only two cars in the lot. As they walked inside, David noticed there wasn't a noticeable change in the temperature. A woman walked out of a side office to greet them. Before she could say anything, Stephanie asked if Sandy was available, as they had spoken on the phone.

"I'm Sandy, so nice to meet you Stephanie. And this must be David. Nice to meet you as well. Are you ready to buy some furniture? Well, let's go see what we have." Sandy appeared to be in her early fifties, with reddish-brown hair and a square face, and her expression was cheerful. Stephanie and Sandy walked ahead, and David trailed like any man would while shopping with a woman who was making furniture decisions.

Stephanie gave Sandy her list, and they walked around looking at the various pieces. As Stephanie was making her choices, she couldn't help but ask David for his opinion, even though he told her several times he didn't have one. But she still asked with each piece. Everything Stephanie chose was met with little discussion and quick acceptance by David, with the only exception being the fabric on the living room couch, which was a dark green and red-orange flower pattern. It wasn't so much the pattern, but the combination of green and red and orange wasn't very pleasing. David suggested a solid-color couch, maybe even a faux-leather one, and they continued their search towards the back of the warehouse. Sandy located a different couch similar to David's suggestions, and started explaining how this was a very well-built couch, and how it was eight-way hand tied or something like that. David did not care what it meant or why it mattered. To him, a couch was a couch. But Sandy was very excited about this selection. David feigned excitement as much as he could.

The furniture buying took a little over three hours. The warehouse was unbearably hot, and David was sweating profusely. The outer walls of the store were flanked by eight six-foot fans embedded on the sides of the warehouse. But the fans only blew hot air from outside all over the showroom floor. Sandy had apologized for the heat several times, but Sandy didn't appear to be breaking a sweat, a fact David found to be odd. She stated the air conditioning was broken and the repair man was due any day now, but David guessed there wasn't a need to run the air conditioning in such a large warehouse when you had a short supply of customers. He speculated they probably only turned on the fans as customers drove up to the building.

The shopping was finally finished, and Sandy went into the office to tally the bill. Once Sandy learned of David's Party status, he was able to finance the purchase. It seemed if a business had something to sell, and if you were a member of the Party, they could finance it for you. Any and all Party-approved loans were also Party-guaranteed loans. If you stopped making payments for a considerable length of time, the Party would pay the loan off for you. Of course, the Party retained the option to come back to you for retribution, but David wondered if they even bothered to do that. He could envision the higher-level Inner Circle Party members buying all sorts of things on Party credit, only to quickly renege on the loan. And the Party probably wouldn't even come looking to collect, at least not for these higher-ranking individuals.

Sandy finished the online paperwork, and David digitally signed the loan document. She said they would have everything delivered to his cabin tomorrow around noon, give or take an hour. David noticed as Sandy explained everything, her voice was even more excited than before, and she talked faster than when they first met. He guessed she should be excited, as they just purchased a large amount of furniture.

Sandy mentioned it would probably take two trucks to deliver it all. David surmised if a customer bought two truckloads of furniture from you, it might put a little spring in your step. Maybe he should have paid a little more attention to how much they were buying. During the three-hour buying marathon, all he could think about was escaping the heat.

David and Stephanie left the store, and drove back to the car dealership. David asked her to wait in his car, so he could leave the motor running with the air conditioner on. Stephanie obliged and didn't say a word. As David stepped out into the afternoon heat, he started sweating again. He wondered if he should have stayed in the car for another ten or fifteen minutes to cool off. But he wanted to finish everything and beat the traffic back to his place, so he could take a shower.

David found the manager, who led him through a maze of hallways to the back of the dealership. His truck was outside, all clean and shiny. The manager opened the truck's door, and showed David a very small button on the dash, with a faint green light on it. The manager explained that when the green light was on, the tracking device was enabled. When you pressed the button and the light went off, the device was disabled. David reached into his pocket, and pulled out two thousand. He brought a considerable amount of cash with him for the furniture, and he was glad he was able to finance it instead. Paying for all of the furniture in cash wasn't something he wanted Stephanie to witness.

David thanked the manager, and stepped up into his new truck. The dash was very similar to his work vehicle, except it didn't have any wood trim, and the console display wasn't as large. He pushed the button to start the engine, and at first he wasn't sure if the engine was on, as it was quiet. He assumed the sound of the truck's engine would be similar to the one he bought in the mountains, but it wasn't. The manager gave David a polite wave, which he returned, as he drove around to the front of the lot. Pulling up beside his car, Stephanie rolled down her window. He asked her if she would drive his car back to his place, and he would follow behind her in the truck. She gave him a wink and a thumbs-up.

Chapter 25

Stephanie and David arrived back at his apartment. Stephanie packed a small bag, which David mistook for a large purse. They really hadn't discussed any plans for the remainder of the night, or at least he didn't say anything specific to her. Stephanie mentioned earlier in the week something about having plans, but he didn't even bother to ask what her plans were or why she canceled them. Once inside, he said he needed to take a shower, and they would order food to be delivered. The shopping and the heat and the sweat drained him, and all he wanted to do was to sit around and watch whatever was on the television. Stephanie followed him into the bedroom and placed her bag on the bed. As David started towards the bathroom, she was standing in front of a chest of drawers, and asked, "Do you mind if I have this bottom drawer?"

David responded without looking at her. "Yeah, of course. Use whatever you need." She thanked him, and then started taking things out of the bag and putting them in the drawer. David didn't bother to even look to see what she brought, the only thing on his mind was a shower.

After his shower, he put on shorts and an old t-shirt before going out into the living room, where Stephanie was already on the couch watching television. Before their evening started, he decided this would be a good time to tell her what they would be doing tomorrow, which was part of his plan to be able to continue his mission, without having to hide his actions from her. The story was plausible, and it didn't require him to be dishonest, and the truth didn't matter in this situation. Also, it was better for her to not know what he was doing. Sitting down on the couch, he asked her to mute the television.

"Okay, here is what we need to do tomorrow. If we leave here around eight hundred, we can make it up to that area before ten. But, I have a few errands I need to run before we get to the cabin. I have some Party business to take care of at several of the banks. I can't really tell you what I need to do, but it won't take much time, a half-hour or less. So, I can either drop you off at the cabin, a cabin which has no furniture, or you can ride with me. But, if you ride

219

with me, you can't ask me anything about what I am doing, and you can't tell anyone either. Or, I can go up there by myself, and you can follow me up there later." The last option was added as he knew she wouldn't want to drive up to the red zone by herself, and it would almost force her to choose the option of riding around with him. And he already knew she wouldn't ask him what he was doing if he said it was Party business. Also, giving her more options made what he needed to do sound more plausible, as far as it being work for the Party.

"I don't want to drive up there by myself, are you kidding me? No, I will ride with you, and sit in the truck while you do your business. And yes, you can trust me. I never ask about Party business or discuss whatever you might be doing with anyone. I know better than that."

David was content with her answer, even though it was predictable. The need to start making his withdrawals again was on the verge of being urgent. He still needed to recruit more associates, and he probably wasn't going to be able to do that this weekend. But another trip out of town next week, under the same guise of reviewing the conversion projects at more of the hospitals, would provide him with recruiting time. Phase one was quickly approaching, and there wasn't much time left for recruiting and David had squandered what precious time he possessed. Time was needed to find associates who were willing to say yes, and then the new associates needed time for their own planning.

After some discussion, they decided to order Chinese food, mainly because they couldn't agree on any other type, and to simply watch whatever happened to be on the television. Stephanie could tell David was tired, and she decided she would try her best to not be chatty tonight. David sat on the couch, and Stephanie cuddled next to him and put her head on his shoulder, with her arm around his chest. For the first time, David didn't feel uncomfortable with her, or scared she would find out about the mission. Maybe it was because he was able to fool her about his plans tomorrow. Perhaps he felt like he could really trust her, or he could trust her enough to do what he needed to do. The mission would still remain a secret, he would definitely not tell her about that, at least not yet.

The food arrived, and Stephanie placed it on the dining room table. David didn't have a dining room table at his old place. Eating alone, he never considered spending money on a table and four chairs. Years ago, he was shopping for a set, but instead opted for a single barstool, using his kitchen counter for a table. If he wanted to watch television during a meal, the couch and coffee table was a good substitute. Having a real table was almost like eating in a restaurant. Normally he felt rushed when he ate any meal, and his eating habits were as if he was starving. But with Stephanie here, he didn't feel the urge to gulp down his food like he normally would. There was nowhere to go, no clients to visit, no roads to drive, and he had a beautiful woman sitting next to him. Life was good.

They slowly ate their food, in relative silence, and then moved back to the couch to watch a comedy series marathon playing all night. The show was one David had never watched before, as he didn't watch much television, but it was one of Stephanie's favorite shows. David rarely watched more than an hour of television a day, and it was usually when he traveled. The televisions in the Party hotels usually only accessed Party-approved channels, which were mostly news programs which praised the Party's actions on whatever the Party did that day. There were only a handful of broadcast channels which didn't tow the Party line, but these weren't available in the Party hotels, nor were they available on David's television in his new apartment. Because this was a Party-owned apartment complex, those obscene and dangerous free-thinking channels wouldn't be available here either. At least he had some Party-approved entertainment and sports channels which the hotels didn't have.

They went to bed a little after twenty-two, and David was surprised but disappointed Stephanie didn't try another bathrobe-dropping move. David assumed she knew he was tired, and while he didn't appear to be in the mood, if the situation presented itself, he certainly wouldn't have said no. The only satisfaction in this disappointment was that he was tired and needed sleep as tomorrow would be stressful enough. Even though she bought into his story about him doing Party business with the banks, he couldn't get over the fact she would have information which could implicate him. But it was really the only choice he had. The outcome of any day during the mission was unknown, so there was a chance he would be in hiding in a few months anyway, and he didn't want to lose out on spending time with her. Even though she made quite an impression on his emotions, he needed to remember the mission was or should be his top priority. Preparation was key to survival.

Stephanie snuggled close to David, with her head on his chest and her arm around his body. David normally slept on his side, but tonight he didn't have any problems falling asleep on his back. David could smell her hair, and her own scent along with her warm body was very soothing. As he tried to fall asleep, he was thinking of a way to continue his mission and still spend time with her. He would have to be very careful. Maybe the teller idea for tomorrow wasn't such a good one after all.

After an hour of not being able to sleep, David went into his closet and retrieved one of his tablets, which contained the notes on the associates he wanted to try and recruit. In order to prepare for his recruitment attempts, he needed to review each story in order to start working on what he would say to them. Retreating to the bathroom, he turned on the tablet, and after it booted, he started reading the information on the next potential associate.

The *Guide* stated you needed to recruit associates who were harmed by the various groups that fully supported the Party. This included the media, the courts, local and regional politicians and even celebrities. These were all potential targets of phase one. Phase two was going to be more difficult, as the targets involved the Outer and Inner Circle Party members. His first recruit, Gary, besides having to deal with the pain of his wife's death, had been harmed by the courts, or in particular, by a single judge. His next recruit had his life nearly destroyed by the uncaring media and a rookie police officer. David began reviewing his notes.

George Taylor was an unemployed construction worker. He was in his mid-thirties, and had filed for the worker's union benefits after a stack of lumber fell on his leg, breaking it in two places. The leg healed nicely, but after his benefits elapsed, George was laid off from his job. His manager stated they didn't have enough work for him to do. And now George was living entirely on his Prosperity Benefits. George was lucky as he was single, but he barely made enough money from his benefits to survive. After losing his job, he moved out of his apartment and was living with a friend, renting a room in his friend's basement.

His friend worked as a construction foreman, and his friend's wife had a part-time job as a maid at one of the local Party hotels. They had two kids, a ten-year old boy and a fourteen-year old girl. Even with his benefits, George wasn't content with the life he had, and was constantly looking for work. But the unemployment level in construction was extremely high, and George didn't have any marketable skills other than carpentry. He considered trying to get work as a day laborer, but if you were caught working, you would lose your Prosperity Benefits immediately, and possibly forever. So, he spent most of his day looking through the job postings online, and applying to as many jobs as he could.

One afternoon, George was in his basement bedroom watching television when the house phone rang. On the other end was his friend's wife, Jill, who was still at work. Normally, around this time of the day, she would finish work and pick up her daughter Meagan from school. Today she was offered work on the second shift as a banquet waitress and she couldn't pass up a chance to make extra money. Her son rode the bus home earlier and was upstairs. Jill said he was okay staying by himself for ten or fifteen minutes, and asked George to drive to the school and give Meagan a ride home. Meagan was a cheerleader, and her practice was after school. Since Jill was twenty-minutes late, she was afraid her daughter would give up waiting and walk home. They lived in the area where the red zone met the blue zone, and it wasn't really safe for her to walk home by herself, even in the afternoon.

George told her he would drive towards the school and see if he could find her. Jill thanked him and hung up the phone. George grabbed his wallet and keys, and went out to his car, which was an old sports car that at one time was painted a bright cherry red. The original paint was all gone, and the exterior color was now more rust than paint. George really loved his car, and it was his only luxury, even though it was falling apart. He started the engine and headed down the street towards the school.

The school was only seven minutes away, but George drove slowly as he noticed a lot of kids playing outside, throwing or kicking balls and riding their bikes on the sidewalk. Even though the car was a piece of junk, George babied it like it was new. So, he took his time as he was driving, looking at all of the kids, while at the same time keeping an eye out for Meagan.

Just a short distance from the school, he saw Meagan walking down the sidewalk, on the opposite side of the street. George lightly tapped his horn, and Meagan noticed him and stopped. George drove past her, with his head out the window, and turned around in a driveway. He started driving slowly towards Meagan, who was waiting with her arms folded around her books, in her cheerleading uniform, with a large purse hanging down off her shoulder.

When the car was right beside her, he stopped and she bent over to look inside the car. George explained that her mom sent him to pick her up, and for her to get in the car and he would give her a ride home. Meagan was a little embarrassed about getting into such a junky car, so she looked around to make sure none of her friends could see her. With the coast clear, she opened the door and slid into the front seat. George started casually driving back to the house while asking her how her day had been. Meagan said very little, and she reached over and turned on the radio. She was a typical teenager, as she really didn't like talking to her parents or their friends. She was hoping the music would help end the one-sided conversation.

While trying to coax Meagan into talking, George didn't see the police car watching him. Earlier, the officer was wondering why this car was driving so slowly, and the officer was surprised to see a young woman get into the car. Considering how she was dressed, the officer couldn't tell if the girl was a student or a prostitute. Besides prostitution, crime was rampant in this area, especially since the only people with guns were the police and the criminals. Over the police radio, the officer told the dispatcher he thought a potential crime was in progress. He also stated he was trying to decide if the person of interest was a prostitute, or a young girl, and either way he was worried the driver was going to harm this person. The police car quickly caught up to George's car, and once the officer was right behind them, he turned on his blue lights.

George was still casually driving, watching the kids playing near the street and in their yards, to make sure one didn't dart out in front of him after a ball or a toy. Meagan increased the volume of the music to a level he could barely stand, but he figured they only had a short ride remaining and they would be home. He didn't notice the police car or the blue lights behind him. Finally, the office hit the siren with two short bursts.

George glanced at the rear view mirror, noticed the lights, and a wave of disbelief ran over him. As he pulled to a stop, his mind went through a list of what he could have done wrong. He wasn't speeding, and his registration didn't expire until next year. It wasn't dark, so it couldn't be a broken light. He really didn't need a ticket, and he certainly couldn't afford the fine.

Meagan was oblivious to the entire scene. As he pulled over, she asked him why he stopped. Over the loud music, George shouted, "Cop", and pointed to the back of the car. Meagan turned around, and saw the officer stepping out of his car.

"Oh, he is cute." She flipped down the sun visor and looked at herself in the mirror, licking her lips to make sure her lipstick appeared fresh. She opened her purse, searching for a hair brush. George rolled his eyes and thought, "Does she think this cop is going to ask her out on a date?" He rolled his window down, and his license and registration were already in his hand. He reached over and turned off the music.

As the rookie police officer approached, he was being cautious with this potentially dangerous situation at hand. With one hand on his sidearm, he was trying to see into the car, but the windows were filthy. He noticed an object that was round and black in the passenger's hand, and it looked like the barrel of a handgun.

The officer drew his weapon, pointed it at the passenger and yelled, "Get your hands up in the air!" George knew the drill, and he instantly stuck both of his hands out of the window.

Meagan was unaware as to what was happening. She turned around to see what was going on behind her. The police office saw her turn and point the black object in his direction. He fired his gun once through the back windshield, striking Meagan in the back of the neck, at the base of her skull, and killing her instantly. George turned towards Meagan, began to scream, with his hands still out the window. George was yanked out of the car by the officer and onto the ground, where he planted a knee in his back, and put him in handcuffs. George was taken down to the police station, and charged for participating in a crime where a death was involved. It didn't matter that the police officer was at fault and George had done nothing wrong.

The media outlets had a great time with this story. Since this was early in the day, the details of what happened, as the police reported it, appeared on the early news, and both hour-long nightly news programs. The media reported that George was arrested for attempting to have relations with a minor, the girl was a prostitute, and because of his actions, the girl was shot and killed. It didn't matter to the media that when Meagan's parents received the news, Meagan's father was able to explain to the police why George picked her up in his car that afternoon. And it didn't matter that George was released the next day, without even an apology from the police, and all charges were dropped. The media decided to ignore this part of the story, and they didn't release a follow-up story or any additional information, as the next day there were more exciting stories to cover. And the media didn't even mention the fact the police officer was a rookie and was suspended for a week without pay. Nor did they mention the officer was back on the job soon after this incident without any further consequences. A fairly common occurrence was for the media to only present the side of the story which fascinated their audience.

Because of the attention the media gave to this story, George's life was nearly destroyed. His friend was too distraught to have George around, as he was a constant reminder of what happened to his daughter. After the funeral, George was asked to move out of his friend's basement. A case worker from the Prosperity Office saw the story on the news, and revoked all of his Prosperity Benefits as if he were a felon, even though he was never convicted of a crime.

Now George was homeless, and he had resorted to living out of his car, taking day jobs from people who didn't recognize his name or his face. Almost two years passed before he could find steady work as an hourly warehouse worker without any employer benefits. And since David had access to the hospital's computer system, he was able to easily locate George's work and home address. George would be the next recruit.

Chapter 26

David and Stephanie woke up at seven hundred, and he took another shower as he always did every morning, regardless if he took one the night before. The hot water helped to revive his senses, but the main reason was his short hair was thick, and was easier to brush when it was wet. The bathroom door was left open, as a subtle invitation for Stephanie to join him, but the hint was not recognized. By the time he was finished, she was already dressed and in the dining room. Like his previous trips to the mountains, David was dressed in jeans and a t-shirt, but he was wearing his old sneakers. The sneakers should suffice, as he didn't anticipate going anywhere near mud or water, but he would bring his boots just in case. The old boots hurt the back of his feet, and if he was going to be spending time in the mountains, a new pair of boots would be necessary.

David walked into the dining room, and Stephanie was sitting at the table. She made a pot of coffee, and placed a mug for David on the table, along with a small pile of sugar packs from work. She was eating a banana she brought from home. David sat down to drink his coffee.

Stephanie asked, "Are you going to eat anything?"

"No, I think I will just have some coffee. My stomach doesn't feel right." David was still worried about this plan, and whenever he worried, it would cause his acid reflux to return. He was hoping he would feel better after visiting the banks and having time to calm down. If she didn't say anything or ask any questions about his teller run, then he would feel better about the situation. He was wearing one of the hats he bought for when he made his withdrawals. Stephanie asked him why he was wearing a hat.

David laughed to himself. The question reminded him of his ex-wife, and her need to know everything. "Well, I like wearing hats on the weekends." She didn't respond and went back to drinking her coffee.

After finishing their coffee, they left the apartment and went down to the garage. David told her they would be taking the truck to the mountains. He then remembered the switch to disable the vehicle tracking, and he would need to turn it off before she noticed it. They approached the car together, and he unlocked the doors with the fob, but didn't walk around to open her door for her. He thought maybe she wouldn't care, since this wasn't really a date. Either way, he needed to turn off the switch. In the darkness of the garage, the faint green light would probably be noticeable. And even though she didn't question his Party business, a green light might attract her curiosity. The little things and the minor details were what you had to worry about, as ignoring the minutiae is how you are caught. He quickly opened and jumped into his seat, and as she was opening her door, he felt around under the dash, found and then pressed the button.

As she climbed into the truck, he feigned an apologetic expression. "Oh sorry, I should have opened your door for you. I wasn't thinking."

Stephanie climbed into the truck. "Don't be silly, You don't have to do that for me every time." She gave him a wink, and he was relieved. Her getting mad was such a small thing to worry about, but at times his insecurity was tough to shake.

The drive north to the mountain cabin should have only taken an hour and a half, but the traffic was unusually thick for a Saturday morning. After an hour of driving, Stephanie noticed a small wooden shack on the side of the road and asked what it was. David replied it was a stand for buying fruit and vegetables, and he suggested stopping at the next one, but Stephanie was reluctant. David spotted another one a hundred meters down the road, and he pulled over. They stepped out of the truck, and walked over to the stand. Stephanie was amazed at the quantity and quality of the fruit. David asked her to pick out what she liked, and she grabbed a bagful of apples. The apples were nice and fat and dark green in color, and were much larger than what was available at the co-op food stores. David's stomach problems subsided for now, and so he decided to eat one. The skin was thin, and the apple was juicy. David was amazed at how much better it tasted than what he was accustomed to eating. He would have to remember where this place was located, as if one fruit stand was better than another. On the way back to the truck, Stephanie noticed a huge iron pot, with a fire underneath and a sign which read, "Boiled Peanuts."

Stephanie nudged David and pointed over to the pot. "What are boiled peanuts?" David remember what Susan said about boiled peanuts, and was surprised Stephanie had never heard of them before.

"You've never eaten boiled peanuts?" Stephanie shook her head no. David went over to the man standing by the steaming pot, and bought a gallon bag of them. "We will have to sit out on the deck and eat these. You are going to love them. I haven't had any since I was a kid. My grandfather used to bring these whenever he would visit. I think I enjoyed the peanuts more than visiting with him. He was a grouch more often than not, always complaining about life and his health and telling war stories."

Hopping back into the car, they continued with the drive. After forty more minutes, they reached the small town near David's cabin, and this area was already part of David's mountain route for visiting the teller machines. He knew the location of all of the teller machines in this city, but didn't think he could get away with visiting all of them today, so he decided to go to the ones within walking distance of the town square, where he met the real estate agent. David parked the truck, and turned his head towards Stephanie. "I will be back as soon as possible." He parked on the outer side of the square, with the truck facing the wall of stores opposite the square, as this would prevent her from seeing where he went.

David left the truck, put on his sunglasses and walked across the square to the first teller machine. From each machine, he withdrew a thousand, and stuffed the money in the front pocket of his jeans. The route took twenty minutes to complete, and he headed back towards the square. As he approached the truck, he noticed Stephanie was not inside, and he began to panic. He kept walking and started to search the square, expecting to see black Party vehicles or perhaps a drone overhead. As he was almost at the truck, he saw her through the window of one of the shops, and was very relieved. The sign above the window read, "Bunny's Leftovers" and he wondered what they sold. As he went inside, a little bell attached to the side of the door shouted with a short but loud ring.

Stephanie turned around to see him. "Hey there. Over here." Stephanie was standing by a clothes rack, flipping through the items, with a pile of clothes on her left arm. She motioned for him to come over.

"Look at this. These are used clothes. But these aren't like the used clothes you get at the Second Chance store. Most of these look like they are new. And they are so cheap." She held up a pair of jeans. "This would cost you three or four times as much at Second Chance, and ten times as much as a new pair. And this one is all cotton. I hope you don't mind, but the truck was getting hot. I noticed the sale sign in the window, and so I thought I would give it a look."

David was amused. Given the style of her clothes, he didn't think she would ever shop at the Second Chance store. But it probably made sense. She couldn't be making any more money than what he made at his old job, and clothes, especially natural-fabric clothes, were very expensive.

"No, I don't mind. Take your time. We still have almost two hours before the furniture arrives." Taking the clothes off her arm, he said, "Let me carry this for you, and you can keep looking. I am going to see if they have anything for me." Stephanie turned her attention back to the clothes rack. David started walking towards the back of the store, and as he looked around, he could see it was mostly filled with junk. There was a shelf filled with old and rusty tools and a line of worn-down furniture along the wall, but the rest was nothing but decorative items.

David found what he assumed was the men's area of the store, which was much smaller than the woman's section up front. He always had a difficult time buying clothes, as he was very tall, and never knew what was in style. Plus, he avoided spending a lot of money on unnecessary items like new clothes. His wardrobe was limited to the nice clothes for work, and then older and dingy but comfortable clothes for the weekend. On the side of the back wall, he noticed a metal shelf lined with a stack of large shoe boxes. Once he was closer, he noticed the boxes contained boots. Searching through the disheveled stack, he found a pair in his size. The boots didn't appear to be used, as they still contained the tissue paper stuffed inside each boot, and the outside was clean. The price appeared to be reasonable, but he really had no idea how much a pair should cost, as he hadn't bought boots in a while. But they seemed cheap enough, and he needed a pair.

There wasn't anything else which caught his attention, so he ambled back towards Stephanie. She finished rummaging through the clothes rack, and was now looking at a box of costume jewelry. When she noticed David was close to her, she asked without looking up from the box, "Ready to go?"

David said yes, and he placed the clothes on the checkout counter. As he took out his wallet, the woman behind the counter started writing a receipt and punching in the prices on a calculator. Stephanie opened her little purse, and was fumbling for her credit card.

David nudged Stephanie with his elbow. "I will get this."

Stephanie objected. "No, no, David. I can buy my own clothes."

David countered. "This can be a thank-you for helping me with the apartment, the furniture and the truck."

Stephanie seemed or at least acted surprised. "Are you sure? I wasn't expecting you to buy me anything."

"I know. Don't worry about it. You really helped me out of a tight spot. And I appreciate it." As David held out his credit card, the woman glanced up from her work. "Sorry, we only take cash." He placed his credit card back in his wallet, and noticed he didn't have much cash inside. Stephanie returned to fumbling through the box of jewelry. David casually reached into his pocket which contained the money from the teller machines, and carefully pulled out three bills. Since Stephanie chose the clothes, he wasn't sure how much the total would be, and he was mentally pushing the woman to finish the tally faster, but her fingers were having a difficult time working the keys.

The total was just under two hundred. David gave her the money and put the change in his other pocket. The woman stuffed all of the clothes in a large black plastic garbage bag with a yellow drawstring, and handed it to David. David thanked her, tapped Stephanie on the shoulder, and they walked out to the truck. David threw the bag in the back seat, and as he started to climb inside, he noticed the store next to Laverne's. He didn't know how he missed it before. The sign over the door read, "Mountain Randy's Gun and Pawn." The insides of the window were lined with rows of security bars, and a big red sign hid behind them and flashed, "Open."

David had heard of pawn shops, but had never visited one. The next time he was here alone, he would have to check it out. If he ever decided to hunt, he would need a gun and whatever else you needed for hunting, and he didn't want to buy any of those types of items from within the blue zone. He sat down in the seat and closed his door.

Stephanie was putting on her seat belt. "I really appreciate the clothes. It wasn't necessary. When I helped you, I was only doing my job."

David didn't know if she was saying this because she meant it, or if she was trying to be polite and appreciative at the same time. "I know you were doing your job. But, I can't give you a bonus at work for helping me with personal things. So, consider this a bonus from me." As he said the last sentence, she let out a small giggle. David put the truck in reverse, drove around the square, and headed towards the cabin. On the way, they stopped at a little store, much like the one where he called Stephanie to rescue him that night. He bought a bag of ice, a carton of diet cola, and a bagful of snacks to eat.

David noticed Stephanie had been very quiet on the trip. And of course, he wondered if buying her the clothes was a smart thing to do, and maybe she really didn't like him doing that for her. Party-supporting women like to be thought of as being strong and independent. But only until they caught a Party member, and then they expected to be pampered and treated like a queen. As for this situation, he was always overthinking things about her and trying to guess her reactions. Stephanie spent most of the time looking out the window, at the buildings and the houses and the scenery. David couldn't figure out if she was deep in thought, enjoying the drive, or if she was simply scared she was in the red zone. Earlier, when they were at the office, Stephanie let it slip she didn't know why anyone would want to visit the red zone, much less buy a cabin there. Maybe she was on the lookout for someone who would force them off the road and then rob or even kill them. David couldn't figure out what she was thinking.

David's curiosity finally got the best of him. "Is anything wrong? You have been very quiet all morning."

She kept looking out the window. "Oh no, nothing is wrong. At first, I didn't know what to expect out in the red zone. I was really thinking of the worst things I could imagine that might happen to visitors out here. But the scenery is beautiful. There are so many trees and flowers. And the houses are so small and cute. And I don't know if you noticed, but we passed a field with a bunch of cows in it. I can't remember the last time I saw a cow. At the national zoo, they had an old animal which looked like a cow, but I think it had more hair and was dark brown. I don't remember what it was called. And then I saw a bunch of really big birds on the edge of another field. I think they were turkeys. They looked too big to be chickens. I don't know if I have ever seen a live turkey before. I know I haven't eaten turkey since I was a little girl."

The majority of the traditional holidays were gradually banned by the Party starting nearly two decades ago. These old holidays either focused on religion or an ancient or historical event. The older people in the red zone still celebrated these holidays, but only Party-approved holidays provided people with a day off of work. And stores within the blue zone only focused their sales events around the Party holidays.

The Party holidays usually celebrated a political event, or a leader or group of leaders within the Party. And the significance or supposed origin of each holiday might change from year to year, given the current political agenda the Party was pushing at the time. Or, if one of the celebrated Party members fell out of favor, or if that person was replaced by a larger persona, then the holiday name and purpose would change. Previously, turkeys were consumed at these old holidays, but now the main and more importantly, the most socially-acceptable animal consumed were chickens. Turkeys fell out of favor a dozen years back. Plus, their cost increased to where people didn't purchase them anymore. The turkey farmers all switched to raising chickens, as did most of the ranchers who raised cattle. At one point, the Party tried to ban eating all animals, and wanted people to eat their conscious-approved vegetable-based protein products, but that didn't go over so well, even with the majority of the die-hard Party members. So, chicken and a select group of fish were the main politically and socially-acceptable animals to kill and eat. Beef was still consumed, but the price was so high very few could afford it on a regular basis. At least this is how it was in the blue zone. David was unfamiliar as to what the rules were in the red zone.

Stephanie kept staring out the window as David drove down the winding roads, and her spirits seemed to be lifted since David's question. She was more talkative, and it was almost as if she was playing a game where she would score points if she spotted an animal or a flower or a pretty house. She expressed her excitement when she saw a large bird, or when she saw a rabbit or another small furry animal she didn't recognize. David was noticing the details of the scenery more than the last time he was here. Her excitement made David wonder if many people from the blue zone ever visited the red zone. Were the residents of the blue zone afraid of being robbed or killed in the red zone, as Stephanie was? The red zone certainly had a bad reputation. The Party maintained firm control over the news and the media, and when possible, they would exaggerate any negative story coming out of the red zone. And if nothing negative happened, they would invent stories of crime run amok, of red zone citizens being slaughtered, or whatever story they thought would cause people to fear the red zone. The reality was the blue zone experienced at least ten times the amount of crime, but it rarely made the newscasts or electronic papers. The red zone was the only place where the citizens could still own weapons, and criminals knew this. But the stories of people using these weapons to defend themselves were never made public.

David took a right turn off the main road, and drove slowly down a narrow road. Small houses were perched on either side, nestled in between large trees, and surrounded by overgrown bushes with grassy yards needing to be cut. As they slowly crossed the bridge over the stream, Stephanie asked him to stop. She stared out and down at the stream, soaking in the scene and mesmerized by the water rushing over the rocks, and the view reminded her of watching a nature program on the television. She rolled down her window and a gentle breeze whipped by, and the air was clean and sweet. She gave him the okay to go ahead, and David continued driving slowly, along the narrow road, through the woods and past the clearing, until they reached the top of the mountain. With the new truck in a low gear, he didn't need to drive as fast as the real estate agent had driven, as his truck had no problem navigating the steep hills. He parked the truck on the right side of the asphalt area, near the end of the separate three-car garage, so the furniture trucks would have room to back up to the front of the cabin. He would have to figure out how to open the garage doors later.

Stephanie hopped out quickly, and took four steps before stopping to look around. She was in awe of the surroundings and mentioned this resembled a park, but one without any grass or trash or cars or other people. David opened his door, reached into the back for her sack of clothes and grabbed his luggage, but couldn't reach over to get the other bag on her side of the back seat. Her bag would require a second trip. She was still admiring the scenery and view as he walked up beside her. "Ready to go inside?" She smiled and nodded her head. She put her arm around his, and they walked up to the front door. David placed the bag of clothes down on the wooden porch, then unlocked and opened the door. Stephanie eagerly went inside first.

She took a few fast steps, and then started walking slowly until she was in the middle of the family room. As she surveyed the room, she turned to David. "David, this is incredible. And you own this, right?" David nodded.

"Wait until you see the view." David placed his luggage and the bag of clothes on the floor and walked over towards the dining room table, to the sliding glass doors. As with Susan, he had trouble with the lock, and it took him longer than it should have to remember how to unlock the doors. As he finally popped the lock and slid the door to the right, a friendly rush of air flowed inside. He motioned for her to go first, and they walked outside onto the covered deck.

Stephanie went over to the edge of the railing, and the wind began to play with the ends of her long hair. "David, the view is gorgeous. This is a lot better than I imagined." David wondered what she was expecting, if this isn't what she imagined. When a person says, "a mountain cabin with a view", what else would it look like?

Stephanie performed a quick pirouette, and noticed a little wooden table with two chairs. David glanced over and wondered why they were there. He didn't remember seeing them when he was here the last time. Stephanie walked over and sat down, with her legs out straight and crossed. "Do you mind if we sit here for a while?" David noticed a little card attached to one of the chairs with a piece of ribbon. Opening the card revealed a note from Susan, his real estate agent. "David, I hope you enjoy your cabin. The table and chairs are a house-warming gift. I appreciate your business, Susan."

David was thankful for the gift, otherwise they wouldn't have a place to sit until the furniture arrived. David slipped the card into his pocket and sat down in the other chair, and stared out into the valley. Since the deck was on the back of the house, and on the north side of the mountain, the temperature seemed to be at least ten degrees cooler than the front of the house. And the mountains were always at least five or six degrees cooler than the city. The subtle breeze was still blowing, and he thought this was the perfect weather to sit outside and do nothing.

As David stared out at the trees and up at the clouds in the sky, he remembered the food he bought from the store. He told Stephanie to sit there and relax, and he would be right back. Walking through the house, he went out onto the driveway, and retrieved the food from the car. The ice had melted a little bit, and there was a small hole in the bag. David made a the hole a little bigger with his finger, and let the water flow onto the asphalt. When he was satisfied, he grabbed her bag and carried the ice and the groceries inside.

David walked into the pantry, and placed the non-perishable food up on a shelf, before heading into the kitchen, and putting the ice in the freezer and the rest of the food in the refrigerator. He then noticed what appeared to be a small dishwasher near the refrigerator. Opening the door, he discovered it was an ice maker full of ice, and he recalled Susan mentioning an ice maker. David assumed it was the kind normally built into the freezer, and he was thrilled with this surprise, as he was a big fan of ice. The ice maker at his old apartment had been broken for several years, and the apartment manager didn't seem to think repairing it was a priority. And buying ice in the city was expensive, so he rarely enjoyed ice at home. And he loved drinking his diet cola over ice.

He joined Stephanie back on the deck, with a red plastic cup of ice and diet cola, and she declined when he asked if she wanted anything to drink. Relaxing in the chairs, their silence was enhanced with the sound of the wind attempting to strip the leaves off the trees, and the occasional bird call off in the distance. The serenity of the scene was very calming, making one believe all was right with the world. A small road could be seen in the distance, and a car would pass by every once in a while. The valley was flat, and was dotted with houses and red barns surrounded by what appeared to be farm land. David could make out the lines of crops in the fields, and wondered what they were growing this time of the year. A trip to one of those stands for some fresh vegetables might be necessary later this afternoon. It was difficult to recall the last time he purchased a vegetable that wasn't from a can.

They had been sitting outside for over an hour. Stephanie would point out a bird or a squirrel when she saw one, but for the most part, they sat in relative silence. Off in the woods below the house, David heard a low rumble. He stood up to see what it was, and walked over to the edge of the deck. The road was partially covered by the trunks and leaves of the trees, but he could see two large white trucks coming up the hill. The furniture had arrived.

Turning to Stephanie, he mentioned the trucks, and they went back inside and out to the front of the house. The cabin's entryway had double doors, so David opened both of them. The intermittent breeze kept trying to close the doors, so Stephanie held them open while he found two large rocks from the side of the house to serve as door stops. The first truck drove into the round asphalt area, whipped around, and started backing up towards the house. David walked out to provide guidance, and the truck slowly approached in reverse, and stopped a meter from the front porch. Two very large men climbed out of the first truck. The first man introduced both of them, while the other man opened the back of the truck, which was full of furniture, either wrapped in plastic or in large cardboard boxes. The second truck maneuvered into place next to the first truck, and two more very large men appeared.

As they began unloading, Stephanie took over and directed them to where each piece belonged in the cabin. David grabbed a dining room chair from one of the trucks, and took his place on the front porch. He suffered from a bad back and occasionally a bum knee, and even though his knee seemed to be better, he wasn't going to risk hurting either one by helping. Plus, they were probably union members, and wouldn't allow him to help anyway. Besides, Stephanie was doing a good job directing the flow, and she seemed to be enjoying her role.

The four men took almost two hours to place the furniture in the house, and then another hour to adjust everything to where Stephanie thought each piece should go. As the men finished, David offered them water, but they declined and said they had drinks in the cab. As they were placing the moving blankets and empty cardboard flats into the truck, David realized he should probably tip them, but all he had were hundreds. He really didn't know how much would be an appropriate amount, so he gave each man a hundred. Their excitement told him he probably tipped them too much, or maybe they weren't accustomed to being tipped at all and any amount would have sufficed.

The trucks took off, barreling back down the mountain road. David walked over and closed both of the double doors, and locked the deadbolt. Walking back into the family room, he was surprised by how much better the room looked with the furniture. He didn't see Stephanie, so he walked into the master bedroom. She just finished putting the sheets and a comforter on the bed. David was surprised. "Sheets. I didn't even think about buying sheets. Or pillows. Or that top cover thing. Did we get those at the furniture store?"

"Well, yes and no. Since they didn't sell sheets, bed pillows or comforters, or bath towels, I asked Sandy if she could buy these for us and put it on your bill. She knew of a store nearby, and was so excited from all of the furniture you bought she said she would take care of it. She said she would add an approximate total to the amount you financed, and then adjust afterwards. I don't know where they came from, but I am glad she was able to help us out. I was a bit worried she would forget."

Stephanie was smoothing the wrinkles on the comforter, and David simply stood there, once again amazed at her efficiency. David didn't even consider sheets, or a comforter, or pillows, and certainly not bath towels. It probably would have taken him numerous trips to the store to get everything. He would have bought the sheets and pillows, but not the comforter. And then he would remember he needed towels and have to go back to the store. Looking around the room, he noticed four framed prints lined against the wall. As they were shopping, he didn't even remember looking at any art or pictures.

The cabin was now more than simply a hideaway in the woods. Stephanie had transformed it into a place more like an actual home. Even though he would have been content with any type of furniture, the items she selected were perfect. Watching her making the bed reminded him of when he was first married, and how he felt towards his wife at that time. But this new feeling was more than admiration. He was suddenly aware of his desire for her, a feeling beyond the passion they embraced. His heart was having a difficult time comprehending what was happening. Remembering his relationship with his ex-wife, he did love her and he believed he was in love with her, but their time together didn't seem to generate this same level of intensity.

David's eyes wandered across the room, and Stephanie noticed he was staring at the prints. She interrupted his reflection. "We will need to go to a store later and get a hammer and nails. I didn't know what we would need to hang these." Even with this slight oversight, she did a much better job than he could have ever done. Standing on the other side of the bed with her hands perched on her hips, she was admiring her work. She looked over at David, until she caught his attention. She had a sly look on her face.

David said, "Well, what do you think?"

She grinned. "I like what you have done with the place." Stephanie sat down on the bed and then tapped the top of the comforter with her hand. David smiled and closed the bedroom door.

Chapter 27

David and Stephanie spent Saturday and most of Sunday at the cabin. He finally convinced her into venturing out into the red zone for sight-seeing and shopping. The afternoon was spent visiting a park with a long hiking trail which ended at two side-by-side waterfalls, a scene which delighted Stephanie. On the drive back to the cabin, they discovered a flea market and Stephanie was amazed at all of the handmade goods for sale. She was just as excited as when she found the used clothes. Despite her hesitation for wanting to venture into the red zone, she was sad when the weekend came to an end.

On Monday morning, David arrived early as usual at work. He mentioned to Stephanie on the drive home last night he needed to get back out into the field and visit more hospitals, when in his own mind he really needed to finish his recruiting. As he arrived at work that morning, she was already in her office, making travel arrangements for him. They enjoyed a cup of coffee together in his office before he left for his trip.

David needed to finalize his remaining associates. Upon arriving at his first destination, he stopped by the hotel to check in and drop off his luggage. His recruitment list contained eight good potential associates from his research, and he discovered the last known mailing address and employer for each person via the medical records application. His first attempt for this trip was to meet a man named George Taylor. George's last medical visit was at a clinic in the industrial side of town, on the outskirts of the blue zone. David didn't like having to recruit in the blue zone, but he was running out of options. He wasn't sure what George did for this company, he only knew the company name and location, which was in a large warehouse down by the river. David didn't have any idea how he would locate him. He was hoping he wouldn't have to go to his house.

David left the hotel and drove to the clinic near George's place of work, and parked his car in the lot. It was a given his car was being tracked, so to provide a cover for why he was in the area, he decided to drop in and visit this particular clinic. According to his project plans, this clinic was not scheduled to install the new software in the near future. He went inside, introduced himself to the staff, and met with the clinic office manager. His purpose for the visit was to update her on the delay in getting the software installed, and he would be in touch once they determined a firm installation date.

David anticipated a quick visit, but it didn't take long for the manager to go off on a tangent about everything wrong with the current software product. The main problem wasn't really software-related. Their problem was the large number of paper forms they still needed to complete. She didn't understand why these forms weren't available on the network. David asked for copies of all of their forms, in order to determine which ones were to be added to the new software. David believed this also would help corroborate his alibi, if he needed one. It also provided him with a good idea on how to get in touch with George. As he was leaving the manager's office, he noticed a stack of various business cards on the receptionist's desk. He took one of each, and put them in his pocket before thanking the clinic manager for her time and walking out the door.

David left his car parked at the clinic, and walked three blocks over to the warehouse. The front office door was on the side of the building, and he opened the door and walked up to an administrator who was sitting behind what at one time could have been called a desk. It appeared to have a metal frame, with a thick piece of rough plastic sheeting on top, but it wasn't large enough to cover the entire desk, and the cracked original surface peeked out from the sides. The administrator half-heartedly greeted David, and he could see her wrinkled skin looked like she spent too much time in the sun, and her face also appeared to be covered with a thin film of grease. David wondered if the oily substance was supposed to be makeup.

"Can I help you?"

David smiled and extended his hand. "Yes, good morning. My name is Steve, and I am with the SoCare medical clinic down the street. I need to speak with George Taylor for a moment."

The woman's face grew perplexed and as her head moved, the oily substance glistened under the dim lights. "Yeah, okay, hold on." She picked up the phone, pressed a button, and babbled some incomprehensible words to the person on the other end. After a short wait, a man in dingy and grease-covered overalls walked through a door on the side of the room. The woman nodded in David's direction, and the man walked over to him.

"Yeah, I'm George." David stuck out his hand, and the man gave it a firm shake. David tried to ignore the dirt and grime that was transferred to his hand.

"George, my name is Steve, and I am with the medical office down the street. The last time you visited us, we forgot to get you to fill out a new medical benefit form, so I need five or ten minutes of your time to get this corrected."

George wasn't happy with this information. "I filled all that stuff out the last time I was there, and the time before that. Can't they get it straight what needs to be filled out? Every time I have to fill out more stuff."

David kept up his act. "I know, I know, it is frustrating. There are some minor details on the form we missed. You know, health benefit regulations and all of that. I know you are busy, so if you want, I can come back at the end of your shift and get it all finished. Again, this shouldn't take long. I don't want to keep you from your job."

George looked at David with his head cocked to the side. "How long will this take?"

"Five, maybe ten minutes, at the most."

George paused, as if he was struggling with the answer to a complex question. David was wondering if his cover wasn't going to work. George finally said "Well, I gotta be somewhere after work. But I got a lunch break here at eleven-thirty. Do you want me to come down to the clinic?"

David looked at his watch, and the time was eleven-sixteen. "I don't want to keep you any longer than necessary, so I will wait outside and save you a trip. Come on out when you are ready." David then tapped the stack of papers he held under his arm. "I've got all of the paperwork right here. I will make the process as quick as possible."

George nodded and glanced over at the admin, who was busy ignoring them and angrily typing on her keyboard. As George was leaving, he slowly took a few steps backwards, as if he wanted to keep an eye on David, before opening the door leading back to the warehouse. David reached into his pocket and removed the business cards he lifted from the clinic. Flipping through the stack, he found the business card for the clinic's manager, and placed it on the corner of the administrator's desk. "If you ever need any medical help, here is the clinic manager's business card. We are right down the road." The woman took the card and appeared to read it. David knew she probably already used this clinic, but he thought it was a good addition to his ruse. George was sure to come back by her desk, and maybe she would mention the card.

David thanked her for her time, and went back outside. The sky was overcast, but the temperature was still hot outside, and the clouds only provided minor relief. Searching for a place to sit and wait, David couldn't see anything viable nearby. He took out his tablet, and was reviewing his notes on George. Since George now had what appeared to be a steady job, he wasn't sure if he would be willing to join the mission. David filled his time waiting by reading about George and the other potential associates. His plans for the week were to visit the cities of his next three candidates, and he was hoping to get the remainder of them on board as soon as possible. If not, then he would have to take another trip next week.

David was deep in thought when he was startled by the sound of a metal door clanging loudly behind him. He turned to see George strolling towards him, and his face was wearing a sour look. "Okay. What's this really about? You don't work at that clinic. I've been over there enough, and I know most of the people who work there. Whatever you are selling, I ain't buying. You got about thirty seconds here to explain to me why you are bugging me at work." From the look on George's face, David could tell he was on the verge of walking away, or punching him in the face. David couldn't determine which one it was going to be.

"George, you are correct. Sorry about that earlier, but I didn't want the woman to know what was going on. I'm not selling anything. But I do need to talk to you about something very important. How about I buy you lunch and we can talk about it?"

George was eyeballing David, and wondering who he could be, standing before him and dressed in his fancy suit and tie and shoes. There weren't too many people dressed like that around this area. But a free meal was hard to turn down. Almost anyone or any pitch could be tolerated for a free meal. "All right. There is a diner about a block over, we can walk to it. But I better like what you want to talk about. I haven't had a good day so far."

"Yes, I hope you do like it. Lead the way."

David followed George to the diner, walking right beside him, but not too close for George to feel uncomfortable. Neither one of them said anything. When David saw the diner, the building reminded him of an old diner down the street from his house when he was a kid. The exterior was made of a type of metal that at one point, was probably so shiny you could see your reflection. The years of being planted in the industrial park defiled any shine that was once there, or maybe the owners didn't bother to take the time to maintain the appeal. David was having second thoughts about actually eating any food they served, but he decided it couldn't be any worse for him than Party-hotel food.

Walking up the sagging plastic stairs in the front of the diner, David followed George through the hazy glass door. George selected a booth towards the back, far away from the kitchen and cash register. A waitress came over, said hello to George by name, and handed them two menus. Not quite a minute later, she was back with a pot of coffee and asked if they were ready to order. George ordered a medium-rare steak with scrambled eggs, biscuits with honey, red potatoes and a side of bacon. David stated he would have what George ordered, but he wanted a diet cola with lots of ice. He wasn't going to take a chance on the diner's coffee.

David started with the same strategy he used with Gary, mentioning he read about what happened to him, and how he thought it was a horrible thing. David stated his empathy, and George wasn't alone as this type of thing has been happening all over the country. But instead of sitting back and doing nothing, David had a solution for him. Given George's disposition, David didn't believe he would open up like Gary had. Even though both had their lives nearly ruined, Gary appeared to be friendlier than George. Maybe the reason was something to do with where he met Gary. Or maybe it was because Gary wasn't as old as George. David didn't even try to figure out the reason, but he predicted he would have to do all of the talking.

David proceeded to explain it was time for people like George to get together, to stand up for what was being done to them. He provided George with examples of other similar situations. The food arrived, and David continued his spiel while George started making quick work of the steak. After David said something he thought George would reply to, he would pause for a moment to take a bite of food. Like George, David started with the steak, and the taste was incredible. It actually tasted like real meat, and was almost as good as the steak from Christopher's. David was baffled, wondering how a restaurant like this could serve real meat, and then he noticed the bone along the edge. Yes, this was real meat.

George didn't reply to any of David's statements, he simply kept eating and drinking coffee, so David continued with his pitch. George finished his meal before David even finished his steak. George stacked his empty plates on top of each other, and topped off his coffee from the pot. He took a long sip, and then placed his mug back on the table. George had a look of discontent on his face, despite having eaten a nice meal, and David was getting a little uncomfortable. There really wasn't a backup plan in place, nor did David know what to do if someone turned down his offer. During the meeting with Gary, David had been a bit naive, as he assumed everyone would jump at the chance to be a part of this mission, everyone would want to be a part of history, and everyone would want to put their personal demons to rest. Maybe George was different. The waitress came over and took George's plates away. George kept staring at David, so he decided to keep eating, before the food became too cold to enjoy.

While he ate, George appeared to be contemplating the offer, thinking about the situation being presented to him. Here, a strange man in an expensive suit shows up at work with a fake story. Then the man lures him to lunch in a public place, and offers him a chance to join a covert organization. An organization which is basically trying to start a coup or a revolution or a widespread act of defiance, to begin a process of overthrowing the government, even though those exact words weren't used. Here is a man asking him to possibly lay down his life if he is caught. And for what? This man mentioned killing flowers to stop the bees or a hive or whatever. David inhaled the eggs and potatoes, and was working on the biscuits and honey. The biscuits were fluffy and soft, and the honey was good and sweet. The waitress brought him a refill of his diet cola.

As David ate, neither one said a word. David finished the biscuits and moved on to the bacon, which was nice and crisp, with a smokey flavor. The taste was one David couldn't quite place, but it was amazing, and he considered ordering another batch to take with him. The quality of the food caused David to finally break the silence.

"This food is incredible. Where in the world do they get this from? You can't get food this good anywhere in the city. At least not anywhere I know about."

George let out a chuckle combined with a small belch. "Well, it probably won't hurt nobody to tell you this, plus it ain't like it is a big secret around here. You see, everybody in this area works near the docks on the river, or in the trucking warehouses. And most of this food is destined for other places. But every so often, depending upon what it is or what we need, a pallet or a box of it falls off a truck or a forklift and is, uh, damaged. We can't ship it to the destination if it is damaged. So, since most everyone around eats here or over at Tommy's place, they wind up getting the damaged food, at a bit of a discount, and we make a little extra money in the process. If you ignore the obvious fraud or whatever you want to call it, this is a win-win. Well, at least we win. And I guess the restaurant wins as well." The waitress came over and removed David's plates, ripped the bill from her pad, and placed it face down on the table.

David finished the last piece of bacon and he licked his fingers, and even the grease from the bacon was tasty. He wiped his hands on a napkin, and took another drink of his diet cola. If George doesn't hit him over the head with a pipe and throw his body in the river, he might have to come back here again. George was still silent, and his expression was blank and rough. The years had not been kind to his face.

David surmised George wasn't the talkative type, so there was no reason to ask him if he had any questions. "So George, what'll it be? Are you in?" George continued his icy stare at David, as if he was indeed figuring out where he could hide the body. After a minute, his chin dropped, and he stared down at the table, as if he was remembering what happened to him, or what happened to the girl in his car, or how his friends were hurt beyond repair. When he finally looked up, he said, "Yep. I'm in."

David reached into the stack of papers, and pulled out a thick green envelope which contained copies of the guide, the cash and the prepaid cell phone. He placed it on the table in front of George. "Everything you need to get started is in here." David grabbed the check, and stood up. George was holding the envelope in his hands, feeling it as if he was trying to guess what it contained. David looked at the bill, and then down at George. "Good luck George." David reached into his pocket and threw out two bills on the table for the tip, walked over to the register, paid cash for the meal and left the diner.

As David walked down the sidewalk, back towards the clinic and to his truck, a feeling of great pride came over him. He was proud of himself for being able to successfully recruit another associate, especially one like George. Given that George had been a little grouchy, he was proud in how he handled the situation, but this feeling was even better. With his first recruit Gary, it was nervousness first and then pride. With George, it was pride all the way. As he strolled back to his car, he was replaying in his head everything he said. Even though George was fairly non-responsive, he tried to notice if he could detect from George's subtle reactions if certain phrases had been more effective. Did anything specific strike a nerve with him? Could this analysis be transferred to the next recruit? Maybe everyone says yes, but none of them follow through with it. Neither of them were told in advance they would be receiving anything like the money, so money couldn't be what persuaded them. While he thought his pitch was pretty good, was it really good at all? He now only had two references to consider. But were people so desperate in their lives, so angry at the system, wouldn't everyone jump at the chance to participate, even if death was a factor?

After all, death was a possibility and should be a concern with missions like this one. The mission wasn't really a coup at this point, but more like individual widespread acts of revolution against a corrupt national government. But then again, the sum of the acts couldn't be considered a revolution, as a revolution involves replacing one form of government with another, and David wasn't certain another form of government was to be

247

implemented. The goal was they simply wanted their current government to go back to the way it was, forty or fifty or more years ago, back to a time when the government actually protected the freedoms of their citizens. Back to when the government was once heralded as the best platform of ideas and beliefs in centuries. Back to a time where the people could become anything they wanted to be, but only because the government did nothing to intervene in their lives. This period was when capitalism was king, and the means of production were privately owned and operated for profit, and profit was still a good thing. It was also when socialism and communism were evil, but only because the people understood the principals and fallacies of both.

Maybe these people, these recruits weren't blind after all. Maybe the daily propaganda being fed to them wasn't really working. Perhaps when you place a population in a situation where the outlook is so bleak, the future so unknown, they are simply waiting for the right person, or any person, to provide them with an opportunity worth fighting for, and the only thing they needed was a little push and a little direction. Yes, maybe this was more than a coup, maybe this was simply the beginning of a revolution, but a revolution to go back to the beginning, and not necessarily one with a new set of rules. But would it work? It had to work. If it didn't work, then would all of this be for nothing?

Chapter 28

David had a very successful week, both in visiting the medical centers and in his recruitment efforts. Now it was Thursday afternoon, and he was making the long drive back home. In addition to meeting George, he was able to meet and recruit Thomas and Lewis Chambers, a set of twins who were star football players as well as academic scholars at a local high school. Their only fault was they were outspoken against the Party and publicly criticized the standardized testing being given to juniors and seniors at their high school. They believed the tests were created in a way so any idiot could pass them without a problem. They both aced their tests without studying, as to them the answers to the questions were too obvious. They also argued the tests were only geared towards making the teachers look successful, versus actually trying to gauge how well the students were learning. This didn't sit well with the teachers or the teacher's union. Even though the school was in the red zone, the educational system was one of the only things tightly monitored and controlled by the Party regardless of the location.

During their last week of high school, there were many celebrations and parties during the previous weekend. It was now Monday morning, and Thomas and Lewis only needed to endure one last normal day of school before final exams. They were sitting in their homeroom class when the school's principal walked in, flanked by two police officers. The principal stood in the doorway, and motioned for the teacher, who shuffled over and stood beside him, with her back to the class. He whispered in her ear, and she nodded. Turning around to face the class, she asked for Thomas and Lewis to step outside. The principal and the officers stepped back out into the hall. Thomas and Lewis stood up, looked at each other, and walked outside.

The principal, with a smug look on his face, said, "Boys, we have a report you have a weapon in your vehicle. We need you to follow us so we can take a look." The twins were puzzled as to what the principal was talking about. They didn't own any weapons, so they knew there couldn't possibly be a weapon in their car. The group started walking down the hallway towards the front entrance. Everyone went outside and headed towards the parking lot, as the boys lead the way.

When the group arrived at their car, the principal asked for the keys. Thomas gave him his set, and the principal handed them to one of the police officers. This particular officer was a tall and husky man with a shaved head. The other officer was short and fat with a high-and-tight military-style haircut. Both officers were already wearing thin black gloves. The tall officer pressed the key fob to unlock the doors, and he opened the driver's side door. Thomas and Lewis stood there, incredulously wondering what in the world they were looking for.

As the tall man sat down, he reached over and pressed a button to unlock the trunk. As the trunk popped open, the short fat officer walked over to open it. Thomas followed him, but he stayed a good distance away. The trunk was filled with all sorts of papers and boxes and trash. The short fat officer started rooting through the mess. After a quick search, he shouted, "Hey, hey, hey! Jablonski, I think I got it. Come take a look at what I found!" Thomas walked closer, but he still couldn't really see what was in the trunk. The officer reached towards the back and pulled out a small six-inch hunting knife in a sheath, and it looked more like a toy than an actual weapon.

Officer Jablonski climbed out of the front seat and started walking towards the back. With a melodic and sarcastic tone, he said, "Hey Webb, what do you got there?" The officer held up the knife for everyone to see.

Thomas and Lewis, in near unison, immediately said with a surprised tone, "That's not mine" as they looked at each other, wondering if the knife belonged to the other twin.

Officer Webb arrogantly said, "Yeah, of course it isn't. We hear that a lot." He then turned to the principal. "Let me give this to you for evidence." Holding the knife in one hand, he reached into his pocket and pulled out a plastic bag with a zipper enclosure. The officer placed the knife in the bag, closed it, and gave it to the principal. The principal held up the baggie by the top.

"Thank you, Officer Webb." He turned to the twins. "Follow me to my office. We are going to have a talk."

Because the officers found this weapon in their car and on school grounds, the twins were expelled. They weren't allowed to take their final exams or participate in the graduation ceremony. Even with failing grades on their exams, they still managed to have more than enough credits to graduate from high school. The larger problem was because of the expulsion, the academic scholarships they received to their local national college were withdrawn. Of course, they both knew this was a setup, probably in retaliation for their speaking out about the standardized testing, but there was nothing they could do. Their parents filed an appeal, but the expulsion was upheld by the local school board. They filed a lawsuit in the local court system, but the judge killed it at the first hearing. The zero-tolerance policy against weapons at school was just that, zero-tolerance, no exceptions.

The twin's parents couldn't afford to send them to college, so they found jobs working as auto mechanics at their uncle's repair shop in town. They hated the work at first, but soon found they were good at diagnosing and repairing almost any problem, especially if it involved the car's computer system. Even after working with their uncle for four years, they still hadn't found a way to let go of their anger. While it didn't consume them on a daily basis as it did in the beginning, they were still bitter and blamed the event on their current situation in life.

The twins were a bit younger than what the *Guide* suggested, as far as the qualifications for suitable recruits. They recently turned twenty-three, and the recommended age was at least twenty-five, but David thought he would take a chance. Because of their high intelligence, David thought they might have found a way to control their emotions and to get over what happened. However, David also believed he might be able to use their intelligence to his advantage. While they might not be ideal candidates, he was running out of possible recruits, and more importantly, he was running out of time. David located them working at the shop.

The auto garage shop was in a small town an hour and a half south of the city, and it was located in the red zone. The *Guide* didn't specify that all recruits needed to be from the red zone, but it suggested recruiting in the blue zone was too dangerous. The multitude of cameras and listening devices were too well-hidden and numerous to locate and avoid. The Party still held the belief that what happened in the red zone didn't matter. Plus, the red zone was too spacious to effectively monitor at this time. This would all change, but for now, the red zone was a safer bet.

David walked into the shop right before closing time. The building held three garage bays, and a small waiting room off to the side. There was one office with two large glass windows which provided views of the shop and waiting room. David didn't see anyone in the office, so he made his way through the door on the side and took a step into the garage, where he spotted the twins. A large sedan was up on a lift, and one of the twins was pointing out something to the other. David cleared his throat to get their attention. Thomas looked at David, and then looked over at the clock on the wall.

"I'm sorry, we are about to close. What can I help you with?"

"I know it's quitting time, but I would like to talk to you about the knife they found in your car." The twins looked at each other, and a slight frown appeared on both of their faces.

Lewis was the first to speak. "Who are you?"

David casually walked over, until he was a few feet away from them, and they appeared to be a lot older than twenty-three. None of these recruits seemed to age well. Maybe the years hadn't been good to them, or maybe working under cars all day sucked the life out of them. And once David was closer, he also noticed they were large individuals. David's height was over two meters, and they were as tall as he was, but with broad shoulders and thick necks. David surmised in this case, age didn't matter. These guys were brutes.

David looked at one twin, and then the other. "Well, you don't know me. But I am very familiar with your story. I believe you were framed, and I am guessing you agree with me. I know your life's intention was not to work in a garage. You were destined for much, much greater things. I am here to provide you with an opportunity to be a part of something much greater, to be part of something meaningful. A mission with a greater meaning than you could ever imagine. A chance to literally change the world."

David had worked on this speech for a while. With Gary, he waited for him to tell his story and to become emotional. But that strategy didn't work with George. David figured perhaps, instead of emotion, logic would work better with these two. Sure, emotions would play a part. But right now, he would focus on trying to provide them with a goal greater than what they could ever achieve working as mechanics.

The twins didn't take long for David to convince them. As soon as David mentioned revenge with a purpose, for what happened to them, they were in. They confessed they had been thinking about revenge for the past four years, starting from the day it happened. And even more so during the appeal and then again after losing the lawsuit. But deep inside, they had a conscious, albeit a small one. David's mention of a mission probably gave them the excuse they were looking for. Once they accepted the offer, David gave each one their own green envelopes, with copies of the guide, along with the money and cell phones. For the first time, David left knowing he made the right choice. He wasn't going to have to worry about these two.

Chapter 29

Tim was driving in the nation's capital city moving with the thick traffic along the busy streets and taking his time. A meeting was scheduled for eleven hundred this morning, and he left from his hotel three miles away. Since he was retired from the hospital, he preferred mid-morning appointments. A new but unwanted habit of staying up late, working on his part of the mission had taken hold of him, and the result was he was sleeping as late as possible. His cancer treatments gave him insomnia, but once he fell asleep, he had a difficult time waking up. Even though the treatments were finished weeks ago, he still didn't possess the energy he used to have. And he couldn't attribute this to simply getting older.

Making a right turn off the street, the car slipped inside a dark parking garage, forcing him to use the headlights, and he drove around until he found a good spot to park. Tim hated parking garages. They were always so dark, and he was paranoid someone was going to sneak up behind him and shoot him in the back of the head. He made it a habit to park as close as he could to one of the light fixtures which still worked, then to leave the car as fast as possible, and walk quickly to the exit. For his age, he possessed excellent hearing and vision, and he attributed this to his paranoia. His sense of smell wasn't good, and he decided his other senses compensated for this loss. Plus, he didn't think he would smell anyone sneaking up behind him.

Tim made it to the exit, and walked up two flights of stairs to the lobby. Elevators were avoided for the same reason as the dark areas of the parking garage. Even though all elevators were equipped with cameras, if the Party wanted to shoot you in an elevator, getting rid of the video evidence wouldn't be a problem. His shoes didn't make a sound as he walked on the concrete steps. He changed all of the soles on his dress shoes from synthetic leather to rubber, so they wouldn't make any noise as he walked. Paranoia was his best friend.

Once Tim made it to the lobby, he walked past the elevators and over to the entrance to the main stairs. Thankfully, given his distaste for using the elevators, the meeting was on the third floor. Exiting the stairwell, he walked down the hall to suite 300. As a force of habit before any meeting, he reached for his tie to straighten it, but then remembered he was only wearing slacks and a button-down shirt. For him, wearing a suit was a necessity of the past.

The entrance to the suite consisted of two big glass doors, which allowed for plenty of visibility from both sides. He opened the right door and quickly stepped inside. There wasn't a receptionist, so as usual, he sat down on the leather sofa to wait. They were expecting him, and he always waited for them to come for him. The waiting room was much nicer than the one at his old office at the hospital. At least the magazines and periodicals were newer. A copy of the Party newspaper sat proudly on top of the magazines spread out across the side table. Picking up the paper, he wondered why they bothered to print these anymore, since everything was available on the network. Maybe it was so the Party could scatter the papers around all of the stores, hotels and businesses, as a constant reminder to the general population the Party existed and was in control.

The newspaper was half real news and half sensationalism. To get people to read the paper, the cover headline read more like a tabloid, with an outrageous or eye-catching tag line, in large bold type. Today's headline read, "Twelve Die In RZ Fire - Building Violations Found." RZ was an abbreviation for the red zone, and nearly every negative story occurred in the red zone. The article was about a hotel fire, and the hotel apparently skipped the implementation of an obscure national building code, one which was not related to anything dealing with fire safety. Even though the origin of the fire was probably caused by another reason, the Party always found a way to relate a disaster to the blatant disregard of the regulations the Party established and constantly tweaked. Every disaster was tied to not being a good Party follower.

Tim skipped down to the bottom, to a story of a Party member who was found dead in a hotel with an unidentified but also dead woman. The story didn't mention the cause of death for either person, but they made sure to specify this occurred at a hotel in the red zone. Tim knew this was a lie, as Party members had access to really nice hotels in the blue zone, and would never take a woman anywhere else. Plus, if you were a Party member and wanted privacy, a Party hotel was where you went. In fact, a Party member could pretty much do anything they wanted to do in a Party hotel and get away with it. This member would have gotten away with whatever happened, if he hadn't died as well.

Tim opened the paper to read page two, when a man walked around the corner. He was startled by the sound of the man saying his name.

"Tim." He raised his head up from the paper. "Good to see you again. We are ready for you."

Tim half-cheerfully replied, "Good morning Johnny." He folded the paper and placed it back on the side table, stood up and followed him. They quietly walked down the hallway, passing the exterior offices on one side, which were all dark and empty, and the empty cubicles on the left. They arrived at a corner office, and Tim followed the man inside.

As Tim went through the doorway, he was surprised to see another man sitting in a chair off to the side, almost in the corner.

Johnny pointed towards the man. "Tim, you know Howard, don't you?" Howard was an older man, probably in his late sixties or early seventies, with a thick head of red hair combed backwards. Despite the fact Howard was probably born with fair skin, he always seemed to have a nice tan, even in the winter. Tim always speculated it was a chemical tan. Howard was a nice dresser, wearing expensive silk suits and real leather shoes, but he had a difficult time choosing the appropriate coat size. Every time they met, his coat always appeared to be too large for him, as if he lost a considerable amount of weight since its purchase. His shoes always needed a shine, and he never wore a tie. There was a disconnect in his appearance and his selection of clothes. Howard stood up.

Tim looked over at the man, with even less enthusiasm than when he saw Johnny. "Yes, I know Howard." Tim took his place in one of the chairs in front of the desk. Johnny went around and sat down behind his desk, and leaned back in his chair. "Howard is updating me on the project. I hope you don't mind if he sits in with us. From this point forward, he will be participating in the discussions with all of the primary-level players."

Tim forced himself to put on a fake smile, and moved his face from Johnny over towards Howard. "No, of course I don't mind."

Johnny didn't bother to make small talk, as there wasn't time for that. "I hope you have a good progress report for us." Tim looked away from Howard and back at Johnny. Howard always gave Tim an uneasy feeling. Even though Howard was a former legislator like Tim, he was still a high-level member of the Inner Circle and worked for the Party within one of the many clandestine departments, and no one ever mentioned his official title. The title was really irrelevant, as whatever job or title he presented to people was a cover for his real work within the Party. Tim worked with him over twenty years ago, but he never felt like he could trust Howard. Tim's primary concern about him was he wasn't honest, even to his fellow Party members. It was an unwritten rule, Party members were to be as honest as possible with each other, but they could take advantage of anyone else.

Tim sat straight in his chair. "Yes, I have made considerable progress. Since the last time we met, I finished recruiting my last associate. I now have eleven who have agreed to join. The majority of them have been very steady in their withdrawals, and nine of them have finished their first round of recruiting as well." Johnny's face tightened. He didn't like to hear Tim wasn't at one hundred percent of his task.

"Well Tim, what about these other two, how many have they recruited?"

Tim stopped as if to think for a moment. Even though he had not been in direct contact with any of his recruits, he knew David recruited four people, and he was working on his fifth. The other man only recruited one person, and hadn't really made an effort to recruit any more. "Well, David has recruited four people, but since we put him in the new job, it has taken him a bit longer than we expected. The good news is he is four-for-four. We were correct in assuming he would be good at recruiting. We still have time left. I am confident he will finish his last assignment."

Johnny seemed pleased at first, but then his face once again showed a slight concern. "And what about this other associate, the one with only one recruit. Are you talking about Scott?" Scott was an employee at Tim's hospital. Tim had known Scott and his family for over ten years, and he trusted Scott more than anyone else at the hospital, and he certainly thought Scott would perform well. At first, Scott was very excited, but he grew doubts about the mission's purpose, and then he encountered a run of bad interviews with candidates. His first two recruits turned him down, and it caused him to second-guess as to why he was part of the mission. Scott was lucky with the third attempt, but the fourth recruit also turned him down, and threatened him with bodily harm. Scott was now too scared to approach anyone else.

Tim replied, "Don't worry about Scott. I will go and have a talk with him. It might be it is tough for him to work a full-time job and finish his recruiting. I can talk with his manager and arrange for him to take time off work, so he can finish everything on schedule. And David, I know he has identified his candidates, and he has a fifth and final recruit lined up to visit, and he should be able to talk to him in the next week or two. I don't see David as a problem. He will finish in plenty of time."

Johnny leaned forward, and put his elbows on the desk. "Tim, I don't have to tell you how important it is for Scott to fulfill his requirements. And, I think David is far enough along, and even if he doesn't get his fifth recruit, he can proceed to phase two as planned." Phase two involved recruiting an additional five associates, but neither Johnny nor Howard knew David was not assigned a project task for phase two. Tim was the only one who knew after phase one, David was finished with his part of the mission. And Tim knew what Johnny's response was going to be about David's status. But he could tell by Johnny's expression he wasn't pleased with Scott.

"I will talk with Scott. I can get him to finish his job." said Tim.

Johnny gave Tim a hard look. Johnny was aware Tim knew what would happen to Scott if he didn't complete his part of the mission. Johnny voiced his opinion in an earlier meeting that he thought it was a mistake choosing Scott. Scott was Tim's youngest recruit, and he still had over ten years left of his work benefit time at a decent-paying job he enjoyed before he would be forced to retire. And Scott was married, which was frowned upon as far as recruits go. Single recruits were much better. Recruits such as Scott were also more likely to accept the challenge if they were angry, full of revenge, about to retire or resented the Party. Scott had none of these qualities. Tim knew he made a mistake, but he wasn't going to admit this to Johnny, especially with Howard in the room.

Johnny cocked his head towards Howard. "Do you have anything to add?" Howard had been sipping on an alcoholic drink, and his only contribution so far was staring at Tim, and he shook his head. Tim could feel Howard's eyes on him, and knew he wasn't going to say anything. Howard was the type of man who didn't say much when he didn't approve of a situation, but he would gladly stick a knife in your back when you weren't looking. Or have another person do it.

Johnny turned back to Tim. "Well Tim, is that all you have for your report?" Tim glanced over at Howard, who was still nursing his drink. Tim really didn't like him being there. He would much rather have this conversation alone with Johnny. Tim looked back at Johnny. "How are the other principles doing? Are we all set for phase one? Do you mind giving me an update?"

Johnny sat up and leaned his head towards Howard, and Howard gave him a slight nod of approval. "Yes, phase one and phase two should be a success. We have our principles in the forty-two targeted regions, and the majority of them have met their quota. The average second-level recruitment rate is about eighty-seven percent. Our reports show we should have a little over seven hundred and forty at the second level. And after that, we will have over thirty-two hundred third-level associates. Phase one should yield a success rate of seventy, maybe seventy-five percent, perhaps more. And phase two, if we are lucky, about fifty percent. As usual, we set our expectations low so we can surpass them when we present our final results to the project committee."

Tim did the math in his head. If seventy percent of the combined four thousand recruits for phase one are successful, then a little over twenty-eight hundred targets will be successfully eliminated across the country. You could round up the total as there were always extra casualties, consisting of non-targets and bystanders. And these numbers didn't include the additional associates to be recruited after phase one. The final numbers could be four or five times as large. Perhaps sixteen to twenty-thousand individuals would be targeted, and over half would be eliminated.

Tim asked, "And what about phase three? Have we finalized on a date for phase three? The last I heard, it was going to be in mid-December. Wasn't it going to be the seventeenth?"

Johnny sat back, swiveling his chair to the right, and again waited for Howard's permission before divulging any information. Howard spoke for the first time in the meeting. "Tim, December fourth is the new target date for phase three. We decided to move it up a bit. We figure the news will still be fresh for about a week after phase two ends. We wanted phase two to still be on everyone's mind as we launch phase three. And phase three has been modified. We were able to secure a little over two hundred devices, versus our original request for a hundred and fifty. And the yield was increased to eleven, instead of six."

This news bothered Tim, but he couldn't let it show in his face. Despite what one thought of a given situation, it was always good to not show your emotions. "Okay, good, two hundred or so devices. But why the increase in kilotons? The yield, is what, about half of Fat Man?" Tim was referring to one of the first atomic bombs used at the end of World War II.

Johnny answered, "Tim, we didn't think the original devices were going to provide the height we needed for the visual display. We need people to be able to see these things going off from a long distance. And it seems the smaller devices weren't powerful enough in some of the cases to do what needed to be done. We went over this at our last meeting, didn't we?"

Tim maintained his lack of emotion, even though inside he was getting perturbed. "Well, I wasn't at the last general meeting. If you remember, I was receiving my first round of cancer treatments that week, and I wasn't able to travel. And I haven't been able to make it to any other meetings, as well, because of the treatments."

Johnny responded as if he had forgotten. "Oh, that's right. I remember now you weren't there and haven't been around. How were the treatments? Were they successful?"

Tim wondered why he was asking this question. He knew Johnny had probably been updated by the doctors, or by someone else in the Party. They both probably knew more about his medical status than he did. Tim started to ask himself if Johnny was trying to tell him something in front of Howard.

Johnny and Howard both probably knew the results of the treatments before he did. But he decided to not worry about this for now. If Johnny had something important to tell him, there were other methods he could use. No use in making Howard suspicious.

"Yes, the treatments were fine and apparently successful. The cancer appears to be in remission. I should be fine, at least for a while."

Johnny smiled, and Tim could tell the smile was forced. When the Party first offered to cure Tim's cancer, he started to believe the Party had given him the cancer, so they could offer him a cure if he helped them. And once they had him, once he agreed to this mission, he couldn't quit. The cancer arrived about two years ago, and after failing to gain approval to receive the treatment benefits, he was approached by the Party with a deal. Help them out with this mission, and they would treat him, and they could possibly cure him. Once he agreed, he would have to follow through with the mission, or the cancer might return. The old saying, "Once a Party member, always a Party member" was true, but Tim wasn't ready to die yet. The mission would have gone on without Tim, so it was better for him to agree to be a part of it and get cured. Otherwise, he would either die from the cancer, or from a bullet in the back of the head in a parking garage or the stairwell or perhaps even in an elevator. And, there were other personal reasons for wanting to stay alive.

Johnny looked at Howard again, as if he needed Howard's permission to close the meeting. "Howard, anything else?" Howard shook his head. Johnny turned back to Tim. "Anything else Tim?" Tim shook his head as well. "Well then, Tim, thanks for stopping by. Send me a note when you have Scott straightened out. And I am sure David will finish his job as well, and your part will be labeled a success." Tim stood up, turned and gave Howard one last look, and walked out of the room. Howard rose from his chair, and moved to the door to watch Tim walk down the hallway towards the lobby. Closing the door, he sat down in the chair in front of Johnny's desk.

Howard was always trying to discover anything about a person which would point to Party disloyalty. "Did it look like Tim was a bit concerned about the changes to phase three?"

Johnny thought for a moment. "I don't think so. What difference is an extra kiloton here or there? The damage will be done either way. So the end results might be a little more devastating than the original plan, but the outcome will be all under our control. And it doesn't matter what he thinks. He will be finished in a little while, and then he won't be a concern."

Howard nodded in agreement and asked, "What about Scott? Do we wait?"

"No. Scott is a liability at this point. We shouldn't have waited this long to solve this problem. Don't worry. The problem will be cleaned."

Tim walked quickly down the stairs and to his car. He got inside, started the car, and drove off, making it safely out of the parking garage, and then he headed south. The decision to drive to the meeting instead of flying was due to the fact he felt safer in a car than on an airplane. Besides, when he flew, he would have to leave his car in a parking garage at the airport, and he didn't want anyone to have access to his car for a day or two while he was out of town. Now he had a good ten or eleven-hour drive ahead of him, which would give him plenty of time to think.

As Tim drove, he started going over the plan for what he was going to do next. Scott was definitely going to be eliminated, so he certainly wasn't going to waste any time in talking to him like he stated. Besides, Scott knew what he was getting into, he was aware of the risks, and since Scott failed, there was nothing he could do about it. Plus, he didn't have the time nor the willingness to save Scott. He didn't have to worry about David, he knew David would pull through. The other recruits didn't matter, as they were on target. Now his last meeting with Johnny and Howard was over, he only needed to make it home alive, and then he would disappear. He wanted to be long gone before phase one started, and calculated he only needed twenty-four hours to make it happen.

Chapter 30

A little over a month had passed since David met with Thomas and Lewis. A week after the meeting, he finally recruited his fifth and final associate, a farmer named Henry. Henry's farm had been in his family for at least five generations. But the poor economy and escalating gasoline prices caused Henry to take out several farm loans to keep his operation running. After years of hard work and turmoil, he finally succeeded in growing enough crops to make a decent living and to keep the banks off his back. And then the National Environmental Police (NEP) knocked on his door.

The NEP suddenly discovered a rare species of salamander living in the streams running across Henry's property. This salamander was on the forever-endangered list, which meant the salamander was entitled to protection without review for at least a hundred years. A hundred years wasn't quite forever, but it was long enough. The NEP placed a temporary land-use injunction on his farm, and they wouldn't allow him to grow any crops. The NEP claimed since Henry used pesticides and fertilizer on his crops, the rain would cause these chemicals to flow into the streams, and therefore cause harm to this delicate amphibian. After a long and drawn-out series of hearings, the NEP stated Henry could continue to farm as long as it was done without using any chemicals. To ensure Henry played by their rules, they would come out once a month and perform a test of the soil and the stream, the cost of which Henry had to bear. And the tests weren't cheap. If any chemicals were found, then they could prohibit all farming and possibly seize the farm.

Henry tried growing organic crops, and rotating what he grew in a vain attempt to keep the soil fertile. And while the soil was still yielding good growth, without pesticides he couldn't control the insects ravaging the seedlings. Over time, the crop yield was smaller and smaller, and his payments to the bank became delinquent. Also during this time, his local bank failed and was converted to a national bank. The banking relationship he and his family built over the past century was gone. The national bank wasn't as lenient on overdue payments. His farm was seized by the bank before the NEP could shut it down. When David found him, he was living in a single-wide trailer on his cousin's pecan farm, picking up pecans and selling them at a local private farmer's market. His cousin was lucky as his land didn't have a stream on it.

And for unknown reasons, this salamander made a quick and successful comeback. The NEP restrictions were lifted, and the bank sold the land to the Party's National Grower's Union. After a clean bill of health from the NEP, the farm was active again. George didn't require much convincing from David. He was more than willing to join the mission, and his targets would be the local branch and employees of the NEP.

Since David was now finished in recruiting his five associates, he could focus on preparing to possibly go into hiding once phase one started. Unlike his recruits, David didn't have a role after phase one, and he didn't realize he was the only one granted this privilege. His recruited associates still needed to pick and eliminate targets during phase two, as well as continue recruiting, but David's job was finished. The *Guide* didn't specify he would have to go into hiding, but it did mention having a place to go was a good idea. David took this as a subliminal hint. If phase one didn't go well, or if one of his associates was caught, he needed to be ready to run.

He and Stephanie spent the previous weekend at the mountain cabin. David made several trips there during the week, stocking food and supplies in his survival room, which was still a secret he kept from Stephanie. She didn't need to know anything else at this point. Letting her know about the bank visits wasn't the best idea anyway, but it was working and he kept it up during their trips.

His withdrawals also increased during the week, and he was less paranoid about making them near his office in the blue zone. If the Party was aware of his actions and was looking for him, they would have caught him by now. The conversion at Tim's old hospital finished on time, and he received a nice bonus check. The majority of the check was spent on supplies for his survival room, and he was feeling pretty confident he had everything he needed.

It was Monday morning, and he arrived at work earlier than his normal time. Walking into the kitchen, he was glad to see someone brewed a pot of coffee. He poured himself a cup and added his two sugar packets, while slipping a handful into his pocket for use at home.

The offices on his floor were fairly empty as he made his way back to his desk. He was wondering who made the coffee, until he was met in the hallway by another administrative assistant, and she was startled by seeing another person there so early. In passing, she looked at the cup and said, "I see you found the coffee," as she continued down the hall. David previously noticed her scurrying around the office this early in the morning, but he didn't really know her, nor did he know who she worked for. But, like all of the other women who worked for the Party, she was young and pretty.

David walked into his office and placed his briefcase on the side of his desk. He pulled out his laptop, plugged in the external monitor, the mouse and the power cable, and turned it on. As he was waiting for the laptop to boot, he noticed a large white envelope on his stack of papers. The envelope was hand-addressed to him but was without a return address and it didn't have any postal markings either. He didn't remember seeing it on Friday, but he and Stephanie left early to go to the cabin. He held it up to the light, but it was a security envelope and he couldn't see what was inside. Taking a pen, he found the flap on the back, and ran the pen down the length of the envelope to open it. He reached inside and pulled out a single sheet of paper.

At first glance the paper appeared to be an invoice for office supplies. Most of the supplies came from a different department within the Party, and he never had to approve invoices, so this was unusual in that respect. As he read the line items, he couldn't remember ordering any of the office supplies listed. Whenever he needed office supplies, he would ask Stephanie for them. And, the list contained items he never used, such as three-ring binders, reams of paper and staplers. The invoice was puzzling, until he noticed the "deliver-to" name at the top, which displayed the name and address of Tim's hospital. As his eyes went back down the paper, this time a little slower, he noticed the invoice number. It was an eight-digit number ending with a dash and the number seven. The invoice number was in red ink, while the rest of the invoice was in black ink. It was clear to him now, and the invoice number, especially the lone number seven after the dash, was what solved the puzzle.

The *Guide* mentioned in rare cases, if you needed to convey a message to one of your associates, you could use a very simple code included in the book. The code only consisted of ten numbers, from zero to nine. Each number corresponded to an action or an item. If you needed to send a message, you could send the code, but it was better if you could disguise the code within or on another object, like an envelope or letter, or in this case, an invoice. Since this was an invoice for Tim's hospital, David was guessing the message was probably from Tim. David tried to remember what each code meant. The meaning of the codes were relative to the numbers on a telephone. The numbers on the right side, three, six and nine, stood for danger. Three meant you should be careful as you are being watched, while nine meant you were in grave danger, and you should go into hiding. Nine usually meant the Party knew who you were, and they were going to be paying you a visit, one you wouldn't enjoy.

The numbers on the left side, one four and seven, were related to performing an action. The number one instructed you to stop using your teller cards, and four directed you to increase your bank withdrawals. The number seven meant you needed to arm yourself. Seven signified that you needed to buy weapons. The numbers nine and seven, and their related tasks stuck in David's mind when he read the *Guide*. He understood why the number nine had significance, but he wasn't sure why seven made an impression on him.

The note bothered David, and he thought the logic behind the code system was a bit strange. He could see the need for notifying an associate if the Party was closing in, or even if you were being bugged or watched. But if you were being watched, shouldn't you go into hiding? If they were watching you, wasn't a visit from the Party inevitable? But he never understood the need to buy weapons. Maybe this code was for the other associates who needed them for their part in the mission. David had no such requirement. And for David, the only gun he ever shot was a pellet gun. His grandfather owned one for shooting rats and squirrels. But in his personal life, David never even thought about buying a gun. And now, Tim was telling him he needed to buy one, or more than one. Was his life in danger? Was he supposed to carry one with him at all times? If his life was in danger, wouldn't Tim have used one of the other codes? His paranoia, which had relaxed and was almost non-existent at this point, kicked in.

David kept reviewing the information on the invoice, trying to see if there was another message buried in the list of office supplies. When he looked at the bottom of the page, he noticed a small white label with one word which simply read, "Pull," with an arrow pointing to the right. He brought the paper up towards his face, and studied it closely. The label looked like one of those sticky notes with an arrow on it Stephanie would put on documents, marking where he needed to sign. The left side of the label was rounded on the end. He placed the paper on his desk, and held it down with his left hand. With his right hand, he took his index finger, and flipped up the end of the tab until he could grab it with a finger and his thumb, and he pulled it quickly to his right. As the tab lifted away from the paper, he saw a small spark and then a tiny flame appear. The reaction of the flame was so quick, he didn't even have time to move. In an instant, the entire invoice flashed yellow as the small flame ignited the paper and the invoice was gone, vaporized.

David didn't move, and was still holding the tab in his right hand. His left hand was a bit warm from the flash, but there wasn't any pain. David then recalled the letters Tim gave him, the ones he read in his bathroom and then destroyed with the lighter. This invoice must have been written on the same type of flash paper. And instead of needing a flame, pulling the tab discharged an ignition mechanism. That alone confirmed this letter was from Tim, and not a misplaced piece of paper. But why didn't Tim use this same paper, with the auto-ignite tab, in his original letters? Either way, he understood and the message was clear, he would need to buy a weapon, or many weapons. But there was still the unknown purpose. Was Tim telling him he needed these for protection? Or was David going to be asked to participate at a higher level in phase one or phase two which required weapons? Would a list of targets follow the letter? David wasn't sure, but it didn't matter, he was certainly going to do as he was instructed. He would need to buy weapons.

David started thinking of places where he could buy a gun. Since he was a Party member, he only needed to show his Party identification to purchase a weapon. There weren't any background checks, waiting periods or forms to complete. Members of the Party were the only ones excluded from such hassles, but David was positive the purchases were tracked. There was a huge outdoor recreational store on the outside of the main downtown area, but David couldn't remember if they sold guns. Not that he would remember, as he never ventured over to that side of the store. He had been there many times, but only to buy camping supplies and dehydrated food for his survival room. And he would rather not buy weapons in the blue zone. In the back of his mind, he knew the red zone was the place to go. His thoughts turned to the city near his cabin, and he was trying to recall if he had seen any outdoor stores in the area. He then remembered seeing the sign for the pawn and gun store, where he left Stephanie while he made his teller run, and where she found all of the used clothes.

David looked at his watch, and it was a little past seven-thirty. He would wait until around nine, and then tell Stephanie he had errands to run. If she asked any questions, he would say he needed to do business for the Party. She never questioned what he did, but if she did, she wouldn't question him any further after such a response. He checked his calendar, and as usual, he didn't have any meetings or conference calls for the day. Turning his attention back to his coffee and his work, he started working on his weekly reports.

David left the office a little after nine, and told Stephanie he would be back later in the afternoon. As he expected, she didn't even ask where he was going. David drove back to his apartment, changed his clothes and swapped his Party vehicle for his truck. If he was successful in his purchase, he would take the guns back to the cabin, and put them in the survival room. His knowledge of guns was less than nil, and he was ignorant on what type of gun he should buy, or how many. He would have to figure it out later.

The drive north was uneventful. Traffic was still thick on the southbound side towards the city, as it always was, and usually it would clear before noon. The highways in the blue zones were always invaded with these never-ending construction projects, and the construction teams always seemed to work during regular business hours. The national highway projects accounted for a large portion of the work benefits allocated to the population. Of course, most of the work was done in the blue zone, with the red zone left to fend for themselves.

David made it to the pawn shop a little before eleven hundred. As he parked in front of the shop, he stayed in his truck, and was looking all around the area, and trying to see inside the shop. Through the bars on the windows, he spotted an older man, and assumed he was the owner, or an employee. There was another person inside, a young woman, and David wanted to wait until one of them left. He didn't need or want any extra witnesses. As he waited, he studied the sign for the store, which read, "Mountain Randy's Gun and Pawn." The paint on the metal sign was faded, and the red letters were peeling around the edges. A few minutes later, the woman exited the store and walked down the sidewalk, and he watched her until she disappeared into another store. David decided there wasn't anything to worry about. People in the red zone probably buy guns all of the time. Why should his transaction be any different?

David left the truck, took another look around the area, and walked inside. As he opened the door, he heard a soft chime echo and fill the room. The old man looked at David. "Howdy. What can I help you with?" David casually walked over towards him, surveying the contents of the store. Like the store next door, it appeared to be filled with a lot of junk. There seemed to be an abundance of power tools in the racks running down the side of the store. There were guitars and brass instruments hanging on the wall above and behind a glass counter which ran along the right side and across the back. Then he spotted the guns. They lined the far back wall, behind the continuation of the glass counter. David was now at the back of the store, with the old man on the other side of the counter.

"Good morning. Yes, I am going to need help. I need to purchase a weapon." The old man's face looked concerned. David didn't know what that look meant.

The old man started walking over towards the gun display. "Well, I can help you. What did you need a gun for? Hunting? Home protection?" Then the old man cracked a smile. "Caught your wife cheating on you?" The last line shocked David for a second.

"Oh, no, no. I'm not married."

The old man laughed. "I'm only kidding, the last one there was a joke, son."

David politely but awkwardly returned a short laugh. "Home protection mostly. But I wouldn't mind having a gun or two for hunting. But I don't really know what I need, so can you show me what you have, and maybe help me decide?"

The old man stopped and was staring at David, as if he was sizing him up for a fight. "Have you ever shot a gun before?"

"Well, if you count a pellet gun, then yes."

David's response made the old man chuckle again. "Yep, I guess you can call it a gun, but we don't sell pellet guns. And it isn't going to do much for home protection. You might be able to take out a squirrel or a black bird, or maybe even a rabbit if you hit him right, but it isn't what you need." David watched as the old man took a rifle off the rack and held it in both hands. He pulled back a lever on the side of the rifle, and it make a loud clicking sound. David watched as the old man looked inside a slot on the side of the gun. David didn't really understand what he was doing. The man handed the rifle to David. "This here is a good hunting rifle. It shoots a three-oh-eight, and with this here scope, you can take out a deer or a bear from three hundred yards. You don't want to use it on rabbits or groundhogs, because there wouldn't be much left, but you can also use it on feral hogs, at least on the big ones." David had never heard of a feral hog.

The rifle felt heavy in David's hands. It was much longer than he thought it would be, with a long and thick scope on top. It didn't look like the short rifles he saw on television, the ones the police use. David really didn't know what he should be doing with it, now that it was in his hands. He handed it back to the old man. "That looks good. What else do you have?" The old man brought down another rifle, and again he fiddled with the side of the gun, before handing it to David.

"This here's an AR-15. You can use it for both hunting and home protection. It shoots a two-twenty-three or five-five-six. This is a much better gun in my opinion for home protection, but it does cost a bit more. You can still hunt with it, and it isn't as heavy."

Now this rifle looked more like what David saw on the news programs, as it resembled what the national police would use whenever they would surround a house or storm a business. There was a grip on the front and another one near the back. As David inspected the rifle, he noticed the business end of the gun was a lot thicker than the earlier rifle.

David pointed to the end of the barrel. "Why is this rifle thicker on this end?"

"That there is a suppressor. It takes away most of the noise when you shoot the gun. Now, it don't make it silent, but it makes it a lot quieter. People who shoot a lot at the range like the suppressor because it won't hurt their ears as much. And when you are hunting, you might be able to get off a second round before the game runs away. Not always, but it helps to have an option."

This gun was more like what David thought he needed. The rifle rack behind the counter contained at least a half-dozen more which looked like this one. He handed the rifle back to the old man. "This rifle looks like what I will need. Now, what about handguns? What kind of handgun would I need?" The old man put the rifle back, and then fished in his pocket for his keys. He unlocked and opened the door to the glass cabinet, reached inside and removed a handgun. He pulled on the end of the gun, and it popped back into place.

"This here is a nine-millimeter. This is really only good for home defense. And, you can carry it around with you if you have a CWP."

David took the gun in his hands and asked, "What is a CWP?"

"A CWP is a concealed-weapons permit. If you got one of those, then you can carry it in the red zone. Of course, you can't have any guns in the blue zone, not even in your car or in your house." The old man paused, and while looking at David, he added, "Well, unless you are a Party member. Then you can pretty much walk down main street with a machine gun if you want. But I wouldn't advise doing that." The old man's intuition was right. David wasn't from around here, where kids get their first gun and learn to hunt before they go to kindergarten. But a buyer was a buyer, it didn't matter where he was from.

David liked the smaller gun. It was lighter, and it felt good in his hands.

He still wasn't sure what he was supposed to do during the gun-buying process. Was he supposed to pretend he was shooting it? Should he stick it in the front of his pants like they do in movies? His only personal reference to guns, besides the pellet gun, was what he saw in the movies or on the television. The old man probably knew David was a novice at this, so there wasn't any point in pretending he knew what he was doing.

David asked, "Does this gun come with one of those things that makes it quieter? What did you call it, a suppressor?"

The old man cocked his head a bit. "Yeah, I think I have one which would probably fit it. I would have to double-check the threads to be sure. But, you gotta have a special license for a suppressor, and excuse me for saying so, but I doubt you have one of those. And if you don't have your CWP, then we got a background check which takes two or three months, and then there is a waiting period of another month or so."

David figured it was time to tell the old man something which might put them both at ease. Or at least it would put David at ease. "You are correct, I don't have a CWP, and I don't even know what that other license is you mentioned. But, I am a Party member, so it shouldn't be a problem, correct?" As he was talking, David pulled out his Party identification and badge, and laid them on the counter. When the man noticed the credentials, he backed up a half-step, as if he was scared to touch either one. The old man stepped forward and took the badge, and brought it up to his face and examined it. He did the same with the identification card, before handing both back to David.

A look of worry was now on the old man's face, and he folded his arms. "I'll tell you what. Why don't we cut the bull and you tell me what you are trying to do. Then I will decide if I can help you or not. I am not too keen about this situation right here. We don't get many, well, we don't get any Party members in this area. To be honest, I really don't like them very much."

David now knew what Susan meant when she said to keep his Party membership a secret. Maybe he should have stuck to the outdoor recreational store in the blue zone. But then David knew this old man could probably tell if he was lying, so he might as well be a little truthful with him.

"That's fair. To be honest, I have only been in the Party for a short while.

I received a promotion at work, which pushed me into the Outer Circle. For the past forty-seven years, I wasn't a Party member. But now that I am, I'm trying to make the best of it. I bought a cabin near here, and plan on moving here when I retire in a few years. And I want to be able to protect myself, and then do a little hunting for food. I have no idea what I am doing here, as far as buying guns and all. And so, I could really use your help. Now, that's the truth. Do you think you can help me?"

The old man seemed to be deciding if he wanted this business or not. Given the more than sluggish economy, he might want to put his differences and feelings about the Party aside. After all, money from a Party member was as good as any other money from regular folks. And, since David didn't know what he wanted, or what he needed, this might turn out to be a good day after all. The old man leaned over the counter. "I'll tell you what. I'll help you. I can tell you don't know diddly-squat about guns. So, I'll show you what I got, and I'm gonna make my recommendations, and if you have any questions, you ask them. I can set you up so you can do all of the home protection and hunting you will ever need."

David now felt a slight fondness for the old man. Hopefully telling the truth wouldn't come back to bite him. He spent the next hour with the old man, learning all about the guns. The old man explained which guns were good for hunting deer, or rabbits, and which guns were good when a half-dozen people were trying to get into your house. After his mini-lesson on weapons, the old man put away the final gun and turned back to David. "Well David, that's about all I got. Now, I've given you my recommendations, and I hope by now you have a good idea of what you are going to need. So, what'll it be?"

David felt fulfilled in a way, content that in the past hour, he really learned quite a lot of useful information. Even though he still didn't know why he was buying these guns, at least he felt a little more educated about them. "I really appreciate your time and all of your advice on the different guns and suppressors and ammo and hunting tips. I'll tell you what, I'll take it."

The old man didn't understand what he said. "You'll take what?"

"I'll take it. I'll take everything you showed me. And I also want those suppressor things. And ammunition. I'll need plenty of that as well."

The old man's face produced a huge grin. Yes, this was going to be a good day after all.

"For these types of transactions, we only can take cash." David nodded in agreement.

David arrived back at work a little after fifteen hundred. No one would have missed him if he had not returned, but he wanted to check in with Stephanie. He casually walked into his office, and when Stephanie heard him, she strolled in and sat down in one of the chairs in front of his desk. She didn't hesitate to start talking about work. "Okay, your reports all came in. And, I hope you don't mind, but I was bored so I went ahead and completed your reports. They are on the network drive. I was going to submit them, but I thought you might want to review them first."

David looked at her. Once again, he was impressed with her efficiency or job dedication, or whatever it was, and once more, he thought she was incredible. As he sat there staring at her, he remembered that a short time ago, he was alone and miserable. Even with what was happening with the mission, with all of the stress and uncertainty, the paranoia, he felt he at least had a friend. Well, it was clear she was more than a friend. But he hadn't felt this close to anyone in a long time, and it was a good feeling. He wasn't sure if it was love, or infatuation, or what. While he loved his first wife, that was so long ago he couldn't remember how to interpret his emotions. If he did have to go into hiding, maybe, just maybe, she would come with him. But he wasn't sure what he would say to her. Could he tell her the truth, could he tell her about the mission?

Phase one wasn't for several weeks, and he was pretty much done with his part. The withdrawals were being completed in a timely manner, and it was rare if he missed making all ten in one day. There was plenty of time to figure out what he was going to say to her, if he had to say anything at all. After phase two was over, he didn't know if he would be asked to do anything else. If he told her the truth, or if she discovered his participation, would she understand what he had done, or why he did it? People were going to die, and he was the instigator of these deaths. But the deaths were for a worthy cause, correct? The mission's purpose was to try and restore freedom and liberty. And these people, the ones who died, they deserved to be killed, didn't they? But could she get over her love for the Party, and redirect her love towards him, after what happened? This was a question he couldn't answer.

He realized he had been staring at her for longer than normal, and she was staring back at him. And of course, she was showing off her wonderful smile. The smile was key, the smile held all the answers. Yes, he could tell her the truth. He would have to tell her the truth. Maybe this was love he was feeling. After all, she was now too important to him, too much a part of his life for him to go on without her, that much he knew. She would have to understand his side of the story. If not, then maybe he wouldn't run. Maybe he would face the consequences of being involved with the mission. Would he want to go on if she wasn't there?

She interrupted the silence with a statement she never really asked him before. "A penny for your thoughts."

"I was thinking we need to go out to eat tonight, to a nice restaurant. I heard of this place which has great fish, and I hadn't had a good piece of salmon in a long time. I think the name is Ryan's Seafood. Maybe we could give that a try."

Chapter 31

The last month was incredible for David. The past four weekends were leisurely wasted at the cabin. Stephanie swapped her normal habit of volunteering at a Party event for time alone with David. David bought a homemade grill at the flea market, made out of a fifty-five gallon oil drum, and found a local butcher who sold real beef. He also purchased a freezer, put it in the basement, and stocked it full of meat. His favorite was rib eye steak, but he stockpiled an enormous amount of chicken, pork and homemade sausage as well. On Friday afternoons as they made the drive to the cabin, they would stop along the way at one of the many roadside stands and buy fresh fruit and vegetables for the weekend. Tonight they were having rib eye steaks, red potatoes and corn on the cob, and nothing was from a can. The man at the store told David how to cook the corn on the grill, and then add the steak when the corn was almost done. And per Susan's advice, David knew to check each ear for bugs or beetles or whatever. David picked up two bottles of local wine, and the plan was to eat and watch movies all weekend long. If the weather was nice, and if they felt like it, they might take a hike or have a picnic by the lake. David was settling in to a lifestyle he hoped would never change. But in the back of his mind, he understood and accepted the fact at any given minute, he might have to disappear.

At times he wished that he never met Tim. He would still have this new job, this new girl, and this great new life. He hadn't really used any of the mission's money on himself, as his new salary more than covered everything he needed to buy. Keeping his mind focused on the purpose of the mission was becoming more difficult, especially if his part was over for now. He still wasn't sure what he would need to do for phase two, so he needed to remind himself he needed to keep re-reading the *Guide* as much as he could. At one point, two weeks passed without him touching it. When he did read it, the words renewed his spirit about the mission, and he even believed it made him think more clearly. And, despite the fact he wanted his situation to be different, he made the decision to join the mission after seriously considering all other available options for a month. He knew in his mind it was the right thing to do. Someone needed to do something, even if this might not be the best way to do it. He really couldn't think of a different or better plan. The flowers must die in order to kill the hive.

David and Stephanie were sitting out on the deck in two wooden lounge chairs he bought at the flea market. The chairs Susan gave him were too small for relaxing. He was laying back with his feet on top of the deck railing, and she had a small blanket wrapped around her shoulders. They finished their incredible dinner, and were each sipping on a glass of the inexpensive but very sweet local wine. David discovered this wine at one of the farmer's markets, and Stephanie loved visiting and shopping at any of the local stores. She thought the places were tacky at first, but once she started buying knick-knacks for the cabin, her attitude changed. She had grown to think of the cabin as her place as well, and it was now filled with what she called "RZ treasures." Her attitude about the red zone and the mountain people, as she called them, changed even though she would probably never visit the area by herself.

The sun was starting to set, the temperature was dropping and there was a slow breeze blowing. The trees were losing a few leaves as the wind picked them off the branches and threw them slowly towards the ground. The date was September twenty-third, one week before phase one. David had been busy over the past two months filling the survival room with canned food and supplies, and enough dehydrated food for at least three or four years. And to make sure there was clean water to rehydrate the food and to drink, he purchased a special water filtering unit and pump he could use with lake or stream water, in case his regular water supply was unavailable. In the survival room he placed a double bed, blankets, and extra clothes for both Stephanie and himself, should she decide to join him. And he purchased enough ammo to hunt all day and everyday for a long time. He was pretty confident when, and not if, the time came for him to go into hiding, he would be okay for a while. The part where she joined him was still up in the air, but he thought she would say yes. He hoped she would say yes.

As usual, they were sitting out on the deck in silence, enjoying the night air and the closing darkness. Stephanie interrupted the quiet by asking David a question. It was another question she never asked before, and she seemed to forget the unwritten rule about not asking Party members personal questions. Over the past month or so, she had been wanting to say this to him, but she didn't quite feel comfortable until this very moment.

"David?" He leaned his head towards her, and noticed she wore an almost-sad expression on her face. "What are your thoughts on the Party?"

He moved his stare away from her, and his eyes opened wide, and his mind went blank. Of all of the things he prepared for, this question wasn't one of them. Up to this point, he assumed since she never mentioned the Party as far as he was concerned, it would never be a topic of conversation. When they first met, she was always talking on and on about the Party events, or the protests, or the wonderful new laws being passed. And like most young women who weren't in the Party, getting into the Party or marrying into the Party was their top goal in life. But this type of talk had subsided.

David removed his feet from the railing and sat up in his chair, placing his glass of wine on the table. He was unsure how to respond. What was the reason for this question? All he could think of for a response was, "The Party? What do you mean, what are my thoughts on the Party?"

"Well, I used to talk about the Party all the time, and heck, I am not even in the Party. You are in the Party, in the Outer Circle, but you never go to any events or even mention the Party. Every once in a while you will do your bank work for the Party, and of course I have never asked you for any details on what you are doing. I don't know, I guess I was curious as to what you thought about the Party."

David took a deep breath, and tried to disguise it as a yawn. What did he think about the Party? He certainly couldn't say he thought the Party was lawless and corrupt. He couldn't say that he, along with probably at least a few thousand other people, even though he didn't know the exact number, were hard at work with a goal of hopefully destroying the Party. There wasn't going to be an easy way out of this. Maybe he could turn it around and get her to talk about what she thought about the Party first. This way, he could be sure he didn't say the wrong things, and his answers could be tailored to match hers. Or was this a setup? Was she trying to get him to say something negative about the Party, so she could turn him in? He instantly despised himself for thinking that way, after all the time they spent together, but the Party instated strange thoughts and behaviors in their followers. For this moment, he would have to ignore that part of his paranoia. "That's a pretty broad question. The Party is like a big machine, with lots of moving parts. Could you be more specific?"

She responded quickly, as she had obviously given this subject a lot more thought than David, and the tone of her voice changed. "Yes, the Party is big, and they pretty much have their hand in every aspect of our lives. I mean, they provide us with health benefits, work benefits, retirement benefits, grocery benefits when we are hungry, and a place to live. I don't see how anyone could live without the Party. But, as we drive all around here, to the flea market, to the butcher, we see and meet all of these different people out here in the red zone. They really don't have anything to do with the Party. I know from my volunteer work we don't really operate out here. I know their Prosperity Benefit levels are probably a half or even a quarter of ours. They don't have a guaranteed work benefit, and I don't think they even have a housing benefit. Yet, whenever I go to the flea market, and I see these people struggling to live, struggling to survive by selling mostly junk, I wonder how can they be so happy? Most of the people I talk to, the guy at the vegetable stand, the man who sells the wooden birdhouses, or the woman who sold me this handmade necklace, they all seem to be so happy and friendly. All I hear at the Party meetings is how painful and miserable and dangerous it is to live in the red zone. On the news, all of the violent and vicious and horrible crime is out here. The murders, the looting, the unspeakable acts, I haven't witnessed any of it. And to be honest, I feel safer here than I do back in my own apartment complex. None of what I know or have been told about the red zone seems to be true."

The quantity of information she presented was too extensive for David to absorb. From reading the *Guide* and his own experience, David already knew the majority of what the Party said was a lie, especially when it concerned the red zone. The people in the red zone lived happy lives, as they were free from the majority of the Party's oppression. Of course, the laws were the same for both zones, but the red zone citizens either ignored the laws as much as possible, or found a way to survive in spite of what the Party did to them.

The Party was a well-oiled propaganda machine, and it only churned for the good of the Party. The Party made up the rules as it benefitted the Party, and ignored the laws it didn't want to follow. Corruption wasn't only at the highest levels, it flowed downstream and was absorbed by the members of the Outer Circle, who welcomed it with open arms. To be a part of the Party was like having permission to do whatever you wanted, to whomever you wanted, as long as it wasn't taking anything away from a higher-level Party member. And the higher levels made sure to grease the wheels of the lower levels, for they were the ones doing the actual work. Everyone in the party benefitted to a degree, and some more than others.

David had been quiet for a minute or two, trying to think of a response. "I don't know what to say. I joined the Party when I took this new job. So, I guess I am still learning what to do and what to say. I certainly am grateful to the Party for my job. I guess I haven't really given much thought to what you are asking or saying."

This answer probably wasn't what she wanted to hear, but he was hoping this would put an end to the conversation. Of course, he really wanted to take her downstairs, show her the survival room, and have her read the *Guide* so he could expose the Party for what it really was. She would have to understand. She would have to realize and accept the truth. Or was she too far gone, too far indoctrinated to understand and realize what the Party was really like? She wasn't ready to know the truth, and he couldn't do that, not at this point in time.

David placed his feet back on the railing, grabbed his wine glass and took a large sip. The sun vanished behind the mountain, and the stars were starting to appear directly above them. David leaned back and was looking straight up. A small touch of relief soothed his mind, as though he solved a major problem.

But after a short pause, Stephanie continued, and in a much more excited voice. "David, seriously, why would the Party say all of these things about the red zone?"

He didn't look at her. "Why does it matter what the Party thinks?"

She didn't really like his answer. "Why does it matter? David, all of my life, I have listened to the Party talk about the red zone. How their capitalistic free markets and food and everything were horrible. How the businesses took advantage of the workers, and they paid them low wages, and how scarce everything is and how whatever you bought fell apart or could hurt you. About how it is the most disgusting place on earth to live, how it is filled with degenerates, and prostitutes, and criminals and the worst things you can imagine. And the most despicable kind of people you can imagine lived out here. When I had to pick you up that night, from the store out in the middle of nowhere, I almost threw up, coming out here by myself, I was so scared. The only reason I came out here was because I was thinking if I didn't, you wouldn't be alive. I was positive someone was going to rob you or kill you, and I was going to drive up and see your body in the parking lot."

The sound of her voice was becoming more intense, almost hostile. "And then, the first time we came out here to see the cabin, I'll be honest with you, I was still scared, really, really scared. When you left me in the truck to do your Party business, I was terrified. I locked the doors in case anyone walked by, and I kept my head down, as I didn't want to make eye contact. I got out of the truck because I thought I would be safer in the store. The first time you suggested we stop at the flea market, I was sure someone was going to kidnap me or kill me, or worse. And now, we have been coming here for months, and all I can think about during the week, when we are at work, is coming to the cabin and spending time with you and going out and visiting the shops. All of this, it makes me think. If the Party has been lying to me about these people, about what goes on out here, what else is false? What else are they lying about? Why would they do that? What is the reasoning behind it? It doesn't make sense."

David removed his feet from the railing, leaned forward, and turned towards her. Besides the change in the tone of her voice, she was now visibly upset, almost angry. But he couldn't say what he wanted to say. "I don't know. Like I said, I have only been in the Party for a few months. I have worked for the Party for a long, long time. But I never really volunteered like you did. I did my job and I went home. I guess I was too busy trying to live my own life than to worry about what the Party thought or said or did."

Stephanie was now flustered. "You know, you are like my father. He was in the Party his whole life. He was at the highest level of the Inner Circle. And then he gave it all up to take a regular job. Before he left the Party, he was more enthusiastic about it than I ever was, or ever could be. Then his attitude changed, he wasn't negative about the Party, it just didn't mean that much to him any more. He is still in the Outer Circle, and he has a great job, but he stopped talking about it. And whenever I would visit for the holidays, I would go on and on about the Party and all of the work I was doing. He would sit and listen, and he would never respond beyond telling me he was proud of what I did. I've tried to be a good Party supporter, I really have. I honestly, really have."

David could tell she was highly agitated, and he needed to say something to comfort her, to put her mind at ease, but he really didn't know what to say or do. "Look, the Party is huge. It is all-encompassing. It has a grip on pretty much everything we do. If you live in the blue zone, you can't survive without the Party. Maybe they said those things about the red zone to make people feel better about living where they live. If you live in the blue zone and have a miserable life, knowing that other people, the red zone people are more miserable than you, maybe it helps some people feel better about their own situation. I don't think the people out here really benefit at all from the Party. I don't think they support it beyond the heavy taxes they pay. So, the Party favors the blue zone and the blue zone citizens. I don't know why the Party would say things about the red zone which weren't true. Maybe the things they said were taken out of context. Maybe the media is sensationalizing everything about the red zone. Boring stories aren't interesting. People want to hear all of the bad stuff and none of the good."

This seemed to settle her down a bit, or at least he thought it did. She was now quiet, taking a drink of her wine every few minutes. The breeze stopped blowing, and the stars were now everywhere in the sky. David finished his wine, but his mind was still racing. Should he tell her? He had read the *Guide* numerous times and he could easily explain everything from memory. He could tell her the history of the two parties and the reasons they merged into the current Party. He could explain all about the deceit, the lies, the corruption, and the ignoring of laws. But despite her need for comfort, or for answers to her questions, he still couldn't bring himself to do it. While it may have been a good time for her to discuss the Party, he decided he would only tell his side of the story at the last possible moment, and only if necessary. He needed to stick with this strategy.

The pending scenario had been reviewed in his head at least a dozen times. A message from Tim would appear on his phone, a message only containing the number nine. The number nine meant danger was inevitable, it was time to leave immediately, to go into hiding, and you couldn't waste any time in doing so. If he was at work, or out at dinner, or in his apartment, he would simply tell her to come with him. And as they drove out of the city and to his cabin, he would start talking, explaining everything to her. And if she didn't want to go with him, he would drop her off at a store or a gas station with money for a taxi. If they were already at the cabin, he might have more time to talk, to answer questions. If she disagreed, he would give her the keys to his truck and ask her to go home. He would then retreat to his survival room and wait it out. It didn't matter what scenario he played in his mind, to him the only acceptable outcome was if she stayed with him. He couldn't imagine going on without her. But he reluctantly decided he would go at it alone if he had to, if this was his only option for staying alive.

She finally spoke again. "David. What I am trying to say is this. If the Party would lie to me, and you, and everyone else about the red zone. What else is a lie?"

David's only response was, "I don't know. I really don't know."

Stephanie sulked deeper into her seat, and tightened the blanket's hold around her. The wind was absent, and the rustle of the leaves subsided, and the sounds from the woods were restrained. The waxing gibbous moon was attempting to spread its light on the valley below, and for a moment, it was as if time stopped.

Stephanie's attempt to persuade David to open up to her about the Party failed. She was never any good at reading people, and it was even tougher for her to ask direct questions, especially if the answer could be something she didn't want to hear. But she had questions which needed to be answered, and the wine brought out enough courage for one last attempt. She stared at David, who was laying with his neck arched backwards in the chair, and was uncomfortably gazing at the stars.

"David, I know you have less than five years of your work benefit left. And this may not be the best time to talk about this subject, but we haven't really talked about where we are in our relationship. I mean, where we are and how we feel about each other should be a given. I don't think either one of us doubts our status, even if we haven't specifically said anything. We have only been together for a few months, and I can honestly say I am happy when I am with you. Work doesn't seem like work as long as you are there. And when we come here, whatever troubles or worries I have, it is like I leave them at home. I almost wish our office was nearby."

Stephanie paused to take one last gulp of her wine, for added courage. "And I don't want to scare you, and I know this question may be too early to ask, but when you think of retiring, do you see me anywhere in the picture? Do you ever think about making this place your permanent home one day? I always thought I wanted to live in a fancy apartment downtown, right in the heart of the city. A place like what you have now, but a little closer in. But I don't want that anymore. I only hope we can continue doing what we are doing right now. If we can do that, I think I would be really happy. Do you think we are going to have a future together?"

David couldn't believe what she was saying. He had fallen for her within the first week or two, and he never imagined she felt the same way. With this mission, would he even be around next year, much less in five? If she was so enamored with this way of life at this moment, how would she feel towards him if it was all taken away? But now was not the time to disclose his secrets.

"I will be honest. Yes, I have thought about a future together, probably a lot more than you have. And it would be wonderful if we could keep continuing to see each other and spend time together. I agree, work isn't really work when we are together. I don't want to say that five years is a long way off, but it really is. I would rather not worry about the future. There are too many unknowns we can't control. I believe if we think about it too much, we will be distracted from what we have here, right now. But I will promise you this. If anything changes, or if for some reason I no longer have my job, I want you to come with me."

David realized he might have said more than he wanted to say. "You don't have to answer me right now, if you would go with me or not, as I am not going anywhere. But that's how I feel. A future together is definitely in my plans."

Stephanie's eyes felt heavy, and were filling with tears. His answer wasn't exactly what she wanted to hear, as she wanted one of them to say they loved the other one. Maybe the time for such a response was too soon. But she was satisfied with the information she received, and for the first time in a long while, she felt warm inside.

Chapter 32

This was the last full week of work before phase one was to occur. The plan for phase one called for all of the associates to hit their targets on the same date, Saturday, October the first, 2044. Then, after almost two months of endless news stories and assumptions on the reasons for these attacks, phase two would be executed on the last weekend in November. The date for phase two was chosen as the majority of the phase-two targets would be at home, celebrating the week-long fall holiday. And everyone, especially the new targets, would be relaxed and back into a normal routine.

The mission directors planned to have the outcome of phase one be the top story in the news for at least two or three weeks. During the first weekend of reporting, the media would be analyzing the deaths, and providing speculation on what happened. After a week, the funerals would start being held, and those events would garner another week of coverage. And then for the more important and famous targets, workers in the media department at the Party would sloppily put together the biographical stories on the all of the deceased, and those would run for a week or two. After two months of constant news reporting, the stories would gradually begin to die, especially if a good car chase, robbery, gang killing or scandal occurred. And the Party always had plenty of those types of stories ready to go.

David and Stephanie continued their weekend at the cabin. On Sunday, after their discussion about the Party and their relationship, Stephanie was quieter and seemed to be a little distant. She didn't want to really do anything but sit on the couch, drink wine and watch television. David suggested taking a hike or going to the flea market. But she appeared to be preoccupied with their discussion from the night before, or perhaps she was trying to overcome the effects of too much wine. She hadn't mentioned anything about what they discussed, and David certainly didn't bring it up. Now they were both back at work on Monday, and David devised a plan to keep her mind off their discussion, if it was still on her mind.

David arrived early, and as soon as Stephanie walked in, he asked her to come into his office. She was still quiet and not her usual cheerful self. He stated he needed to go and visit more clinics, and he wanted her to make his travel arrangements. He handed her a piece of paper with the addresses, and as she turned to walk back to her office, he asked her a question he knew would make her happy.

"Wait a minute." She stopped and turned around to face him, with a solemn look on her face. "Do you have anything urgent to do for the next two or three days?"

"No, not really. The reports from last week will be coming in, and so I can take care of those for you. Besides that, I have busy work, but nothing really important."

"I am not scheduled to visit the first clinic until tomorrow afternoon. And, since you don't have anything pressing to do, why don't you come with me on this trip?"

She was surprised, and her eyes lit up. "Wait, what? You want me to come with you?"

"Of course. I don't think it would be against the rules. But book two rooms in case anyone says anything."

Stephanie now had a mischievous look on her face. "But we won't be using one of those rooms, correct?" She flashed her incredible smile again, and his plan appeared to work.

"Exactly. If you don't have anything important, we can visit the clinics, and I can show you what we are trying to accomplish with this software, and all the other boring business stuff. We can leave after lunch, maybe around fourteen or fifteen, and try and beat the traffic."

Stephanie giggled before quickly turning away and scurrying into her office to make the travel arrangements. David thought, "That should do it, at least until we get back."

David and Stephanie were busy that morning. David was completing his reports, and contacting the clinics to let them know when he would be arriving. Stephanie was making sure everything was all set. She had never traveled on business before, and she drove home during lunch to pack. David would have finished by lunchtime, but they changed the format of the reports again, and it took him a bit longer than usual to finish his work. But by the time his watch read thirteen hundred, he was finished. Stephanie arrived back at work fifteen minutes later. She walked into his office.

"Okay, I am all packed and ready to go."

David kept staring at the monitor, even though he wasn't working on anything. His mind was captivated with thoughts about the possibilities of what would happen between them. After Saturday's discussion, he hoped she might be turning a little against the Party. And he was thinking if anything was going to derail his plans of going into hiding, it would be her. Her displeasure with the Party, was it a fleeting thought, driven by the amount of wine she consumed that night? What if she turned back to the Party-loving person she has been the majority of her life? When he asks her to go into hiding with him, what if she said no? Would he really be able to leave without her? What would the Party do to her if they found out she knew David was part of the mission? Would it matter if she only found out as David was leaving? The question wouldn't be, "if they would punish her," the question would be, "How severe?" Or, would she know to keep her mouth shut, and not say anything? Could she act surprised? Was she a good enough actress in that regard? The more he thought about it, the more he believed maybe he should prepare her for the news. Maybe there was a way he could test her, to gauge how she would react to the truth.

David's stare at his monitor was broken by her question. "Well, believe it or not, all of my reports are in, and I have finished all I need to do. Whenever you are ready, we can go ahead and leave early. We can stop by your place on the way out and drop off your car."

Stephanie beamed with excitement. "Let's go!"

They walked out of the office and down to the parking garage. David followed her to her car, and she drove him around to his car, and he followed her to her place. She found a parking space in front of her apartment, and he put her luggage into his car. The drive would only take two hours, if they were lucky and beat the traffic in both cities.

David was hoping to avoid talking about the Party during their trip, so he spent the time trying to explain the conversion process, the software and how it worked. David talked about the medical benefits software, and how it was able to link to all of the other national benefit databases, so every citizen's medical and benefit information would be accessible from one source. But the conversion was more complex than simply converting medical records. Since the main database also linked everyone's Prosperity Benefit information together, anyone in the national government could research and find out anything they wanted to know about a person. They could review their work, medical, unemployment, housing - all of their Prosperity Benefits information would be in one huge database. The theory was this solution would cut costs and make benefit allocation and approval much easier. David knew it was nothing more than an easier way to track and control everyone. David didn't know any of the details about the other benefit departments and what information was being stored, but at least the discussion killed enough time to avoid talking about the Party. He could tell she was bored from the conversation, and she really didn't care. But she politely acted like she did, and she even asked questions to appear interested, or to at least keep the conversation flowing both ways, but it was mostly to help ease her boredom. As they spotted the hotel, they both were glad the drive and the discussion was over.

They pulled into the hotel parking lot, dropped the car off at the valet, and went inside to check into their rooms. Like David suggested, Stephanie booked two rooms, and the hotel was able to get the rooms together next to each other on the same floor. A bellhop appeared and took their bags for them. The hotel clerk handed them their electronic keys, and they went up to their rooms. David went into one room, and Stephanie went into the other. The rooms were large and nice, with connecting doors between the two. David was a bit relieved when he saw the doors, as he noticed every hall in the hotel had several cameras mounted in the ceiling. Even though he was sure he wouldn't get into any trouble by taking her along, he didn't want the people watching to see her go into his room and not leave until the next morning. David wasn't sure if anyone would notice or not. It was best to not take any chances.

Once they were in their individual rooms, David opened his side of the connecting doors, and knocked. Stephanie opened her door as well. David said,

"Since you haven't traveled, and even though I don't think it is a problem with you coming along, when we leave the room, let's make sure we each go out our own doors."

Stephanie was perplexed. "Why? Why would it matter?"

"If you didn't notice, out in the hallway, there is a camera every ten feet or so, up in the ceiling. I don't know who is watching, or what they are recording, but it might be better if we leave our own rooms separately. Or maybe I can leave first, and then come to your room and knock."

"I think it is silly, but hey, you're the boss."

David never liked it whenever she said, "You're the boss." While it was true, given their relationship, it didn't sound good to him. But as usual, he shrugged it off. "I am going to try and log into the network, and see if I can pull up the project plans, so I can figure out the progress of the clinics we will be visiting. I should have checked before I left, but I wanted to beat the traffic. You are welcome to come in here and watch TV if you want."

Stephanie responded, "I need to take care of a few things. Give me about five minutes."

David walked over to the desk in the corner of the room, removed his laptop and a small stack of papers from his briefcase, and sat down in the chair. Connecting to the network at the previous Party hotels he frequented with his old job was never reliable. At least once or twice a month, he would have to switch rooms because the connection wasn't even available. However, this time, he was lucky and was connected almost immediately. He brought up the project application, and started doing his research. After wading through useless report after useless report, he finally found what he was looking for, the status updates. The clinic he was to visit tomorrow had been a national clinic for the past four years. They began the software conversion two years ago, and like most of the other clinics, the project encountered numerous problems. While David really couldn't do anything to solve the problems, he decided he at least needed to make an appearance, and pretend he could help.

He was engrossed in reading all of the minutia of the report, and how the project engineers kept having problems with one vendor, so they would cancel the contract and hire another one. To David, this seemed to be the usual reason why these projects were always late and over budget. A ranking member in the Inner Circle would award one of these projects to a friend or to a relative's company, even if they had no experience in this type of work. The vendor would flounder around for half a year or more, collect some consulting checks, and then get fired. And then another Inner Circle member would pick up the contract and pass it along to another friend. The circle of new contractors never seemed to stop.

David was almost catatonic, staring at an endless supply of numbers and notes which didn't seem to make any sense, when he heard a noise behind him. His eyes stayed focused on the screen, as he figured it must be Stephanie, and he continued to read. For this one project, the last company was hired six months ago, and it looked like they were finally making progress. But now they were having problems with the hardware vendor, which put a temporary hold on the project. David thought he should be amazed at the incompetence associated with this project, but he was getting used to it by now, and incompetence was simply another line item in the project plan. But for him, the finish line was not the five-year extension he was given, he only needed to make it through the end of November, after phase two. If he didn't have to go into hiding, then maybe he could actually try and solve these problems, even though he really didn't know what to do. But he liked the fact that maybe, possibly, he could actually be good at this job and make a difference. He was never given the chance to do that in his old job.

Stephanie let out a loud sigh, but he stayed focused and kept reviewing the reports. She then cleared her throat, but he didn't turn around, and kept staring at the screen. Then she cleared her throat again, and this time it was a little louder. Still unfazed, he kept reading until he heard her say in a songful voice, "David." He turned around, and saw she was under the covers in his bed, and her bare shoulders were barely visible behind her long hair.

"Is it quitting time yet?" She gave him a big grin.

David looked at his watch, and then back at her. "Close enough."

David and Stephanie enjoyed a great week on the road. They visited one clinic per day, and only spent an hour or two at each one. The rest of the time was consumed driving to the next town, and spending most of their spare time in the hotel. Even though the food at this level of Party hotels was much better than what David was accustomed to eating, they skipped the Party restaurants and sampled the local fare. Instead of worrying about getting reimbursed or being reprimanded for not eating at the Party restaurants, David paid for the meals himself.

They left work early on Friday for another weekend in the mountains. David was relieved the topic of the Party hadn't been broached again. Stephanie spent most of the drive talking about the fabulous time she had that week. She hadn't really traveled much since college, when she would volunteer to go to an out-of-town event for the Party. And they discovered she stayed at the same crappy Party hotels David had frequented for almost twenty-five years. They swapped stories and tried to best each other by stating they stayed at the worst hotel or ate the most disgusting hotel food. David, only by his sheer length of experience on the road, won that game.

They arrived at the cabin around sixteen hundred, having stopped by one of the stands for fresh vegetables and fruit, and also to buy more of their favorite cheap wine, which seemed to be in abundance no matter what stand or store they visited. David normally purchased two bottles with each visit, but this time he bought five cases, as he said he wanted to take it back with him to his apartment, so they could drink it during the week. But the real reason was he didn't know if he would ever be going back to his apartment, or if he would be confined to the survival room for an extended period of time. Phase one was to start tomorrow, and he was trying not to reveal his nervousness. Luckily for him, Stephanie was a bit hyperactive, and didn't notice he was more subdued than normal. They enjoyed a nice dinner, sat on the deck until dark, and watched a romantic comedy before going to bed. David's mind was racing about the mission, and he couldn't sleep. He also thought he should have had another glass of wine.

Chapter 33

The morning of October the first arrived, the start of the phase-one campaign. The sky was slightly dark, as the sun had yet to peek over the mountains. A man was slowly navigating a large black van down a winding and rough dirt road. As the vehicle came to a fork in the road, it stopped. The man reached over and picked up a piece of paper from the passenger's seat. Reading the directions again, he placed the paper back on the seat, and took the left road. He kept wondering why anyone would want to live out here in the middle of nowhere. The nearest town was over thirty miles away, and the town was a dump. The previous night was spent in the town's only hotel, but he slept on the floor on top of a sleeping bag. He wasn't taking any chances on using the bed.

The destination was drawing near, and the van was continuing at a slow pace, stopping every minute or two while he checked his GPS device and to look at the map and directions, which by now were almost useless. The map on his device showed his position as a blue dot, but the dirt road was no longer visible on the map. The dot appeared to float through the green area which represented the trees. The vehicle stopped about a hundred meters away from the target area. Quietly he opened the door, and reached over onto the floor of the passenger's side and grabbed a small backpack, and then slid out of the seat onto the dirt road. He carefully closed the door so it barely made a noise when the lock caught. The rest of the trip would require him to travel on foot, which would mean leaving the road and heading into the woods.

With his device in hand, he slowly started making his way through the trees. The leaves had already began to fall, but luckily for him, a recent rainfall softened the carpet of leaves on the ground. His heavy boots barely made a sound as he walked, and he paused every twenty meters to verify his position with the GPS. As he slipped through the trees, he would keep the trunks of the large trees between him and the target area. The mission was a little behind schedule, so mentally he was in a hurry, but he needed to take his time approaching. The woods opened and revealed a clearing, which cradled a small cabin nestled under a group of large oak trees, with their thick limbs jutting out over the roof. A wide expanse of camouflage netting was suspended from the limbs, blanketing the cabin on two sides. There was no doubt this was the place. Hunching over, he walked even slower, and leaned behind a large white pine tree. He squatted, and gently placed the backpack on the ground behind the tree. Checking his watch, he only had a minute or two before the sun would attempt to break over the mountains to the east.

He calculated he was about fifteen minutes behind schedule. Driving down the dirt road took longer than he expected. But it was early, and he had plenty of time. There weren't any lights on in the cabin, and he didn't see anyone outside. He placed his device in the bag and at the same time he retrieved a handgun. Out here, there was no need for a suppressor, as the nearest person was seven miles away. He did a quick survey of his route to the cabin. It was flat, and covered in pine needles and leaves up to the wooden steps in front of the cabin door. Moving from his position, he stayed low, and walked very slowly at an angle towards the steps, keeping his eyes fixed on the window on the side of the cabin, verifying the cabin was still dark inside.

Moving closer to the steps on the front of the cabin, he could no longer see the side window. His right foot was gingerly placed on the first step, over towards the right edge so the chance of the old wood making any noise would be reduced. His other foot moved onto the left side of the second step, and he cautiously worked his way up to the small porch area in front of the door. Stopping, he turned his ear towards the door, listening for any sound coming from inside, as he was almost close enough to touch the door. He paused again to listen, but there was no sound. His right foot moved slowly with another dainty step, and he reached up and placed his hand on the door knob, giving it a very slight turn, until he felt resistance. The door was locked.

At that moment, before he could remove his hand from the door knob, he felt a force hit him hard in the chest, as part of the door seemed to explode, and he stumbled backwards, off of the porch and onto the damp ground. As he lay in the needles and leaves, he found he couldn't move, and was gasping for air. The door swung open, and Tim walked out of the cabin with a shotgun in his hands. He chambered another round, and made his way down the stairs, with the shotgun and his eyes focused on the man. The assassin's handgun was five feet away from his body, thrown from his grasp as the buckshot tore open his chest.

Tim walked over to the man, and stood over him. The man was looking up at Tim, with a expressionless look on his face. Tim looked down into the man's eyes. "Really? Seriously? Phase one hasn't even really started, at least not until the sun rises. And yet they send you here to kill me. After all I have done for them. I didn't expect to see you until December. Well, to be honest, I was hoping I wouldn't see you at all." The man attempted to say something, but he couldn't respond. He was clutching his chest with both hands, and the blood that wasn't filling his lungs was slowly pooling onto the ground. Tim walked over to the man's handgun, shifted the shotgun to his left hand and picked the gun up off the ground. Tim examined the weapon, and he recognized this particular model.

"Not even a suppressor. I guess that makes sense out here. But I do hope you have one in your kit, as it would be a bonus for me." Tim studied the man's face, but he didn't recognize him. The Party usually brought people in from other regions to do this type of higher-level work. You couldn't use anyone local, as they might be recognized, especially by someone like Tim. The man's breathing relaxed, and after a few quick attempts to fill his chest with air, he became motionless. Tim didn't say anything else. But in order to be positive the threat was eliminated, he aimed the handgun at the man and fired two rounds into his chest.

Tim examined where the man was on the ground, looked back at his cabin, and then looked out towards the woods. The man's bag had to be out there, not too far away. You never leave the bag far away, as it was easy to lose after all of the excitement. Tim walked in the direction he thought the man might have taken, and after a quick search of the area, he located the bag behind the tree. Kneeling down, he opened the bag, and rifled through the contents. Inside was a suppressor, several passports, and a large manilla envelope filled with cash. He then found the man's device, a satellite mini-tablet. Tim thought, "Nice. A regular tablet wouldn't do a cleaner any good out here." Tim pressed a button, and the tablet's screen came on. The display was now showing what was known as a "clean form", displaying Tim's picture, the GPS coordinates of his cabin, and miscellaneous information about Tim. He knew what needed to be done, and he pressed a button marked, "Status" on the top of the form, and a small window appeared. The window displayed two additional buttons, one with a red X, next to one with a green check mark. Tim pressed the green check mark, and after a small wait, a message popped up which read, "Delivered." Tim had sent verification back to the Party that he was now dead.

Tim looked at his watch. Even though he was a little under three hours away by car, he might be able to make it. It was very early in the morning, but he would have to hurry. He took the bag and began walking as quickly as he could back to the cabin, careful to avoid going anywhere near the assassin. There wasn't time to do anything with the body, and it didn't matter. No one would be looking for him for a while. Tim was positive the man had other targets to hit, but given Tim's location, his next job probably wasn't until tomorrow. And besides, the coyotes and wild boar and other animals would take care of the evidence. He turned off the tablet and dropped it into the bag. He took the cash, the gun and the suppressor, and left the tablet and the bag on the floor of the cabin.

Tim grabbed a large backpack and placed the items from the assassin inside. He knew this day would come, even though he was hopeful it wouldn't, at least not until after phase two, or maybe even phase three. He was always packed and ready to leave in an instant, assuming the outcome would have been in his favor. As he walked out onto the porch, he remembered the need for transportation. Heading back inside the cabin, he retrieved the man's bag, reaching into it and finding a set of car keys. Tim checked his watch again. If he hurried, he should make it in time. He left the cabin and began walking through the woods at a brisk pace, trying to maintain a straight line, looking for any signs of where the man walked. All he needed to do was find the vehicle. If he was lucky, the other cleaner would be delayed with their target.

Chapter 34

An hour north of the city, the honorable Judge William Raymond had a big day planned. William lived alone, in a large house on a huge lake which spanned several miles, and provided water to most of the blue zone to the south. The lake and the surrounding property was one of the odd blue zones rural areas technically located in and surrounded by the red zone. The Party secured control of the lake, and annexed the majority of the prime real estate areas, so they would have more control over the housing, recreation and taxes. The majority of the houses and mini-estates surrounding the lake were occupied by Party members. The recreational areas, which were once filled every weekend with people from the red zone, were now closed off to the general public. This exclusion led to a minimal and controlled use of the lake, and therefore offered protection to the fish occupying the clear blue water. William was going to take advantage of this situation, and he was going to reap one of the rewards of being a Party member.

Living on or near a lake since he was a small child, William found great pleasure in fishing. But he was somewhat of an introvert, and he preferred to fish alone. Despite only being in the Outer Circle, he was one of the Party's most vocal and active proponents. And after a long week of enduring what he considered to be another boring criminal trial, nothing made him happier than spending a relaxing morning fishing. Like most older and successful Party members, he was divorced and spent his non-fishing time chasing young Party-hopefuls. But he was feeling a little tired yesterday, and woke up this morning alone. Plus, he preferred to get out before sunrise, so he could get into position to take some largemouth bass.

William walked from his house across his freshly-cut lawn, and down to his boat dock. His shoes were covered with a mixture of grass clippings and morning dew. A cooler was filled with his regular fare, a six-pack of beer, a handful of cigars, and a sandwich or two. Even though he always packed sandwiches, he normally drank his beer and enjoyed a cigar for breakfast and lunch. A typical day on the lake would end when he would stagger back home before it was too hot, and sleep it off in a hammock stretched under two large birch trees. If the ducks or geese made an appearance, he would feed his sandwiches to them. The drunker he was, the more likely the ducks would eat well that day, and the waterfowl usually ate more often than not.

Climbing into his bass boat, he placed his cooler down behind him, sat in the front chair and used the trolling motor to gingerly back out into the lake. Once free from the dock, he switched to the seat behind the steering wheel, and he started the larger engine but took off very slowly, and maintained a relaxing speed across the lake. The art of taking one's time while fishing was one of his only proficiencies concerning the sport, along with enjoying the morning and the solitude. For him, fishing was never about catching fish, even though when he did, it provided some excitement. Fishing was a reason to get outside, drink beer, smoke some cigars and relax. When he gained enough speed and entered the mouth of the cove right next to his house, the motor would be turned off, and he would drift as far as possible towards the back of the cove, using the trolling motor if needed. Only after opening a beer and lighting his first cigar of the day, would he start fishing.

The cove was narrow but deep, and snaked back through the trees and curved in a direction away from his house. Today's objective was to drift towards the back, where no one from the main part of the lake could see him and ruin his seclusion. The boat was allowed to float, hugging the cattails and skimming over the lily pads, and he would fish on one side before turning around and coming back up the opposite side. If the fish were in a mood to be fooled by his lure, there was a chance to catch one or two early in the morning, or whatever quantity would be enough to satisfy his fishing urge, where he could spend the rest of the morning drinking and smoking. As a custom, he checked to make sure water was in the live well of the boat, even though he rarely kept any fish. Cleaning fish was too much of a hassle and he didn't do much cooking.

After an hour and a half of floating and drinking and smoking, and without any success with the fish, he finally reached the end of the cove, thanks to the kind wind at his back pushing him along. A fishing trip was always nicer when he didn't have to use the trolling motor, which required constant attention and thinking and a deftness he would lose as the morning was spent. After one cigar and three beers, the call of nature that had been building inside him for the past twenty minutes was knocking on the door.

The boat drifted into an irate cluster of cattails, and he decided now was a good time for relief. The anchor was carelessly tossed over the side, even though he probably didn't need it, as the wind carried him close to the bank. The decision to cast the anchor was based more on alcohol-consumption than logic, as the cattails had a secure hold on the bow. He placed his fishing pole on the seat behind him, opened another beer, and then staggered up to the bow to relieve himself in the water. With his hands full, he couldn't figure out what to do with his cigar, so he put it back in his mouth. Only one hand was needed for this particular job.

Standing on the bow, as he was relishing in the comfort of his emptying bladder, from the nearby woods, an arrow flew into his chest and exited out his back. Stumbling backwards, he landed on the front seat near the trolling motor. The beer fell from his hand onto the deck, and with the cigar still clutched in his mouth, there was a slight hesitation, as his body waited for gravity to decide the next move, and he slumped to his left and plunged into the water. Thirty-five meters away, behind a large oak tree, Gary was standing there, with a bow in his hand. The revenge he had been seeking for his wife's and unborn child's murder was finally fulfilled. The honorable William Raymond would not do any more bending of the laws or legislating from the bench. In Gary's mind, the revenge was sweet and harsh, but justice had finally been served. His wife and unborn child could now rest in peace.

Gary walked a couple meters closer to the water for a better look. The judge wasn't moving, and the cattails were preventing him from drifting, and were doing their best to hold him in place. He scanned the horizon, out across the quietly-lapping waves, towards the open water, and no witnesses were visible. Satisfied his work here was complete, Gary turned around to start the long walk back to his truck.

Almost an hour passed before Gary made it to the old store where he parked his truck. Before popping out of the bushes, he looked around to make sure nobody was watching. With the area clear, he quickly walked to his truck, placed the bow and quiver in the back, and sat inside. Closing his eyes, he remained still, to allow his mind and body to became calm, and also to rest from his hike. Reaching over, he opened the glove compartment, and pulled out an envelope, which was addressed to him, but without a return address. He opened the envelope, pulled out a folded sheet of paper and looked down at the name and address hand-written on the inside. Gary would have one more stop before heading home. The address was for Johnson Bryce.

Several hours later, school principal Marvin Armstrong was outside, enjoying the nice fall morning. Marvin was a former teacher, a school principal for the past eleven years, and was a year away from fulfilling his work benefit. Along with his wife and a cat named Belle, he lived in a small but charming house, with a well-groomed yard, located a few blocks down the street from the school. Marvin's wife had gone with friends to go shopping, and he was outside, reluctantly trimming the boxwoods surrounding his house. The weather had been warmer than normal during the past month, and he was hopefully cutting them for the last time this year. He thought the trimming could have waited until the following Spring, but his wife disagreed.

Marvin happily tolerated working in his yard. For the most part, it was mindless work, and he enjoyed being outside, even if the pleasure was confined to his yard. He attended his school's football game the night before, and slept in a little later than usual. That morning, after rising, he went into the kitchen for a cup of coffee, and he saw the note from his wife, stating she would be back around lunchtime, along with the friendly reminder to trim the hedges. Breakfast was a plate of scrambled egg-substitute with a dry piece of toast, and coffee to accompany him while he read the morning news online. After procrastinating for a half-hour, he reluctantly made his way outside. Sometimes, yard work was pleasant and relaxing in an odd way, but his least-favorite task was trimming the bushes. The problem was his lack of skill, in being able to apply the cut at the same height along the long row. But at least he would be done in an hour or two, to allow time for a shower before the college football games started.

The work was finished in an hour and a half, and he checked his watch, and there was plenty of time to go and check on his garden. Like most residents with a back yard, every good Party-supporter grew what they called a "Sharing Garden." Besides providing a way to supplement your food supply, the idea was if you grew too much of one vegetable, you could share it with your neighbor, who either didn't have time for a garden, or didn't have the room or the resources. And likewise your neighbor would share their excess vegetables as well. The concept sounded credible, but most people kept what they grew and canned what was left over. Fresh vegetables were too valuable to share, and certainly too precious to waste on a neighbor.

Marvin had three tomato plants and one bell pepper plant still producing. Separating the long electrical cord from the clippers, he began looping it around his arm. Finished with the cord, he grabbed the clippers and started walking back towards the garden to the old and rusty shed, with the one door dented on one side so it was difficult to open. As he approached the shed, both doors were closed, which was unusual as he left the bad door open earlier to avoid hearing the outcry from the hinges. The wind must have closed it.

Placing the trimmer on top of his wheelbarrow which was leaning up against the side of the shed, and with the bundled cord in his left hand, he reached over and pulled hard on the shed door. The door creaked and hollered, as if it were in pain and resented being touched. As he stepped inside the dark shed, a blue wrapped-up towel was hovering in the air, directly in front of his chest. Past the towel and still in the darkness, a familiar face could barely be seen. Before he could react or his mind could process the image before him, Thomas Chambers put a bullet into the left side of his body. Marvin fell to his knees, still clutching the cord, while attempting to grab the air for support. Thomas placed the towel closer to him, pressing it against the other side of his chest, and fired again. Marvin awkwardly lurched backward, and collapsed onto the dirty floor of the shed. Thomas placed the towel-wrapped gun down on a small table, and pulled Marvin's body towards the back of the shed. Thomas took the gun and towel and shoved both into a plastic bag which he stuffed into a backpack. Walking out of the shed, he attempted to gently close the doors, and vanished into the woods behind the house.

Around eleven thirty, Officers Webb and Jablonski arrived at Alejandro's for an early lunch. Alejandro's had a faded sign in the front window of the restaurant which welcomed police officers, and the sign offered them a fifty-percent discount on their meals. The owner, Alberto Alejandro, lived in a rougher-than-usual area of the blue zone when he was younger. One night as he was walking home from work, he was surrounded by a local gang. As they started beating him, two officers drove up in their patrol car, and the gang scattered. Alberto never forgot that night, and ever since, he has tried to show his appreciation to the police.

But Officers Webb and Jablonski saw his gratitude as an opportunity. At first, they were appreciative and humbly accepted the discount, and would leave a nice tip for the waitress. After a while, they decided a tip wasn't necessary. And soon after that, to them, paying for the meal became optional as well. They would eat here two or three times a week, and instead of paying the check they would walk up to the counter and hand it back to Alberto. They even stopped saying "thanks" after a while. Alberto finally accepted it as a cost of doing business. The other police officers who ate there were not as brazen.

Alejandro's was a small family restaurant. His two daughters were the waitresses, and he and his son swapped the cooking and busboy duties. His wife was in charge of ordering the supplies and doing the accounting. She also had an illegal second job, helping the local neighborhood businesses with their lengthy weekly compliance and benefit forms. Because of her assistance, the small ethnic neighborhood began to prosper. Starting a small business was easy compared to managing the relentless and endless stream of paperwork and regulations.

Webb and Jablonski took their usual seat in the back corner booth. They liked this secluded spot because it gave them an opportunity to talk about whatever scam they were running at the time, without a fear of being overheard. Even though they were in the red zone, they possessed a sort of diplomatic immunity, at least as far as petty crimes were concerned. Along with the majority of their fellow officers, they had several schemes going at once. If you owned a business in their jurisdiction and wanted protection from the local gangs, you either gave them food, merchandise or money. Even if there weren't any gangs in your area, you still were required to pay the police a little extra for doing their job. The officers who didn't partake or approve of this practice simply looked the other way.

Their waitress, Maria, came over to take their order. Jablonski was the first to speak. "I'll take a number eleven, but with extra refried beans, and a coffee. Oh, and a bowl of the cheese dip with peppers, and an extra side of the dark-looking hot sauce. I don't want the red sauce."

Maria turned her attention to Webb. "Yeah, a number eleven sounds good, but I want a sweat tea, no lemon." Maria flashed a smile, took their menus and walked back to the kitchen. Alberto's son, Israel, took the order from Maria and placed it in the ticket holder above the grill. She wrote a small X on the bottom of the ticket, and circled it. She made sure Israel noticed the marking.

After a few minutes, Maria brought the officers two large plates of beef burritos, smothered in cheese, with two large helpings of refried black beans. She interrupted their conversation as she put the plates on the table. The officers didn't waste any time eating. The food at Alejandro's was excellent.

Once they finished their meal, Maria walked over to them. "Officers, this meal is on the house. No ticket today." Jablonski and Webb looked at each other like they solved a big case or won a prize at the fair.

Jablonski said, "Well, it's about time. I mean, how long was it going to take for Alberto to get the message? He should give all of us free meals. We do a lot for this guy. When was the last time he was robbed, huh? You can't get any better insurance from anyone else." Webb snickered. Maria smiled, and cleared their plates off the table.

Jablonski and Webb stood up, straightened their heavy belts, and strolled out to their patrol car. As they settled into their seats, Webb turned to his partner. "It took him long enough to get the message. The guy must be dumber than dirt." Jablonski smirked, turned on the engine, backed up the car, and then headed out onto the street. Webb kept talking. "You know what? I think I might see if Maria would go out with me. What do you think? Huh? She has to be what, twenty-one, twenty-two years old? That's plenty old enough, don't you think? You think she would go out with a old guy like me?"

Jablonski laughed. "No, I don't think she would go out with you. If you lost about fifty pounds and grew a foot, then, maybe. Then again, nah, she would never go out with you. You need to throw your line in some other pond. That ain't gonna happen." Webb responded with a loud and wet belch.

Jablonski kept looking straight ahead as he drove. "Sure is nice when you taste it twice," and he laughed.

The pair continued their leisurely drive through the run-down area of town, passing vacant homes and businesses with their windows covered with plywood and graffiti, until the car turned onto the main highway and headed back towards the more prosperous side of the depressed town. In the past week, the weather had turned cooler than usual, and the day was forecast to be nice and clear, and traffic was oddly light. As he continued to drive, Jablonski noticed his hands were clammy, and the steering wheel had developed a stickiness. Webb then let out a thick guttural grunt, and he grabbed the left side of his protruding stomach.

Jablonski noticed the movement. "Hey, you alright?" Webb didn't respond, except for another grunt. He was bent over slightly and sweat was trickling down his face. Jablonski asked his partner again, "Hey, what's wrong. You alright?" Webb was buckled over, with his head against the dash and his body wasn't responding, although the muscles in his left forearm were involuntarily twitching.

Jablonski reached over and gave his partner a shake. He tried to focus on his partner, but his eyes were watery, and his vision was a little blurry. As he turned his eyes back on the road, his vision temporarily returned, but his thinking was muted. Then he felt a sharp jab in his side, as if a person stuck him with a small knife, causing him to let out a grunt as well, and accompanied by a tiny surge of vomit which settled in his mouth. Another sharp pain stuck, and then another grunt, with this one being longer and higher in tone than the previous one. Immediately, the pain was unbearable and the haze thickened his thoughts, so much so he forgot he was driving. His mind was only concentrating on finding the knife and pulling it out of his side.

His arm kept reaching for the knife, but it wasn't there. The pain intensified, the short bursts now became one long-stabbing pain, and he was still having trouble finding the knife. The pain distracted him to a point where he hadn't even bothered to reduce his rate of speed, and the ability to recognize the approaching red light was lost as well. As the intersection and the waiting cars drew closer, his senses were awaken for an instant, and he jerked the car to the left. The maneuver prevented a collision with the stopped cars, but he failed to negotiate the path of a large cement truck coming from his left side, and the driver didn't see him either. The truck slammed into the side of the patrol car, which shattered into dozens of pieces, along with Jablonski and Webb.

Back at Alejandro's, the lunch shift had been in full swing, and the flow of customers finally stopped. Alberto and his staff weren't graced with the presence of any more officers, only the normal crowd of locals and blue-collar workers. Israel had been busy for the past hour, and now the orders calmed down and he was caught up with washing the dishes, he told his father he was going outside for a smoke.

Israel walked towards the back of the kitchen, past the prep counter and walk-in freezer, and out the creaky steel back door. Pulling his smokes out of his apron pocket, he sat down on an old vegetable crate. He flipped the package upwards, until a single cigarette popped its filtered head out of the pack. Leaning to his right, he offered the cigarette to Lewis Chambers, who was sitting beside him on a crate. Lewis accepted the offer, and leaned closer so Israel could grant him a light. He took a long deep draw, held it, and exhaled slowly. Israel took a cigarette, lit it and took a quick puff, exhaling the smoke through his nose and all over his clothes. Words really weren't necessary at this point. After a few more puffs, Lewis stood up, adjusted his sagging pants, reached into his pocket, pulled out an envelope and handed it to Israel.

"One thousand." Israel took the envelope and put it in his back pocket, and Lewis walked away, flicking the cigarette against the back wall of the restaurant.

Chapter 35

David was still in bed. Sleep had been teasing him off and on through the night, as his mind didn't want to be alone. During the brief periods when sleep won, a bevy of strange dreams ruined each session. When he woke, he couldn't remember the details, which was probably a good thing. Stephanie had risen earlier, and David heard the sounds of someone in the kitchen making breakfast. The plan for the day was simple. They would wake up early and go to the flea market, and maybe do some sightseeing if it wasn't too cold. Some type of activity was going to be needed to take his mind off of today's events. The clock read nine-eleven, which was later than what the plan called for. The flea market was already open, and Stephanie loved getting there early to take advantage of whatever bargains were available. Forcing himself to get out of bed, he ambled to the bathroom for a quick shower. He knew Stephanie would be anxious and would want to leave soon.

After the shower, he put on blue jeans and a long-sleeved camouflage shirt Stephanie bought him. She thought since a lot of the people in the mountains wore camouflage, he should wear it as well, to "blend in with the locals" as she put it. And as always on the weekends, he skipped shaving, as she liked the stubble on his face. He walked out of the bedroom, across the living room, and towards the dining room table. Stephanie was sitting in a chair, warming both of her hands with a cup of coffee, and looking out the sliding glass doors, enjoying the morning view of the valley below. She cocked her head towards him. "Good morning. I heard you in the shower, so I made your breakfast. Scrambled eggs and biscuits with some local honey we bought last night. There's apple butter in the fridge if you are tired of the honey. I wasn't sure if you wanted any sausage or not, but I can make some if you want."

David was impressed. "You made biscuits? From scratch?"

She swiveled her head back towards the view. "Well, yes and no. These were from that jar of biscuit mix I bought last weekend at the flea market. So, if scratch means they came out of a jar a stranger prepared, then yes. But I did mix it all together and made little round shapes and put them in the oven. I should get a little credit for that much."

David sat down at the table. She even poured him a cup of coffee, and it was a given sugar was already added. His chair was on the side of the table, and the view wasn't as clear as where Stephanie was sitting, but he didn't mind if she took the good spot. The view would still be there later. The eggs were perfect, nice and fluffy, and were unlike the runny hotel ones, only because they were real. Everyone around here owned at least a few chickens, and they purchased these at their favorite roadside stand. He couldn't imagine ever eating the fake eggs from a hotel again.

David finished his breakfast, and took his plate into the kitchen. He was still tired, so he poured another cup of coffee. As he stood there slowly enjoying his coffee, he altered his gaze between Stephanie and the view outside. Looking at her, he almost forgot what day it was. All of the thoughts which kept him up last night started flowing back into his head. Would she go with him if he needed to leave? Even if he received a warning, would he even have enough time to leave? Maybe he should leave now. His part of the mission had been over for a long time. Almost a million in cash was in a bag in the survival room. If they could find a place to live here in the red zone, hidden in the mountains, that amount of money would last for a long time. They could get a small house, grow their own vegetables, and maybe have five or six chickens. His mind slipped into another daydream, and he didn't notice Stephanie stood up and was walking to the front door.

As she disappeared from view, the presence of her empty chair broke his train of thought. He walked out of the kitchen, past the dining room table, and into the living room. Stephanie already made it down the small hallway towards the front door.

"Stephanie?"

As she walked, she said, "I think someone is at the door. I thought I heard a knock."

His mind couldn't react in time, and he began to walk quickly towards her. His thoughts were scrambled and he temporarily forgot how to speak. He finally managed to softly blurt out, "Wait!", but the warning was too late, she had turned the deadbolt and started to open the door. As the door swung to the side, David was expecting to see the national police standing there, with guns pointed at them.

Instead of a gang of policemen, there was a lone man, standing there wearing a baseball cap, and holding a backpack. As the man looked up, David recognized him, and he whispered to himself. "Tim?"

At that moment Stephanie recognized him as well. In a questionable voice, she asked, "Daddy?"

Tim cracked a smile, and Stephanie quickly flung out her arms and wrapped them around him. David stood there, in a daze, talking to himself. "Daddy? Tim?"

Stephanie was almost shouting with excitement. "Daddy! Wow! I can't believe you are here. Come in, come in." Tim walked through the door, placed his pack on the floor, and Stephanie took him by his arm, and led him towards David. "Daddy, this is David. David, this is my daddy." David couldn't move as he was trying to figure out what was happening. Was it possible he was still dreaming?

David finally spoke. "Tim. Good to see you again."

Stephanie did a double-take. "Hold on, you two know each other?"

Tim was so relieved to see his daughter and David alive, for an instant, he forgot why he was there. "Yes, we know each other. David used to, well, he used to try to sell me medical supplies at my hospital."

Stephanie was euphoric. "I can't believe you two know each other. Oh, this is incredible." David and Tim stared at each other. David had several ideas on why Tim was there, but he didn't know if he was there to kill him or to warn him or to save him.

Tim then remembered his purpose of coming here. Slipping out of Stephanie's arm, he started walking towards the back of the cabin, into the living room, and he stopped at one of the windows looking out into the valley. Standing to the side, he gently peeled back the curtain on the right side of the window. The deck almost blocked his view of the valley below, but he surmised he had a good enough view without having to go outside. Outside was not a safe place to be.

"Well, we can catch up in a bit. First, David, have you heard anything unusual this morning? Any unusual noises around the doors or windows? Have you been outside yet?"

Stephanie was perplexed. "Daddy, what are you talking about?"

Tim turned to Stephanie, and in a fatherly but commanding tone said, "Stephanie, I need to talk to David right now. Please be quiet for a moment."

David was still staring at Tim. Tim wasn't there to kill him. Tim knew something was going to happen, and it probably wasn't good.

David replied, "No, Tim. We haven't been outside. I just woke up, and took a shower, so I haven't heard anything." Tim checked his watch, and then returned to the window. The only reasonable explanation was they must have gone to David's apartment first. And then realizing he wasn't there, they looked at his file and discovered he owned a cabin. But wouldn't they have already known that? They couldn't have been so sloppy. Maybe the cleaning teams were stretched too thin, as they were dispersed across the country, ready to take out any associates who had been caught or failed. If the Party was going to take you out at your home, they did it as early in the morning as possible. The only other plausible reason for the delay was the cleaner had multiple targets this morning, and David was number two or three. Or maybe there was another unknown reason why this event was delayed. Tim continued to look out the window, scanning the woods and the valley below.

Stephanie couldn't take the silence. "Daddy, please tell me what is going on. You are scaring me."

Tim then saw a movement through the trees, down towards the bottom of the mountain, at least a hundred meters away. The movement was a quick flash of black, followed by another, and then another. The figures were moving to Tim's left, possibly moving up the road. Tim was trying to follow the motion to his left, while trying to notice any additional movement between the trees. There was no doubt, this was a cleaning team. But why would they send a whole team after David? A single man could have easily done the job. Also, didn't they know Stephanie was here? The agreement was they wouldn't hurt Stephanie. They had an agreement.

Stephanie asked again, but in a softer voice. "Daddy, please talk to me."

Tim whispered. "Wait a minute sweetie. Give me a minute here."

Then Tim heard it. A very faint and low rumbling sound, like a large truck engine idling. His eyes moved up from the bottom of the hill, out past the woods and up out into the valley. A large bird, or an even larger black object was moving along the top of the tree canopy, out there, across the fields, far away. His eyes began to water, and he lost his focus. And there it was, a police drone hovering just above the landscape, and it was coming in fast. They might have a minute, maybe less.

Tim quickly spun around and looked at David. "David, we have a group of men and a drone coming in. We might have one minute. We have to leave now."

David froze for a second, trying to comprehend what Tim was trying to tell him, as he wasn't sure, but did he say drone?

Tim yelled "David! We have to move now!"

David tossed his coffee cup onto the floor. "Follow me."

David grabbed Stephanie's arm, whipped around and took a few steps, and opened the door to the basement. "Hurry!" He was almost dragging her while running down the steps as fast as he could go. Tim grabbed his backpack and was right behind her. As David pulled her towards the back of the basement, he flipped open the thermostat cover, punched in the code, and waited as the heavy concrete door started to slowly open. David was muttering at the door. "Come on, come on!"

As soon as the door was open wide enough, David pushed Stephanie inside. Tim followed with his backpack, and David stepped in, and after ensuring both of them were clear of the door, he reached up towards the big red button. The noise, the loud, rumbling noise of a Party drone could now be heard, and the sound paralyzed him for a moment, and he could feel the concrete floor slightly vibrating. David slammed the button with his palm, and the heavy door stopped opening and quickly reversed course, closing with a soft but booming thud.

Outside, the cleaning team made it up the hill, and took a position along the ridge, on the right corner side of the cabin. One of the members held up his rifle and looked through the scope. He located the sliding glass doors, pressed a button, and a green dot from a laser appeared on the glass. With a deep and firm voice, he said to one of the other men, "Target acquired. Ready for go." The other man cupped his hands over the end of a microphone jutting from his ear, and repeated what the first man said.

The sound of the drone hovering overhead was almost deafening. The jet engines from the drone roared, and the wind from the engines tore apart the leaves above. The drone steadied itself, and once the laser beam was acquired, the doors on the bottom opened and released a oblong vaporizing mini-drone, that carefully started winding through the trees towards the cabin. The drone slowly crashed through the glass doors, landed on the dining room table, and then opened ports on its side which quickly filled the open area with an expanding air-gel substance. Once the drone was satisfied with the application, it ignited the air-gel, and the resulting inferno instantly consumed and vaporized everything inside the cabin walls, including the mini-drone itself.

Once the larger drone plotted a clear and straight path to the target, a missile was released. The missile screamed as it raced through the trees, through the shattered glass door and into the cabin. A larger fireball erupted from the openings of the cabin, followed by another greater explosion which disintegrated the walls and the floors and the roof of the cabin. The entire hillside and everything and everyone on it quivered as the shock waves traveled down the valley. The waves impacted the drone, causing it to flutter, before leveling off again. The engines roared once more, and the drone rose rapidly. The back engines turned, shooting the drone forward, and it disappeared over the ridge. After the shock wave passed, tiny chunks of raw meat, in various shapes and sizes, rained down all around the men, as the freezer gave up its precious contents.

As the smoke dissipated, the team moved gradually up the hill, with their senses alert and their weapons fixed on the rubble. One man emerged from the right side of the woods and shifted out onto the driveway. There wasn't much left of the house. The scene was as if the entire cabin, the logs and the furniture and the appliances, was fed through a shredding device, and then haphazardly scattered across the mountain top. Amazingly, the three-car garage appeared to be relatively intact. The drone missiles were very accurate and inclusive in their destruction, especially when the goal was to eliminate any possible evidence.

The only remains of the cabin, besides the concrete walls, were random defiant pipes, rising out of the debris, spewing water over the unrecognizable debris. The man cautiously moved closer, surveying the damage and continuing his search for any survivors. The other two men were stationed at the back of the house, one on each corner, weapons still drawn, and eyes still concentrating on detecting any movement. The man approached the front door area, and was able to look down into the basement, filled with shredded logs and plastic, and scattered pieces of meat. The evidence was satisfying. He adjusted his microphone with his hand. "10-12. 10-12." The man walked around the side of the house towards the back, joined the other two men, and the team walked down the hill.

Chapter 36

Stephanie was sitting on the survival room floor, rocking back and forth, and she had been crying for the past ten minutes. David was holding her from behind, with his hand over her mouth, rocking along with her, and attempting to calm her. It was unclear if the team knew about the room. There was no practical way the team could enter through the basement, but if they were aware of the outside door, there was nothing they could do to stop them. David was trying his best to console her, but his attempts weren't working. The blast violently shook the room, but the damage was contained to the area above ground. The noise from the blast was a heavy and extremely resounding boom, and while the concrete offered a significant amount of protection from the sound of the blast, their ears were still ringing. Tim was sitting on a large box of dehydrated food, with a empty look on his face. The security video monitors on the wall were displaying static.

Tim finally spoke, in a low but stern voice, as if he was scolding her. "Stephanie. Stephanie. I need you to quit crying. Please. I need your full attention. I don't believe they are going to return, but I need you to listen to me. We don't have time for this."

Stephanie kept her eyes focused on the floor, and attempted to obey her father's command, and started taking deep, long breaths. Tim was beyond furious. None of this was supposed to have happened. He was the one who set David up with the new job and arranged for Stephanie to work with him. David was a good man and he knew he would keep an eye on her. He already accepted the fact he would probably die, either from the cancer or via the Party. But the agreement was they were to leave her alone. Their relationship wasn't a secret, but given his situation, he couldn't do anything about it, and not that he wanted to either. He hadn't talked to Stephanie in almost a month, and thought he would have more time to warn her. He didn't think any of this would happen until after phase two.

Stephanie finally calmed down. Tim asked her if she was okay, and she nodded. Tim knew he needed to explain the situation, but in a way which could possibly still isolate her from the mission. From their last discussion, he knew she was in love with David. She shared with him her feelings, and how she never felt this way before. Given his knowledge of that piece of information, he needed to choose his story carefully.

"Stephanie. As you know, I left the Party a long time ago. And even though I had a private job, I was still part of the Outer Circle by invitation. But, because of my past with the Party, I knew too much about how the Party worked, and about the things they did. Apparently, I still knew too much. The Party decided to take drastic measures. Earlier this morning, a man tried to kill me. Luckily for me, he failed. And because you are my daughter, they were going to kill you as well, as a way of punishing me."

"I was the one who had you assigned to work for David. At the time, I didn't know you two would forge this relationship or whatever it is you have. But before that happened, I advised David to buy this cabin with this survival room, and to stock it with all of the things you see in here. I needed a place where he could take you, if I felt your life was threatened. I knew my life was in danger, and I was given a promise by the Party that they would not harm you. But I didn't trust the Party. I didn't trust their promises or their inherent inability to keep them. They made many promises in the past, and they broke them all. David was my insurance plan for you. I hate that I had to drag you both into this situation. This was not part of the plan."

David sat there, listening, in awe of Tim's ability to fabricate such a lie on the spot. Did he really comprehend what Tim has said? Tim arranged for David to have this new job so he could protect his daughter, but what about the mission? Tim didn't even allude to her there was another side to this story. A completely different side David thought had nothing to do with Stephanie, or with this cabin. David decided to buy this cabin on his own. He decided to stock it with survival gear and food. David was the one worried about being killed. David had no intentions of starting a relationship with her. Stephanie was the one who made the first move between them. The only thing which made sense was Tim was now trying to protect him, to make sure he didn't look bad in Stephanie's eyes. Maybe if Stephanie believed his story, she would think this was all Tim's fault. But since Tim's story made it seem like David had been assigned to her, as a protector, how was David going to explain his actual feelings for her? Wouldn't Tim have told David to not get too close to his daughter? Or was this part of the plan as well?

Stephanie temporarily forgot about the attack from the drone, and her anger was now directed at Tim. She wrangled out of David's arms and stood up. "I don't, I don't understand. What do you know about the Party? What did they do? What did you know to make them want to kill you? Or to kill me? For my entire life I was told the Party was good, the Party helped people, the blue zone was where I should be, and the red zone was pure evil. If the Party was bad, why would you let me go on believing all of that? Why didn't you warn me? A drone just tried to kill me, and you, and David. I have always been there for the Party. I spent almost every Saturday for four or five years helping the Party. What could you possibly know that would make them want to kill you and me and David?"

Tim dropped his head, and was now staring down at the floor. Her words along with what he knew about his own actions and his dealings with the Party made him ashamed of his life, of his own selfishness, and of his own greed. If he had his way, he would have never taken the job at the hospital. Back when there were two parties, and the Blue Party made the deal with the Red Party, he should have spoken up back then. He never should have believed what the Blue Party was offering. He knew how they were, he knew they were deceitful and could not be trusted. Even though he held firm to his beliefs and didn't accept their offer to switch sides, he should have walked away. By accepting the job at the hospital, he never really severed his ties with the Party. He thought by quitting, he would keep his honor and his pride, and his belief system would be intact. But instead, he became another pawn in their game of domination. He was hooked on the lifestyle, the money, and even the corruption. The Party never stopped owning him.

Tim raised his head, and turned towards Stephanie. "Because of my job and my past, and perhaps because of my greed, I chose to continue to be a member of the Party. And good little Outer Circle members support the Party. Once you are in the Party, they make it impossible to leave. Yes, I knew they were corrupt. I knew they were evil. But without them, we wouldn't have enjoyed the good life we had. There was no way I could get any other job without the Party's help. And after your mother died, I did what I thought was best to provide for you. To make sure you had nice clothes, a good education, a good job. You came to us so late in life. I was scared I wouldn't be around to take care of you. And as long as I stayed loyal to the Party, you would have a good life. Even if it meant I was required to sell my soul. Which I did, a long time ago."

David was in amazement. Maybe this wasn't about Tim being part of the mission because he wanted the mission to be a success. Tim still might hate the Party, and he still might think the purpose of the mission was justifiable. But maybe the only way for Tim to protect her was for him to agree to be a part of the mission, and to see it through. The mission would have happened with or without Tim. And the only way for Tim to put him next to her, to watch over her, was to get him involved as well. Even though Tim was only in the Outer Circle, he obviously yielded a lot more power within the Inner Circle than he would have otherwise. Was his involvement in the mission really about changing the Party? Did he believe in any of that? Or was it only about protecting his daughter? David still had these questions he wanted answered, but he decided he probably should remain silent for now.

Stephanie started again, and with a scolding tone. "Daddy, you could have left the Party. We could have moved out into the red zone. You could have found a job. I know you used to say the red zone was full of nothing but bad people and bad things, but I have spent a lot of time out here. It is nothing like what the Party portrays it to be. You had to know this, you had to know the truth. Out here, we would have made it. You didn't have to do all of that. You didn't have to sell out to the Party. We would have made it out here. We would have been fine."

Tim replied, "Yes, we could have made it. But it wouldn't have been easy. Ex-Party members don't receive jobs out here. We could have made it, but I didn't want you to have to live through the hardship we would have faced. And to be honest, I didn't want to do that either. This is all my fault, I was lazy and selfish, and I'll admit to it. I could have done something but I didn't. I took the easy way out. But right now, the only thing we can do, is for you to try to forgive me. We are where we are because I failed. And unfortunately, this is going to be your chance to experience what we would have experienced back then. As of now, life isn't going to be easy. You both are going to have to run and hide, and stay hidden. I hope the two of you will do it together. I honestly don't think you will be able to survive if you are apart."

Stephanie looked at David. She already made up her mind that if it was possible, she wanted to spend the rest of her life with him. She always wanted to marry a Party member, but that requirement was tossed a long time ago. She now wanted David because he was David, and not because he was a Party member. She wanted David because she loved him, and she was wishing she had told him how she felt that night. In her naivety, she assumed he felt the same way about her. But after hearing he was assigned to be her watchdog, her quasi-bodyguard, did he really feel the same way? Did she love him more than he loved her?

Stephanie turned to him. "David. I know we somewhat discussed a future together, and this isn't exactly what I had in mind, but can we do this together? I know I haven't said it before, but I love you David. In the beginning, yes, the fact you were a Party member was exciting. But those feelings about you being in the Party went away a long time ago. It hasn't been about the Party for a while. And it didn't take long for me to understand that. It is about you, David, and me, being together. I love you, and I should have told you earlier. Can we do this? I know I can't do it without you."

David stared into her eyes, and couldn't believe what she said. He was so focused on the mission, so preoccupied with battling the paranoia that the Party would discover his role, and what he would do when the time came, he never thought she could have real feelings for him. He knew she did to some degree, even after their discussion at the cabin, but he thought it all had to do with him being a Party member. Why was he so blind, unable to see her feelings went beyond that? Maybe this was what she was trying to convey when she asked him what he thought about the Party. She was trying to tell him she cared about him, and the Party didn't mean anything to her any more. But he was too busy worrying he would be the one saying what she was saying. And his insecurity was holding back any reasons why she would love him for being him.

"Yes, of course we can do this. Yes. I love you too. And I hope you knew this already."

Stephanie smiled and walked over to him, wrapping her arms around his neck, and gave him a long, strong, deep hug. She placed her head on his shoulder, and she immediately knew she would be safe. As long as she had him, life would be good. When they separated, Tim spoke.

"Okay, I hate to uh, interrupt this, but we have to get going. David, I hope this place has a way out of here besides the main door." David nodded. Tim reached into his backpack, and pulled out a large white envelope. "You two are going to have to leave this area, and you will have to go into hiding. Inside this envelope are birth certificates and two passports, with two new names on them. David, you are now Robert James Smith. And Stephanie, you are now Sharon Kay Smith. There is also a marriage certificate, and a sheet with past details about your new identities. You will need to memorize everything. You will…"

Stephanie interrupted. "Wait. Where did you get this?"

"I made these a few months ago. I was hoping I would never have to give them to you, but you always have to be prepared for anything. You need to remember preparation is the key to survival. If you are not prepared, then you will get caught and you will die. But we aren't going to let that happen. I have made the necessary preparations to keep you safe. I have arranged transportation for you. They only know you as Mr. and Mrs. Smith. This is a private transport, so they will not ask any questions nor will they check your luggage, though I would keep your belongings within your reach. David, I really hope you have your money with you."

David replied, "Yes." Right behind Tim, over in the corner, was the large duffle bag filled with cash.

"Good, because you won't be able to get a job for a while. In fact, it might be several years before you can even start looking. You will have to find a way to survive on what you have and maybe if you can qualify, you can apply for whatever benefits are available. I have purchased a place for you to stay. It is sparsely furnished, but you won't have to worry about rent, and I prepaid the taxes for ten years, assuming the tax rate doesn't increase too much. Once you get there, buy as much food and water and necessities as you can. Buy things that will last for a long time. David, if you can remember what was in the *Guide*, that will help. There are going to be some very bad things happening in the next month or two, and so you need to do all you can to be prepared. That's all I can tell you right now."

Stephanie didn't like hearing his last two lines. "Bad things? What kind of bad things? Daddy, what's going to happen? I think we need to know."

"I am sorry sweetie, but I can't tell you exactly what might happen, as I am not sure if anything will happen. But, no matter what, remember the Party is bad, it is evil. You may have to sing the Party's praises to survive, and I suggest you do so, and with great enthusiasm. I am sorry, really sorry it has come to this, but at least you will be alive and probably in a better place than if you stayed here. Life is going to be rough. It will not be easy. I hope whatever it is you two have now, together, it is strong enough to survive the next five or six years. After that, you should be okay."

Tim turned to David. "David, I don't know if your truck is still in one piece. If it isn't then we will have to go into town and buy you a vehicle. All we need is a vehicle to last for the time you will need in driving to meet the transporter. I mean the person who will take you where you need to go. In the envelope is a map, and instructions on where you will be going. Read it along the way and memorize it, and then destroy it. David, the auto-ignite tab is at the bottom of each document. You know what to do with it."

Tim turned around, taking a quick survey of everything in the room. "David, where are your weapons?"

David led Tim over towards the far wall, to a wide row of gun cases, carelessly covered with a mountain of loose blankets. "All of the guns are in these cases. The ammunition is in the green cans inside the plastic boxes on the right. Take whatever you need. I am guessing we won't be coming back here, and where we are going, we won't be needing any of this."

"That's correct. You shouldn't be in any danger. You two don't exist any more. You were just killed by the Party. They will wipe their records clean of you both. It will be like you never existed."

David walked over near the boxes of dehydrated food, and grabbed one of the duffle bags he stocked with spare clothes for Stephanie and himself, and handed it to Stephanie to carry. He went over to the back corner and found the bag which contained almost a million from his teller withdrawals. He now understood why Tim had given him so many teller cards, and why he told him to withdraw as much as he could. Yes, the money was to be used for the mission, but David now assumed Tim provided him with more than the usual number of teller cards. Tim wasn't worried about David, he wanted the money in case Stephanie needed to go into hiding because of Tim's involvement in the mission. David was now kicking himself for being so sporadic with using the cards over the past month or two. He took the bag and grabbed another duffle bag of clothes and necessities, and walked over to the door which led to the exit. David looked at Tim, and then at Stephanie, and took a deep breath.

"Are you ready?"

Stephanie replied, "Yes."

"Well, okay. Let's go."

Chapter 37

The conference room table was littered with paper, assorted food wrappers, and makeshift ashtrays of coffee cups filled with spent cigarettes. The air held a thin fog of smoke and food aromas and body odor. Johnny was sitting at the end, looking at one of the three monitors in front of him. Howard was leaning back in a chair near the far corner, with his feet propped up on another chair. There were eleven other people in the room, all with their own monitors, notepads and personal piles of trash. It was almost three in the morning, and the first day of phase one was nearing an end. The group was busy tabulating the score and preparing for any necessary cleaning of associates who had been apprehended. Years of planning came down to this one night. While the likelihood that phase two would be canceled was zero, the group still needed to know how successful the day had been.

With another phase to complete, the group was to evaluate any possible errors, so they could avoid those scenarios in the future. If nothing else, this group was good at counting the dead and learning from their mistakes. They also needed to see what methods worked, and who escaped. This wasn't the first time a program like this was executed, but it was the first time on their own soil. Every successful mission similar to this one for almost the last hundred years had been monitored by a team like this one. For the ones they controlled, the outcome was always in their favor. And each time, the success rate for the individual phases was higher than before. And now, this program was being executed across multiple nations, and data needed to be compiled as quickly as possible for analysis and review.

A computer program scrubbed the electronic news feeds to identify the success or failure of the attempted elimination of each target. And when possible, every target that was eliminated still required verification by a human on the ground. They had a database of all of the recruited associates, and a list of their potential targets. Since they knew the current and historical home addresses and cities of each associate, another program scrubbed through the news feeds to match a potential target to an associate the best they could. There was an acceptable margin of error, but it was important to do whatever they could to accurately predict the possible targets for each associate, as not everyone was expendable. The information gathered from exercises like this would be used to plan similar future missions, and to predict future crime. The Party executed missions like this before in the past two decades, but it was always in a third-world country and now the years of practice were being put to the test. The analysis and stream of reports would continue at least through tomorrow night, and if necessary, a day or two more.

All of the events for phase one were mandated to take place on Saturday, October the first. But they understood certain targets might not be accessible, and this was the only exception for allowing target elimination on Sunday or even on Monday. The *Guide* explained the risks involved, and the associates were urged to use extreme caution if they attempted anything on day two. It was acceptable to call off a hit on either day, but only if an associate was in danger of getting apprehended. They expected to have a small percentage of eliminations roll over to the second day, but they still needed an accurate count tonight, as any failures needed to be resolved.

Howard was sitting in his chair, with a drink in one hand and a cigarette in the other. He was contemplating if he was getting too old for this type of work, while fondly remembering his past days as a Party member when he was in the legislature. Back then, he could go home at night and on the weekends, and actually enjoy life. But a person with his background and his knowledge, and especially a person in his current position, never retires. There are only two options when dealing with Party members like Howard. They are either relieved of their duties for health reasons, where they retire to a housing center to be spoon-fed mashed vegetables until death took over. The other option was they were eliminated without warning. Howard figured he had another four or five years left until one of these options was played out. And he really enjoyed his work, so it wasn't all bad.

This group of men arrived the day before, and quickly prepped the room for the start of phase one. After a nice meal at a fine restaurant, they slept in the office overnight, and gathered again early in the morning. The first reports started coming in a little after eight. Apparently more than a few of the associates were early risers and eager to finish their tasks. Every detail about each event was carefully monitored, analyzed and recorded. The men doing the work were beyond tired, but they were accustomed to this type of work. They could easily go three days without sleep, with coffee and stimulants to keep them awake. And now, with the clock at three hundred, they decided to call it a day. Cots were brought in the day before, and scattered throughout the empty offices. They were told they could sleep until seven. The men took pills to stay awake, and now most of them were taking pills to fall asleep. It was the nature of the job.

In situations like these, Howard never slept in the command center. First, he had a bad back and if he slept on a cot, he wouldn't be able to walk the next day. And second, his ranking within the Party was well above those who were utilizing the cots. After he received the latest report from Johnny, Howard could make his way back to his hotel and possibly sleep until noon. He would then have a nice lunch before he came over to check on their progress. Johnny did not have this luxury, as he would be sleeping on a cot, and he made the call to quit for the night. His men needed their sleep, and they might not have this luxury tomorrow night.

The men filed out of the room, and were scattering throughout the office to their cots. Howard rolled his chair over to the table, and lit another cigarette. Johnny moved over to a different monitor, and lit one as well.

Howard asked, "Well, how did we do?"

Johnny took a deep drag, held it, and then exhaled. He put on his reading glasses, and then looked at the monitor. "Do you want the details for each section, or percentages of success?"

"Percentages. And round up so I can remember the numbers. It is late. I can read the full report tomorrow."

Johnny turned back to the monitor. "Attempts, ninety-one percent. Success rate, ninety-four percent. Unknown target success, not quite six percent. Failure, if the attempt was made and if we have verified it, was low, not even one percent. Associates apprehended, around twenty-three. Sorry, twenty-three was units, not a percentage. And yes, we have already begun cleaning of this group. The last time I looked, we were successful on eighteen of them. The other five will be cleaned before the sun rises. The maximum window on completing the cleaning from point of apprehension is six hours or less, and we are on target. We had the usual lazy group of associates, and they started late or didn't prep well enough and were caught. And there are the ones who didn't even try, they will be identified and taken out as well. I will have the cleaning report finalized by the time you get here tomorrow."

Howard was more than pleased. He, along with about forty other people, were in charge of the mission in this region, and there were five other regions. It was very difficult to have a plan this complicated executed so well, especially within the Party. They normally would contract out this type of work, but the stakes were too high. The future of the Party was riding on it.

Howard asked "Are those stats for our unit? What about the numbers on the other partners?"

Johnny looked over at a different monitor. "We have preliminary numbers. I probably won't have the final tally until later today. But the other nations are reporting similar results."

The mission wasn't only being implemented in this country. There were a total of seventeen first-world nations participating in this same event. They all joined together in planning what was going to be a world-changing event and time in history. There was a separate plan in place, greater than simply these three phases. A plan which would greatly depend upon the success of each country. If any one country failed, then they could be excluded from the final plan and the final merger. Therefore, the consequences of failure by a single country would only be devastating to the failing country. Every nation was isolated to a degree. But no one expected anyone else to fail. And with the status of the reports coming in, it appeared every partner nation succeeded.

Howard was now satisfied, content he could now leave and get seven or eight hours of sleep. He instructed Johnny he would be in later that afternoon, but if he had any problems, to call him immediately. Rising from his chair, he flicked his cigarette into a coffee cup, picked up his briefcase, and walked out of the room. Johnny was still looking at the monitors. He wasn't ready to go to sleep yet. He wouldn't be satisfied until the final report was written and the results confirmed.

Howard made his way down the stairs to the lobby, and continued to the parking garage to the first level where his car was parked. His back was hurting from sitting all day, and he needed to take the stairs slowly. On second thought, maybe he was getting too old for this. He was looking forward to the hotel bed, and he contemplated even watching a little television, as the news reports of what happened had been flowing all day and were scheduled to be repeated throughout the weekend and the following week. A massage might even be necessary before he came back to the office.

The parking garage appeared darker than usual, even for this late at night, but Howard was too tired to notice. He reached into his pocket for his keys, and unlocked his car from ten meters away. As he approached the car door, he heard a voice behind him say his name.

"Howard."

At first he thought it was Johnny with an important update. He turned around, and was trying to focus his eyes back towards the exit door, but the light from above the door was blinding him.

"Hello? Johnny, is that you?"

A man walked out from behind the car next to his.

"No, this isn't Johnny." Howard squinted, trying to see the man's face. It was dark and the man was wearing a baseball cap. He finally recognized him.

"Ah. Hello Tim. Good to see you. I thought you were finished with your phase one reports. Are you delivering an update in person?"

Tim stepped out of the shadows, and moved closer, stopping at the back of Howard's car. "No, Howard, you should know I am not here to give reports. I have some questions for you."

Even though a meeting like this was highly unusual, Howard was calm. In his mind, he was always in control of any situation. His confidence bordered on controlled arrogance.

Howard said, "Well, make it quick. I have to get to bed. Today has been a long day and I am tired."

Tim agreed. "Yes, it has been a long day, so I will be brief. We had a deal Howard. I would help you with your mission, and you would let me and my daughter live. I would go away, hide myself in a small town in the middle of nowhere, and peacefully live out the rest of my life. Stephanie would keep her job, and in a few years she would receive an invitation to the Outer Circle. That was our deal. But you didn't want to stick to our deal, now did you Howard?"

Howard was standing straight, with his arms at his side, and his briefcase in one hand. He was still at ease with this situation, even though he knew Tim was more than upset. But Howard was aware of the details, way beyond what Tim already stated. Tim was standing sideways so he could look at Howard but keep the garage exit door in view, in case anyone else appeared.

"Yes Tim, that was our deal, and I planned on keeping it. But then you had your daughter assigned to work with one of your associates. You knew all of the remaining associates were to be cleaned after phase two. And you allowed your daughter to get close to him. A little too close in fact. We overlooked your decision at first, but then their relationship became a liability. You know we can't make any exceptions when it comes to this program. All level-two associates and their recruits were to be cleaned. We knew when we eliminated David, there was a good chance we would have to eliminate Stephanie. And then, if we eliminated Stephanie, we would have to eliminate you. It is as simple as that."

Tim was both impressed but infuriated by Howard's calmness, in telling him he was only following the program rules by killing him, and by killing David and his daughter. Such was the mentality of the higher-level Party members. We have rules, and if you break them, you suffer the consequences, and you might have to die. Tim was about to speak when Howard continued.

"Tim, yes, we had a deal. We would cure you of your cancer, and we would let you and Stephanie live. Actually, Stephanie was never a target. You only thought she was."

Tim was holding back his rage as best as he could. He didn't want to raise his voice or show any emotions in front of Howard. Emotions were a sign of weakness. "Yes, I know we try to avoid killing the children of Party members, especially a person like her, one who has devoted the majority of her life to the Party. And yes, I know we use these fears to control people, and you did control me in that respect. And it is my fault I allowed you to do so. But don't give me this story about the Party being kind and curing my cancer. The Party gave me the cancer. You know that, and I know that. The cure was only another stick to prod me into doing what you wanted me to do."

Howard yawned. "Well, Tim, another member may have given the order to give you the cancer, but it wasn't me. I was the one who demanded we provide you with a cure. You are a good man Tim, and we needed your knowledge. Without me, you would already be dead. And we still need your expertise. This mission isn't over yet."

Howard took a step closer towards Tim. "And we provided you with several more favors, really more than we thought was necessary, or even deserved. We created that meaningless job for David. We bumped his pay level up more than what was normal, gave him a nice car, and looked the other way when he bought a cabin. We transferred Stephanie to be his assistant. We bent the rules and helped him get his new apartment, at less than half the cost. We called off drone support when your boy was running from the police in his truck in the red zone. With that stupid act alone, we should have taken care of him right then. Even though the police thought they were chasing the previous truck's owner, we knew David would be worried he was being sought by the Party, and would therefore fail at his part of the mission. And so we directed the cleaning team over to the truck seller's house, to move the blame for the chase away from David. But then he bought what, almost two dozen weapons from the pawn store? His part of the mission never called for weapons. With the gun purchases alone, he became a threat, even if he didn't possess an understanding of how to use those guns. But none the less, we did all we could do for him. We also did a lot for you, and I think you understand how much we did."

Howard took another step closer to Tim. "Tim, we couldn't have done this mission without you. Most of the Party members disagreed with me, but I knew we needed you. And you should have known we wouldn't let you say no. Twenty years ago, this was your specialty. You were the only one still around who had this knowledge and experience. You could execute these types of programs in your sleep. You had the experience and the knowledge we needed, and we couldn't take no for an answer. You should have known that. Now, I am sorry about Stephanie and David, but that call was beyond my control. But the Party can't afford to have any loose ends."

Up until now, Tim knew the Party were the ones who put out the hit on him. But he didn't know if it was Howard or someone else who made the decision. And right now, it really didn't matter. The only purpose for this meeting, for putting his life at risk was he needed confirmation from one of them that they believed Stephanie and David were dead. This was one of his reasons for coming here tonight. It was a dangerous move, but he needed to know if they believed Stephanie died in the cabin. Her survival was the only thing which mattered to him now.

Tim took a few steps towards Howard, so he was close enough to clearly see his face, despite the darkness.

"Yes, Howard. I am a Party man and I fully understand. No one can afford to have loose ends."

Tim raised his right hand towards Howard. In his gloved hand was the gun the assassin had tried to use on him earlier, but this time the gun was accompanied by a suppressor. Tim quickly squeezed off two shots, striking Howard in the middle of his chest. Howard's body shook, and he dropped to his knees before falling backwards, where his body hit the ground with a dull thump. Tim moved and stood over him, and placed another bullet where his heart would be. He dropped the gun onto Howard's chest, and walked away into the darkness.

Chapter 38

The Party viewed phase one as a unprecedented success as thousands of their supporters were eliminated. And like they planned, the media and the public went crazy with excitement. Of course, the Party carefully orchestrated and distributed every news story broadcast to the public. The information Johnny and his team gathered was directed to a separate group which specialized in feeding the news stories to the media outlets. This control insured a steady flow of information on what happened, with the details meticulously outlined by the elite Party propaganda machine. The same task was given to the hundreds of other similar teams across the partner nations which participated.

Phase two was even a greater success than phase one. Like phase one, the aftermath of phase two was precisely calculated and directed. The only outcome of either phase which could not be completely controlled was the public's reaction. But even this was easy to manipulate as needed. The media relished in the flood of murderous and horrid news stories, and in turn, the public was infatuated. The stories were being run around the clock, and the people could not get enough. But in phase two, when these same events were directed at the members of the media, and higher-level supporters of the Party, everything changed. There was still round-the-clock coverage, but normal television programming and sporting events were canceled or suspended. The governments involved were acting as if they were struggling to get everything under control, when in fact they were watching it like it was a graceful symphony, and they were the conductor. And from this day onward, the media would only be allowed to broadcast what the Party dictated. Alternate, non-Party supporting media outlets were forced to comply with the new Party regulations, or they were shut down.

Phase three occurred in each of the participating countries around eight hundred, local time for each nation, on December the fourth. For each country, that moment in time would forever be known as the day of revolution. But, this particular revolution was unique. The revolution generated an outcome which was the opposite of most other revolutions. In this revolution, the government was both the instigator and victor. The revolution was not started by the people to end an autocratic regime, but rather by the government itself to elevate their power and to finalize their control.

At that moment in time, in a slow wave moving across the world, thousands of small nuclear devices were detonated. Each of the participating nations experienced and subjected their citizens to the horror of a small but controlled nuclear holocaust. The majority of the detonations were in the red zone, with a select few in blue zone areas the Party felt needed to be cleaned. The targets were mainly industrial or transportation-related. The goal, besides instigating widespread panic, was to cripple the resources of the red zone, to a point where living there was nearly impossible. The plan was designed to literally blast the red zone back to the stone age. And it worked.

Up until the enacting of phase three, all of the action from both phases was being blamed on the red zone citizens, which to a degree was true. The Party instructed the news outlets to tell the public the red zone was attempting to start a civil war. The Party made it clear this was not the work of any one group of people, but thousands of discontented individuals acting alone. These copy-cat criminals were caught up in the wave of violence, and it simply propagated from region to region.

The Party stressed there was no way the red zone citizens were smart enough to form any type of assembled group, for the purpose of coming together and fighting for a specific cause. Several governments blamed the citizens of another country, including former enemy nations, as the instigators of this world-wide and seemingly-tragic violence. The violence was described to be like the plague, spreading across the world and wreaking havoc on an otherwise peaceful and perfect citizenry. It wasn't until two days after phase three, when all of the governments started directing the media to announce they discovered new information from their joint investigation with the other nations. They announced the Party's spies had infiltrated the terrorist encampments in the red zone areas, and they secured numerous leads. It seemed the Party was misinformed, and there was a connection between these murders and acts of mass destruction. With this new information, everything could now be attributed to a previously-unknown terrorist group. This group was responsible for everything which occurred.

The Party then let the public know this information was only discovered because of the brilliant intelligence gathering of all partner nations working together. This information would have been hidden forever if it wasn't for the unity which was born out of this tragedy. By working together, they identified the truth of who was behind all of these crimes and violence and destruction. The culprit was none other than a secret terrorist group called The League of Patriots. The League of Patriots was responsible for everything. They were the ones who started the revolution, and they needed to be stopped, and they would be stopped at all costs.

An announcement stated The League of Patriots was trying to start a world-wide coup, with a goal of enslaving the common man and destroying his rights and freedoms. The Party spies discovered this group was being spearheaded and funded by the richest men and women on the planet. Their goal was to start a war, an actual war on those in poverty, a war on equality, and a war on fairness. And a war in which they would be the profiteers. These rich zealots viewed the common man as nothing more than livestock, to be slaughtered and consumed when necessary. When they finished using the common man to boost their worth, the old ones were to be cast aside and a new stock was brought in. This revelation only strengthened the Party's platform that wealth was evil, individualism was bad, and capitalists were nothing but greedy old men. But this information came too late, the Party was unable to stop the terror of the nuclear detonations. The Party needed to implement a plan to prevent another wave of destruction, and only they possessed the answer, the solution to this problem. And as always, the public bought the story without question. They demanded the Party find and eliminate the members of the League of Patriots.

The partner nations sent representatives to an emergency meeting, to decide on the best way to handle this threat. They needed to find a way to protect the citizens from further harm, and to restore order and peace to society. During this meeting, many ideas were put forth, and many resolutions were read, discussed, and debated. After two days, the group came to an unanimous decision. Separately, these nations would fail against the League of Patriots. But, if they joined forces, together, they would be victorious against this new menace or any other future threat to society.

The representatives of these nations each carried back a treaty for their respected governments to consider. Every nation's government brought the agreement to a vote, and in every nation, the vote was unanimous. These partner nations would band together as one supreme nation, in order to bring back prosperity, security, equality and freedom. As of January the first, these nations would join governments, would join forces, and would now collectively be known as one. This new band of nations were scattered across the globe, and many new names were proposed. Since a new and perfect society was being born, the chosen name for this new utopia would be "Societas."

But these nations couldn't wait for the ink to dry on the treaty before acting. Their first step was to hunt and capture all of the members of the League of Patriots they could find. And, given that each associate was tracked and monitored from the start, it wasn't difficult. There were a handful who avoided capture and went into hiding, but it didn't take more than a week to capture a majority of them. The trials for the members who were still living were held en masse, and broadcast over every media platform and controlled by the Party. The associates were brought into the courtrooms, shackled to each other, found guilty, and quickly and publicly executed. The only event the public enjoyed more than a good car chase was a good execution.

The official public unveiling of this new multi-national government was to be announced today, January the first. The media outlets leaked information about what was happening to the public, in an attempt to calm the populace. Across the nation, residents were being directed to be close to their televisions. Even with the euphoria of the capture and execution of the majority of the members of the League of Patriots, the public was still scared something like this could occur again, as a few members of the League of Patriots escaped. The Party needed to put their mind at ease. They needed a person, or a presence and a promise that would solve this problem of uncertainty. The public needed to be able to feel safe and secure. Peace needed to be restored. And the Party was the only viable entity who could deliver this sanctity to them.

Chapter 39

David was sitting in a recliner watching the television, with the volume turned down, to a level where he could barely hear it. The power had just been restored, but it was unknown as to how long it would stay on. The power was intermittent during the day, and always turned off at dusk. Cutting the power was an attempt by the Party to deter the looting and to reduce the violence in the streets. Whenever the power returned, the lamps and lights in the flat would come on, and David, along with the other residents of Societas, would immediately turn on the television. The television was the only way to get any information about what was happening outside their flat, as none of the land-line phones or cellular or network services were operational. David didn't know if this was because of the after-effects of the nuclear blasts, or if the Party was controlling their usage. The reality was it could be a combination of both. So, without the television, David, along with every other citizen of Societas, would have no idea as to what was going on with the outside world.

After the assault on his cabin, he and Stephanie were quietly relocated to London, and were now living in a nice three-bedroom flat near Chiswick Park, west of the city. The date was January the first, twenty forty-five. The time was eleven forty-three, and Stephanie was still asleep in the master bedroom. She was pregnant, and over the past three weeks always seemed to be tired. David figured the conception occurred during one of their weekend trips to the cabin in September. She had been taking an oral contraceptive, but medications like that weren't always reliable. The only problem with their current situation was the timing, as they had yet been able to see a doctor. The hospitals weren't fully operational yet, as they were still busy treating the sick and the wounded from the after-effects of phase three. David was unsure when or if the hospitals would get to a point where they would offer any type of prenatal or even birthing care.

They moved into the flat two days after phase one, and settled in nicely, but hadn't left the flat in a long time. The last time they ventured outside was the day before phase two started. The day was pleasant, and they ate lunch at a nice restaurant, took a long walk through a nearby park, and made their way home before dark. David spent the time between arriving and phase two stockpiling the essentials. The process was arduous, but he was successful in converting most of his cash to silver and gold, in the form of coins and various-sized bars, which were more suitable for trade or barter. The *Guide* correctly predicted an economic collapse after phase two, and it stated paper money would be almost worthless. The *Guide* didn't mention phase three, it only alluded that after phase two, every associate should be prepared to immediately go into hiding, if their plot was discovered. And now, with paper money no longer viable, the rampant inflation made silver, gold, food and water the currency of choice.

As David stared at the television, his thoughts drifted back to the after-effects of phase two. He decided to not tell Stephanie anything about phase two. But since he knew the date, he arranged for them to be at home on that day. He remembered the media's reaction to the second wave of endless violence and murders. The majority of the targets mentioned on the news programs were unfamiliar to him. But inside he felt a sense of pride when he would listen to how these people, who were staunch supporters of the Party, had their lives tragically cut short. When they would describe the manner of death, to him, the more graphic the details, the better. Even though he was in hiding, and was not privy to any more details about the mission, he never lost hope it would be successful. While phase two had a starting date, it was never designed to have an ending date. Phase two would continue until the mission was successful.

David and Stephanie had stayed inside their flat since phase two started. He cautioned her it was too dangerous to go outside at this time, as the killings appeared to happen at random places and to random people. She was still unaware of what was happening, or the reasons for the violence, and she was in a state of constant shock and fear. She didn't mind staying inside, and had welcomed her own sense of paranoia at the same time. Tim's purchase of this particular flat in this location wasn't by chance. Tim knew the target areas for phase three, and this area was the safest he could find. There were other reasons as well, but David was unaware of them.

David remembered the destruction on the day of phase three and the following chaos which occurred. The electricity had gone out for a few days, and it wasn't until the stream of military vehicles passed by, with their loudspeakers blaring information and orders to stay inside, that they learned a little of what happened. Since that day, with all of the looting and riots and responding actions by the military and national police, they were both content to not go outside.

A couple days after phase three, after the majority of the nuclear fallout dissipated to where people could go outside of their homes, there was a run on the banks, stock values plummeted, and food prices soared. Retail businesses were looted, riots erupted, and the hospitals were overrun with casualties. Not all cities were this clean so quickly, as the oily and sticky black rain fell and tainted large amounts of land and drinking water, while at the same time cleverly spreading radiation poisoning throughout both the red and blue zones. Death for these victims would be slow and painful.

The bodies which filled the streets were being cremated in huge numbers outside of the city. Marshall law was imposed, and the Party deployed national troops to the troubled areas, where rioters and looters were shot on sight. The Party recognized that the people who stayed inside their homes, out of the chaos, those who didn't take to the streets, they were the ones the Party wanted to survive. The ones who were obedient and listened to the emergency radio and television broadcasts and the commands from the police and military and helicopter loudspeakers, these were the obedient ones, the sheep. The people who were quick to join a crowd and protest against the situation, these people had no value to the Party. The logic was maybe one day, these same disobedient people would direct their actions against the Party, and therefore these types of people needed to be eliminated. Plus, to justify their own violence, many of the victims were conveniently identified as members of the League of Patriots, and no one doubted the labels being placed upon the dead.

A week after phase three occurred, and after the shock of what happened wore down, Stephanie fell into a state of depression. Besides the anxiety from the nuclear explosions, she was concerned about Tim's safety, and was still worried they would be caught by the Party. Even with all of the precautions

Tim had taken, David couldn't convince her they were safe. After a while, David gave up trying to persuade her. He switched his focus to keeping them both alive.

David wondered how long it would take before life resembled anything even close to normal. He left the living room and walked down the hall to the master bedroom. Stephanie was still asleep. A recurring thought kept running around in his head almost constantly, day after day. Where would he be if he had not joined the mission, if he said no to Tim and simply retired? The simplest of everyday tasks, such as going to the store, being stuck in traffic, even going to work, were activities he now craved. Would it have been any different if he said no to the new job? Would he have moved to the red zone, to live in the basement of a stranger, only to be disintegrated by a nuclear blast? Maybe it would have been a blessing if they had not been able to get out of the cabin before the missile hit. He tried to not dwell on what could have been, but it was difficult at times. His thoughts were interrupted by his stomach rumbling again.

David heard the sound of water rushing through the pipes, the pipes knocking, and then water splashing. He quickly walked into the small kitchen, and the water was gushing out of the open faucet. There was an extreme water shortage, and the water flow was sporadic at best. David left the faucets in the kitchen and bathroom open at all times. A bucket was in the kitchen sink underneath the faucet, to capture the water before it escaped down the drain. The water would, without warning, come on every other day, and it would flow for only a minute or two, and during this time David would work to fill the buckets, which were lined in a row in the kitchen.

As the water filled the first bucket, he moved the faucet over to another bucket on the other side of the sink. Reaching down , he grabbed a third empty bucket, to swap it out for the first. During the transition, the bottom of the full bucket hit the edge of the sink, and a small wave of water splashed onto the floor, and David cursed himself under his breath. He had stockpiled plenty of food, and he thought he bought enough water, but he never imagined the water service would be unavailable and so unreliable. As the second bucket started to fill, he reached over and took a plastic cup from the counter, stealing a bit from the faucet as he filled the cup halfway. The water stopped flowing as quickly as it started, and David looked into the sink. The water only reached the middle of the second bucket, but it might be enough for a day or two. He removed the half-empty bucket and carefully replaced it with another one, and placed the buckets with water on the kitchen table. Conserving the bottled water he purchased and hoarded was critical, and so far he had been successful.

David walked down the hall to the bathroom. The tub collected enough water to barely cover the bottom. They would have to wait until the water ran two or three more times before attempting another cold bath. Staring at the tub only reminded him of how much he missed taking a hot shower. The toilets were inoperable, so they resorted to using a bucket and the waste was disposed out the window into the alley behind the flat. There was no other choice.

David returned to the living room, and flopped down in the recliner. The television was set to a Party news channel, which continuously ran stories of the looting and the killings, and periodically it would run the numerous videos taken of the atomic blasts. A red banner was continuously running across the bottom of the screen, warning residents to stay inside, especially after sunset. The private television channels were gone, and the majority of the other Party channels suspended their usual programming, and were only relaying the video feed from the news channel. As the noon hour approached, one of the news anchors stated they would now switch over to a special news bulletin from the Party. The faces of the two news anchors faded, and a new scene appeared, one of a man standing in front of a podium, with the flags of all the partner nations in the background. David didn't recognize this man, and no introductions were made on the screen. The man was simply standing behind a podium with a large red V on the front. The man paused for a second, as if he was waiting for a person off camera to tell him to start. Someone gave him a signal, and he nodded his head, leaned over to get closer to the microphone, and started speaking as the camera zoomed closer, until his face almost filled the entire screen. David turned up the volume.

"Today marks a great day in history. Today, we will witness the birth of a nation of nations. Today will forever be known as the day when peace, security, equality and prosperity were restored to this earth. As of today, a league of nations have come together with the same goals, hopes and dreams. We will no longer cower in fear from terrorism. We will no longer endure the hardships thrown down upon us by the wealthy and the privileged. We will no longer have to worry about where our next meal will come from, or if our families will be safe, or if our children will be able to get a good education, or if their parents will be able to find a decent-paying job."

"For today marks a new era, a rebirth of mankind, and a rebirth of history. We will no longer be subjugated to the will of the capitalists who control everything, only providing what they feel is necessary or deserved. We will no longer be bound by a society where one class rules another. No longer will one group of men control the wealth of a single nation. We will finally have a society where all men are free, where all men are equal, and where no man shall have a need which can't be fulfilled. But furthermore, we will no longer have a society that is afraid. A free society doesn't cower in the basement, or hide in their attics, wondering if they will see the rising of the sun on the next day. A free and just society doesn't put a negative emphasis on the color of one's skin, or where a person lives, or what career they have chosen. A free nation is a nation of equality, of fairness and most importantly, a nation of security and prosperity."

"This type of journey has been attempted before. And this journey has concluded with the same horrible ending we all have witnessed. In the past, nations have risen, only to fall again. In the past, man has made many mistakes. In the past, instead of learning from those mistakes, men had a tendency to look back and reflect on what occurred, and then foolishly, they would repeat these same atrocities. A free nation must be free from their past, must be free from their mistakes, if they are to start new again. A free nation can only look towards the future. The past is no longer necessary or relevant, only the future matters. We will forever be in control of our future and our destiny."

"As of today, January the first, we will erase from our past and from our memory, these sins and failures of man against society. No longer will men be able to reflect upon these obscenities they called capitalism. We are remaking history today, and to ensure we don't fall backwards into the abyss, and to ensure our nation of nations will only look and move forward with progress, we will forget and erase the past. We will strike it from our history books, and blot out these failures. Today is not January the first, twenty forty-five. No, it is not. Because if we truly want to forget the horrible acts of abomination which have occurred, these acts which the capitalists and wealthy and terrorists have committed against us, we the people, we can't continue forward by dragging along the chains and the anchor of the past. Our society will no longer be subjected to a past filled with failure and oppression."

"How will we move forward? What will we do to ensure peace and tranquility are restored? Who can do this for us? This dream may seem like an impossibility now, but we have the solution, and we have the answers. When many of you were younger, you relied on others to protect you. Your parents, who often labored under the tyrannical thumb of the capitalists, weren't always there when you needed them. For many of us, an older sibling was our only source of our comfort, our protection, and our guidance. Our new nation is a family made whole again. As of today, we will all rely on our family, and this family will provide assistance, comfort and protection to those in need. To achieve our goals, we will all have the same protector, the same leader, the same friend. There will be no one closer to you than this person, this leader, our leader. For as of this moment, your life will have true meaning because of him. No one will want or need or suffer, because of him. The events of the past several months will never be repeated, all because of him. Everything we do, everything we own, everything we care about, will all be because of his grace. Our new leader, our All-Father, will guide you, he will comfort you, he will serve you and most importantly, he will protect you."

"As of today, January the first, we will erase our past. Today, January the first, will be known as the day the great new and powerful nation of Societas was officially born. January the first is our first day of our rebirth, of our independence from greed and tyranny. And to ensure we do not fail in this endeavor, as of today, we will turn our calendars back to a time of great success and triumph. We can't turn back the hands of time and erase our mistakes, we can only prepare for and control our future and our destiny. This past, our soiled history, will be forgotten, and these failures will never be repeated."

"We will succeed. We will prosper. We will be secure and safe. In order to achieve this, as of today, our calendars will show today is January the first, nineteen forty-five. And you can rest assured, the past one hundred years of abject failure, poverty, oppression and misery will be forgotten and never repeated. You can rest assured for the next hundred years and beyond, we will not fail. Long live Societas, and long live All-Father."

With the last closing remark, the man stepped away from the podium, and the camera panned out. The individual flags in the background were replaced by one new flag, the flag of Societas. An unfamiliar song started playing on the television, and the small red V on the podium morphed into a larger red V for "Victory" as it filled the screen. The song was reminiscent of a marching band, with a heavy emphasis on the drums and brass instruments. The screen then dissolved back to the news anchors, who along with their panel of commentators, were scrambling to discuss and praise and regurgitate what had just been said.

David pressed the mute button. Everything was clear to him now, and the true purpose of the mission was uncovered. The mission wasn't about hurting the Party or restoring the country to its former greatness. It wasn't even about restoring freedom. The mission simply provided the Party with a justifiable reason for wielding absolute control. And the majority of the citizens gladly traded whatever freedoms remained for the security of being controlled. He had been used and fooled, along with the thousands of other associates, who were simply pawns in a game. The citizens of these partner nations and billions across the world had been deceived.

But had the citizens really been deceived, and were they even capable of recognizing such deception? This outcome, a new nation of nations, with the All-Father at the helm, is probably what the majority of the people wanted anyway. Freedom didn't matter to them anymore. They only wanted security, three meals a day, a new car every seven or eight years, and improved technology when or if they could get it. They wanted to be coddled, to be spoon-fed, to be safe, and to have anyone or any entity besides themselves to take care of their needs. Individual responsibility died a long time ago and was replaced with individual dependency.

And was capitalism really evil? David worked for the Party his entire life, and really had no concept of capitalism. His professors in school all branded capitalism as the scourge of society. The large private businesses with their corrupt and destructive practices, stealing monies from the common man so they could play golf, live in palatial mansions and fly around in their private jets. The nasty executives who paid their workers in pennies while they raked in all of the profits. The malicious and greedy men who hoarded all of the money while the poor starved to death in the streets. Was it fair that some people accumulated more wealth than others? What did these rich people do to deserve such comfortable lives? Their wealth could only have been built on the backs of the workers. What did they contribute to society? Was this capitalism?

Of course, when he was in college, he shopped at the private grocery stores and bought items from the private stores at the mall. But he kept his expenses to a minimum, and he couldn't remember if the items he purchased were any better than the items available now from the Party-owned businesses. The cost of everything had risen dramatically over the years, but wasn't inflation natural? The quality of food, either fresh or canned, was certainly much worse in the blue zone. Or was it only worse because he didn't want to spend the money to buy higher-quality products? On his previous salary, he could barely afford the cheap goods. He then remembered the bag of apples they purchased from the fruit stand on the side of the road. The apples were much greener and juicier than what he normally purchased, and now when he thought about it, the price was indeed much lower. Was capitalism the reason the red zone residents were much happier with their lives?

But why didn't the Party simply seize control of everything, instead of going through this elaborate scheme? They had been headed down this path for the past five or six decades. Maybe they simply grew tired of absolute and complete control taking so long to obtain. Or they needed a reason to bring the people together, give them a cause to fight for, and to weed out the people who really didn't worship their ideals. Perhaps it was easier to secure their goals with fraud than by force or by legislation. Or possibly they needed to cull the herd, and to bring the favorite stock home. David couldn't figure out the reason, and it didn't matter anyway. What mattered now was survival. And Stephanie's survival was important.

David stood up, and his stomach rumbled again. Hunger was an constant and unwanted feeling which never subsided. Even though they had plenty of food, he had been trying to eat as little as possible. He wasn't sure when the shops would open and the flow of food to the stores would begin. He left the living room and walked down the hallway towards the door which led to the inside foyer and stairs. A new obsession was to check the iron bar locks he installed, to make sure they were secure. His paranoia forced him to do this task several times a day, and the bars were always locked. The flat across the hall seemed to have numerous visitors or residents, coming and going at all hours of the day and night. David and Stephanie tried to maintain silence in their home, as they didn't know who or what occupied that flat. Paranoia was invaluable, and it was still his friend, his only friend.

David went into the first bedroom, which faced the street below. This room was filled with his survival supplies, along with boxes and crates of canned and dehydrated food. Five-gallon jugs of water were stacked along the back wall, closest to the hall. The contents of the second bedroom was almost a mirror of the first. Another routine involved performing a mental inventory of what was there. Nightmares of survival replaced his pleasant dreams, where he would wake up and all of the food and water would be gone. There were periods of time in which he thought he was slowly losing his mind. The only calming thought was insane people don't know they are insane. The ability to confirm he wasn't insane was still intact, at least for now.

Surrounding the window and upright against the walls, several thick sheets of plywood were strategically placed, stacked flat against the wall on both sides. The plywood wouldn't provide defense against a drone hit, but it might help shield them, their food and water from a stray bullet from the rioters or the police. The *Guide* listed several suggestions for reinforcing your home, and this was the best he could do. Before phase two started, he managed to travel outside of the city and buy a shotgun, and the precious weapon was laying on the floor beneath the window, with several boxes of shells beside it. He really didn't know if it would do any good or not, but he felt better having it there. The only relief was their flat was located on the top floor of their building.

He pressed his body against the plywood, and slowly peeled back the curtain to see if there was any activity on the street. The street had been fairly quiet these past two days, and when the power wasn't on, the window served as his entertainment. At night, with the power out, he could barely see the people scurrying around below. The Party implemented a mandatory curfew, and if you were caught outside after dark, you would be arrested or shot. He witnessed one person being chased by the police, who once cornered, was shot repeatedly, and he died in the middle of the street. At this moment, the streets were eerily calm. David watched the sky above the flat across the street, to see if he could see any drones or helicopters. One or the other would usually appear once or twice an hour. When he heard their distinctive noise and if they were nearby, he would close the curtain and remain motionless until it passed.

David heard the tinny noise of a motor, a distinct and unique sound, unlike the commotion spewing from an aircraft. Pressing his face harder against the plywood, he attempted to get a better view of the street. As he was straining to see what was happening, a small box truck came into view. The truck pulled up and stopped across the street, almost even with his window. The side of the truck displayed a crudely-made sign which read, "National Prosperity Information Services." The driver quickly stepped out of the truck, and walked towards the back, where he met a fat man at the back of the truck. The driver reached over and unlocked the back door, while the fat man watched. The sliding back door rose into the top of the box, and the fat man climbed inside. A few seconds later, the end of a long tube appeared. The driver took the tube and balanced it on his shoulder, and the fat man jumped out with a tool which appeared to be a large broom. Reaching in, the fat man brought out a bucket and a flat pan, which he placed on the sidewalk. Opening the bucket, he poured some of the contents into the pan. The driver removed a large piece of heavy paper from the tube, unrolled it, and placed in on the sidewalk. The fat man took the broom, moved it back and forth in the pan, and then applied the substance to the back of the paper. When he was satisfied with his work, they carefully picked up the poster and moved down the sidewalk, disappearing behind the truck.

David's view was now obstructed by the box truck. The men didn't appear to go past the other side of the truck, so he thought they must still be behind it, and he couldn't figure out what they were doing. He tried to look up and down both sides of the street, but the angle from the window made it difficult to see anyone else, and he didn't want to expose himself to anyone watching from another flat. Finally, after a few minutes, the men appeared at the back of the truck and they placed their tools inside. The driver closed and locked the back, and then walked around to the door and climbed into the truck. The man appeared to be reading or looking at a device, and after a minute or two, the man started the truck, and went down the street, out of David's view.

Once the sound of the truck's motor dwindled, David turned his gaze towards the building on the other side of the street. The men had applied a large poster to the side of the building, in between two windows on the opposite row of flats. The poster was brightly-colored, with one half red and the other half blue. In the middle was a large picture of a man's head, and it almost filled the poster. The look on his face was stern, but David imagined the face had a slight appearance of friendliness. The man on the poster was looking straight ahead. David squinted through the greasy and dusty window, to try and read what was on the poster. Once his eyes were able to focus, David read the poster out loud.

"All-Father Will Protect You." David repeated it, as if he didn't understand the words. "All-Father Will Protect You."

David adjusted his stance, leaned against the plywood again, and opened the curtain a little more, so he could use both eyes. Staring at the strange face, surrounded by the vibrant primary colors, he was mesmerized by its appearance against the dreary and dirty white paint of the building. The poster was almost as captivating as watching television, even though the face or the message did not change or move. David immediately felt a slight comfort by the presence of this simple but large sheet of paper. As David stared at the poster, the face seemed to convey strength, but the words also helped the face summon a feeling of compassion inside David. His thoughts turned back to what the man on the television said, about today being a new day, a new beginning, a new future of hope and plenty. David repeated the poster's slogan in his mind. "All-Father Will Protect You."

David let the curtain fall back into place, and he slowly and quietly made his way back into the living room, and he gently sat down in the recliner. He was remembering what the man with the deep and compelling voice stated earlier, in what was certainly a powerful and moving speech. Maybe the Party wasn't so evil after all. Maybe the mission, even thought it was directed by the Party, maybe it was justifiable. After all, it was designed to bring a group of nations together in harmony and peace. Maybe the citizens needed a tragedy to finally come together as one, united in equality, tranquility and justice.

Perhaps he was wrong this past year. After all, for the majority of his life, the Party provided him with a job, money, benefits and a nice place to live. And, the speaker on television sounded sincere and honest. What he said in the speech, it now started to make sense to David. Maybe life was going to be better this way. No more suffering, no more want, everyone would have a job and a place to live, with plenty of food to eat. Maybe All-Father could accomplish what others failed to do. All-Father certainly seemed to have the solution, the answer to everyone's problems.

Maybe he simply needed to give All-Father a chance.

347